Praise for *The Last of the Seven*

"A gripping look back at WWII through the eyes of a war-torn unit of European Jews who are sent behind enemy lines to strike back at Hitler, Steven Hartov's *The Last of the Seven* opens fast and never lets up for a second. Impossible to put down. Fans of Robert Harris and Andrew Gross will want to get their hands on this one the second it hits bookstores."

—Ryan Steck, *The Real Book Spy*, author of *Fields of Fire*

"*The Last of the Seven* is a story that is as beautifully crafted as it is tragic and brutal. Steven Hartov moves beyond an impeccably researched recounting of historical events, tapping into the vivid memories and raw emotions of one who lost everything under the Nazi reign of terror. It is deeply personal and highly compelling—a memorable novel of survival and revenge during the tumultuous era of World War II."

—Taylor Moore, author of *Down Range*

Also by Steven Hartov

The Soul of a Thief
The Heat of Ramadan
The Nylon Hand of God
The Devil's Shepherd
In the Company of Heroes
The Night Stalkers
Afghanistan on the Bounce

THE
LAST
OF THE
SEVEN

A NOVEL
OF WORLD WAR II

STEVEN HARTOV

HANOVER
SQUARE
PRESS

HANOVER
SQUARE
PRESS

ISBN-13: 978-1-335-05010-6

The Last of the Seven

Copyright © 2022 by Steven Hartov

Gertie From Bizerte
Words and Music by James Cavanaugh, Walter Kent and Bob Cutter
Copyright (c) 1943 Shapiro, Bernstein & Co., Inc., New York and Walter Kent Music, California
Copyright Renewed
International Copyright Secured All Rights Reserved
Used by Permission
Reprinted by Permission of Hal Leonard LLC

Hanover Square Press
22 Adelaide St. West, 41st Floor
Toronto, Ontario M5H 4E3, Canada
HanoverSqPress.com
BookClubbish.com

Printed in U.S.A.

For Sergeant Shalom Kamin, BDE, and the boys of Company C.
You were the best of us.

And for Lia, Oren and Jesse, my lighthouses in the storm.

THE
LAST
OF THE
SEVEN

AUTHOR NOTE

Most of the incidents and characters in this book
are based on historical events and real people.

PART ONE

TOBRUK

But man is not made for defeat.
A man can be destroyed, but not defeated.

—ERNEST HEMINGWAY
The Old Man and the Sea

One

North Africa, Spring 1943

IN THE SAHARA, THE SUN COULD MAKE A MAN bleed.

It was hard to believe at first, especially if you'd ever trekked a frigid winter landscape somewhere, boots slogging through alpine snow, limbs shivering and aching bone deep. It was a challenge to imagine it, such a murderous sun, when December memory recalled teeth chattering like a Morse code key, toes and fingers numbed and raw, eyebrows stiff with frost, till all at once that blessed star emerged from charcoal clouds to save the day.

The sun was a holy thing then. The breath of God on your frozen face.

Ah, but in the vastness of that empty desert, when spring fell prey to cruel summer, when the cloudless sky was nothing but a silver mirror, the sand an iron griddle, and there was not a tree or cave or cactus to throw a shadow's sliver. Nowhere to run from the sun. It was then that heaven's jewel became a hunting thing, its furnace eye unblinking, merciless, and pounding.

You could shade your skull with a cap, drape your blistered neck with burlap, but still you had to see your path as your squinting eyes filled with flies who'd found the only liquid in the land. The lancing light bounced off the dunes to slowly broil your face, lips turned plaster white and split, and the oils of your nose and cheeks fried patches there like poultry on a spit. And then, the crow's-feet wrinkles at the corners of your bleary vision turned to brittle parchment, until at last they cracked, and the most unnatural happened...

The man across the dunes was weeping tears of brine and blood. But they were not of sorrow or self-pity, for all of his emotions had hollowed out so many weeks ago. They were simply the last vestiges of all the fluid he had left, squeezed from the ducts by that relentless sun.

He was small there in the distance, and nearly weightless now, though from the way he moved it seemed he wore a yoke of iron. He was no more than an upthrust child's thumb against the umber sands, shimmering in the steaming light of the fata morgana, an illusion where horizon met the sky.

He wore a Bedouin burnoose, tight about his oily blond curls and rough against his bristled jaw. His German staff sergeant's tunic was girded with white salt lines of evaporated sweat, a single bandolier of ammunition, and the lanyard of a camel skin water bladder, now shriveled like an ancient's scrotum, nothing left. One *Feldwebel* rank was on his collar, his Afrika Korps palm-tree shoulder patch was bleached into a ghost, and in one pocket were two lizard tails he'd chewed from time to time, though all the meat was spent. The right waist of his tunic was punched through with a bullet hole, its fringes black with dried blood, and in the left thigh of his trousers was another one just like it, the reason for his crooked limp.

In his dangling right hand, below a ragged sleeve, he clutched a German MP40 Schmeisser machine pistol, barrel down, its leather strap dragging through the sand. His left hand held nothing, the nut-brown fingers capped with broken nails with which he'd tried and failed to dig some water from the heart of a dying oasis. His breaths rattled like an asthmatic's, yet he came on, another half an hour, another mile.

A pair of British soldiers from Montgomery's Eighth Army watched him. They knelt behind a berm of sandbags, Tommy helmets buckled tight, sleeves rolled up and neat, shorts revealing sun-browned thighs above knee socks and tanker's boots. They were alone, the western guards of a garrison south of Medenine, Tunisia, and they raised their bayoneted Enfield rifles to bear down on the stranger, like twins who often read each other's minds.

At twenty feet the German sergeant stopped, unmoving, only breathing. The Cockney Tommy on the left aimed the rifle at his chest.

"Drop the bloody Schmeisser."

The German jolted, as if surprised to hear a voice aside from his own mutterings to himself, unsure if these two Brits were real or cruel mirage. Yet he obeyed, as after all he knew it didn't matter. The machine pistol was choked with grit and only the first shell would have fired. He opened his fingers and let the gun slip, like the hand of a dying lover, and it fell to the sand and was still.

The Tommy on the right said, *"Hände hoch."* Hands up. He was a Scot and it came out as "Handerr hook."

The German tried, but he couldn't raise his arms higher than his waist, and his leather palms fluttered there above the sand like a maestro urging his musicians to play the passage pianissimo. His cracked lips formed a trembling "O," though no sound emerged, and he mouthed *Water*, and then again— a goldfish with its face pressed to the glass of an aquarium. The Scot, keeping his Enfield trained, pulled a tin canteen from his battle harness.

"Don't go near him, Robbie," warned the Tommy on the left.

The Scot pitched the water bottle, cricket-style, where it pinged against a rock before the German's boots. But the man could hardly bend his wounded leg and leaned in half a fencer's lunge, snatching the canteen two-handed. He unscrewed the cap and brought it, shaking, to his mouth, and raised his face to heaven as the water gushed into his swollen gullet and dribbled from his filthy beard. His body trembled, and he looked at the two men and said, in nearly perfect British English, "I am not a German."

The Tommies glanced at one another, then back at their intruder.

"You don't say, Klaus?" the Cockney said to him.

"Looks like a bleedin' Jerry to me, Harry," the Scot growled to his partner.

"He's bleedin' all right, mate," said Harry sideways. "Got a couple of nicks."

"Nicks?" Robbie snorted. "Coupla hefty caliber holes. Can hardly see 'em for the flies."

Cockney Harry craned his neck to peer beyond the German's head.

"You all alone, mate?"

"Six others," the German managed in a brittle whisper.

"Don't see 'em."

"All dead."

"Right," said Robbie. "And where'd ye come from then?"

The German dropped the canteen. His fingers wouldn't hold it.

"Borj el-Khadra, by way of Tobruk."

"Bollocks," Harry spat. "That's three hundred miles." He thrust his buckled chin above the sea of endless dunes. "Across *that*."

For a long moment, the trio regarded one another like drunkards sizing up opponents for a brawl. The Tommies watched the German's hands, for they hadn't searched him yet, while for his part he struggled to stay upright. Cockney Harry gestured at Robbie the Scot, but only with his head.

"Fire the Very pistol, Robbie. Green flare, not red. Let's have the captain up here for a chat."

Aside from Robbie's flare, which arced into the silver sky and fell to earth somewhere, the trio stayed immobile until at last a throaty engine loomed. A four-wheeled open command car appeared from the north, its peeling fuselage bristling with petrol jerrycans, pickaxes, and Bren light machine guns snouted at the sky. It spewed a cloud of dust as it hove to and an officer dismounted, his captain's cap stained with sweat, Webley pistol lanyarded to a holster. His left hand tapped a swagger stick against his muscled calf while his right fingers smoothed a short mustache. His large driver followed close, hefting a Thompson submachine gun.

The captain ambled up and stopped, his bloodshot eyes squinting at the strange tableau. Robbie the Scot turned and dipped his helmet brim, but Harry kept his rifle trained, and there were no salutes.

"What's all this then, lads?" the captain said.

"Captured us an Afrika Korps infiltrator, sir," said Harry.

"Sneaky desert serpent," Robbie sneered.

"Good show then." The captain nodded and scanned the prisoner head to foot. "Right. Summon a firing party."

Harry turned and looked at his commander.

"Execution, sir?"

"Affirmative, Corporal." The captain flicked his stick toward a distant rise. "And let's stake his corpse on that hill. Perhaps it shall keep the other vultures at bay."

"Yessir," said the captain's driver, and he turned back for the car to muster up a firing squad.

The captain wasn't barbarous, but more than worn and weary, and his men were not quite sure if he was serious or bluffing. In the past few weeks, despite the routing of the Germans in the westward push for Tunisia, spies of every kind had probed his lines, including one Bedouin woman. They were often followed by marauding Stuka fighter-bombers. He'd lost four men, most painfully his major whom he'd buried and replaced, and had a fifth now dying in a tent, legless and weeping for his mother. So much, he thought, for Erwin Rommel's *"Krieg ohne Hass,"* war without hate.

"I am *not* a German." The intruder spoke again, and his voice spasmed with the effort.

The captain raised his chin. His driver stopped and turned. The prisoner's accent was British, yet with a certain Berlin curl.

"That's quite a claim," the captain said, "given your costume."

"He told us that shite too, sir," said Robbie.

"Says he hoofed it from Borj el-Khadra," Harry said. "By way of Tobruk, no less."

The captain raised a palm to hush his men and squinted at the prisoner.

"What are you, then?"

The prisoner tried to swallow. The water hadn't been enough. It would never be enough. His body quaked in feverish ripples now, his ragged clothing fluttering like gosling feathers. It was the proximity of rescue, now turned to sudden death, coupled with his famish, thirst, and wounds.

"SIG," he said, tunneling in his delirium for the words. "Combined Operations."

The captain raised an eyebrow. Harry asked him, "What's ess-eye-gee, sir?"

"Special Interrogation Group." The captain stroked his mustache corners. "Top secret commando unit, attached to LRDG and SAS. Mostly German Jews, but they were all killed at Tobruk, and that was many months ago."

"Not I," the prisoner croaked. His right hand reached into his tunic. The captain fumbled for his Webley and the Tommies' Enfields stiffened, as the prisoner fetched a pair of British identification disks, one green, one amber, like autumn leaves on a threadbare lanyard, and they fell against his chest.

The captain glanced at them, and at the hollow bearded face again.

"Tobruk, you say. And where've you been since then… allegedly?"

"Captured. Escaped a month ago, or two, perhaps, I think."

"You *think*." The captain closed his fists and put them to his garrison belt. "And why, pray tell, if you were in this uniform, were you not executed as a spy? Those are Hitler's orders, after all."

"Because I had tea with Erwin Rommel," the prisoner said, yet without a hint of irony that the German field marshal would have thusly intervened.

"Had a pint meself with Churchill just last week," the captain's driver quipped. The Tommies laughed, but the captain didn't. There was something in the prisoner's eyes—a sincerity of madness, or truth.

"What's your name and rank?" he asked.

"Froelich, Bernard, second lieutenant." He pronounced his given name as "Bern-udd" and his rank as "left-tenant." Then he added, "Six seven two, four five seven."

The captain produced a small pad and pencil from his tunic pocket—ink was useless in the desert. He wrote the details down, tore the page off and flicked it over his shoulder for the driver, his eyes never leaving the desperate gleaming blue ones there before him. They were bleeding from the ducts, but he'd seen that once or twice before.

"Sergeant Stafford," he ordered, "take this to the wireless

tent and have Binks get onto Cairo. Tell them we'll need our answer double quick."

The driver sped off amidst a cloud of dust, but his return was far from quick. A grueling fifteen minutes passed, while the prisoner teetered on his feet. He could no longer keep his head erect, and he fought to stay awake and straight. He told himself he'd stood this way before, for hours in formations, and he dredged up images of bucolic pleasures, the Danube and the Rhine, and even Galilee. He longed for rain and felt its kisses on his face, while rivulets of something else crawled down his beard and touched the corners of his mouth. But he tasted only brine, and then the armored car returned.

He raised his chin as the driver handed back the paper to the captain, who perused it, then spoke again.

"Lieutenant Froelich, if that's you," he said, "do you remember your last passwords?"

"I shall try," the prisoner whispered as he stumbled through his memory, unsure if he could find the thing to save him from a bullet.

"If I said Rothmans cigarettes," the captain posed, "what would you say?"

The prisoner's sunburned brow creased deeply like a cutlass scar.

"I'd tell you I don't like them, sir…that I fancy Players Navy Cut instead."

The captain nodded, and offered his first thin smile of the week.

"That is correct."

And Froelich slumped to his knees in the sand, a collapsed marionette, strings cut. And then he slipped from consciousness and toppled forward, knuckles in the desert, his palms turned up to the sun he hated.

"Fetch a stretcher, lads," the captain said. "It's him. He's the last of them. He's the seventh."

Two

Tunisia

THE STORM WAS LIKE A SAILOR'S NIGHTMARE, except there was no ocean to be found, and all the waves were roiling sand dunes spitting stinging grit into a howling wind.

What had been, only hours before, a still and bright and shiftless afternoon, had turned with dusk into a tidal wave of tumbling thunder, rising from the northern lips of Libya and threatening to swallow all of Africa. It rose from the horizon, a giant black-brown serpent, arching its spine and obliterating earth and sky as it swept toward Medenine, and until it had its fill, no one knew when it might leave again.

The scorpions had gone underground, the desert beetles burrowed after them, the vultures crouched in the lees of Bedouin stone graves, tucking bloody beaks beneath their wings. Some British tents held firm, those that were well-staked, while others flapped and flew away to choruses of curses no one heard. The Brits pulled tanker's goggles on and fixed them tight, grimacing with teeth glued thick with sand, and the men of Captain Randolph Hood's "A" Squadron, 22nd Armoured Brigade, Seventh Armoured Division, capped the guns of their Crusader tanks and wondered if this Jew they'd rescued, Second Lieutenant Bernard Froelich, might be another Moses who'd delivered God's wrath with him.

But Froelich wasn't bothered by their superstitious glances, nor the pelting sand or thunder. The relief of being saved was like the first breath of a drowning man bursting to the surface of a clawing sea, a glorious feeling that no clash of earth and heaven could diminish.

He lay there on a canvas cot inside the squadron's infirmary, close to the listing fuselage of a Bedford QL transport truck. The vehicle, long dead from ripping Panzer shells, formed the field hospital's northern wall, sheltering its wounded from the winds that smacked it from the distant coast. Its two side walls were formed of mortar ammunition crates filled with rocks, and the roof was a silk cargo parachute, crisscrossed with spiderwebs of ropes to hold it fast. There was no fourth wall, giving easy access for the medics with their litters.

His eyes half-hooded and unfocused, Froelich watched the undulating canopy as he rode a gentle wave of morphine and listened to the wind. There were other wounded in the shelter—he'd seen them when they brought him in—but they made no sounds above the storm. A glass infusion bottle dangled from a makeshift pole, its needle dripping lukewarm liquid in his vein. His uniform was sliced away where they'd cleaned and stitched his waist wound, but they'd barely touched his thigh wound, only wrinkled up their noses at the stench.

He decided not to speculate on that and reveled in his luck instead. It all felt strangely pleasant, like a sailing trip he'd taken with his father as a child. And since there were no German guns, for now, he smiled in his stupor and thought about Berlin, though soon those reveries would darken.

It was *Deutschland im Herbst* again, Germany in autumn, that balmy eve in 1938. The breezes whistled in the trees, there behind the high school that Bernard and Lili called *gymnasium*, nestled in their lovely little town of Gestern just astride the River Havel. The senior class lovers' bench was like a secret throne, perched beyond the rose garden that was pruned and petted by Frau Koch, the high school secretary, and it faced the emerald soccer pitch that gleamed with sunset dew, where Froelich had led his team to glories and won his shy and pretty queen.

They sat there alone, thigh to thigh, she in a white button dress, he in woolen trousers. Lili wore a burgundy sweater, her blond hair braided in a wreath above her ears, her scent like lavender and honey, and Bernard wore a gray felt *Jacke* with its cuffs and collar girded in soft leather. Yet tonight, unlike all the other nights they'd stolen after school, they didn't kiss, or grasp each other's fingers, or whisper of their surely blissful future. Lili chewed her lip and stared across the field, her hazel eyes brimming, and Froelich gripped a sheet of onion skin paper, a letter from their headmaster.

"Are you *sure* he means it, Bernard?" Lili asked, as if that staunch Germanic bureaucrat might have suddenly turned jokester.

"He means it." Froelich waved the wrinkled paper. "The swine won't let me graduate."

Lili laced her small fingers in her lap, as if a prayer to one of their two gods might save their love from tragedy. "But you are second from the top in class," she whispered.

"It's not about my grades, *mein Schatz*." His fingers fluttered to her thigh, a touch he knew he'd never feel again. "It's about my blood."

Her brow knit deeply, the same expression that he'd once seen when they'd kissed too long and almost went too far. Now a tear rolled off her nose and shattered on her knuckle.

"Vielleicht wenn du in die Kirche gehst, Bernard..." Maybe Bernard, if you went to church...

Her suggestion faded with her shame, and Froelich snorted half a laugh.

"I think it's too late for that. We've never gone before, and besides, these Nazi goons are godless." He flicked a finger at the paper square. "These are the Führer's holy commandments, for everyone like me."

"But he seems to know what's best," she said, and then blushed hard. "I mean...for other things."

"Perhaps. But in the last war, my father served the kaiser just like him, and earned two Iron Crosses, and no one asked or cared who was Jewish."

"Have you told Herr Montag that?" She meant the high school headmaster.

"It won't matter. Montag wears the Party pin." He tipped his right hand up, as if waving a farewell to his beloved soccer pitch, and muttered, *"Heil Hitler."*

Lili began to cry. She covered her mouth and trembled

with it, and Froelich turned and hugged her quaking shoulders and said, "Kiss me once, Lili. And then you have to go."

"I'm so sorry, Bernard." She grasped his face in both small hands and kissed him long and desperately, until her tears had lacquered him and run into his mouth. And then she spun away and grabbed her purse and books and fled across the garden's pathway cobblestones, the clicking of her heels a fading drumbeat of her grief, until Froelich heard no sounds except the breeze, crawling through the trees.

He sat there alone, for a long while. He wept for everything, his loss and love and youth, and then he stopped it. At last, with the deeper darkness, he rose and walked and took the tram home, to find his father's dry goods store engulfed in fire...

Froelich shuddered on the cot, vengeance misting his blurred vision. There was no refuge in his reminiscence. It had been that way for years now. Whenever he sought solace in a childhood scent or sweetness, a roadblock always turned him back toward retribution, another kind of thirst he'd never quench. And so he closed his swollen eyes and slept inside the storm's black cloak, to its symphony of creaks and rattles, gone from the world for at least one blessed night of not stumbling through the desert.

The storm was gone at dawn, as the *ahsif* often were, leaving in its wake an altered landscape of battle implements that had to be unearthed again. He woke to light and heat and a furnace breeze, and his ears pricked up to sounds of clicking shovels tossing sand and the mutters of men working. A pleasant scent he hadn't smelled in months curled through his nostrils. Someone had acquired eggs, perhaps through barter with the Bedu. With just an hour of the desert sun baking a command car's engine cover, you could slather it with piston oil and fry them up without a fire or skillet.

"Good morning, Froelich. I see you're still with us."

Captain Hood stood above him, peaked cap pushed back on a balding pate and holding a mess tin cup.

"Tea?" he offered.

Froelich couldn't speak yet so he dipped his chin. A corporal medic slipped a helmet underneath his head to prop it up, and Hood tipped the tin to his cracked lips. The lukewarm liquid tasted like all sorts of things, most of them not tea. The corporal brushed his lips with some sort of salve he thought might be rifle Cosmoline.

"Thank you, sir," said Froelich in a voice that sounded far away to him.

"Not at all," said Hood. He gestured toward the foot of Froelich's cot. "Lieutenant Colonel Pritchard here's the brigade intelligence officer. He'd like to ask some questions."

Froelich peered beyond the thin gray blanket covering his legs, where his naked feet looked like a Bombay fire walker's. The socks inside his German boots had worn through long ago, so wherever leather rubbed his skin the boots had won the day. His toenails looked like broken teeth because he'd tried to file them with rocks, and all the flesh was Salmon-belly white with blackened scabs, some still oozing blister water. At one point in the Sahara, he'd actually tried to drink it.

Past his feet stood Pritchard, an older man of thirty-five, hatless in the medical tent, thick black hair combed back. His uniform looked rumpled and unkempt. He had a cluster of tubular map cases tucked inside one armpit, dusty binoculars hung below his neck, and his tunic pocket sprouted grease pencils and a divider compass whose prongs had pierced the cloth like fangs. He smiled with gray teeth.

"Morning there, Lieutenant," Pritchard said.

"Morning, sir," Froelich rasped. Captain Hood made to offer him more tea, but Froelich nodded thanks, took the cup himself, maneuvered up onto an elbow and sipped. His cup hand trembled.

"I've been told quite a tale," the intelligence officer said. He laid his maps down, upended an ammunition crate and perched on it, which left Froelich with the image of a disembodied fellow floating above his gnarled feet.

"What you've learned thus far, sir," Froelich said, "is accurate."

"Right." Pritchard pulled a notebook from a pocket, while Froelich looked around the canopied infirmary. He counted six others on litters, mostly swaddled in oozing bandages. Three of them were quiet, one moaned and muttered, one chortled with the corporal medic and the last was covered up and dead. Yet besides the corpse, they all had ears, and he was full of secrets.

"So then," Pritchard said, "you're the last of Haseldon's SIGs?" He meant Lieutenant Colonel John Edward Haseldon of the ultrasecret Special Operations Executive and Combined Operations, to whom the Jewish commandos belonged.

Froelich hesitated. "The last I know of, sir."

"German Jews, all of you? Some Austrians into the bargain, perhaps?"

Froelich only looked at him. Throughout his training with

the SIG, odd officers had been tasked to ply the commandos with such questions, just to see if they would slip. Only Haseldon himself, or Bertie Buck, the captain who'd devised the whole SIG gambit, could clear them for such chat, and Haseldon was dead. Pritchard understood Froelich's reluctance.

"Well, let's try this then," he said. "You chaps have English cover names. Yours is Harold Dempsey, correct?"

"Yes, sir," Froelich said. If Pritchard knew that much, he likely knew the rest.

"And in your German guise?"

"Hans Kruger, sir."

"Very good." Pritchard smiled and produced a pencil. "Shall we hear about Tobruk, then? Top to bottom?"

"I'm afraid I can't, sir."

"I'm assuming you were captured by Sixth Panzer." Pritchard pressed on, ignoring Froelich's reticence. "And there's this lovely bit about your rescue from a firing squad by the Desert Fox himself."

Froelich finished his tea and Captain Hood recovered the cup. Propped on both his elbows now, jaw clenching underneath his ragged beard, he looked at Pritchard with defiance.

"I cannot tell you more, sir. Apologies."

Pritchard flipped the notebook closed.

"Pray tell, why's that?"

"I expect to return to Middle East Commando, where I shall be thoroughly debriefed. If I say too much here, I shall be rejected there."

The lieutenant colonel looked at Captain Hood, then cocked his eyes off to where the battalion surgeon hunched above a wounded man. Hood said, "Shelley, if you don't mind," and the surgeon came to Froelich's cot. He was short and bald and wore a bloodstained white frock, with a fruit tin in one pocket filled with reeking disinfectant, from which he pulled a soggy sponge and wiped his fingers. His name wasn't Shelley, but due to his unaesthetic stitching, they'd dubbed him that in tribute to *Frankenstein*'s author. He touched Froelich's forehead, humphed and thrust his hands into his frock pockets.

"I'm afraid you needn't worry about secrecy, Lieutenant," he said.

Froelich looked at him.

"You've got a bold infection," Shelley added, as if bacteria had personalities. "Gangrenous, in fact." He looked down at Froelich's covered legs. "And this."

The doctor peeled the blanket and a bandage back from Froelich's thigh wound. The fibers pulled and made him wince. The wound had been debrided, but the fringes of the exit hole were black and creamy crimson, and the itch he'd felt that morning seemed to be a living, crawling thing.

"The femur's fractured. Haven't a clue how you walked on it. And I'm afraid the sepsis is raging there and well below. You've got a host of maggots. I left them there because they dine on putrefying flesh."

He covered up the wound and patted Froelich's arm.

"I'm terribly sorry," he went on. "You're most certainly going to lose that leg. There's nothing for it. But I cannot do that here. You'd not survive it. At the very least, Lieutenant, your war is over."

Froelich's jaw went slack as if the surgeon's words had fired like a pistol in his mouth, and all the joy he'd felt at being rescued shattered into horror.

"Whenever we take Tunis, perhaps this week or next," said Captain Hood, "a transport aircraft shall appear down here. If the weather holds, you and some others will be off to a proper hospital." He tried to smile. "And perhaps some very fine nurses."

"They shan't be able to save that limb," Shelley added. "But they'll save *you*."

The surgeon walked away to other tasks, while Froelich's heart pounded up into his throat and all his morphine comfort flushed away. His leg, his life, and any meager future now dashed with nothing left. He slumped back on the helmet, its steel resounding in his skull, and he barely kept the tears at bay and only that because other eyes were on him. A plane was coming, his salvation and damnation. He heard Lieutenant Colonel Pritchard's voice again, like the echo of an evil ghost rattling the halls of a medieval castle.

"Well then, Froelich, it appears your secrecy indeed is moot. So, let's hear about Tobruk."

Three

Cairo, June 1942

IN THE SHADOWS OF THE PYRAMIDS, IN THE land of Tut and Nefertiti in their gloomy tombs, Froelich woke one day to irony, a Jew returned to Egypt.

He'd loved those many Passovers at his parents' house in Gestern, listening enthralled as his father read the *Hagaddah*, the Legend. With the table set for twenty guests and *Mutti* flitting and fussing, each spring they heard again the ancient tale of liberation, passed down through generations. The Hebrew slaves, the ten plagues, the uprising of young Moses, a dash across the Red Sea and forty years of wandering in the desert, until at last they crossed the River Jordan.

He'd been a happy careless German youth, with thoughts of milk and honey lands arising only once a year. But then, while stumbling into early manhood, another pharaoh had arisen, like a demon from a hellish well of history, this one adorned with swastikas instead of golden serpent cuffs.

They'd murdered his father, taken his sister, and crushed his mother, who begged him to flee to Palestine, a place he'd never really wanted to go. And there, with nothing of his past surviving and no future he could see, he'd drifted to Jerusalem's German Colony as just another refugee. He washed dishes at the King David Hotel, drank arak with the ruffians in Katamon, and roamed the streets with visions in his head of conquering Berlin, murdering Gestapo thugs and rescuing his tortured family. He sharpened up his high school English and tried to join the occupying British Army, but the recruiters at Camp Schneller rebuffed him for his ravings of revenge, until at last he shut his mouth and they relented. The Royal East Kent Regiment trained him up for months at Sarafand and attached him to a Palestine Buffs Infantry Company. But then, of all the luck, they shipped him off to Cairo—the bloody wrong direction.

It was the Bible in absurd reverse. It was as if his sullied Hebrew God had chewed up the Old Testament, gulped it down, then spewed it out all over him with a sadistic sneer.

Welcome back to Egypt, Jew.

Cairo, in 1942, was like Berlin's Kurfürstenstrasse district, flipped upside down and broiled in the sun. The city teemed with Allied troops, British and Australians, Indians and Africans, all soaking up the heat and sloth of garrison life while indulging in the perfumed prostitutes and the smoke of the *nargilas*. Hunched astride the Nile, the market souks rang with twangs of strumming ouds and clicks of *Shesh Besh* dice, as Arab shopkeepers brayed their deals and soldiers bar-tered back in twenty tongues yet always overpaid. The place was terribly exotic, full of spies and sheiks and beauties, but Froelich, sucked of joy, relished none of it. He wanted desperately to fight, but there was no fight yet in these colonial conscripted tourists.

At British Army headquarters, a sprawling complex of marble floors, gurgling fountains and suites of clacking typewriters, the officers behaved as if still wafting through their motorcar clubs beside the Thames. All labors stopped from noon till five while they made off for polo jousts or cricket matches, or took their lunch at Shepheard's Hotel or the Continental, where the lower ranks were banned, or copulated in the Berka district with their Arab mistresses, ignoring the German and Italian cannons just west and lurking in the desert. When they were at their desks, they requisitioned further tanks and guns and men, until the army bloated like a feasting tick and Froelich's spirit simmered with frustration. He was made a corporal driver to a prissy captain, a Cambridge graduate who prattled on about the wonders of the ancient world, but didn't do a damn thing for the war.

So Froelich drove, and smoked, and tore the pages from his pocket calendar like a prisoner marking days till liberation. He gnawed his lips and listened to the urgent crackles coming from his captain's wireless as pitched battles raged across the western desert, and he saw how armor officers, plucked from their silky beds at Shepheard's, never returned their keys to Ismail the concierge. He heard the upper ranks' wry jokes about Field Marshal Erwin Rommel landing in Tripoli to save Mussolini's brigades from humiliation. After all, the Italians were smartly uniformed, yet more adept at subjugating Africans than dueling the King's own regulars, *wot*? But all that bluff fell flat before the truths of racing motor- cycle messengers as Rommel ravaged Libya. He'd conquered Benghazi and Gazala and laid siege to Tobruk, wiping out its Allied garrison, and now his panzers were storming El Ala- mein. In Cairo British noses were at last sniffing shell smoke, and Froelich heard the panic in the pitches of the nightclub singers at the Scarabée and Kit Kat, while he sat outside and waited for his captain to stop dancing.

Privy to murmured dispatches, he discovered a battalion that was his rightful destiny, 51 Commando, composed of Palestinian and European Jews like him. They'd fought in Abyssinia and Eritrea, and many had died hard, and now the rest were folding into Middle East Commando and going after Germans. They were rough men, desert warriors, at- tached to elite units like the Special Air Service and the Long Range Desert Group, and whenever they appeared out of the dunes at the Gezira Club or Groppi's in their keffiyehs and thick beards, all voices hushed and glasses were raised up, and Froelich longed to be one of them. With all his heart he wanted in, but his captain's tepid and pedantic soul wouldn't let him out.

So Froelich fled, abandoning his chauffer's seat—away without leave. Soon captured by the MPs in the market, he was remanded back, berated by his scowling captain, and for- given. Apparently the man had failed to glean his fervor, so he escaped again, this time at night, and wound up drinking in a dank saloon in Cairo's slummish Dar-Al-Salaam.

The place was dark, misted in thick smoke, and packed with Allied troops of every stripe, with laughing whores perched on laps stained by sloshing beers. Brooding over what he might do next, he leaned against the crowded bar and nursed a Burton Ale, until a Coldstream master sergeant spun him around and finger-jabbed the Palestine olive tree badge on his field cap.

"What's a dirty Jew like you, doing in my purview?" the drunken sergeant growled.

"*This*, you bigot bastard," Froelich spat as all his compressed rage detonated, and he gripped the bottle's gooseneck and smashed it on the sergeant's skull. He was dragged away still kicking, tossed into the brigade's barbed wire stockade, and didn't give a damn because, at least for now, he was no longer anyone's feckless driver. Early the next morning, an Irish provost marshal called him to the fence.

"A scrapper are ya, lad?" he sneered. "Well then, in an hour you can join the brigadier's Friday morning pugilists. Do well and ya might not spend the rest o' the war whitewashing every fecking rock from here to Sharm-el-Sheik."

So Froelich fought, in nothing but his desert boots, khaki shorts, and a set of thinly padded boxing gloves, on a gravel pitch surrounded by a cheering throng of officers all placing bets. His opponent, a beefy beet-faced Scottish private, had no idea that in him Froelich saw his high school headmaster and every Gestern Nazi neighbor who'd betrayed his family and his father.

The private circled in the dust, shoulders hunched, gloves up and jabbing in short feints, his feral eyes gleaming with sure triumph. Froelich didn't even raise his fists, but only turned in concert with the dance. He let the private's first hook slam the left side of his face, due punishment for abandoning his sister, then took a shocking blow to his right jaw, fair pain, though not enough, for leaving his poor mother to those dogs. Then Froelich punched him in the solar plexus, with so much force the crowd exhaled a gasp. And when the private found his feet again, Froelich smashed his nose until the blood gushed in his teeth, then blackened both his eyes with blurring blows until he toppled on his spine and the officers leaped back to keep their uniforms from being crimson-splashed. The poor Scot left the contest moaning on a litter.

Afterward, as Froelich stood there snorting like a Spanish bull and hoping for another go at someone, he was shocked by the euphoria of violence. In all his life he'd never looked to fight, not even on the soccer pitch when bullies fouled him, or even when some cruel remark was triggered by his lineage. His mother bade him use his wits and not his fists, so he'd obeyed and played the good Jewish boy. And what the hell had that gotten him? How had that helped *any* of them? Now he felt the power of vengeance and adrenaline surging in his veins, and he was plowing up his garden of passivity and cultivating fury.

He whipped around as fingers touched his sweat-slimed shoulder. There stood Captain Herbert "Bertie" Buck, an officer from Middle East Commando, with his hands inside his pockets, smiling at Froelich's rage. The Irish provost marshal stepped up to escort Froelich back to prison—his fate for cracking a Coldstream skull had yet to be decided—but Captain Buck raised a rifle-calloused hand and staved him off.

"Stand down there, Sergeant Major," Buck said. "He's mine now, though I'm sure he'll soon regret it."

The provost snapped a stiff salute and sauntered off. Buck spoke to Froelich through a sniper's grin.

"I see you're learning, Corporal, that sometimes in this army, to get the orders you deserve, you have to disobey the ones you have."

And so, with Bertie Buck's renegade slogan still ringing in his boxed-up ears, Froelich learned his deeper twist of fate, imagining the giggle of his callous Hebrew God as he volunteered to join a counterfeit unit of the German Army. Buck's secret "Wehrmacht" training camp was tucked away beside the sapphire waters of the Suez Canal, sandbagged, barbed wired, and removed from prying eyes, where some forty other Austrian and German Jews goose-stepped in perfect Nazi kit. The vision chilled him to his guts, yet also warmed his wounded heart, for the scent of looming payback was as sweet as the summer bougainvillea mixed with sea salt marinade.

English was verboten there, only *Hochdeutsch* spoken. Every bit of uniform, from boots and socks to shorts and caps and blouses, had been stripped from German POWs and freshly stamped as Afrika Korps. Their Mercedes trucks and BMW command cars had been captured after desert fights and towed back through to Cairo, and their weapons, from Mauser 98 rifles to MP40 Schmeissers, had been cleaned of blood and all polished back to flawless. Love letters in their pockets were penned and perfumed by British female linguists, along with *Soldbücher*—the soldier's identification booklets—forged and stamped with recent pay dates, and the well-worn photos of their German lovers were really English beauties who had that Aryan look.

They goose-stepped to the mess, singing "Deutschland

Über Alles," "Panzerlied," and "Die Fahne Hoch." They greeted one another with *"Heil Hitler,"* read only German papers like *Der Stürmer* and *Berliner Morgenpost*, and their dusty gramophone played "Lili Marlene" and "Erika." They sweated on their cots at night, dreaming in the native tongue they'd longed to leave behind, and whenever Captain Buck ambushed them at 2:00 a.m., God help them if they failed to snap awake and answer him in proper Wehrmacht slang.

Some of them were newly minted, some already bloodied veterans of wild German airfield raids. Before them, many had been killed in action, but Buck had filled the ranks again with stalwart, angry Jews. Froelich fell right in, rebaptized now as Feldwebel Hans Kruger, despising what he had become while loving the intent. They called themselves the Lions of Judah, while Buck told them with a grin, "You are my Trojan horses," and promised soon they'd know exactly why. Formally they were the SIG, the Special Interrogation Group, but that was nothing more than cover. They weren't going to be interrogating anyone.

One bright Sunday in September, as beyond the camp's high sandbag walls the sails of fishermen's feluccas drifted by, Buck faced the troops in stiff formation. Another of their British charges, Lieutenant David Russell, a six-language linguist, had just snapped *"Achtung!"* and in their spit-shined jackboots they looked right enough to escort Hermann Göring. Buck stood above them in a Nazi Kübelwagen, knuckles to his waist, and spoke to them in English.

"As you all know by now, comrades, the Germans have taken Tobruk, which, given its position at the northern coast of Libya, places our supply lines in mortal peril. The good news is, they've only got a modest troop of fifty thousand men and four hundred tanks."

His Germans smiled, yet they didn't quip or budge. They were no longer Brits, who'd wisecrack at such comradely bravado. The remainder of Buck's speech was brief.

"Pack your kit, gentlemen. We're off to take it back."

Soon thereafter, Froelich found himself again a driver, this time at the wheel of an Opel Blitz canvas-covered troop truck. There were four of the Afrika Korps–marked lorries, his in the lead, each packed with "prisoners of war" who were in fact commandos of David Sterling's Special Air Service— their bandaged uniforms and expressions of defeat belied by Brens and Sten submachine guns tucked beneath the benches. Lieutenant Colonel John Edward Haseldon, commander of SAS Troop B, huddled in one lorry as a forlorn private, and all were guarded front and back by SIGs with Schmeisser machine pistols, ostensibly escorting them to a stalag in Tobruk, to which they would never arrive.

The trek, across eight hundred miles of searing desert, led by the bearded sand pirates of the Long Range Desert Group, had begun at the Kufra oasis in southeastern Cyrenaica and was nearing its fourth night. Each day was a brutality of heat and wind and stinging sand, their vertebrae grinding on the bouncing benches, while at night they froze and cuddled up beneath the trucks and chewed their bacon biscuits, lumps of cheese, dried fruit, and tinned herring, and sipped a draught of rum and half a cup of overheated water, their only daily ration.

On the third day they'd been strafed by German Messerschmitts—despite the Wehrmacht stripes stenciled on their

lorry bonnets—which had only stopped when the SIGs unfurled a Nazi battle flag and pumped their fists in skyward
fury. But now, at last, they were close, with the lights of the
forbidden city glowing in the underclouds, readying themselves to destroy the German coastal guns just prior to the
British landings. But emerging from the desert meant that
German sentries would soon be popping up along the roads,
and Froelich, for the first time in his life, felt the nausea of
likely death.

He drove the heavy Opel truck along a snaking two-
lane tarmac. It was deeply night, the lenses of his headlights
dimmed with amber stain, the norm for German convoys, and
he gripped the wheel and squinted through blue eyes made
bloodshot pink by days of wind and sand. Captain Buck, now
Hauptmann Schiller, sat beside him in the cab, both in full
Wehrmacht regalia. They hadn't spoken in an hour, except
when Buck unfurled the map and said "this way" or "that."
But then he shared some thoughts, beginning with a smirk.

"You needn't choke that wheel so tightly, Frock." Buck
nicknamed everyone, himself included, which was how he'd
come to be Bertie. "Save your muscles for the fight." He spoke
in English, though his German was fluent.

"Yes, sir." Froelich eased his grip.

"We'll soon be in it," Buck said, "so I'll impart some combat wisdom."

"Please do, sir."

Just then the right wheel dumped into a rut, the truck
bounced hard and Froelich reined it in again. An SAS commando in the back muttered, "Froelich, bloody *hell*," and then
some laughter and it quieted again.

"I have an uncle who's a thespian," said Buck.

"A thespian, sir?" Froelich thought he meant a Greek or some sort of sensual deviant.

"An actor, with the Theatre Royal. He told me once, that in preparation for a role, he studies every aspect of that person's past, his mannerisms, quirks of dress and his emotions, and imbues himself with such details for weeks before the play. And then, on opening night, he simply tosses all of that away and takes the stage."

"I see, sir," Froelich said, though he wasn't sure he did.

"Soldiering's much like that," Buck went on. "You train and train until you've got it in your muscles' memory, and when the shooting starts you toss all that aside, trust your instincts, and improvise to seize the day. After all, no battle plan survives the opening salvo. Right?"

"As you say, sir."

Buck lit up a German cigarette, an Eckstein N°5, leaned back and streamed a contrail. "So far it's stood me well."

Froelich knew that was true. Buck never spoke of it himself, but David Russell had whispered tales of his adventures. Before Froelich's arrival, Buck had taken Russell and three SIGs and strode into a German army camp, where the SIGs lined up with the other Wehrmacht troops to draw their weekly pay, while Buck and Russell dined inside the officers' mess, the epitome of chutzpah. Once, after a disastrous airfield raid at Martuba, Buck had been captured and taken away in a Kübelwagen to be executed. He'd killed the driver, donned his German uniform, and walked all the way back to British lines. The lesson was to stick in Froelich's mind.

"Cigarette?" Buck offered.

"No, thank you, sir." Froelich craved one, but didn't want his captain to see it trembling in his fingers.

"You've got leadership potential, Frock," Buck said. "Good head on you, disciplined, not too chatty. There's no officer amongst you SIGs, and I think it's time."

Froelich's brow furrowed as Buck opened his tunic pocket and removed a folded sheet of signals paper.

"Promotion orders here, Froelich. Subaltern, second lieutenant. Have a look."

Froelich squinted at the paper and saw his name and fresh rank. His stunned gratitude emerged as a feeble "Thank you, sir."

"It's not a gift," Buck chuckled. "It's a burden of responsibility. But one of you must carry it and you'll more than do. Not quite Sandhurst," he said, meaning the British Army's officers academy, "but this war's ample substitute for all that stuffy education."

With that he tore up the orders in strips. He rolled his dusty window down a crack and fed the paper feathers to the wind.

"We shan't be caught with this." Buck rolled the window up again. "But have no fear. There's a proper copy stamped and signed back at HQ. Congratulations."

"I don't know what to say, sir," Froelich managed to get out.

"Say nothing, but do well, and earn it."

The compliment swelled Froelich's heart, while the battle-field commission gripped it in an icy fist. On the precipice of such a bloody fight, it felt more like a posthumous reward, a brevet for a corpse. Yet he forgot all that as a hundred yards down the midnight road, a sentry's lantern swung a lazy arc, signaling the convoy to pull up. Buck tossed his cigarette away, straightened his German tunic and said, "Here we go."

Froelich slowed the truck, reached back and rapped his knuckles on the cab's rear window. *"Strassen Wache."* Road guard, he called out, knowing that behind him SIGs were gripping Schmeissers tight. His hands were wet and trembling, his pulse beating in his throat, and because he knew that nothing in his posture was as casual as it should be, he pushed his *Feldmütze* field cap back on his head to reveal blond curls and feign bored disregard.

The figure on the highway's shoulder grew larger, his helmet and rifle gleaming in the lantern's light. Just beyond him, a weighted sentry pole was dropped across the road, and farther off into the dunes and gloom stood a small radio shack, its whip antenna bending in the breeze.

"Damn," Buck murmured. "He's got communications."

Froelich braked the Opel as the other trucks behind him stopped as well. He rolled the window down. The sentry crossed the road and held his lantern up. He had blond Nordic eyebrows and a teenage gap between his two front teeth.

"Guten Abend," Froelich said. He clenched his bladder.

"Guten Abend." The young German scanned the lorries. *"Was haben Sie hier?"*

"Gefangene." Froelich told him he had prisoners.

"Wirklich?" Really? The sentry seemed impressed.

"Ja, wirklich." Froelich felt his smile trembling.

The sentry stretched and looked at Buck, who perused a map and ignored him.

"Anweisungen," he snapped.

Froelich pulled forged orders from his pocket. The sentry

took them and said, *"Einen Moment,"* and turned and marched off toward the shack.

Froelich looked at Buck, who shook his head and sighed. They both knew the forgery would do for casual perusal, but not if someone called them in to check their bona fides.

"They won't pass muster," Bertie said, and he reached into his boot for a Fairbairn-Sykes commando knife and exited the truck.

Froelich watched Buck cross beyond the headlights and disappear into the dunes. He wiped his right hand on his trousers and gripped the handle of his Schmeisser, praying Buck would be the only one he'd see again, and knowing what that meant if it were so. *That boy's a German kid, like me,* he thought, then reasoned fast that boys like that were digging shallow graves for Jews back home and dragging them from ghettos. He set his teeth and told himself, *Feel nothing.*

He squinted at the shack. Its wooden walls tilted once and shivered, and he thought he heard a thin cry like the whimper of a dog. Then Buck emerged again, his mouth set hard and tight, carrying the sentry's rifle. The captain freed the roadblock pole, tipped it up, came back around the cab and climbed inside. He dropped the German rifle on the floor.

"He shan't be needing this again," he said, then closed the door, wiped his dagger with a handkerchief, crossed himself and ordered, "Carry on."

It was all lightning after that. Buck knew there wouldn't be much time till someone found his victim, and he raced the trucks until the rolling sands turned to rows of palms and stucco houses at the city's southern outskirts. He stopped them there and snapped out whispered orders.

The SAS in Froelich's truck split up and climbed into the others, then Froelich drove his Opel off the road and down into a wadi. Along with six more SIGs, he was to hold there in reserve and make the lorry look disabled. They jacked the carriage up, popped the bonnet, unscrewed the radiator cap and let the engine steam, so that even a passing German colonel wouldn't try to make them move it. Then they watched as Buck and Haseldon took their Trojan horses and roared off for Tobruk, heading for the guns.

Froelich and the other six sipped cold tea and waited, feeling awful tension yet no impatience. They knew that soon enough their turns would come. The only boys who thirsted for a battle were those who'd never been to war, but these had had a taste of it and knew how quickly soldiers turned to ghosts. Froelich felt affection for them all, although he'd tried to keep his distance. Kurt and Otto, Fritz and Erich, Heinrich and Franz, late of Salzburg and Berlin and Frankfurt, were all so much like him. Otto was the youngest, who looked upon him like an older brother. He'd taken Otto under his wing and tried to toughen him, but thought the boy could hardly harm a butterfly, let alone kill Germans. He'd let his guard down someday, if they all survived, but for now he told them not to worry, and kept his field promotion to himself.

An hour later, the sky above Tobruk burst ablaze with German searchlights lancing at the heavens, British bombers defecating ordnance, Wehrmacht antiaircraft batteries spitting fire, and airplanes spinning from the clouds in flaming wrecks. Froelich's radio sputtered only static and told him nothing. He didn't know the German guns had been successfully destroyed, but that the British warships, HMS *Sikh*, *Coventry*, and *Zulu*, were all afire and sinking, and the Royal Marines had never come ashore. There was no word of failure or success, nor that Buck and Haseldon and all the rest had been surrounded, cut off and decimated, the dead left where they fell, the wounded scattered to the winds.

At 3:00 a.m. the first came in. They staggered from the night like drunken scarecrows. Some were weaponless and limping, some draped across the shoulders of the stronger, some dragging Stens and Brens that gleamed with sweat and blood. Froelich and his SIGs laid them down and watered them and tended to their wounds as best they could. None of them could speak, except for one commando, who said that Buck had bravely run to rescue Haseldon, and had never showed again.

Froelich ordered the truck made ready. His men eased the wounded SAS into the bed. Then he waited, until no more of them appeared out of the night, and he climbed inside and raced for Cairo.

But there was only one road from Tobruk, the same one that they'd followed in, and as Froelich reached the sentry's pole it was down again and they were ambushed. A pair of MG34 machineguns shredded all his tires into hissing scraps of rubber. Inside the cab, Froelich and Otto flung themselves to the floor as the windscreen exploded and bullets laced the Opel's ringing fuselage and filleted its canvas cover, while the remainder of the SIGs in back smeared themselves across the wounded SAS and yelled in German, *"Fertig! Fertig! Nicht schiessen!"*

Shooting back was useless. It wasn't a fair fight.

The gunfire stopped. Its echoes rattled off into the desert. Boots tramped across the tarmac and a harsh voice ordered, *"Raus! Hände hoch!"*

Froelich crawled up from the floor, opened his bullet-ravaged door, and trembling like a lamb in a slaughterhouse, stumbled to the road. The searchlight from some vehicle blazed in his face and through his twitching squint he saw rushing, stamping figures. Then, just in front of him, a pair of icy eyes below a helmet scanned his German uniform from boots to throat and the man's mouth spat, *"Verdammter Spion!"* Damned spy!

And then the butt of a Mauser rifle slammed into his skull and sent him to a deeper darkness.

Four

El Adem

THE FINGERS OF A GECKO WOKE HIM TO A cold desert dawn as the small creature skittered past his face, tail swishing sand into his fluttering right eye. He lay on his left side, eyebrow buried in the grit, knees curled up to his chest where they'd sought fetal warmth in his unconsciousness. His wrists were bound behind his rump with hemp that bit and numbed his flesh. His boots were gone, stripped off by the Germans. Without boots, escape was hopeless in the Sahara.

The light was thin and aluminum gray, showing him a high sand berm that stretched from left to right like the buttress of a firing range. Beyond that he saw only muted sky and the flickers of some failing stars. On his side of the berm German voices muttered speculations and complaints, just like all troops everywhere, and the windless air was laced with cigarettes, boiled coffee, desert dysentery, and scorched cordite. Spoons and mess tins clicked and clacked, someone was telling a joke about a pig and a nun, and like most German humor, it had a filigree of cruelty.

Froelich heard a broken whimper, its octave twisting upward in a plea. He looked down past his toes, where in the gloom a *Feldwebel* and a private gripped the elbows of another barefoot man and marched him on his jellied legs toward the far tail of the berm. He thought, *My God that's Otto*, though the boy's blindfold hid his twisted features, and Froelich wanted to cry out and beg for mercy for his friend, but his voice was paralyzed like in the worst of nightmares, and they disappeared around the bend.

There was nothing for a minute, until he heard the racks of rifle bolts, and then a volley of gunshots clenched his guts and sent a flock of desert snipes into the sky, as if escorts to a freshly slaughtered soul.

The terror flooded through his body like poison from an asp and he felt his bladder lose control, then realized from the dampness in his crotch that it already had the night before. A voice nearby grunted with executioner's relief, *"Weiter und zuletzt, Gott sei Dank."* Next and last, thank God.

Hands gripped him from behind and dragged him up, his legs like stalks of licorice, his heart pounding in his rib cage, his mind racing through a labyrinth of tricks to stop the clock. What could he say to halt this outrage? What ploy could he invoke? He saw his happy childhood in bursts of desperate longings, his friends and girls and joyful celebrations, and knew he'd never see them anymore and they'd never know his fate.

Should he tell these Nazis he had secrets only he could give, if they'd just let him live? *No*, he'd give the bastards nothing of the kind, not even one last shameful claim that he was not a Jew and they were all mistaken. He saw his mother as he'd seen her last, standing in the charred doorway of their savaged home, clutching her wooden cooking spoon, and the tears sprang to his eyes and he began the Lord's prayer, but only in his head. He'd be damned if he'd let these monsters hear it.

"Shma Yisroel." Hear, Oh Israel...

He stumbled toward the berm, and a young German appeared with a strip of gun cloth for his streaming eyes.

"Keine Augenbinde." No blindfold, Froelich gasped as the idea of that darkness only surged his panic more.

"It's better if you have one," someone said behind him.

"How would *you* know, Fritz?" another quipped and they roared with laughter.

And then, the approach of a roaring motorcar stopped them all in their tracks. Someone yelled *"Achtung!"* and there were stomps of boots and rifle butts, and the hands released him and he fell to his knees, slinging drool as the tears rolled from his chin onto the sand. He turned his head and looked up to the right, where a mustard-colored Kübelwagen had halted in a cloud of orange dust.

Standing in the passenger side, gloved hands gripping the windscreen, was a familiar figure in a buttoned leather frock coat, peaked cap, and tanker's goggles, with a black Knight's Cross below his throat.

Froelich squinted up through bleary eyes, sure this vision had to be delirium. But Field Marshal Erwin Rommel looked down at him, then off to someone else, slapped the windscreen top and ordered, "Take this man to my command tent."

And Froelich dropped his forehead to the sand, and swore he'd never doubt his God again...

Rommel's tent was like an outsize wedding canopy. Its walls were rolled up tight and tied, while at each corner pole a private gripped the stanchion just in case the wind picked up. But there was, of course, no bride or rabbi, only a German general of nearly royal rank, reclining in a camp chair before a folding wooden table, his cap cocked back as he perused reports and sipped tea from a pewter bottomed glass. To Rommel's rear, tucked into one corner, a clerk perched ready at a typewriter on a table made of ammunition crates, fingers posed to hammer keys if the field marshal chose to dictate.

Froelich stood there just inside the entrance, steadier than before, though hands still gripped him upright. The enlisted escorts to his disrupted execution had been replaced by officers, a major and a captain. He was still barefoot, wrists still bound, and having no idea what Rommel wanted of him, he teetered on the precipice of fate. He thought that truth might be his only hope.

"How many of these were there?" Rommel asked the officers without looking up, as if speaking of a flock of hens who'd fluttered from a poultry truck.

"Seven, in our sector, sir," said the major on Froelich's right. His breath stank of cigarettes and cheese.

"Only seven?" Rommel dropped a file on the table, his hawkish eyes examining his men as if searching for their weakest fissures. That practice stood him well and was how he won his conquests.

"Yes, Field Marshal. We heard that there were more inside Tobruk, dressed as Germans, but we captured only these, along with their wounded."

Rommel sipped his tea, his eyes unblinking at the major. "And the other six?" he asked, though he already knew.

"*Der Kommandobefehl.* The Führer's orders, sir," the major stammered. "About…not…leaving British commandos alive."

"Yes, yes, I know the order." Rommel flicked his fingers up as if to stay stupidity. "But tell me, Major. How does the Führer expect us to glean intelligence from dead men?"

The major said nothing. Froelich felt a hitch release inside his chest. He thought the legend might be true and prayed it was, that Rommel slaughtered tank brigades without mercy, but once the fray was over, treated his defeated enemies like honorable Olympians. Rommel frowned as he realized Froelich was still trussed, and snapped, "Untie his hands." The captain did it quickly and stepped back.

The field marshal's posture shifted and he smiled, revealing chipped teeth and that renowned sun blister on his lower lip. He cocked his head as if he'd just encountered this young man on a park bench in the Berlin zoo.

"What's your given name, boy?"

"Froelich, Bernard, sir." He didn't dare lie or pretend to not know German.

"From?"

"Just outside Berlin, sir. A small village called Gestern."

"Yes, I hear the accent." Rommel didn't ask if Froelich was a Jew. He seemed to assume so. "Where is your family now?"

"I do not know, sir."

The general's smile faded. He reached for a metal finjan and poured some amber tea into another glass. He pointed at it.

"Drink this. Your mouth is dry from fear of death."

The major and the captain tensed, but Froelich stepped forward, raised the glass with trembling hands, sipped half the brew, and put it back. He nodded thanks and retreated to his place.

"Which commando are you with?" Rommel asked.

"The 51st, sir," Froelich said and blushed with shame at his revelation. He'd have to carry that betrayal, but he could live with it.

"You're safer here with us," Rommel quipped, and his typing clerk snickered because he thought he should. The field marshal waved a finger at Froelich's filthy German uniform. "Put him back in British kit," he ordered his officers. "I might want to interrogate him further, in due time."

The major clicked his heels as a flush of merciful relief crawled up Froelich's neck. Rommel had just issued an order to spare and keep him whole, and all within that tent had heard it, and none would dare defy it. Rommel got up from his chair, took his gloves and slapped the dust from them against his breeches.

And just before he left he said, "Come and see me, Froelich, when this war is done, if we're both alive. We'll tell each other where we've been, and how it's so much better that it's over." He smiled like a fox. "That part will be a lie for me, but likely not for you."

Five

Ayn al Gazala

FROELICH LOST HIS SENSE OF TIME IN LIBYA.
Time had been a precious thing for all his youth, perhaps
due to the Teutonic culture of his fatherland, where utmost
joys and even basest tragedies were measured by the clock. But
here he had no watch, and since each day of prisoners' activi-
ties mirrored the one prior, and all the ones thereafter were
the same, a timepiece lost its value. Some of the other British prisoners, mostly armor crews and cocky airmen, notched
their wooden tent poles with each day, perhaps so they could
someday boast of what they had endured. But Froelich saw
no point in that, for he suspected no one that he loved was
left alive to hear his tale, if ever he would tell it.

The prisoner of war camp was west of Tobruk, astride
the coastal road to Darnah, but it was no more than a dozen
twelve-man tents surrounded by barbed wire. Bleached parch-

ment white by the North African sun, the tents resembled
unmarked gravestones hulking on a barren plot of sand and
scree, without a single flower. There were no barracks for the
German commandant, only a large troop truck with a canopy
of interwoven palm leaves, which often had to be replaced
after sandstorm winds assailed it.

During the day, the commandant sat in the shade of a camouflage net, on a canvas folding chair, issuing desultory orders and reading Nietzsche and Goethe. At night he slept on
a comfy cot in the cargo bed of the truck, a kerosene heater
kissing his feet, while his men shivered on the hard-packed
sand in mothy blankets, bodies tensed for horned vipers and
yellow scorpions. The only hard structure in the camp was
a wooden tool shed stuffed with pickaxes and shovels, from
which a crooked branch of Acacia raddiana poked skyward,
and a Wehrmacht battle flag whipped itself to tatters.

Strictly counter to the Geneva Convention, the POWs used
the tools to build a new road from Tobruk's border toward
the distant southern town of Jalu and the Messla oil fields, and
they made decent progress under threatening Mauser rifles
and the promise of the day's lone meal of camel meat at sunset. They labored dawn to dusk, survived on meager water
rations, swooned beneath the pounding sun, at times passed
out and were kicked awake again by jackboots, ate little and
grew brown and bony. Their ranking officer, a Lancaster
pilot, objected to the commandant of Mobile Stalag Nine—
so titled because the camp was taken down and moved each
month. Red-faced and ramrod stiff, the British major fumed,
"Colonel Messer, it is absolutely *forbidden* by the Geneva Con-

vention to force my men to break up rocks and build your bloody road!"

The commandant merely smiled from his chair and pointed toward the coast.

"Major, I believe Geneva is that way, by perhaps two thousand kilometers. Should the Red Cross ever visit us, which I doubt, you may file a complaint."

Froelich made no friends at Mobile Stalag Nine. After Otto's execution, he'd sworn that evermore, throughout this war, he'd make no friends again. Besides, no other SIGs were there and his tainted English accent made him suspect, and his arrogant retorts in perfect German to the sentries only made it worse. The only reason the Wehrmacht goons didn't flail him bloody with their truncheons was the rumor that Erwin Rommel had some interest in his health.

All in all, he wasn't loved by either side.

The British internees at such POW camps quickly formed committees, as if they were a social welfare club. One was for escape plans, another for men's health, a third for games and entertainment, and the last, Committee X, to glean intelligence and root out spies. Early on, he woke up in his tent one midnight to find his tentmates gone, instead surrounded by four Brits perched on cots, smoking cigarettes and staring in his eyes. The questions came staccato, a crossfire meant to trip him up.

"Where'd you train in England, Froelich?"

"I've never been. I trained in Palestine."

"Haifa was it, then?"

"No, Sarafand."

"Ah, the walkways there are paved and awfully neat."

"They aren't paved. Only bordered with neat rocks."

"Yes, those brightly painted red ones..."

"They aren't red. They're white."

"Where's the windmill in Jerusalem?"

"It's on Mount Zion. Overlooks the Kidron Valley."

"Really gets some speed up in the wind, what?"

"No. It doesn't turn."

"You claim to be a subaltern, second leftie. Who blessed you with that pip?"

"Captain Herbert Cecil Buck, 1st Punjab Regiment, then later the Scots Guards."

"Handed out the ranks like candy, did he?"

"The orders are in Cairo. Look them up."

"We shall indeed. At the very first opportunity."

"Take me with you when you go."

"You must've had a drink or two at Shepheard's then in Cairo, Froelich. They've got a lovely bar."

"I wasn't yet commissioned. Lower ranks were not allowed."

"You're looking awfully Aryan for a Jew."

"My ancestors were raped by Cossacks. You look more a Jew than I do."

It carried on that way another hour, but Froelich knew they weren't satisfied, and didn't sleep a wink. At the morning formation his four interrogators clustered to one side, talking and regarding him like vultures, and he thought he might be murdered in his sleep. But just then, as the hundred some odd captives formed up to fetch their tools, a German truck arrived to deliver a fresh prisoner.

He was large and lanky, bushy bearded, wearing a keffiyeh

around his neck, with muscled legs and arms bursting from his shorts and shredded tunic. It was Sergeant Stafford Owen, one of the Long Range Desert Group who'd guided the commandos from Kufra to Tobruk. Owen marched right up to Major Haworth, saluted with a grin, then spotted Froelich, threw his arms up high and bellowed, "Frock! You bloody awful driver!" He rushed to Froelich, clapped his arms and crushed him in a hug, and Froelich's fate reversed and for just that moment, all was right with the world.

It didn't last for long. Owen wasn't there to make friends either. Two nights later, he crawled under the wire and raced into the dunes. The Germans chased him, gunned him down, and for breakfast left his corpse upon a hillock, bloating in the sun for all the prisoners to see.

Few men tried escaping after that, for there was nowhere to go, and those who did were quickly hunted down and shot like Owen, a sport that broke up the Germans' monotony. But having nowhere to go did not discourage Froelich's plans, as he had no home on earth in a wider sense than simply the Sahara.

The Allies reconquered Tobruk in November, which Froelich knew because he heard the Germans whisper, and he became the prisoners' only link to truth because they had no wireless or newspapers. Rommel's fuel lines were smashed at from the air and ground, and he rolled back on his heels into Tunisia as Montgomery's tankers pounded at his face. Mobile Stalag Nine moved farther south, and then again toward Borj el-Khadra, building roads and airfield strips that wouldn't last the winter. December and then January broiled them all by daylight and froze their bones with cold at night, and Froelich often found that he fell onto his cot drenched in sweat, and woke at dawn with his pathetic blanket stiff with ice.

The monotony tormented him, leaving too much time to brood, day after day, week by week, month by month. There were no books or music, and the improvised chess games made of German ration crates and empty rifle cartridges didn't interest him. His hands were blistered black and raw, his arms and legs ached day and night, and he felt his body losing every cell of fat. Once a water truck appeared, and the prisoners lined up naked to be deloused with spray that stank like sewage, and he looked down to see his pelvis bone bulging through his skin. He felt that he was going mad and death was lurking just around the corner.

And still, he bided his time, worked the road gangs, caught and killed and ate whatever slithering desert creatures he could find, and watched the Wehrmacht sentries and their routines like a zoologist. Then at last, he pickpocketed a folding knife from one of his German charges and traded it for a pilot's wristwatch. He had to know the timing of the sentries' stints at the gate, where the concertina wire fences left a gap for lorries. And gradually he used his German wiles and chatted up the guards, and approaching his sixth month he'd made something like friends with a boy named Franz from Stuttgart. The boy he was going to kill.

Franz was helpful in this regard, at least in terms of soothing Froelich's conscience, whatever there was left of it. He'd joined the Hitler Youth in '39, worshipped fervently the Führer and his Reich, and knowing Froelich was a Jew, made no apologies, but only explained with cold detachment how all his kind had to be exterminated. With his straw hair and ice blue eyes, Franz looked like a cover model for *Signal*, the Nazi propaganda rag, and when Froelich visited him at his post he ranted on about the Jews as *Untermenschen*, expecting Froelich the subhuman to accept his place in a superior society—which was no place at all. And Froelich listened, feigning understanding and apology, while the Nazi's ravings filled his cup of hatred. Froelich felt that he was fattening a lamb.

Franz stood the watch at night, in four-hour stints. He had a makeshift lean-to at the gate where he could shelter from the wind, but only for ten minutes at the top of every hour. At the bottom of each hour, a sergeant on a motorcycle rumbled by to check as he rode a circuit around the camp, and Froelich noted the precision of the timing. He reckoned there would be a ten-minute spell when no one expected to see Franz outside, then twenty minutes more until he was discovered.

Finally, and even though he felt foreboding surging in his guts, Froelich knew that it was time. A prisoner who kept a mental calendar had mentioned it was Saturday, the Jewish Sabbath meant for rest and peace and prayer, but Froelich took it as a starter pistol's signal, his day to murder slavery.

At the end of that day's labor, he made sure that he was tasked with five other men to return the road tools to the shed. He lagged behind to be the last one out and slipped a ball-peen hammer down inside his baggy trousers, where he'd fixed a bootlace through a waistband hole. He tied the hammer's head and let the handle dangle, and the German guard outside looked only at his empty hands and waved him by. He didn't sit amongst the other POWs to eat the evening meal that night, but stood outside his tent and slurped his putrid stew, awash in jangling nerves and spinning up his hatred.

There were no stars out when Froelich walked to Franz's lean-to at eleven, but the air was clear and cold and he shivered in a Red Cross sweater, with the hammer freed now of its lace, tucked inside his waistband and covered by the wool. The three-sided shelter was pitch-dark inside and all he saw was Franz's grin.

"What are you doing here, Jew dog? You know it's forbidden to leave your cage except to piss."

Froelich returned the grin, his back teeth grinding. "I have American cigarettes from a Red Cross package."

"Keine Lüge?" No lie? Franz stepped forward, and Froelich saw to his horror that the Nazi was wearing a helmet, which he'd never done before at post. Froelich's heart doubled its already racing rate.

"Ja, wirklich," he said, and offered Franz the Lucky Strikes. He stared at Franz's helmet, his mind screaming for solutions as the German plucked a cigarette from the pack and craned his neck outside the lean-to.

"If Colonel Messer sees me smoking here he'll cut my dick off, and then I'll be a filthy mushroom head like you. Did you bring matches, Jew?"

"Yes," said Froelich as he produced the matchbox. "And actually, I'm not cut."

"You're not? Why not?"

Froelich shrugged. "My mother didn't want it."

Franz laughed. "She probably liked Christian cocks and wanted you to have one."

"Maybe." Froelich's smile was a death's-head grin. He cocked his head. "Why are you wearing a helmet tonight?"

"Orders," Franz huffed as he lit up and sucked.

"Really? I heard you had a fight."

"A fight?" Franz pulled his chin back.

"That's what they're saying in the camp." Froelich glanced aside in innocence. "That Sergeant Pakow beat you up, and you're wearing that helmet to hide where he crowned your skull."

"*Scheissedreck!*" Franz spat. "You fucking Jew, who's spreading all that shit? Is it you?"

Froelich raised his palms. "I'm only saying what I heard."

Franz yanked the cigarette from his lips, shot it at the dirt, and stamped it out. He tore the buckle open at his throat, cranked the helmet off, dipped the top of his blond skull at Froelich, and pointed at his cowlick. "There, you stupid Jew. *See* anything?"

And Froelich hit him right there with the hammer, as hard as he could, a full arcing swing from his waistband and over his head and down. The skull crack was so loud it echoed in the shelter, and Franz collapsed like a horse in a French slaughterhouse. Froelich's chest was heaving, sweat bursting from his armpits, as he stared down and grunted, *"Eigentlich, ja."* Actually, yes I do. And even though he knew Franz was already dead, he bent and hit him again, and once more, then stopped because he didn't want the bastard's Nazi uniform soaked in blood.

He was wearing it within a minute, and he took Franz's water bottle, battle harness, and ammunition pouches and scrambled into those as well. Then he grabbed Franz's Schmeisser, and a Bedouin burnoose hanging from a nail, and squinted at his watch. He had nineteen minutes left until they'd find the corpse, and he looked at Franz once more and nearly vomited, but swallowed it instead.

He sprinted that entire time into the desert, and never stopped. Not when he heard the distant engines roar behind him, knowing they'd be flailing out in all directions, nor when he heard the rageful shouts or saw the arcing flares to left and right and overhead. His physique was a mere shadow of what it had been in high school, but he felt that he was running twice his soccer speed and knew that after what he'd done, if he were captured, even Rommel couldn't save him. He never slowed, not even to take cover when the gunfire started. He knew the shots were wild and that meant they'd almost given up.

He barely felt the Mauser bullet bite his waist, or even the machine gun round that cracked his thighbone.

The pain was nothing but a sting, compared to the euphoria of freedom.

Six

Sahara

IN THE MIDST OF NOWHERE, IT WAS EVERY-
where. In the midst of nothing, it was everything.

For the first time in his life, he understood the universe, because this had no end and no beginning. Sometimes there were dunes, soft and deep and clawing at his boots like desperate fingers. Sometimes there were baked lakes of dried brown mud, spidered with mosaics of cracks and hard as marble. Sometimes there were rocks peppering long slopes, promising sure footholds and hope beyond the top, but when he crested, only more dunes. And always there was water, pools of it far away, shimmering with reflections of a scudding cloud or vulture, but as he neared, they always fled, until he knew these were a devil's tease of cruel mirages.

For a while he kept on around the clock, before the adrenaline evaporated and the liberation waned. He gripped his waist wound underneath his tunic, pinched the flesh until the seeping and the bleeding stopped, and at last that one scabbed over. But there was nothing he could do to help his leg wound. He didn't even touch it. Each step was like a dentist's pliers twisting a rotten tooth, shooting lightning bolts up through his hip into his skull. He could stop it if he'd just lie down and die. He wasn't ready yet.

By the third day he knew he couldn't duel with that sun and should only walk at night. He remembered things from Sarafand, about the stars and ways to navigate, and when at dusk the sun gave up its daily quest to kill him, he crawled out from the slice of shade he'd found beneath an outcropping, where he'd lain all day just breathing and thinking things he shouldn't. The sand and rocks sucked heat from dawn till dusk, then quickly breathed it back at night, and his fevers turned to shivers. The sky cloaked over, deeply black, more so than any sky he'd ever seen, and it filled up with a million points of light and he knew he had to choose just one, and wisely. There it was, Ursa Minor, the Little Dipper, and out beyond its handle end, the brightest star, Polaris. He staggered northward after it, each night, all night, and prayed the clouds would stay away, then prayed they'd come and bring him rain, and he often almost wept for it, but didn't.

Franz had half a bar of hardtack in his battle harness. He finished it. His *Feldflasche* canteen was half full of hot water tinged with beer. It didn't last. His thirst turned desperate. His hunger turned treason, devouring his remaining fat. He saw small darting creatures in the night, their gleaming eyes mocking him and laughing, but he wasn't fast enough, or steady enough, to shoot them. He came upon a cactus full of prickly pears and without thinking snatched a flowered fruit, tore it open with his thumbs and ate the orange flesh. But then his hands and lips were full of stinging needles, and he mewled at the sky like a dog quilled by a porcupine.

His pilot's watch stopped working. He saw no point in winding it.

At last it rained one night. It never rained in the Sahara in the summer, or so he thought. He lay down on a hillock on his back and was quickly blanketed in fat black buzzing flies, slurping at his nose and ears and eyes, but he didn't mind and opened his mouth wide and drank the rain for hours. He woke up bloated in the morning, and feeling fueled up, he chose to brave the sun and staggered north, or so he hoped, until his bladder couldn't take it. He stopped and pissed into his dry canteen, and then he stumbled onward, and soon he drank that too.

Panzer tanks appeared, and British lorries here and there, but they were all burned out, looted and empty, except for skeletons, charred corpses rank like spoiled lamb, more flies and slithering fat snakes too quick to catch. Once a single Messerschmitt winged out of the blank cerulean sky and circled and explored him. He looked up at it through the slit in his burnoose, not caring if it killed him, then remembered he was wearing Nazi kit. But anyway it wagged its wings and flew away as if the pilot were gloating, *"Viel Glück!"* Good luck! I'm happy I'm not you.

His skin began to shed everywhere it touched something. It peeled in patches from his face and arms and oozed inside his boots, and his nipples bled where they rubbed against his salt stiffened tunic. His lips split. He had no spit to heal them, and the sand invaded every fleshy crevice, like ground glass filing him raw.

He was falling often now, rising up again, but slower. He knew that he was going mad and it was almost over.

On the tenth dawn, he was on his knees because he couldn't find one shelter. No shelf of rock, no cave, no tree, no shade. Only flat, brown, broiling packed sand and nostril searing air. The pain was eating half of him and he was thinking of his grave, marked by nothing, but he was blinking at a date palm tree a hundred feet away, and a small, white bellied Dama gazelle plucking at its fruit. And even though he knew it was the madness of imagination, he shot it.

She was a thing of beauty, magnificent in death, and real, when he eased himself onto the ground beside her corpse and touched her. So soft. Maybe fifty pounds. The topside of her fur was colored like delicious caramel cream, and her underbelly was white like freshly fallen snow, yes, snow. She had a ballerina's muscled neck, a lovely deer's face sloping to her still wet nose, with a pair of light cream stripes painted to her lashes, and long velvet ears like a giant rabbit's. Her two black horns were straight and perfect, like a pair of children's shofars for Yom Kippur.

He sat there stroking her, thanking her, for maybe half an hour, nothing else around for fifty miles. Just a burnoose hooded German soldier, his machine pistol propped on a small boulder, rocking back and forth and weeping for his pet.

He named her Elsa. He had no knife. But besides the single magazine locked in his Schmeisser's well, there was another one in Franz's battle harness. He took it out, stripped out all the bullets, popped the little floor plate off and for another half an hour, sharpened its steel lip on a flinty rock, while he hummed "Ach du lieber Augustin," a ditty of the plague, then sliced her jugular open. He drank her blood, retched it up and drank some more. He saw that she still had half a date palm in her lips, and he popped it in his mouth and chewed it. And then he ate her eyes.

They left together, late that morning, after he'd plucked the last few dates from the palm and stuffed them in his pockets. He dropped the useless battle harness, forgot the water bottle, and laughed at the small pile of bullets gleaming in the sun, because they looked like some metallic creature had shat brass droppings. With the Schmeisser strapped along his back, he hefted Elsa's corpse across his shoulders, grasped her long fine legs in front, her head upside down and lolling, and they walked.

Too hot when the sun was high, they spooned together in whatever shade he found, inside a wadi or the lee of an acacia. At night they carried on, one foot in front of the other, and just one more, and another. He sliced her belly open and ate her, piece by piece, even though sometimes she made him vomit or shit his watery guts. She kept him warm there on his shoulders like a cloak and shielded his neck from the whipping sands of the haboob.

They found the carcass of a camel. He made a water bladder and a lanyard from its neck folds and its sinews, and filled it from a pool of filthy runoff after a midnight drizzle. It leaked. He came across a peyote cactus and ravaged its meat, which made him more delirious and dreamy but camouflaged his pain, and in his reeling mind, Elsa became his sister. He knew that if his sister was suffering or lame, he'd carry her like this forever, and that was how he walked, and walked, and walked into another month.

But her meat was waning, her maggots bored and wanting more of him than her. Still he made her last by giving her a respite when he found wild desert gourds, or thyme or tamarisk to chew. He dove into the sand to snatch up grubs and spiders, and ate them whole while moaning because the shock of leaping set his leg bones grinding. He caught lizards when their backs were turned, baked their parasites away on the steel of his machine pistol in the sun, then chewed and stuck them in his pocket. Three times, just after short dawn rains, when flash floods ripped through skinny wadis, he flung himself on his stomach and opened his mouth as the rushing wild streams pelted his battered face but filled him. The water made the Schmeisser rusty, and every time he dropped Elsa to save himself with drink, vultures large as pterodactyls tried to take her.

Never. She was going with him to the very end.

But at last, she was nothing, just bones and stinking matted fur, no longer pretty and never answering what he said to her. He buried her beneath a pile of rocks, with a muttered prayer and a scarlet desert rose for a marker, and gave up trying to go on in just the cool of night, because the leg was done and if he stopped at all he'd never rise.

And in the bloody burning horrid heat of one last day, when he was hoping that the Schmeisser's clotted breech would work just one more time and let him put a bullet in his brain, he saw that last mirage on the shimmering horizon, just another encore of delirium, a pair of wavering chess pawns behind a berm of beans.

And the pawns turned into Cockney Harry, and Robbie the Scot.

Seven

July 1943
His Majesty's Hospital Ship *Kensington*

A HUNDRED LOVELY NURSES DESCENDED from the main deck after dinner, bouncing down the stairwell like a Busby Berkeley entertainment, costumed-up in olive-drab fatigues, bellies full of British Navy stews and singing "Over There," a ditty from another worldwide war.

Froelich's bed was tucked into the last row of the empty patients' ward, but he could see them at the other end as they flowed around their bunks like clownfish in a coral cove, smoking, laughing, tossing army purses on their beds and finger-combing curls from pretty faces shiny with the summer's heat. With them came a heady waft of sea salt, perfumed soap, and raw tobacco, and he watched them for a while, then turned his gaze back to the ceiling. Even girls like these, he thought, to whom gore was the norm, would likely want a man with two good legs. But his morphine haze had caused all sorts of visions, so he assumed they weren't real, and when he looked again they all were gone.

The *Kensington*, however, was real as steel. From an airstrip in Tunisia, he'd been flown in a Lockheed Hudson airplane to Algiers, where four corpsmen had bounced him on a litter up the gangway to the ship and dropped him on a bunk below the decks amongst a score of empty metal beds. Right after that the ship had set sail with an armada for the invasion of Sicily, heading toward a beachhead that he'd never heard of, Gela.

The sea was like a living thing, a quilt of breathing liquid, and Froelich's vessel crawled across its undulating skin like an insect hoping not to itch its calm. Much like the fickle desert, the ocean had its moods, from meditative stillness with the dawn to roiling madness bullied by the midnight winds. At times the ship motored straight and true, at other times it rolled and pitched and yawed, and longing for stability, Froelich didn't like it. Yet drunk with drugs and feeling little pain, he accepted being nothing but a passenger, with a ticket to wherever fate would toss him.

The *Kensington* was unarmed and unremarkable. Four hundred feet from prow to stern, her flanks of soiled white were emblazoned with red crosses and her decks were packed with crates and rucks of medical supplies, above which lifeboats swayed from davits like salamis in a butcher's kitchen. Her crew was meager, though game and optimistic, and in addition to six British medical officers she had a hundred nurses, mostly American girls eager to be put ashore. For the moment, the surgeons all ignored their only patient. Preparing for invasion, they had no time or interest in amputating Froelich's leg, for soon, they knew, they'd all be under fire.

And Froelich had no curiosity about the bigger picture. He didn't care that Rommel, the man who'd plucked him from the teeth of one hell and dropped him in another, had been finally trounced in Africa. He felt no victor's pride to hear from one old salt that the *Kensington* was just one of three thousand vessels steaming toward the Allies' first strike on Europe's "soft" Italian underbelly. His war had shrunk to very small six-foot bumpy mattress on a patch of metal springs, illuminated by a swaying light bulb painted blue, with a porthole rarely open to the breeze. The losses and the wins were someone else's game.

The second day at sea was rough. The Mediterranean grew restless for midsummer and seemed to balk at warships that thought they'd ride her back for free. The engine thrummed and clanked as the ship rose and fell and cleaved through clawing crests of gray-green waves. Froelich didn't sleep a wink, despite the ampule needles in his veins, and at times he had to grip the siderails of his bunk to keep from flopping out. He lay there staring at the ceiling of black steam pipes and top-deck under-timbers, where green musette bags hung from wire hooks swayed back and forth like canvas udders, and below him nurses' Tommy helmets slid and screeched across the tilting deck like turtles fleeing from a fire.

No one spoke to him, except the captain's cabin boy, who checked his welfare every other hour and brought him crackers and canteens of soda water for his nausea. A lad of just fourteen, Timmy's skinny frame was lost in sailor dungarees, which made him look like a red-haired freckled head popping from a denim sausage. His summer-pinkened face was bright with thrills of upcoming adventures, things that Froelich knew a boy should never see. He should have been at home in Liverpool, practicing for Sunday choir.

Timmy wore a brimless British sailor's cap with *Kensington* embroidered on the band. He took it off whenever officers or ladies were about, and gesticulated with it like a pointer. Now he twisted it and thrust it out at Froelich.

"You all right there, sir?"

"Just fine thanks, Tim."

Timmy's wide green eyes crinkled. "Had a gander yet at all our Yank birds?"

"You mean the American army nurses?"

"Right!" Timmy twirled the cap like a circus dinner plate. "There's some Brit birds and 'bout a hundred Yanks, some of 'em *real* posh."

"I saw them once down here," Froelich said, "but thought it was a dream."

"Oh no, they're bleedin' real!" Timmy clapped his fingers to his mouth. "Sorry, sir, shouldn't say it that way."

"That's all right, Tim."

"You haven't seen 'em, sir, 'cause they've been topside for lifeboat and fire drills. We're putting 'em ashore in Sicily, along with you, I think."

"Right," said Froelich, although he couldn't fathom why they'd drag his helpless form up to a beachhead hospital, just to make him useless for all time. Often now the panic of impending amputation dredged up desperate thoughts, some even close to suicide. But then he'd judge himself pathetic, knowing just how much his friends who'd lost their lives would give to live again with just one leg.

"Don't know why the Cap wants all those drills." Timmy shrugged his bony shoulders. "We're seagull white with twenty-foot red crosses, and at night we're all lit up from bow to bum like a Christmas tree. No one's gonna bomb us. It's the *rules*."

Froelich only smirked and raised a thumb.

"Well, ta-ta for now!" Timmy spun around and bounded up the stairwell toward the light, and Froelich watched him go and thought, *You don't know the Germans.*

Sometime later in that second evening, the sea becalmed as if Neptune had quelled his indigestion, and Froelich heard that happy chorus line tumbling down the stairs again. He closed his eyes and tried to push them from his mind, but then he heard the clops of small boot soles approaching and he rose up on his elbows as a pair of nurses flanked him.

"Oh, don't get up for us, Lieutenant," said the American one who'd walked up to his left. "We're *so* low class." She had a wide grin, chestnut eyes, and lovely curling auburn hair.

"Speak for yourself, Yank," said the other girl as she grinned too and braced him on the other side. She had short blond hair, a button nose, and an English schoolgirl's gap-toothed smile.

Both were wearing fatigue pants with flapped front pockets, but they'd shed their tunics in the heat and sported only clingy undershirts, their dog tags hanging from fine necks that looked as smooth as Greek sculptures.

"I'm Dorothy," said the Yank as she unwrapped a tab of Dubble Bubble gum and tipped it in her mouth.

"Vera here," the blond Brit said, as from somewhere behind her came a curse, a giggle, the squeal of a wireless set, and the crackling of Glenn Miller's "In the Mood."

"A pleasure." Froelich nodded once at each, then fixed his gaze on their eyes to keep from glancing at their curves. "I'm Froelich, Bernard."

"You mean, 'sir,' right, Lieutenant?" Dorothy snapped a salute, then popped a small pink globe of gum and sucked it back into her lips.

"We've brought you dinner," Vera said. She held a metal tray with a steel water cup and a plate piled high with fish and chips.

"It's really swell." Dorothy nodded at the meal, and Froelich raised a brow at Vera.

"She means it's good," Vera translated for him, and she placed it on Froelich's lap.

"Thank you very much," he said, although he had no appetite. He looked at them and thought of Otto, and the oath he'd sworn to never make a wartime friend again, but then he reasoned that these girls were noncombatants, so perhaps their amity was safe.

Dorothy touched the bottom of the bedsheet covering his legs. "Mind if we take a peek, sir?"

"If you can bear it," Froelich said.

Dorothy and Vera peeled the sheet away, their eyes expectant as if they might find some strange creature trapped beneath. He was grateful that the corpsmen had left him in his shorts, and also that they'd plucked the maggots out.

"It's all splinted up," said Vera.

"Yes, it's broken," he said, and winced as Dorothy peeled

the heavy bandage from his thigh. She wrinkled her nose, but tried not to look alarmed.

"It's kinda stinky, but we've seen worse."

"Just take your penicillin, sir," Vera said. "It's on the tray there too."

"Of course, mum." He smiled, relishing the nurturing.

Vera tilted her blond head. "You've got an accent."

"So do *you*," Dorothy said to Vera, and both girls laughed.

"Born on the Continent." Froelich offered nothing more.

"Oh, I see." Vera winked. "Someone mentioned that you're all hush-hush." She looked down and fingered a manila card tied to Froelich's splint. "What's all this, then?"

Dorothy squinted at the card and its grease pencil scrawl: Schedule Amputation. She looked at Vera, pulled a face like a child rejecting spinach and said, "Heck, no. It's *way* too early."

"I fully agree." Vera nodded. "Let's tend to that, shall we?"

While Vera held the card, Dorothy slipped a pair of scissors from her trousers, snipped it off, tore it up, and stuffed the remnants in her pocket. She clacked the scissor blades.

"There!" Her smile was angelic. "All better."

Froelich frowned. "But at the Eighth in Libya, the field surgeon said..."

"*Shh.*" Dorothy put a finger to his lips and whispered, "You've got at least three days, maybe even more before they get to you again. Invasions keep docs hoppin'. We'll drown it in sulfanilamide and pump up your penicillin."

Froelich stared at her and swallowed. "Are you married?"

Dorothy blushed and Vera laughed and said, "You heard her, sir. It's way too early!"

They replaced his bandage and his sheet as another nurse

appeared, handling a folding surgeon's curtain on a tri-piece metal frame. She opened it across the foot of Froelich's bed and walked away. Vera shrugged at him.

"Terribly sorry, sir, but we ladies need our privacy."

"It's a shame, too." Dorothy grinned. "We've got some gals with great gams."

"She means girls with lovely legs," Vera translated again.

Dorothy squeezed Froelich's arm and said, "See ya later," and the pair disappeared beyond the curtain. Then Dorothy's pretty head poked out again.

"Call us if you need the potty." She wagged a warning finger. "But no peeking! It's so damn hot down here, we all sleep in the nude."

She winked and they were gone for good, and for a moment Froelich wondered if he'd dreamed them up. But there the food tray sat, all too real and unappealing. He picked at a few chips and the pink feathers of cold fish meat, took the pills, washed them down, and slipped the tray onto the deck. Then he fell asleep to the strains of Miller's mood.

In the arms of the morphine and the witching hour, Froelich found himself again in Germany.

He didn't know the place at first, only that the sky was silver blue, and clouds that looked like feathered pillows teased the morning winter sun. The air was full of pine and woodfire smoke, and the wind flicked icy fingers at his face below his raccoon hat and goggles. Where was this now? The trees were tall and spiky, with fat green needles coated in white cream, and there below him in the valley matchbox houses embraced a church's spire with a cap just like a plum. Then he looked down at his woolen pantaloons and skis, and knew.

It was the hill between Gestern and St. Augustin, where he and his little sister had cut their hiking teeth in summer and skied all winter long. It was just two hundred meters high, but to them it was an Alp, and Papa wouldn't let them use the horse to tow them to the top. He was a mountain man, a climber, and a soccer coach, and he wanted them to have good legs and healthy lungs. So, for every run, they had to haul their wooden skis and poles up to the top, just to get a single minute's rush.

"Komm, Bernard!"

There was Greta at the bottom, waving her red mittens. Even far away he saw her dimpled smile, red wool cap, matching double-buttoned coat, and her long caramel braids whipped up by the wind. She annoyed him, and adored him, and he felt the same depending on which day it was. But days like these were always good.

He pushed off with his poles and slalomed down the hill through runnels of fresh snow. And then he raced right for her, sliced a curve and sprayed her head to foot as she jumped back and yelled and laughed, *"Blöde Kuh!"* Stupid cow!

He laughed in triumph. "You have to react faster!"

She pelted him with snowballs, and he let her and pretended that they hurt.

"Mutti's making vanilla Kipferl!" Greta cooed with glee about the cookies. "And hot chocolate."

"Good. Let's go in," he said. "It's damn cold."

"No." Greta pouted like a schoolmarm and raised a warning finger. "Papa says we have to do five runs, and that was only four."

"You think he's really watching?" He squinted at their distant house.

She put her small fists to her hips and pinned him with her bright blue eyes. "Yes, with his field glasses."

Froelich smirked. "You might be right, for once."

"Koffer," she said, the German word for suitcase, but in school slang it meant dolt.

"Here comes Lümpy," Froelich said as their dachshund returned from peeing on a tree. The small brown sausage dog bounded through the drifts and barked.

"Sit, Lümpy," Greta ordered with a mitten. "And *stay.*" The dachshund sat, but whimpered a complaint. He'd tried to climb up with them once, but was so exhausted that Froelich had to ski down with him tucked under an arm.

They shouldered skis and poles and started trudging for the summit. Greta fell behind, but her legs were so much smaller and he secretly admired her resolve. At last they made it to the top, panting foggy funnels, and strapped their skis back on. Greta fixed her goggles as she stood beside her brother and looked out at the picture-perfect vista, and a flock of honking winter geese cleaved the sky above.

"It's pretty," she said.

"So are you," said Froelich, with no idea why he'd uttered such a thing, but he turned away and blushed.

Greta's smile stretched her lips and she said, "I love you, Bernard," and she pushed off before he'd have a chance to take it back or ruin it.

He watched her go, and then he heard the train.

THE LAST OF THE SEVEN

Which was curious, because no railroad tracks ran through Gestern. Yet there it was, the heavy warning whistle, the growing Doppler of iron wheels clacking over ties, the heavy thumps of giant pistons and the hissing spews of steam. Greta was a small red figurine shushing down the hill, and somehow sensing danger with the dichotomy of things that shouldn't be, Froelich took off too but couldn't catch her, and he saw a blur of freight cars screeching to a halt behind her tiny form as she tumbled in the snow and lost her skis.

The freight car doors screeched open and Nazi soldiers spewed from their black maws, but their faces were horrifically half human and half wolves, and with heavy rifles swinging from their shoulders and hands like clawing talons, they snatched up Greta as she kicked and screamed. They dragged her back inside the train, and its black steam funnel belched a plume of copper fire.

He tore his skis off and tried to yell, but nothing of his voice would come because his throat was packed with sand, and he ran past Lümpy's trampled little body, and then the train began to clank away. He stumbled through the drifts and tried to stop it, but collapsed because he only had one leg, while from inside the monster Greta's small red mittens gripped a window's iron bars. Her tiny face thrust out and she shrieked as if something horrible was happening to her inside the train, "Bernard! Please *help* me, Bernard!"

And he snapped up in his bunk aboard the *Kensington*, soaked in sweat and yelling, but they'd reached the shores of Sicily and no one heard him for the shelling.

The whole ship shuddered with the cracks and booms of naval guns, and Froelich gripped his sodden sheet and tried to orient from one nightmare to another. To the right his porthole had been closed, its beam of morning light swirling with dust devils swatted from the ceiling by concussions. His mouth was dry and thick, and he reached down to the deck, snatched his water cup, downed all of it, slithered down the bed and kicked the surgeon's curtain over.

No one else was in the hold. All the nurses' helmets and musette bags were gone, and for a moment panic gripped him as he thought he'd been abandoned and forgotten. Then, at the far stairwell, a pair of boots appeared across the handrails and Timmy zoomed down from the top, landed like a cat, and ran across the deck.

"Morning, sir!" The boy's grin beamed below a giant helmet, and he wore a life belt like a rubber doughnut.

"Where the hell are we, Tim?"

"We're just off Gela Harbor. You slept all bleedin' night! That pretty Yank bird shaved you proper, but you didn't even stir." Timmy winked as if he'd witnessed something pornographic, and Froelich touched his jaw to find it smooth.

"Where are they all?" He had to shout above the gunfire.

"Up top, waiting for the landing boats, but we can't get in for all the ruckus."

Froelich struggled up. Timmy came around the bed to help him twist his splinted leg, and Froelich slung one arm across his bony shoulders and they staggered to the porthole. Froelich hauled it open, and a gale of sights and sounds smacked their faces.

To the left, a line of battle cruisers, hulls turned broadside to the beachhead, belched out cannon fire, each shell lurching from a ring of smoke as if a row of fat men were puffing on cigars. To the right the rocks and palms of Gela's craggy shore endured wild eruptions, and the maelstrom rolled across the emerald waters with a sound just like the train in Froelich's nightmare. The bay was packed with landing ships, from twelve-man fragile craft to giant hulls replete with tanks and trucks, all belching smoke and honking horns and sirens, as if a horde of barnyard hogs were surging toward a tasty swill. The morning air was laced with nostril-stinging smoke and salt and cordite.

"It's a *terrific* show! Right, sir?" Timmy yelled above the booms, but all Froelich could think was that the women on his ship should not be there, nor should this child.

"Who's that over there?" Froelich gestured where another hospital ship rocked amongst the swells and shivered with explosions.

"The *Talamba*," Timmy called. "She's got a flock of birds aboard as well, but they can't get in either."

Just then a buzzing hum encroached upon the gunfire. Out to sea and high up in the sky, a clot of twisting shapes winged over in a screaming dive.

"Look, sir!" Timmy thrust a finger up. "Yanks!"

"Those aren't Yanks, Tim. Those are *Stukas*." He gripped the boy and pulled him back as all across the bay, batteries of antiaircraft guns swung around and up, spewing tracer bullets at the sky. Fifty-caliber machine guns and furious sailors' rifles joined the fray, but nothing stopped the German pilots from loosing their black bombs. One of the finned missiles whistled down, smacked into the waves between them and the *Talamba* and exploded. The shock waves were enormous, and the *Kensington* rocked hard and Froelich tumbled on his back onto the deck, with Timmy falling right on top of him.

"Jesus!" Timmy wailed. "Don't those wankers see our bleedin' red crosses?"

"I believe that's what they're aiming for," Froelich said.

"Hardwick! Where the hell are you?" a voice boomed.

They craned their necks and saw a boatswain's face, upside down and poking through the stairwell hatch.

"Right here, sir!" Timmy squeaked.

"Well, get your arse up to the bridge. Captain wants you quick. We're putting out to sea until this show's safer for the nurses."

"Right, sir!"

Timmy shot up on his feet. The boatswain scared him more than bombs, and he darted for the stairwell, then spun around and said, "So sorry, sir, but, it's the captain…"

"Duty calls, Tim." Froelich waved him off.

"Ta-ta for now, then!" Timmy yelped, and was gone.

Still sprawled there on the deck, Froelich turned his head and saw that some kind soul had tucked a crutch beneath his bunk. The hold was very hot now, his singlet soaked and sweat beads dripping from his chin, but he crawled to it and pulled it out and staggered to the porthole. He gripped the rim and watched the mortal contest as the *Kensington* reversed and began to pull away.

"You haven't got me yet," he called out in defiance to the diving German aircraft, and in the pounding of their bombs he thought he heard their answer.

Give us time, Jew. Give us time…

Eight

Mar Di Sicilia

MONDAY WAS A LANGUID LOVELY DAY. FORTY miles out at sea, to the *Kensington* the beachfront battle was a distant thing. The waves were lakefront gentle, the air bright blue and cleansed of gunfire smoke, and the portholes were all thrown open to the Mediterranean's breezes and its golden dazzling light.

Froelich had an egg and sausage breakfast in his bunk, with black coffee in a brass mug fashioned by a sailor from a cannon shell. Timmy helped him to the toilet, then draped his bad leg in a poncho liner and perched him on a stool for a cool shower. He hadn't felt that clean in months, and Dorothy came to check and change his bandage, and her lyrical voice played strains of hope he dared to entertain.

"I oughta warn you, sir," she said as she brushed his swollen wound with purple tincture. "When they finally get you

off this tub and to whichever kinda hospital, they might have
to bust this leg again. Not sure it's setting right."

He'd never heard the word "bust" used that way, but he
got the gist and murmured, "Marvelous, can't wait." He was
on his elbows watching Dorothy work, and she glanced up
and smiled.

"It's Vera's birthday today," she said brightly as she finished
up. "Twenty-two. Ship's cook is baking her a cake, heaven
knows from what."

"Plaster cast icing?" Froelich ventured. "Signal flare can-
dles?"

"You're a *card*, Lieutenant." Dorothy grinned and pulled
a small booklet from her trouser pocket. On the cover was
the title, *Soldiers' Guide to Sicily*, with a drawn image of the
island and a black hand pointing at its middle. "Sorry, it's all
I've got for you to read." She pulled a frown. "Those girls
pilfered all my Pearl Bucks."

"Well, thank you very much." Froelich smiled and took
the booklet.

Dorothy focused on his leg again, looking down and
smoothing a fresh bandage. Froelich snatched the chance to
look at where her dog tags disappeared into her khaki blouse,
then quickly at her eyes again when she looked up and curled
a lock of hair behind her ear.

"Sir, I gotta ask a question," she said, though it sounded
more like asking for permission.

"Go right ahead," he said, suspecting it might be about
religion.

"Well, are you…?" Just then the ship's horn blasted. Dorothy jumped, looked at her wristwatch, exclaimed, "Jiminy

Cricket I gotta go, see ya later!" And she squeezed his bicep hard and took off for the stairwell, and he watched her bound away.

Perhaps this angel's right, he thought. *My fate is in my hands, not some cold uncaring surgeon's*, and he dared to think perhaps someday a kind and loving girl like her might have him as he was—one leg, none, or two. He touched his bicep where she'd squeezed it, lay back and fell into a long deep nap, and his slumber carried on all day, as if he knew he'd have to store it up...

The German bomb struck the *Kensington* at 5:00 a.m., just as the sea and sky were paling from ink to sunrise silver. Froelich sensed that it was coming, because he heard the first one miss.

The girls had been up top on deck all evening, celebrating Vera's birthday and the news that soon at last they'd go ashore, playing cards and singing everything from "I'll Be Seeing You" to "Chattanooga Choo Choo." Tim had brought him supper, though no one delivered cake, but he assumed with all those healthy girls the cook's dessert had not survived six feet from the galley. He was simply pleased to listen to their laughter, for he knew what they were going to, and at last the American throng parted from the smaller group of British girls, who slept topside in a single cabin near the bridge. The Yanks descended, put his curtain up, giggled as they stripped and slipped into their beds, and then the only lights left on were tiptoe blue.

His eyes flicked open in the darkness, as somewhere in his dreams he heard the distant thrum, unlike the flitting Stukas and more like the heavier rumbles of Dornier bombers.

He tensed and gripped the bedrails as the whistle of a lancing tailfin grew, and the nearby thump and water geyser rocked the hull. He heard some mutters as a few girls stirred, and he wished the bridge would give up their illusions of fair play and douse the bloody running lights. He doubted that it all would pass, but he laid his head back down again.

Just after that, the detonation was like two enormous frying skillets being banged together just beside his ears.

Deck timbers cracked and crashed from overhead. Steam pipes ruptured and sprayed the air with hissing tongues. The wooden toilet door went spinning off its hinges and pirouetted onto someone's legs. The hold was plunged into darkness, the ship's engine groaned one last turn and stopped, flames began to spit and crackle somewhere, and Froelich realized he was on the floor. Not a soul had screamed, but the girls were calling for each other.

"Marion, are you all right?"

"I'm okay. Where's Betty?"

"I'm here! I've got a pile of wood on me."

"June, I can't find my helmet or my life belt."

"Just crawl until you scoop some up, it doesn't matter!"

"I'm *buck* naked. I can't find my darn fatigues."

"Who cares, Mary? Throw a blanket on!"

He listened to the female cries and wanted to jump in and join the roll call, but had the inane thought that his male voice amongst the urgent chatter would intrude. Then he heard their chief nurse shouting from above.

"Girls, grab whatever the hell you can and get topside! Cap'n's calling for the lifeboats!"

The ship began to list, stern down and port side, and Froelich felt it and he smeared his sweat-slickened palms against the deck. Smoke was rolling through the hold and watering his eyes. He reached out for his crutch and couldn't find it, but somehow got his battle trousers on, the left leg sliced away to fit his splint. He rolled onto his chest and started crawling toward where he thought the stairwell was. They'd forgotten he was down there, and he wasn't going to make it.

"Lieutenant, are you here somewhere?"

Dorothy's voice was rent with coughs and wheezes, but she was moving toward him in the swirling blackness, just as she'd been taught to under fire, on her belly and her elbows.

"Here, Dorothy." He saw her eyes as a searchlight from another vessel swept across the portholes. Her hair was wild about her face and her full lips trembled, but her jaw was set with the determination of the role she'd chosen for her life.

"Let's get the heck outta here!" She grabbed his arm and spun herself around to his right side, and in a flash of light from something bursting in the hold, he saw that she was wearing just her tunic top and nothing else. She pressed her naked hip against his and they crabbed madly toward the stairwell, with Froelich's bandage snagging on debris and sending lightning bolts up through his spine.

Another nurse came tumbling down the stairwell on her rump, and Froelich saw the stairs and rails had all been twisted from their bolts in the explosion. She was plump and barefoot, wearing just a helmet and a blanket, gripping a wet washcloth over mouth and nose, and she looked to Froelich like some demon diva in a Wagnerian opera.

"Dorothy, what the hell?" she called out in a muffled cry.

"Allison," Dorothy gasped. "Help me get him topside."

Froelich hauled himself up and gripped the handrails as something burst above and shrapnel pinged off metal. Dorothy jammed her shoulder to his rump and Allison reached down and gripped his sodden singlet, released a yell and pulled with all her might. In three long yanks of strains and coughing epithets, they got him to the top, and just as all three collapsed onto the deck, the stairwell bolts gave way and it collapsed and crashed into the hold.

The deck was something from a Dante dream. Froelich lay there on his side, his eyes emblazoned by the awful vision. The ship's entire bridge was gone, leaving nothing but a cracker box of crackling flames and splintered timbers. The ship's steam stack was a lifeless silhouette against the brightening sky, but just abaft of that, her twin air intakes were spewing flames like hellish trombone bells as the diesel tanks below were set alight. On the port side, the gunwales had been shredded by the bomb and drooped like slack-jawed lips, and Froelich saw that forward, all the wooden lifeboats were burning like dessert flambés.

All across the stern deck scores of nurses wandered in a daze, tending to each other and some wounded members of the crew. Many of the girls were still half-naked, and as soot-caked British sailors fought the flames with fire hoses and hauled up buckets from the waves below, they took the time to strip off smoldering trousers and give them to the women, as if their modesty was equal to their lives. Froelich searched for Tim but couldn't find him.

"Ahoy there, *Kensington*!" The distant voice was tinny, calm, and British. "We are coming alongside. Ropes and boats, if you please."

Froelich turned to see the masts of the *St. Andrew,* a sister hospital ship, drifting up the starboard side about a hundred yards off. Her crew was crowded at the gunwales, cranking at the pulleys of her lifeboats, and the voice came from her bridge's megaphone. Closer by, amongst the chaos and debris of his ship's deck, Froelich saw the *Kensington*'s chief nurse, a stout redheaded woman, waving her arms as a boatswain's whistle pierced the air, rife with burning diesel, smoke, and sweat.

"Everyone to those boats!" the chief nurse yelled, and she pointed to the only two still left intact, swinging from their davits near the starboard stern.

Froelich pushed himself off the listing deck, got up on one foot, reached down for Dorothy's armpit, and hauled her up beside him. The nurses were all struggling to their feet, a pathetic sight of mismatched uniforms, flushed nude skin, and cockeyed helmets. Some had lifebelts drooping to their ankles and one girl clutched a precious, useless wireless, but Dorothy stood there frozen beside Froelich, fists clenched white, tears brimming in her smoke-burned eyes.

"Where's Vera?" she shouted. "Vera!"

Allison appeared and gripped her quaking shoulders.

"Their cabin's gone, honey. It's all *gone.*"

"No!" Dorothy spun around and shook her off. "Vera!"

Froelich followed Dorothy's stare. Just behind the burning bridge, a large deck cabin had been crushed in the explosion, its steel hatch twisted like a pig's ear and jammed shut. Spirals of black smoke were pouring from its blown-out portholes, and instantly he understood that was where the British doctors and their nurses had been quartered. Dorothy collapsed onto her knees, sobbing in her hands.

"We must get her to the *boat*," Froelich barked at Allison, and they both reached down and gripped Dorothy's arms and pulled her hard to switch her focus. She looked up at them and cried "Oh God" as they dragged her upright, turned her around and staggered toward the lifeboats.

The one boat closest to the stern, packed full of survivors, had already gone overboard, its pulleys being cranked by British sailors, leaving one boat left. Froelich's leg was screaming at his brain to stop as he and Allison dragged Dorothy over shrapnel shards and smoking timbers, but he just bit his lip to bleeding as he watched a British midshipman calmly loading up the hull with struggling nurses. The sailor had one broken arm flapping by his side and blood coursed down his face from something in his scalp, but he only gritted his teeth and said, "Quickly now, young ladies. And you there, sir, as well."

And then they were squeezing into the open hull, a tangled mass of trembling limbs and boots and fire-singed hair. The sailor shouted, "Lower away, lads!" and the pulleys turned and the hawsers moaned as the boat descended toward the waves in jerky fits.

Froelich slumped back against a pair of someone's bony knees, sucking in the sea air that was finally clear of choking smoke. But up above, across the *Kensington*'s decks, he saw the fire bursting up in places where it hadn't been before, and knew the ship was lost. A flock of seagulls ranged and circled overhead as if they knew that there would soon be tasty treats to pick, and then the lifeboat jolted hard and splashed into the waves, and someone at the helm yelled orders and the oars unshipped and they began to pull away.

Dorothy slouched beside him, her body shaking everywhere, with her small palms lying upward on her bare and battered thighs. He slipped an arm around her shoulders, and then he heard a distant horrid scream, and looking up at the *Kensington* again, he spotted Tim.

The boy was standing by a porthole of the British nurses' cabin, where flames were licking at its shattered roof now from inside. The screams were coming from one girl still trapped within, and she'd thrust her face outside the porthole, its ring too small for her escape, screaming for mercy.

He saw Timmy clamping both his palms against his ears, spinning around in place, searching desperately for something. And then Froelich knew the girl was Vera, and he pulled Dorothy into him and crushed her face against his chest, covering her eyes, as Tim found a timber, and with all his trembling might, swung it at that poor girl's skull, and she disappeared inside the cabin as it vomited its fire to the sky.

Froelich didn't know if he should pray for Tim's survival or demise, for he knew that what the boy had seen and done would last until his end of days. No, there was no salvation here for Vera or for Tim. And as for him, between the sand and sea, the guns and fire, it seemed that he was always at the mercy of the Germans, or the earth.

Nine

Sicily

THE ITALIANS BOMBED LICATA ON A SUNDAY morning.

The summer skies above the seaside town were Forget-Me-Not blue, and the rising sun had just begun to edge the stucco silhouettes in lemon peel fringes, when the surviving airplanes from Guzzoni's Sixth Army flew down from Foggia to punish the Sicilians for their surrender. The church bells in the central medieval spire of Sant'Angelo had rung a pleasant call to prayer, and soon thereafter, a frantic peal of warning, and then a thousand starlings rose up in twisting murmurations as the spire exploded into clouds of dust, shattered sacramental wafers, and raining stone.

Froelich lay there in the flatbed of a rusting poultry truck, on the long and winding road from Gela, where the thorny fields surrounding Ponte Olivo still sprouted abandoned Allied parachutes, like dying jellyfish in a summer baked lagoon. The truck was packed with wounded British and Americans, and he'd spent the night shivering beneath a threadbare woolen blanket, back-to-back against some moaning stranger. The road was clotted up with vehicles of all kinds, jeeps and trucks and half-tracks, and between them braying donkeys weaved with wagons full of refugees hoping for a peace that wasn't there. The truck was roofless, with nothing sheltering the bed or cab, and only cedar side slats to keep the poultry crates, or now the wounded men, from rolling out.

Froelich, lying just behind the driver's tractor-style seat, heard the bombs, pushed himself erect and twisted around. They'd climbed into the hills just north of Gela off the coast, and below them in the distance he could see Licata burning, while just beyond the carnage morning fishing sloops of pastel hues still cast their nets into a tranquil sea. The driver, a young Italian officer who'd surrendered on the first day of the landings, clenched his fist and punched it at Licata and the sky.

"*Bastardi fascisti!*" he cried out, then spit a gob of something onto the broken road and yelled again, "*Bastardi!*"

Froelich only knew a few words and phrases of Italian, from preparations for a high school trip he'd taken once to Rome, but he understood "fascist bastards."

"*Sì, bastardi,*" he agreed.

The driver turned his head. He had oiled black hair, handsome hazel eyes and a sad mouth, and he spewed a tirade of frustration in Italian, both hands off the wheel as he waved his arms and cursed. Froelich raised apologetic palms.

"*Mi dispiace,*" he called above the rumbling engine. "*Non parlare Italiano.*"

The driver sagged, disappointed. *"Inglese?"*

"Sì." Froelich nodded. *"Parli inglese?"*

"No." The driver shook his head, but then confessed, *"Un po."* A little.

"Parli tedesco?" Froelich asked if he spoke German.

"Mai!" Never! The driver huffed and slammed the brakes as an old man on a donkey laden with bulging leather suitcases darted between the truck and a British half-track just ahead. *"Idiota!"* the driver yelled, and the old man countered with *"Imbecille!"* and they flicked each other off with fingers under chins. The driver shifted gears and drove again, and he and Froelich both looked up as three Italian Picchiatello dive-bombers, the twins of German Stukas, winged away in search of other heretics.

"Traditori," the driver spat, then touched his chest as if they'd stung his heart. He was still wearing his Italian officer's tunic, but it was open to a soiled singlet and all the buttons had been sliced off. *"Sono* Fabrizio," he introduced himself.

"Sono Bernard," said Froelich.

"Piacere, Bernardo." The driver smiled and Froelich did as well, though neither of them thought it was a pleasure here.

"Sei un ufficiale?" Fabrizio asked.

"Sì," Froelich said because he knew the word meant officer, and inquired in kind, *"E tu?"*

"Sì!" Fabrizio raised his chin in pride. *"Tenente."* Lieutenant.

"I'm a lieutenant as well," Froelich said in English.

"Ottimo!" Fabrizio saluted, British style, as he focused on the road, and then he dredged up some English. "I join *Italiano* army for food. Now I have no army, *and* no food."

Froelich smirked. "I joined the British Army to kill Germans." He briefly thought of Franz and realized he felt not a stitch of regret. "But so far, I'm not very good at it."

Fabrizio shook his head. *"Non capisco, Bernardo."*

"That's all right," said Froelich.

"Acqua?" Fabrizio offered water.

"Oh, yes please."

Fabrizio came up with a glass bottle, popped the wired-on ceramic cap with a thumb and handed it rearwards to Froelich. The water had a taste of olive oil but it was cool and good.

"You go *hospitale*, *sì*?" Fabrizio asked.

"Yes, I think so."

Fabrizio took the bottle back, swigged a pull, swished his mouth, and spat some in the road.

"You go Agrigento, a *villagio* by the sea," he said. "Agrigento is *bella*, if it is not bomb-ed."

"Yes," Froelich agreed, though he'd never heard of the place and knew nothing of it. "If it is not bombed."

Fabrizio concentrated on the road, where clouds of ocher dust were rising from the wagon wheels and donkey hooves and clanking armor treads. The grit swirled in corkscrews across the rumbling truck, crawling into squinting eyes and nostrils and causing coughs and curses. Fabrizio came up with a pair of black-rimmed tanker's goggles and pulled them on, which made him look like a motocross competitor at a San Gennaro festival, the kind who'd make the village girls swoon.

Froelich hunkered down again, taking cover from the dust, then remembered something and fished inside the pocket of his battle trousers. Somehow, he still had Dorothy's guide-book, though he had no idea how he'd managed to retain it in the sinking of their ship and violent rescue.

Once aboard the *St. Andrew*, the surviving nurses, battered, bruised, and traumatized, had been taken off to quarters by doting British sailors, perhaps to spare them witnessing the final gasps of *Kensington*, whose crew had fought the flames so bravely but without success. Froelich and some other wounded had been left atop *St. Andrew*'s decks, where they'd watched a destroyer escort stand off from the *Kensington* and sink her with its guns, like some pitiable old farmer's mare who'd broken all her legs.

He and Dorothy had parted with a trembling soaked embrace, and he sensed he'd never see her after that, and she had wept for everything and he had touched her face just once and she was gone. But he'd come to think the war was like a bustling railway station. Sometimes you'd take a bench between arrivals and departures, and briefly know some stranger, learn her story and her warmth, and then your trains would come and you'd be pulled apart, strangers once again. Sometimes addresses and even telephone numbers were exchanged with hopeless smiles, for bombings everywhere were obliterating homes, and phone lines were as fragile as spiderwebs to a typhoon.

The girls had all been shipped back to Africa for treatment of their injuries and trauma, while some days later he and the other wounded had been loaded on a landing craft and gone ashore. He'd ceased to wonder at the logic of it all, sending broken men back into the fray, like a steamer trunk of shattered dolls from which you'd salvage a few parts and assemble bright fresh new ones, ready to be fractured once again.

The book, still damp with seawater, had many pages stuck together. Froelich pulled them gingerly apart until he found a key to useful street Italian. He ran a finger down the list and called out to the driver.

"Tenente Fabrizio."

"*Sì*, Tenente Bernardo?"

"*Quante ore?*" Froelich asked.

Fabrizio thought the Englishman was asking the time, so he glanced at his scratched wristwatch and said, "*Nove del mattino.*" Nine in the morning.

"No," Froelich said. "*Quante ore ad Agrigento?*"

"Ah!" Fabrizio flicked a finger at his skull as if for dullardness, then switched to English, an opportunity to practice. "On a *bella* day like-a this one, two hours."

"Two hours." Froelich nodded. He could endure that much more of having his spine and legs bounced on the steel bed of the truck. "*Bene.*"

"*Anzi, no.*" Fabrizio raised a corrective finger. "On a *war* day like-a this one, maybe *six* hours." Then he added, "*Mi dispiace, ma questa è la guerra.*" I am sorry, but such is war.

"*Sì, questa è la guerra,*" Froelich agreed. "*La guerra è brutta.*"

"Yes, Bernardo." Fabrizio nodded. "The war is bad."

The sun was rising higher now as morning slid away, beating through the dust and causing sweat to break on skins. The wounded men, packed hip to rump aboard the truck, felt their serum tainted bandages begin to tighten in the heat, and then to steam like kitchen wenches' rags laid out upon a stove. The most severely injured had no choice but to relieve themselves in trousers where they lay, and a rank perfume of copper laced with urine hovered there and wouldn't drift away, as the convoy crawled in fits and starts and the day was still and windless. Fabrizio gave the water bottle back again to Froelich, then tossed an oily paper bag over his shoulder. It plopped in Froelich's lap, and he saw that it was full of fat green olives.

"*Grazie, compagno,*" he called.

"*Buon appetito!*" Fabrizio waved a hand, then cursed at someone in the road again.

Froelich popped an olive in his mouth. The spongy meat was full of juice and wonderful, and he spat the pit into his palm, flicked it overboard and made to take another, when he felt a pair of eyes upon him. Sitting to his right was a young British soldier, back against the lorry's wooden flank, elbows hooked between the slats. The lad had greasy blondish hair, which he was combing with a wooden salad fork acquired from somewhere, and above a bony Roman nose his brown eyes crinkled down at Froelich's treasure. Froelich popped another olive, then offered him the bag.

"Thought you'd never ask, sir." The soldier grinned, took an olive, closed his eyes in rapture as he chewed, then spat the pit across the truck and off the other side. Froelich offered up the water bottle. The soldier swigged a long draught and shuddered. "Like water for wine." He wiped his mouth with a ragged tunic sleeve.

"Froelich, Bernard, second lieutenant," Froelich said by way of introduction. "Late of Monty's Eighth."

"Robbins, Tommy, private. Late of the Queen's Own."

They both leaned in enough to shake, then sat back again.

"Queen's own what?" Froelich asked, waiting for the regiment.

"Queen's own royal gimps now." Robbins gestured at his splayed legs, which Froelich saw were swaddled in thick, bloody, mummy-style bandages, from his shoeless feet to his hips. The private jutted his chin at Froelich's splinted leg. "Looks to me you're all cocked-up as well, sir."

"Just the one side," Froelich said. "The other works."

Robbins laughed. "Anyway, I was Agile and Suffering."

He meant the Argyll and Sutherland Highlanders, who were mostly Scots. But Froelich heard a heavy London East End accent and prepared himself for a string of torturous slang.

"How'd you earn your leave, Robbins?"

"My *leave*." Robbins grunted, folded his arms and squinted at the sky. "Well, we was all in Egg-wiped having a good draft, then we piked off for El Alamein in those bloody gin palaces, half of us still swamped, mind you. Then the Jerries stonked us in the open." He looked at Froelich and smirked. "Maybe I'll get me a gong."

Froelich had to translate quickly in his head. *We were all in Egypt on a cushy assignment, then were sent off to El Alamein in armored command cars, half of us still drunk. Then the Germans shelled us in the open. Maybe I'll get a medal.*

"I think perhaps you shall," said Froelich.

"Where'd you get your ticket, sir?" Robbins asked.

"Tobruk."

The private whistled in respect. "Heard that was a bloody awful show."

"Indeed it was."

"Maghoon!" Robbins chortled the British version of the

Arabic word for "crazy," and both being veterans of the madness of North Africa, they shared a wry grin.

"Bamboo wireless says we're off to hospital in some posh seaside spot called Agrigento." Robbins meant the rumor mill.

"Right. So it seems."

"Don't let 'em lop that leg off, sir." Robbins wagged a finger.

"Nor yours," Froelich agreed.

"Mine? Not a bleedin' chance. I ain't no Douglas Bader!" Robbins meant the British fighter ace who'd lost both legs in a fiery crash, then went on flying Spitfires with a pair of wooden limbs.

By then the other men around them had spotted both the olive bag and water bottle. Froelich, remembering his officer's manners, declined another swig or fruit, and Robbins took one more of each and passed the treats on with a sad salute. "Farewell, my lovelies," he said, and soon it all was gone.

Another hour passed as the convoy swung away to skirt Licata's fringes, as if the town's morning sufferings might prove contagious. A pair of army ambulances left the train and headed seaward toward the blasted church, just in case some Allied troops had unwisely chosen prayer on that day. And then the convoy found the road again, the 115 that ran astride the sea en route to Agrigento, its shoulders swollen with prickly pear cactus and palms, and a blessed breeze rose off the waves and cleared the dust and stench, easing rasping lungs with oxygen and summer flowers.

They stopped just once, about halfway, where the road curved very near a stony beach and barefoot women clad all in black yet wearing merry headscarves were washing un-

derclothes and sheets just in the shallows. Froelich saw another cluster of them bent around a glossy, swollen chestnut
mound, then realized they were slicing fillets of raw meat
from a bullet-riddled horse.

"Filthy Eye-ties," Robbins scoffed at the desperate Italians.

"Judge them not," said Froelich. "If we don't see a mess
lorry soon, you'll be wanting some of that."

"S'pose you're right on that one, sir," Robbins conceded.

A few American GIs appeared, emerging from their
trenches and pup tents, wearing grimy, baggy battle uniforms and turtle helmets, chin straps dangling. Slinging M-1
rifles and a few grease guns and Thompsons, they ambled up
onto the road to chitchat with their Allied counterparts, and
Lucky Strikes were swapped for Woodbine cigarettes, and
chocolate bars for jerky.

"How's the birds 'round here?" Robbins called down to an
American buck sergeant.

"A-OK, if you can catch 'em."

"He means the girls," said Froelich.

"Oh, yeah." The American laughed through a stubbly
smile. "They're swell, if you like old wrinkled mamas."

"No, thanks," said Robbins. "Got some water for a parched
mate?"

The sergeant pulled his canteen from a pouch and handed
it up over the side rail. Robbins finished half of it until the
American reached up to snatch it back.

"Take it easy, buddy. The war's not over till next week."

"Sorry, Yank! Much obliged. And who you with, mate?"

"Big Red One." The American meant the First Division.

"Never heard of it, but it sounds a bit naughty, mate."

"Crazy Limey," the GI laughed. "Okay, so long, gotta get crackin'." And he drifted back amongst his men.

At last a mess truck appeared beside the flanks, its tenders tossing cardboard boxes packed with cans of bully beef and corn, along with one full jerrycan of tepid water. The wounded tore into the food, then those who could helped the others down onto the ground so they might find a bush behind which to relieve their gurgling guts. And then the convoy rolled again.

At four o'clock that afternoon the sun was sinking toward the sea, having done its work of thickening tongues and frying arms and noses. The convoy left the coastal road and turned northwest along the 118, a shell-pocked lane embraced by war-scorched trees and thorny bushes that looked like heads of porcupines, and it twisted up into a brace of hills and granite knuckles, making for the still contested fates of Prizzi and Corleone. The engines of the vehicles strained against the gravity, and Froelich watched as all at once the refugees on mules and carts turned away from their armed escorts and disappeared into the forests, like cattle birds abandoning the coats of snorting Brahma bulls.

They'd heard it first, the Sicilians, for they'd come to know those screeches from the skies. The Germans had affixed their awful Stukas with wailing sirens, and the Italian *Regia Aeronautica* had done the same, and now two of those shrieking Picchiatellos winged over at the convoy's head. The men in Froelich's truck sat up and twisted around, and a wounded American pilot shouted, "Get those goddamn bastards!" and up ahead the riders in a half-track thrust their Thompsons and Browning Automatic Rifles up and hosed the heavens in a torrent of mad fire, and one black winged predator loosed its bomb and the earth thundered and a plume of stones and some poor vehicle's shredded skin went spinning up to purgatory.

Fabrizio needed no encouragement to choose the better part of valor. He spun the poultry truck's wheel hard left, bounced the lorry off the road, and dove the nose into the trees. The wounded in his truck were tossed this way and that, hanging on as he found a venue of escape that only he could know was there. Bent forward like a stagecoach driver Froelich had once seen in cowboy films, Fabrizio raced into a long dark tunnel of citrus trees and cypress, their branches interlocking overhead for cover, as behind him and his charges automatic rifles and machine guns banged like drumsticks on an anvil and the Picchiatellos dove and swooped and strafed like iron eagles hunting salmon in a stream.

Then all at once the tunnel ended and the truck emerged through clouds of dust onto a vast plateau of pink- and mustard-colored sandstone. The battle fracas faded, Fabrizio calmed his speed and all the men sat up and stared across the landscape, blinking in amazement. Ranged all around the treeless plain, which went on for a mile in the distance, ancient Doric columns rose into the pewter evening sky, and right there on the left, like some mythic apparition, an enormous perfect temple sat, as if the Acropolis in Athens had been dropped there from the sky.

Fabrizio relaxed, wiped his fevered brow, turned his head to Froelich and said, "Even those *fascisti* will not blaspheme in the Valley of the Gods."

But for the rumbling of the engine, they rode along the dusty thoroughfare in silence, as if trespassing in this place of ancient warriors and worship that no one had disturbed for a millennium. More temples rose up to the heavens, magnificent and otherworldly, of Zeus and Hera and Athena, and so pristine and perfect they looked as though their toga wearing congregants had left only the day before. Froelich had seen the ancient aqueducts in Europe, but never anything like this, and neither he nor any of his wounded mates uttered a whisper.

Near the end of the plateau, Fabrizio stopped the poultry truck where an enormous statue lay upon its back. Its granite feet were thrust up at the sky, its chest of tonnage stones swelling from its spine, its muscled arms posed above its massive head to grip a giant globe that was no longer there. Fabrizio crossed himself as Froelich saw that modern men had prayed there too, and freshly, just before their final battle.

Piled all about were the detritus of hasty combat preparations. There were empty ammunition crates, cartridge boxes, ravaged ration tins, and smoldered cigarettes. Threadbare boots had been discarded, broken useless rifles left, torn-open bandage boxes and even books and Bibles that no one would have time to read. There were no helmets there or bayonets, things too precious to be left behind as these men had faced whatever fight would come. But letters they'd already read, perhaps from family or desperate lovers, skittered in the breeze across the plain. He knew, somehow, that all these men were dead or captured, and no one would return for what they'd left or lost.

Poor souls, he thought as Fabrizio raised a palm out toward the fallen statue and said mournfully, "Poor Atlas... Even he could notta hold this world."

He drove again, and the truck tipped off the precipice

onto a gently winding road, bound at last for Agrigento. And there beyond the valley, Froelich saw a city where he'd never dreamed to be, a cluster of summer burnished stone and stucco houses and cathedral spires, ranged across a braid of undulating hillocks, shimmering upon its perches by the sea.

"That is my home, Bernardo," Fabrizio said to him in something of a loving declaration. "And soon it will be yours."

PART TWO

AGRIGENTO

We groped our way in perfect darkness, descending into the pure heart of Sicily. The smell was good, in this heart of ours...a smell of new dust, of earth not yet contaminated by the world's wrongs, the wrongs that take place on this earth.

—ELIO VITTORINI
Conversations in Sicily

Ten

August 1943

IN THE GRAND COURTYARD OF THE MONES-
tero Santo Spirito, the waters of the ancient stone bowl
fountains, once clear and blue and brimming, had dried to a
melancholy muddy trickle, and the lush emerald face of the
monastery's garden of palms and pomegranate and prickly
pear now wore the powdered makeup of war.

The courtyard was large in breadth and width, a hundred
meters each side, bordered by three-story structures of medieval umber sandstone and sun-bleached flamingo plaster. All
of the doorways were sculpted arches, tall enough to accommodate giants, and some of the windows were archer's slits,
while others were wide and hinged and opened onto filigree
wrought iron balconies. But all the window glass was gone,
long shattered by concussions, and the abbey and rectory facades were pocked by bullets, and the terra-cotta roof tiles

were cleaved by shrapnel scars. High above the monastery's main entrance, which opened its arms to the town across a wide slab stone drive, a trio of iron church bells hung below curved Spanish caps, and whenever they rang now, splinters of glass and the scabs of plaster wounds tinkled down into the courtyard garden.

Before the war, the garden had been carefully pruned on its raised granite stage in the courtyard's middle, a place where the sisters perched on shady stone benches and studied their biblical catechisms, all the while entranced by the sweet scents of olive and fir. But now the garden was crowded with combat litters, between which medics and surgeons flitted, deciding who might live, and who would surely die. If the Santo Spirito, the Holy Spirit, indeed walked here, then his only voice was the moans of the wounded, and the hems of his vestments were fringed in blood.

Many of the monastery's nuns had fled, more than a few were dead, and for the most part the ones who remained were ancient and had cast their fates to the winds. The priest, a rotund baldy called Castillo, was only an occasional Father, and over the last chaotic month had appeared on a single Sunday and only twice for rites of confession. Yet none of his flock questioned his cautious faith, as he lived near the top of Via Giardinello and had to bicycle, while directly outside the monastic walls furious uniformed foreigners had street-brawled with guns and grenades, and the town's once fastidious cobblestone roads were clotted with aerial bomb rubble.

The battles had stilled now with liberation, with the exception of occasional bombings or shells, but if it all started up again, then those within the monastery walls would feel safely cocooned by its godly parapets. That was all illusion, of course, as ordnance paid no heed to religion, but at least the occupants inside the holy fortress would be the last to die, and already had a leg up to heaven.

Second Lieutenant Bernard Froelich, Private Tommy Robbins, and some fifty other Brits and Yanks lay in the garden on rows of low canvas litters, or the creaky iron beds donated by the remaining nuns from their own cenobium. They were shielded from the Sicilian sun by a patchwork skein of artillery camouflage netting strung from palm tree to stone pine, though it gave no protection from the errant rains of late summer, and they were often damp and shivering at dawn, then parched and breathless in the heat of noon, like helpless plants at the mercy of a drunken gardener.

The Allied Expeditionary Force's 7th Field Hospital was comprised of a mixed bag of Anglo-American medicos, cobbled together from General Sir Bernard Montgomery's British Eighth Army in the east and Lieutenant General George S. Patton's American Seventh Army in the west. There were two junior officer surgeons barely done with their residencies, a handful of exhausted orderlies and medics, and a single dentist whose only task was to repair shattered jaws, all commanded by an American captain physician. There were no female nurses to dilute the male hormonal wash, as they were needed at the four hundred bed 10th Field Hospital at Palermo. A pair of British military policemen were attached, wearing puttees, Sam Browne belts, Tommy helmets, and Webley revolvers, though the wounded posed no threat of a ruckus.

The men had been laid outside in the courtyard, because

the only interior space large enough to accommodate them was the monastery's magnificent medieval church of bone-white plaster walls, marble arches and columns, and scores of sculpted saints and cherubs, but it had suffered decimating artillery hits from the Italian 10th Bersaglieri Regiment as the US Army's 3rd Ranger Battalion conquered the town. The hospital's commanding captain might have ordered the broken pews and collapsed roof frescoes cleared, yet he thought it best not to further desecrate the nave with a sacrilege of sputum and blood.

However, having no other choice, he'd selected a large meditation parlor as the surgery. Located up on the second floor of the monastery's northeast corner, it was inconvenient, yet lovely, pristine, and flooded all day with sunlight dappling its orange walls through its high stone windows. Two patients at a time could be tended to up there upon gleaming steel butcher tables, while a thirteenth century Christ on a towering Orthodox cross looked down with openmouthed pity as the men screamed under the scalpels.

At dawn of the second day, Froelich emerged from yet another torturous dream, but this time without alarm. He'd never dreamed so much in his life, or at least had failed to remember, and was becoming accustomed to his psyche's attempts to repair the irreparable, and accepted these horrors as the cinema of his nights. His eyes fluttered open, and through the patchwork above of green, tan, and brown cloth camouflage leaves, he saw the morning's royal blue sky and heard the chirps of a hundred hungry finches, and remembered.

The dream had been the recurring one that had no beginning, and never ended. It was about his father, whom he admired and adored, and he'd found himself running, breathless, on a cold November night in 1938, from his high school soccer field to his house in Gestern, through a jungle that did not exist, though it clawed at him and tried to stop him nevertheless. He had no idea that this was *Kristallnacht*, the Night of Broken Glass, for that evil nomenclature would only come later. But he sensed great danger, and it fueled his panicked sprint.

His father's house was the most prominent and popular in their quaint town of wooden villas and a single *Gasthaus* inn, for its ground floor was also the general store. It was a happy place where neighbors often paid with promises and *Mutti* cooked for many in the bustling kitchen where she reigned, and the large salon held a Knabe grand piano on which Greta blasphemed Mozart, and all the bedrooms above each had a green ceramic woodstove and brass beds with feather down quilts. *Schloss Froelich*, as the fulsome townsfolk called it, had been Bernard's childhood cocoon of love and warmth, replete with scents of bratwurst, goulash, and ladies' sweet perfumes. And tonight, it was burning.

He'd stopped, once again, hyperventilating in the town's main square, facing his house and frozen, as the flames raged inside and licked at the broken windows from all the bedrooms and devoured the green tile roof. And just as he yelled and crouched and made to lunge to the rescue, his father's best friend, a Christian, Heinrich Auer, had appeared from somewhere, gripped him hard by the back of his neck and whispered, *"Hier gibt es nichts für sie, Bernard."* There is nothing for you here...

And there, as always, the nightmare had woken him up.

"You were talkin' Jerry, Lieutenant," said Tommy Robbins.

Froelich wiped his eyes and looked to his left, where two feet away, Robbins was propped on one elbow in his litter, his bright eyes crinkling as if he'd captured a pickpocket. Froelich blushed.

"Yes, I suppose I do that sometimes," he said. "Born in Berlin."

"Ya don't say? Thought I heard an accent, but guessed you were a bleedin' Welchman."

"No." Froelich smiled. "A bit east of that. But it's all right, HQ knows."

"Right. One o' them commando sorts, then?"

"Something like that."

"Well, that's a bleedin' relief." Robbins lay back on his makeshift pillow, a drool-stained, folded field jacket. "For a minute I thought I'd been nicked by the bloody Germans."

Froelich laughed. "No, you're quite safe with me. Such as safe may be."

Froelich and Robbins had been relegated to the last infirmary row in the garden along the monastery's southern wall where, over the past two days, they'd often propped themselves up and watched the hospital proceedings with scrunched up noses, like dukes of a fiefdom rife with the plague. This morning the sun was just coppering the monastery's trio of bells above to the left, yet already the patients were waking to a bustle. Two orderlies wearing cocked side caps and red cross armbands were collecting glass milk bottles sloshing with urine, while a third visited those unable to stand and scooped the excrement from between their legs with a garden trowel into a metal pail.

A pair of surgeon lieutenants, who Robbins had already dubbed the vampires, walked the rows clutching clipboards and metal coffee mugs, with lit cigarettes plugged in their lips as they thumbed eyelids open and peered at pupils, in particular of those swathed in head bandages. At least three cats and a scrawny spotted pup wandered between the cots and avoided kicking boots as they mewed and whined, while a hopeful gull from the sea squawked in a palm tree for a cracker, and a thousand fat summer flies thirsting for tears began to hum. And at last breakfast arrived, carried on a stretcher by two more orderlies, but the repast was nothing more than cans of American Spam, cold corn, and water.

"It's a bloody Bruegel," Froelich muttered as he scanned the scene.

"What's that, sir?" Robbins asked. "Some sort of rugby scrum?"

"No. He's a painter. A Dutchman with an odd sense of humor."

Robbins thought for a moment and said, "Isn't that what they call redundant, sir?"

Froelich did a doubletake and looked at Robbins. "You know, Private, I think you might be smarter than you look."

"That's what me mum says too." Robbins winked.

They both smiled and regarded the waking panorama, their moods lightening along with the square of sky above and what was sure to be a warm and breezy day. The breakfast-bearing littermen reached them at last and handed each a rectangular mess tin full of mealy slop, along with a steel canteen of warm water.

"Lovely, gents!" Robbins exclaimed. "Now we'll have the

scents of shit and flowers, along with the delectable tastes of a hog farm."

"Don't fancy it, don't eat it," one of the privates huffed.

"I'll suffer it," Robbins said, "but whenever our wandering captain finally shows, I shall file a ruddy complaint, and for the lack of entertainment as well."

The breakfast bearers grunted and moved on. The morning was already growing warm, and Robbins shifted in his litter and pushed the thin woolen blanket off his legs. Froelich glanced at the limbs swathed in iodine-stained bandages. They were terribly swollen, like a pair of Polish sausages left too long in the sun, but he said nothing and they both scooped their meals with mess tin spoons.

Without looking at Froelich, Robbins munched his meal and said, "You've got yourself a crop of nightmares, sir."

"Yes. Watered by my childhood in the fatherland, I expect."

"You're a Hebrew, are ya?" Robbins guessed.

"I am."

"Thought as much. You've got that straw hair and you haven't got the beak, but you're a bit of a brooder."

"Is that what we Jews do? Brood?"

"Pensive, more like, and bloody right to be so these days, sir. That's what me mum'd call me whenever I was glum and thinkin'. Pensive. Course I thought she meant I should be in a cage." Robbins chuckled with his self-deprecation, then adopted a tone of respect. "My parish father says you're all the chosen ones."

"So the legend goes," said Froelich. "But chosen for what, I haven't a clue."

"For you are a holy people to the Lord your God," Robbins

intoned like an altared priest. "And the Lord has chosen you of *awl* the peoples who are on the face of the earth… That's Deuteronomy fourteen-two, I believe."

Froelich blinked at him. "I'm impressed, Robbins."

"I was a choir boy." Robbins smirked. "But the rebellious sort. Got me equal parts the head pats and the switch. And *I* only dream about birds, and I don't mean the kind flittin' about in the trees."

"That's all you Londoners think about," said a gravelly voice, and both men looked up to see a large MP poised beside their litters. He wore a brimmed cap, a slim blond mustache, khaki sleeves rolled up, and his fingers rested on the holstered grip of his revolver.

"Morning, Charlie!" Robbins chirped.

"Top of it. And it's Private Harris to you."

"We're of equal rank, and I'm doubly wounded, so bugger the formalities."

"Sorry you're stuck with him, sir," Charlie said to Froelich.

"He's an entertainment," Froelich said.

"And you needn't finger that Webley." Robbins gestured at Charlie's revolver. "No scrappers here, and who'd want to escape this Garden of Eden?"

"It's a habit," Charlie said, but he kept his hand on the butt.

"You're gonna be a bobby after the war, ain't ya?" Robbins teased.

"That's what I was before."

"Couldn't a guessed."

"You men all right then, sir?" Charlie said to Froelich. "Need the loo?"

"I can hobble to it, thanks," said Froelich. He'd been given a crutch by an orderly, and while the toilets inside behind the nuns' small galley were far, he preferred the long trek over the urine bottles or excrement pails.

"Well, I can't slog to it," Robbins said to Charlie as he patted his lower abdomen. "So I'm saving it all for you."

"Tosser," Charlie grunted, and just before he left, he pulled a pack of Players from a breast pocket, along with a box of matches, handed them pointedly to Froelich and said, "Enjoy the day, sir."

They finished their meals, placed their tins on the stone floor, lit up and smoked and watched the gruesome circus of darting medics, emotionless surgeons, and mewling wounded until noon.

A quartet of the remaining nuns appeared after lunch. It had been a light fare of hardtack crackers, figs, and Messina Caprino goat cheese, which Robbins said was much better than the "Government Cheddar" rationed back home. He'd also quipped that the meal was so meager because the orderlies "figured if they shoveled less in, they'd have to shovel less out," though the wisdom of adding figs to the mix belied that logic.

The four nuns, who'd been engaged in their meditative rituals all morning, were middle-aged, stout, and surprisingly spry and jolly. They wore white wimples cupping their faces and brown coifs and veils for their hair, high-buttoned white blouses, dung-colored sweaters, long black skirts, and clogs that clicked on the stones, and each had metal spectacles, no doubt from decades of squinting at ancient texts. They wandered amongst the wounded troops, clicking their rosaries and gracing damp foreheads with gnarled knuckles, and though they spoke no English, many of the men had Sunday Latin, so they were able to converse and were happy to be blessed.

When the nuns finally left, the mood of the infirmary rose in chatter and pitch, as two huge cooking pots were set upon the steel tripods of discarded Italian beach landing obstacles over at one courtyard corner, and wood fires were stoked beneath them for tea. The orderlies dumped piles of loose combat ration tea leaves in the boiling water, then strained the muddy mix through bandage squares and passed the brew around in mess cups. Cigarettes popped, playing cards appeared, and bawdy jokes were slung about. And then a wounded American airman, lying prone amongst the rows, began to sing the dirty version of a ditty from the North African campaign in a surprisingly mellifluous Bing Crosby tenor.

"'Oh, Gertie, from Bizertie, you're as purty, purty, purty as can be!

Gertie, from Bizertie, don't you never, ever dare desertie me.'"

Twenty more men then joined the bawdy chorus.

"'Tho' your lingo, I don't know, when we screw you make me holler Bingo!

Oh, Gertie, from Bizertie, you're the lay, for, me!'"

Greatly encouraged, the airman then sat up on his rack and solo sang the verse.

"'There's a lovesick magoo in the army, who's in love with a sweet desert rose.

When the moon's shining bright, he sings to her each night, and here's the way it goes…'"

At that point, the entire hospital joined in.

"'Oh, Gertie, from Bizertie, they all pucker up and whistle when you pass.

Gertie, from Bizertie, no other skirtie in Bizertie's got that...

(Tell ya' bout it later!)

When I squeeze ya, I can't stop. You're the top, temptation in Tunisia...

Oh! Gertie, from Bizertie, you're the lay, for, me!'"

The men roared the finale, applauded the airman and showed extra approval by banging their spoons on their mess tins, until MP Charlie Harris stomped up onto a stone planter and shouted, "All right stand down, ya mongrels! There's holy sisters about!" He failed to hide his grin, but still they all obeyed him and eventually, calmed.

Robbins, still elated with the mood of the racy ditty, stretched and fetched the Players pack from Froelich's cot, plucked out two with his lips, lit them up and passed one back to Froelich without asking. He lay back on his field jacket pillow, and Froelich did the same, and they smoked and watched the sky through the camouflage netting, where a platoon of steamy clouds from the sea marched across the aluminum blue, giving intermittent shade from the afternoon sun.

"Those legs are paining you, aren't they," Froelich said.

"Like fingers in a coal fire, sir. How'd ya know?"

"It's in your eyes."

"Well, that morphia's 'bout as hefty as a lemon drop."

"Agreed."

"And yours, sir? Got the thunderbolts like mine?"

"Only when I laugh," Froelich said.

"Stay glum, then." Robbins smiled, and smoked, and thought for a while. "So what's your peacetime plan then, sir?"

"Peacetime?"

"Ya know, after the war."

"I think you might be jumping the gun, Robbins."

"Hate to say it, Lieutenant, 'cause I can tell you're the hard charger, but I'm thinkin' you and me might both be done with the guns. Can't charge out the trenches with a limp, ya know."

"Perhaps. But I've still much to do."

"I can tell," Robbins said. "It's in your eyes." He turned his head and looked at Froelich, his pain-racked squint empathic, as if regarding a close friend who suffered unrequited love. "My mind's focused on the parties and the peace, while yours is on the payback, ain't it so?"

"I suppose you're right, yes."

Robbins cranked himself up once more on his left elbow, which caused him further pain as he twisted, yet he had something to impart.

"I know I'm younger, sir, and not as bright as you by half, but I got some wisdom 'bout the last war from me dear old dad. Not that I don't love the Union Jack, but you and me, we're just Churchill's chess pieces on the board, just like the Yanks are Roosevelt's, and all those Jerries that we've stonked are Hitler's too. Those big boys won't have suffered but a scratch when it's all over, but lots of teary mums'll be clutchin' mourning flowers and weepin' over empty boys' beds."

Froelich blinked at the young private, but found he had no retort for such brutal truth. He had no clear impressions of a life beyond the war, while the private had already traveled to that time. Robbins grinned and offered up a conspiracy of optimism.

"I reckon we've had it with these legs, sir. They're gonna pack us off to Merry Ol' England for girls and gongs! I think we ought to partner up for riches, maybe open up a pub off Piccadilly."

Froelich arched an eyebrow. "Something tells me you've already got the name."

"I do, sir!" Robbins raised a eureka finger. "Gimpy's, or maybe, Cripples' Cove. The vets'll flood our doors, we'll fill 'em all with beer, the birds'll tumble at our feet, and Bob's your uncle, everybody's jolly!"

Froelich couldn't help but laugh, and both men lay back again and smiled with the images that curled skyward with their Players smoke. The men in the infirmary were still heady with their jokes and song, their laughs and chatter comforting to Froelich, like evening swallows chirping in a marsh.

Yet not long after, in the longer light of late that day, a shroud of silence fell as the surgeons reappeared. Their names were Pennington and Hedges, which Robbins had remarked sounded like a firm of crooked barristers, and the second lieutenants might have been twins—both dark haired, bespectacled, slim, and grim. But their arrival wasn't what stilled the joy. It was that Father Castillo followed behind them from the monastery's arched entrance.

He was sweating with his rotundity and had arrived on his bicycle, wearing his soiled collar, a velvet vest, and baggy pantaloons pinned up for riding above worn leather ankle boots. His spectacles were fogged from the effort, and he clutched a large wooden crucifix on a rosary and a small cowhide pocket Bible. Fifty pairs of silent eyes followed the old priest as he trailed behind the doctors to one corner of the courtyard, and dabbing holy water from a tiny bottle on the forehead of a boy who was unconscious to the world, he prayed there for a while, then trudged off, stooped and muttering, to find a meal.

Pennington and Hedges made the rounds and checked some charts, but Froelich watched them with a gnawing sensation in his guts, like a lamb exposed to wolves upon a meadow without cover, soon to be discovered. Robbins watched them too, yet without Froelich's alarm, and when they turned and started their approach he said to Froelich, "Ya see, sir? The vampires have come to pack us off back home at last!"

It wasn't so. Pennington and Hedges flanked Robbins' litter, and together roughly unswaddled his terribly swollen legs, prodding at his stinking shrapnel wounds with wooden tongue depressors as he bit his lower lip and winced. Neither looked at Robbins' face as Pennington muttered, "How'd you catch it only in the lower quadrants, Private?"

"I was leapin' headfirst into a little wadi by the road, sir. Legs were still up and out when the 88s hit. You should've seen the boots. Like fish fillets on the grill." He was bravely smiling, yet sweating profusely.

"Right," said Hedges as he and Pennington loosely rewrapped the bloody bandages. "Well, I'm afraid you've got an awful lot of steel here that we can't get out. Plus, it's all rather gangrenous. Smell it?"

"Hard to tell with all these stinks about, sir," Robbins mumbled, but already he was breathing faster. And Froelich, as he watched, was too.

"It appears we'll have to take them both," said Pennington, with all the emotion of a motorcar mechanic. "Surgery, in the morning." He looked across at Hedges.

"Quite right." Hedges nodded. "Good news is, all's not lost. Just below the knee, for each."

Robbins swallowed, but he could not speak, nor barely breathe. His eyes filled up and tears rolled down his ruddy cheeks.

The surgeons turned on Froelich, who would have run had he been able, but he was frozen in his litter like a toddler in a bassinet with horrid monsters looming over. Hedges tapped Froelich's bandaged thigh and splint with his tongue depressor.

"And I'm afraid we'll be having yours as well, Lieutenant. But just the one."

"Apologies, gentlemen," said Pennington. "Do try to get some sleep tonight. You'll need your strength."

And they walked away to further gruesome tasks.

Froelich's head spun. Foul waves of nausea rose up from his gullet. He couldn't grasp the sudden shock of it, the turning of his fate again, nor that of this boy to his left who was even more damned. He felt as if they'd been condemned by the gavels of a pair of demon judges, but there was no appeal, no second opinion, no overarching power who could overthrow the ruling. He looked over at Robbins, who was lying prone again and staring at the early-evening sky, his tear tracks running to his ears. With terribly quaking fingers, Froelich lit two more cigarettes, kept one in his mouth, leaned across the void and plugged the other one in Robbins' slack lips. Then he lay back again, reached out and gripped Robbins' damp limp hand tightly.

"I used to fancy dancing," Robbins whispered. "Ballroom type, ya know. Never told me mum, just sneered and fussed when she made me do it. Friday evenings down the school, church jackets and ties, white gloves and all so you don't print your pretty girls with sweaty palms. Heart's racing, ya know, seeing who they'd pair you up with. Pretty eyes, all that shiny hair, perfume like Easter flowers. Pretended that I hated it… But I loved it, ya know… I loved it."

They didn't speak again, nor did they eat the evening meal. Froelich finally slept at midnight, but Robbins never did.

Sometime later in the witching hour, well before the dawn while all were deeply in their dreams, Robbins rolled in silence to the cold stone floor. First he crawled to Charlie, who slept at the southwest corner of the garden with his kit beneath his cot. But Robbins was an expert surreptitious crawler and had been well-trained in combat stealth, and he stole Charlie's revolver without a twitch in the MP's sleeping cheek.

Then he crawled across the courtyard, between the rows of boys moaning in their slumbers, sweat dripping from his brow and chin and the cold steel of the Webley tucked into his shorts at the small of his back, and he made it to the monastery's northeast corner, and inside a darkened archway there. A slim doorway to the right opened onto a steep stone staircase rising to the roof of shell-shattered timbers, but first arriving, three floors up, to a small iron balcony that overlooked the garden, and beyond that, the star-dappled sea. It took him half an hour.

And then he was there at last, standing fully up, gripping

the wrought iron railing, smiling at the moon across the parapets, with the belfry to his right poking at the sky. He leaned slightly back, as he didn't want to fall and cause a fright or further injury, and he cocked the revolver, placed the barrel against his left temple, and closed his eyes.

The bullet exited his skull, and rang the monastery's bell.

Eleven

FROELICH LOST HIS MIND THAT MORNING.

All the men had woken to the gunshot, except for those too gravely wounded for their brains to care, and just like battle-shattered combat troops everywhere, they jerked and scrambled for their rifles, but their rifles weren't there. The gonging church bell was incongruous before the light of day, and they dragged themselves from twitching dreams and looked around and muttered, *"What the hell?"*

Had one of the four sentries posted in the rubbled streets outside the Holy Spirit clumsily discharged his weapon in a fluke? Had German or Italian snipers slithered back into the town, taking potshots at the hospital for nothing but pleasure? The speculations flew, but it wasn't very long before they gleaned the awful truth.

Froelich sat up straight and scuttled backwards on his litter, grinding his spine against the courtyard wall, his body tensing for the flurry of gunshots that were sure to follow just that one. But aside from all the mutters and the echo of the bell, there was only silence, and right away he turned to talk to Robbins, and saw he wasn't there. His eyes met nothing but an empty cot, a skewed blanket, a neatly sealed envelope and a pencil, and even without knowing yet, some instinct told him and his heart began to race.

Over in the courtyard corner, Private Charlie Harris was performing a strange dance in the flickering light of oil lanterns that the orderlies had hung about. He twisted like a corkscrew, searching desperately for something underneath his cot, and then he tossed it over furiously, like a man flipping a card table on which cheaters had just stolen his fortune. Charlie cursed and burrowed in his battle kit and threw his things in desperate search, until someone somewhere yelled, "There!" and he stopped and snapped his head around, and so did Froelich.

Hands were pointing up from litters at the northeast tower and its ornate balcony just below the splintered roof, where a pair of upthrust bandaged feet were jutting through the iron uprights. They were fish-belly white in the fading moonlight, and tinting blue with the crawl of dawn.

"Robbins, *damn* you, boy," Charlie keened, and charged across the courtyard, dashing madly toward the shadowed archway as he hurdled over litters and crashed an urn of tea onto the stones. A pair of orderlies raced after him, half dressed and shirts askew, and Froelich watched them all with horror in his eyes, and gripped the side rails of his cot with bone-white knuckles, and tried to swallow but he couldn't, and prayed to no one he believed in that it wasn't so.

Pennington and Hedges appeared from somewhere else,

tucking in their blouses and slinging medical kits, and they disappeared inside the arch. Froelich heard their boots pounding up the stairwell and then Pennington was standing on the balcony beside the ivory feet, his fingers clutching at his hair, and he called down something to a medic in the garden, who quickly slung a mattress cover over one shoulder and rushed inside and up. Froelich watched with brimming eyes as Robbins' feet were dragged from sight, and shortly after, when he reappeared again, he was nothing but a lifeless sack of flesh inside the bloody mattress cover, as two sweating orderlies dragged him bumping down the stairs and dropped him on the stones.

Just inside the archway, the surgeons vented all their rage on Charlie Harris.

"You damned *fool*, you let him have your Webley!"

"I didn't *let* him, sir."

"Well how the hell did he get it, then?"

"He…he must've nicked it while I was asleep."

"You bloody well should've had it secured then, Harris. Isn't that what your blasted military police instructors teach you, man?"

"Leave the poor sod alone!" one of the wounded British officers called out to Pennington and Hedges.

"Right!" another wounded American joined in. "Can't you see the poor guy's had enough?"

The ruckus grew as further wounded men defended Charlie. Then all at once, Pennington and Hedges were waving them all off and marching through the garden straight for Froelich. And Charlie, even in his grief and guilt and certainty that he'd be tried for mortal negligence, raced after them and tried to stop them.

"Not now, sirs, for pity's sake!"

"We shall *not* have this happen to another man," Pennington snapped.

"Prep him for his surgery at once," Hedges hollered at two orderlies and grabbed one by the shirt.

Froelich whipped his blanket off and leaped up from his litter. He snatched his wooden crutch from where it leaned against the wall and gripped it near the bottom and swung it madly in a buzzing arc.

"You're not taking it!" he yelled as the stalking surgeons and their orderlies jerked rearward in alarm. "You'll not have my fucking leg!"

"Strap him down!" Pennington yelled, and the orderlies tackled Froelich, even as he conked one on the skull, and they smashed him down onto his litter.

"Not this way, sirs," Charlie pleaded, though part of him had had enough, and he slapped his palms to both his ears as if he couldn't bear to hear the rest.

"Belts, men!" Hedges bellowed, and the orderlies tried to parry Froelich's swinging fists as they yanked their belts off and straddled him like a bucking bull to tie him to the litter.

"You bastards, you'll not have it!" Froelich shouted underneath their crushing weights, and his fists flew and cracked one in the jaw, and he yelled again as the other's rump mashed his wounded thigh and the belt tips whipped in the air like electrocuted snakes. And through it all a chorus of the wounded raged at the horrid melee.

"Leave him alone, you heartless sons a bitches!"

"Ya rear echelon dandies, we oughta take *your* bleedin' legs!"

"Get off him, let him breathe, you wankers! The man just lost his mate!"

"You bloody *vultures*. One's not enough for you today?"

Some of the men, though wounded themselves, were cranking their bandaged bodies up from their litters and grabbing crutches and infusion poles and threatening to join the fray on Froelich's side. They'd all been shot or shrapneled and had little fear of military justice, and the morning's tragedy had cracked their laminate of discipline.

"Officers or not," an American corporal yelled at Pennington and Hedges, "we'll hang your asses from the fuggin' belfry!"

"Shut up!" Pennington yelled back as he and Hedges tried to help the orderlies pin Froelich down, and as the shouts grew into a thundering crescendo, he screamed, "You'll all be bloody court-martialed!"

And then a shot rang out.

It was very loud, and very near, and the ringing boom and all its echoes instantly froze every man in the courtyard to a silent stark tableau. Standing in the garden's western quadrant, a few feet from the monastery's arch, was the field hospital's American commander, Captain Leo Lefkowitz.

He was all of five foot eight, built like a fireplug, with salt-and-pepper close-cropped hair, steel-rimmed spectacles, a somehow-ironed US Army field uniform, and half an unlit cigar clamped in his teeth. He was holding a smoking .45-caliber pistol pointed at the sky, and he growled in a smoke-drenched Brooklyn, New York, accent, "What in the goddamn *hell* is goin' on here?"

No one answered the furious captain's query, but his was the second gunshot of the morning, and it was as if his bullet had cauterized the hemorrhage of the first. After a long moment, a courageous British private croaked from his litter, "We lost a bloke this morning, sir. They were gonna take his legs, but instead he nicked Private Harris's revolver and finished himself off."

Lefkowitz turned his head and blinked down at the private. Someone else pointed over at the bloody mattress cover and Robbins' corpse, and the captain looked and saw that too. He holstered his .45, snapped the leather cover closed, and boomed across the courtyard, "Well, stand the hell *down*."

The wounded rebels melted back onto their mattresses. Lefkowitz, though often called away to other tasks at local Allied headquarters, had a brook-no-bullshit reputation and a rough vernacular born of the Brooklyn truck drivers amongst whom he'd been raised. He strode across the garden between the litters, heading straight for Froelich's corner, where Pennington and Hedges now stood at stiff attention and the orderlies had shrunk back from their victim and were cowering behind the surgeons' backs.

The captain stopped at the foot of the litter, placed his calloused fingers to his hips, and looked down at Froelich, who was still red-faced and breathing hard and slick with panic sweat. Then he glared at his lieutenants.

"Pennington, Hedges, get the hell outta here and go torture some kittens or somethin'."

"Yes, sir," Pennington said and saluted, palm out and up, British style.

"And for Christ's sake, don't salute me in the field," Lefkowitz snapped. "Not even here. Get me?"

"No, sir... I m-mean, yes, sir," Hedges stuttered, and both lieutenants spun on their heels and slipped away.

"And you two clowns." The captain flicked his fingers at the orderlies like he was batting off a bee. "Go clean some piss and shit."

The orderlies scurried off.

Lefkowitz snorted, shook his bristly head, pulled a Zippo from his breast pocket, fired up the end of his soggy cigar, and blew a plume of smoke at the sky.

"Jesus Christ," he muttered. "If the Nazis don't get us, these friggin' guys'll do it for 'em." He looked at Froelich and cranked one thumb back over his shoulder. "Did ya know that kid who offed himself?"

"Yes, sir." Froelich swallowed. "Private Tommy Robbins. They were going to take both his legs."

"Fuggin' waste." The captain spat a glob of cigar juice on the stones next to his spit-shined boots. "Sometimes you gotta do it, 'cause ya got no choice. But you also have to watch the guy and use your goddamn head. You tell some kid he's losin' his legs, he ain't gonna take it so good."

He pulled a canteen from his belt pouch, unscrewed the cap and handed it to Froelich, who nodded thanks and gulped the blessed water down, diluting his adrenaline. "Take it easy. It's a quarter schnapps," the captain said, and took the canteen back. "And what's your story?"

"Well, it's this leg, sir." Froelich nodded at his bandages

and splint. He was still trembling from his battle with the vampires.

"Lemme take a look."

Lefkowitz moved to Froelich's wounded side, yanked a Ka-Bar combat knife from his belt scabbard and sliced the bandages from Froelich's hip to knee, while Froelich gripped the litter sides and clenched his teeth in silence. The captain rocked the wooden splint planks from the bloated leg, then ran his calloused fingers up and down astride the gutted exit wound, his fingertips digging deeply and exploring.

"That hurt?" The word came out as "hoyt."

"Yessir," Froelich hissed as more sweat beaded on his brow.

"Good. You still got nerves in here. How'd you catch this bullet hole? It's through and through."

"Escaping from a German POW camp, sir. They had me at Tobruk."

"Tobruk, huh? Ya don't say? Almost as bad as the Bronx." The captain cocked his head toward where he'd shunned his lieutenants. "And those young meat cleavers wanted this leg too?"

"They did, sir, yes."

"Nuts," Lefkowitz growled. "What's the big idea with these kids? We ain't at friggin' Gettysburg."

Froelich had no idea what that meant so he declined to comment. Lefkowitz scabbarded his knife and came erect again, his fingers back at post on hips.

"What's your name, kid?"

"Froelich, sir. Bernard, second lieutenant."

"You sound a little like a Kraut."

"Born in Berlin, sir."

"Yeah?" Lefkowitz pulled his cigar from his teeth. A string of brown drool rolled down his boot-heel chin and he back-handed it away. "You one a them special Brit commando guys?"

"I was, sir, yes."

"You a Yid?"

"A Yid, sir?"

"A Jew, Froelich, like me." The captain poked a thumb at his own chest. "Ya know, a Landsman."

"I'm, well, yes, I'm Jewish."

"Good." The captain offered up a twisted grin. His teeth were yellow from tobacco. "Ya got some gumption, and we don't need no legless Jews. We need 'em in the fight."

Froelich pulled himself up to lean against the gritty court-yard wall.

"Sir, are you saying...no amputation?"

"*Hell*, no. We ain't cuttin' legs off like we're makin' crab salad. That Nazi round punched you good, cracked your femur and it's setting wrong and crooked. I can't do an in-tramedullary nail here—that's a long bone rod and I ain't got that sorta drill. But I got a better idea."

"What would that be, sir?" Froelich asked with rising hope.

"I'm gonna bust it up again, set it straight and right and rack it for a coupla weeks. After that, you should be right as goddamn rain. Get me?"

"Absolutely, sir."

"Swell. We'll do it after second chow." The captain jabbed a finger at Froelich's face. "But no lunch for you, just water. Don't want you pukin' all over me. Roger?"

"Wilco, sir." Froelich nodded at his eccentric savior, who seemed to have appeared out of the blue.

Lefkowitz turned to walk away, then stopped, turned back, and aimed a pistol finger at his patient.

"And forget about your buddy, Lieutenant," he ordered, and he locked Froelich's eyes with his flinty squint. "He's gone. You ain't."

The meditation room, now the surgery, a story up inside the northeast tower, was August hot and stifling in the early afternoon, the hard sun lancing through the windows and firing up the stony floor and stucco walls like pizza oven bricks. There was no power there, and therefore no electric fans, but Froelich, so buoyed with his rescue by this strange American captain whose crude vernacular he barely understood, didn't care. Four orderlies had lifted up his litter, carried him upstairs, slid him onto one steel butcher's table, and left him there. He looked up at the medieval Christ, who stared back down at him in silence, and then the first of Lefkowitz's cutting crew appeared.

Two medics wheeled a crash cart in, its top tray piled with gleaming instruments, some of which looked to Froelich like auto shop garage tools, including a large drill powered by a foot pedal, like a sewing machine. Then they fetched an infusion pole and a pot of freshly boiled water and set it on a wooden table, where its steam clouded up the room and added further to the heat. When Pennington and Hedges strode in through the doorway, Froelich tensed and feared that Lefkowitz had changed his mind. But soon thereafter the captain marched inside as well, and Froelich breathed relief and thanked his lucky stars.

"All right," the captain boomed. "Let's get this show on the road."

He was wearing a white surgeon's smock, clearly boiled and washed many times, yet so spotted with dried blood and sputum stains it looked like a snow leopard's coat. A surgeon's mask hung below his chin, his bristly hair was cupped in an olive bandanna, and already he was wearing rubber gloves. But for all his attention to sterility, a fresh cigar was clenched between his teeth.

"You good, Lieutenant?" he asked Froelich.

"Right as rain, sir."

"Swell. That's my kinda English." The captain flicked a rubber glove at Pennington and Hedges. "You two, go stand there in the corner and loin somethin'." The vampires backed away and Lefkowitz turned to the medics. "You guys, drop all those instruments in the pot for one full minute. Get me?"

"Yes, sir."

"Too bad we ain't got a lobster," the captain quipped, and both medics swallowed snickers and did as they were told.

"Okay, now strip him to his birthday suit, sponge him down, tape his wrists and the good leg so he don't start floppin', hang me a sucrose bottle, give him a right vein drip and a BP cuff on the left biceps."

The medics went to work, and soon Froelich was lying there completely naked and gleaming from the sponge bath. He felt no twinge of modesty, only glorious pleasure from the coolness of his skin. Lefkowitz circled the steel table to his wounded side, scanned his form and pinched his right waist.

"You got another puncture here, kid. Looks healed but what's the skinny?"

"That was the first bullet, sir." Froelich's neck was angled back over a rolled up towel and he could barely move. "But through and through, sir, as you would say."

"You're like Swiss cheese, ain't ya? What's your blood type?"

"B-positive, sir."

"Hey, that's my motto. Pennington?"

"Yes, sir?"

"Go out and find me a donor. We prolly ain't gonna need it, but just in case I slip. And make sure it ain't some kid who's already half bled out. Get me?"

"Yes, sir."

Lefkowitz looked down at Froelich's crotch and raised an eyebrow.

"Hey, you ain't circumsized."

"No, sir." Froelich blushed.

"You sure you're a Yid?"

"Quite sure, sir. Some of the German families decline the ritual. Prevents the bullies at our schools from having a go at us."

"I get it. Catholic camouflage."

"Something like that, sir."

"You want me to snip you while I'm fixin' your leg?" Lefkowitz grinned with mischief. "Two-for-one sale."

"No, thank you, sir." Froelich smiled at the ceiling.

"Smart. I ain't no mohel. You allergic to anything?"

"Only the Nazis, sir."

"You're a card." The captain looked over at his medics,

who'd plucked the steaming instruments from the pot and were pulling on their masks and gloves. "You men ready?" They nodded.

The captain bent over Froelich's face. He made to remove his cigar, then remembered that he shouldn't touch it.

"Hedges, get over here and take my stogie. And don't smoke it."

Hedges stepped in and carefully retrieved the smoking butt, as if easing a bone from a bulldog.

"Medics, drape Lieutenant Froelich's dick with a wet wash-cloth," Lefkowitz ordered. "Don't want him pissin' in my face."

"Righto, sir."

"Okay, kid," Lefkowitz said to Froelich's rapt attention. "Here's the drill. We're gonna give you ether till you're out. Then, the medics here are gonna grab your leg above and below your screwed-up fracture, and I'm gonna break it again, with this."

And almost like some morbid magician, Lefkowitz was suddenly gripping a very large, gleaming ball-peen hammer. Froelich's eyes went very wide.

"Then I'm gonna set it so it's right, and drill one hole through the bone above, and one below, and hammer a couple a steel bolts through so we can set you up for traction. For a coupla weeks you'll wish you never met me, but after that you'll be swingin' to Benny Goodman. With me?"

Froelich nodded. He could barely swallow.

"Any questions?"

"May I have the ether now, sir? A double if you please."

Lefkowitz grinned with yellow teeth. "On the house," he said, and pulled his mask onto his face.

Froelich jolted as he felt a cold damp washcloth drape across his crotch. Then, a large square of gauze loomed above his face, and he shut his eyes as it settled on his nose and mouth. He heard a bottle cap unscrew and cold rivulets of something that smelled like tarnished silver soaked the gauze. He breathed in deeply once, and then again, and disappeared.

Twelve

WHEN FROELICH WOKE THAT EVENING, HE saw a thousand stars winking in the courtyard's August sky, which made the undulating net between him and the heavens look like it was sewn with diamond jewels. A soft breeze carried scents of iodine and bougainvillea, the whispers of some orderlies, the flutters of their playing cards, and the moans and mutters of the wounded midnight dreamers. But Froelich felt no curiosity about his leg, nor the need to move just yet, and simply lay there reveling in sight and smell and sound, because his senses told him he was still alive.

He realized that his brow was draped with a damp washcloth, perhaps to stem a fever, though he felt cold from head to foot—two feet, in fact—and reveled in it. He curled his toes yet felt no pain and knew that he was sailing on a skiff of morphia, and that was all delicious too. At last he tried to lift his arms and found he could because they were no longer strapped, and saw that one was hosting an infusion line, and a crooked smile crossed his lips as he mused that maybe that fine Captain What's-his-name had ordered an injection of straight gin. He didn't try to raise his head and look down at his leg. He knew that it was there, and that was fine enough.

A shadowed face obscured a patch of stars and loomed above his own. It was Private Charlie Harris, and his smile trembled at the corners.

"Hallo, sir."

Froelich tried to speak but couldn't so he blinked. Harris tipped a canteen to his lips. The warm trickle in his parched gullet tasted like champagne.

"You've no idea how glad I am to see you, sir," Charlie said.

"Same," Froelich whispered.

Harris smiled wider and looked across the litter.

"And you've got another mate here too, sir. Says he was your driver, but I think he's more than that."

Then Froelich turned his eyes and saw Fabrizio, and thought for sure he must be dreaming. The Italian's sad and handsome face was floating to his right, his oiled hair gleaming in the starlight and his teeth ivory white.

"*Buona sera, Tenente,*" said the Italian officer.

"Fabrizio," Froelich managed.

"*Sì,* Bernardo. And your *compagno* isa correct. I driva the trucks, but I am also a carpenter."

Froelich's brow creased, as none of that made sense, until Fabrizio and Charlie slipped their fingers underneath his head. They gently lifted it and propped it on some sort of pillow, and he looked down at his leg.

It was swathed in fresh white bandages and tractioned at an angle in a contraption of bolted timbers. The underknee was laid across a stunted tree trunk stripped of bark, with his ankle elevated higher and resting in a canvas sling, which hung below a pulley at the apex of a tripod. A short steel rod that pierced his femur was wired down to something underneath his litter, and from a second rod, just above his knee, an automotive drive train cable ran up and through the pulley. Its other end was tied off to a dangling counterweight—a can of .30-caliber machine gun ammunition.

"She's a good, no?" Fabrizio folded his arms and regarded his construction proudly.

"She's very, very good," Froelich whispered.

"It's a bleedin' work of art," said Charlie.

"Non è vero." Fabrizio wagged a finger. "I am not a artist, just a simple carpenter. But is respectable profession, like it was for Jesus, *sì*?"

"Sì, Fabrizio," Froelich said. "Like for Jesus."

"Grazie." Fabrizio smiled and patted Froelich's bare shoulder, and Froelich realized he was still naked but covered with rough sheets. "We go now, Bernardo, and give you rest. Your *capitano* says no *mangiare*." He touched his lips to mimic eating. "But the ice girl isa here."

"The ice girl?" Froelich's brow creased again.

"Right, sir," Charlie said. "Seems like every town's got a brood of them, the birds who carry ice about. Captain wasn't keen on having them in hospital, but changed his tune. Thought we might behave ourselves with skirts about." He saluted with a steadier smile. "Ta, for now."

Charlie and Fabrizio turned away and left, then Froelich realized that a third person had been standing there just beside his feet. He blinked again, wondering if perhaps it was a morphine apparition.

A girl was looking at him, her head cocked as if in sympathy. She seemed to be about eighteen or so, with long dark hair that fell in curls about her shoulders and the white collar of a short-sleeved, flowered summer dress. She had slim dark eyebrows above large hazel eyes that gleamed in the orderlies' lanterns, a small nose and full lips, and there were dimples in her cheeks above a lightly cleft chin. Her slim arms hugged a metal cooking pot below her chest.

"*Buona sera,*" she said. Her voice was alto for a girl with a soprano form.

"*Buona sera.*" Froelich nodded.

"I am Sofia," she said in lilting English. Her smile was shy yet perfect, except for one small canine that was chipped.

"I am Bernard."

"Bernardo, Fabrizio calls you. And also, *Tenente.*"

"Yes, he calls me that."

"You wish some ice, *Tenente*?"

"Yes, please."

She moved closer, but with some tilting in her gait, then pulled a sliver of ice from the pot and waited for Froelich to open his lips. She slid the ice over his tongue as he stared at her, still not quite sure if she was real, and she stepped back again and looked over at his tractioned limb.

"He is a very good carpenter, Fabrizio," she said.

"Yes, he is. Your English is very good also."

"From the Catholic school." She didn't look at him, but only at his contraption. "It hurts you?"

"No. I have morphia."

"Yes, the morphia." She nodded. "I had none."

Froelich didn't understand what that might mean, yet didn't ask. The girl turned back to him and smiled in a way that held a hundred thoughts, none of which he could discern, but her expression pierced him in a strange way.

"You are so very lucky, Tenente Bernardo," she said.

"I am?"

"Yes, you are. Good night. I will bring you more ice to-morrow."

"Good night, Sofia."

She turned and retrieved a wooden crutch that had been propped against his litter. It was crude and looked like it had been fashioned from a tree branch, but its bark was gone and all the wood was lacquered. She tucked it underneath her left arm, hugged the pot with her right, and limped away into the darkness.

And Froelich saw that she had only one leg.

Thirteen

September 1943

AN AUTUMN RAIN ARRIVED ONE NIGHT AND stayed for three whole days.

It was a rare occurrence for a temperate Mediterranean island, yet could not be dissuaded by the weakling moon that tried in vain to steam the thunderclouds away, nor by the desperate prayers of the sisters, who gently entreated their Christ to give their wounded charges respite. The heavens banged and bolts of lightning flashed the monastery's towers white, just like artillery, which flinched the soldiers' eyes and cheeks as fusillades of water struck the town.

The orderlies took down the useless camouflage nets and replaced them with a brace of foraged parachutes, but the white- and olive-colored silk and nylon mushrooms only drooped and cupped and gathered troughs of downpour, until at last they all collapsed and spilled it through their folds, drenching everything and everyone. Water runnels dashed across the courtyard to a symphony of curses, carrying syringes, cigarettes, and bandages, as if the monastery could bear no more and had finally heaved up everything it knew should not be there.

Captain Lefkowitz, who'd seen his share of weather in the war, seemed most enraged because he couldn't keep a cigar lit, and none of his brave wounded could smoke either. He ordered that every single litter be sheltered with a poncho, and all the orderlies jumped in jeeps and raced to the nearby forest of San Giusipuzzu, and returned with scores of hacked-off branches, and twined and roped them to each cot until every wounded man had a slicker perched three feet above his head. After that the courtyard garden looked like a crowd of stubborn outdoor concertgoers clutching their umbrellas, refusing to be banished from their music by the storm.

Word arrived of further wounded needing care, and Captain Lefkowitz ordered that they be retrieved, on the double, to fill the beds of those who'd died. Three GI drivers with armed escorts took their jeeps to fetch them at a handoff north near Campofranco. They had no maps and navigated there and back using only landmarks, as all the province's street signs had been torn away by Germans in their furious retreat.

Returning from their mission, they raced the looming darkness, helmets dripping, ponchos drenched, jeeps laden with bouncing litters. They recognized Piazza Vittorio Emanuele by its clumps of broken monumental stones, then weaved through those to find their crucial waypoint, an enormous ficus tree with gnarled arms and drooping vines like the shawl of an old woman.

From there they turned hard right and gunned their engines, bouncing up the cobblestones of Via Atenea, then right again and impossibly tight up Via Porcello, both streets they couldn't name. They plunged into a labyrinth of claustrophobic alleyways, with shell-pocked walls so close they had to pull their elbows in, until at last they made the final switchback and burst onto the monastery's apron. All their jeeps were bruised and scraped and dented, and they set their brakes, released their breaths, got out and lit their smokes as if their Chesterfields were Highland scotch.

Lefkowitz was standing there to greet his drivers and their patients, and one young brave GI asked him why he'd chosen such a place with its "fuggin' screwy" access.

"It makes it tough to kill us," the captain said.

"Sir, on the level, you think the Krauts would bother rustling up a blitzkrieg on a church?"

Lefkowitz examined the soggy tip of his cigar and said, "Kid, you don't know the Germans."

On the morning of the fourth day, a short barrage of long-range cannons struck the town. The unaimed shells fell wildly outside the monastery walls, on fragile roofs and in the alleyways where women strung their wash from crumbled house to house. The shrapnel sang and pinged off stone, and Froelich recalled how the Germans had mercilessly targeted the *Kensington*, and thought that they or their Italian fascist brethren were once again hunting for the helpless.

The wounded men, unable to take cover, tensed beneath their ponchos and waited for the blows. Yet soon the shelling halted, and with that nature's thunder also beat retreat, as if a section of mad kettle drummers had crescendoed, ending a

Wagnerian opera. The rain stopped, the sun came out, and all was blessed silence but for the chirps of grateful happy birds.

Captain Lefkowitz made the rounds, with Pennington in his trail, and the hospital commander's gait seemed chipper, perhaps because his stogies were no longer soaked. He stopped at Froelich's bedside, untied the poncho and flicked it off to have a look. He jammed his knuckles to his garrison belt.

"How's it going, kid?"

"I think just fine, sir, though I haven't moved in days."

"Patience, patient. We'll getcha up soon enough." The captain pulled out his cigar and sniffed the air. "You're stinkin' like a moldy sheep." He turned to Pennington. "Lieutenant, have somebody get this Limey a dry blanket."

"Yes, sir."

Pennington slipped away and Lefkowitz winked at Froelich.

"Gotta remind these young meat cleavers who's the boss, right?"

Froelich smiled back. "I think they know, sir."

Beginning with Froelich's upper thigh, Lefkowitz explored the leg, checked his traction bolts, made certain that the bandages showed no signs of sepsis, and dug his fingers deeper into the fracture line. Froelich gripped the cot and clenched his teeth, but uttered nothing. The captain stepped back, nodding at his handiwork.

"*Ausgezeichnet.*" Excellent, he grunted in German.

Froelich raised an eyebrow.

"Yeah, I speak Kraut," said Lefkowitz. "Did my residency in Vienna. Even snagged myself a pretty Austrian Jewish girl

and brought her back to Brooklyn. She writes me letters tellin'
me how all the 4-F guys come around sniffin' at her skirt."

"Four-F, sir?"

"It's Yank lingo for all those slobs claimin' flat feet so they
can get outta the army."

"Oh, I see."

"But I ain't worried." The captain patted his holstered pistol. "When this is over, I'm bringin' Betsy here home with
me."

Froelich knew he wouldn't want to be some unsuspecting
gigolo facing Lefkowitz's jealous .45.

The captain moved to Froelich's pulley, checked the
ammunition-can counterweight and said, "You need more
stretch, kid." He slipped a pineapple hand grenade from his
belt, wrapped the spoon three times with a roll of white sur-
gical tape, and dropped it in the can. Froelich felt the extra
pull right way, then Lefkowitz glared at him.

"Wait a minute. You ain't depressed, are ya, kid?"

Froelich pulled his chin back. "Well, no, sir."

"Ya sure? You ain't gonna pull a Robbins on me and eat
this fuggin' egg, right?"

"Of course not, sir."

"Swell. 'Cause if you do, I'm gonna have you buried in a
Catholic cemetery under a cross, and mark it Stinky O'Reilly.
Get me?"

"Yes, sir." Froelich grinned. "Not to worry."

"Okay." Lefkowitz opened a breast pocket and dropped
a small brown packet on Froelich's chest. It was a Hershey's
chocolate bar. "Keep your chin up." He walked away.

An hour later, Sofia the ice girl reappeared. Froelich hadn't seen her in four days, even though she'd promised to return, and he'd come to think she was indeed a morphine dream. Yet there she was, limping through the monastery archway with her metal pot, expertly maneuvering her crutch, one slim leg below her flowered dress ending in a small brown shoe. She wore a yellow kerchief in her flowing hair to fend off rain, because she couldn't handle an umbrella, and many pairs of lonely eyes turned to watch her, and Froelich's did too.

She smiled and doled out ice as she weaved between the cots, and as her delicate form grew larger, Froelich touched his face and wished that he had shaved. She passed the final litter in the last row before his, where a wounded man seemed to be sleeping, and she would have tiptoed if she could. Yet then a sallow hand reached out and brushed her dress, and she stopped and smiled down, said something softly Froelich couldn't hear, fed the boy a chip of ice and then came on again. Her face was slightly dipped, but her large doe eyes were fixed on his, as if they were the lantern of a lighthouse.

"*Buongiorno, Tenente.*" She stopped beside his bed and smiled with closed lips.

"*Buongiorno*, Sofia." He saw how the crutch top stretched her underarm and hiked up her small shoulder.

"*Mi dispiace* that I did not come," she apologized. "It was the rain, and then, how you say, the mortar bombs."

"It's all right." He smiled back at her, more to keep her expression and her dimples exactly as they were. "It was a bit too cold for ice."

"*Sì*. Did you have drink?"

"More than enough. I merely had to hold my cup out." He took his mess tin cup and extended it to arm's length, mim-

ing how he'd caught the rain. She grinned fully then, and
that vision warmed his throat and flushed his face, and her
cheeks pinkened also when she saw it.

"Do you want the ice, *Tenente?*"

He almost nodded, then thought to have her fingers at his
lips would be too much.

"No, thank you."

Her smile faded and she nodded once, as if she knew a man
like him would only want a girl with two good legs, and she
began to turn away. He quickly grasped the chocolate bar that
Lefkowitz had given him and held it out.

"But I have something here for you."

She looked at it and shook her head. "No, *grazie,* I cannot."

"Please," he said, and snapped the bar in half, tearing its
paper wrapper. "At least share it with me."

She hesitated, and then as if not wanting to insult, took
her half and dropped it in her dress pocket. *"Mille grazie,"* she
said, and turned to go again. Froelich desperately wanted her
to stay, but couldn't think of any way to do it, except to rush
across a bridge of intimacy he had no right to broach.

"Sofia," he said. "How did it happen to you?"

She turned back, hesitating for a moment. But both of them
were crippled by the war.

"The Germans, they bomb-ed Agrigento," she said. "It
was some months ago, though I do not recall which date because I slept so much after. I do remember it was a Sunday,
because my mama and papa, we went to church to pray and
rode our bicycles to home." She hugged her metal pot and
looked up at the square of sky above the courtyard. "We lived
in a house in the hills, near the Valley of the Temples. It was a

small house, with olive trees and flowers. It was such a sunny day, like this will be. I woke up in hospital, alone, because they were gone, Mama and Papa."

"I am so sorry," Froelich said, his breath hitching in his chest and hating himself for asking. He watched a single tear roll down her sunglossed cheek, like a drop of oil on a porcelain olive, though nothing changed in her expression.

"I live now with my uncle," Sofia said. "Near to here."

"Your uncle." He felt relieved she had some family still.

"Fabrizio is my uncle. He is very good to me. He has seen so much and suffered much, and is very wise and sad from all of this." She took her small hand from her crutch and waved it over all the wounded, but she didn't wipe away the tear. "My uncle says that war is an unforgiving beast. He says that it will drag a soldier to its lair, let him bleed a bit and rest until he thinks that it is over, and then all at once return and take his limb, or life." She looked at Froelich's tractioned leg, then at the empty space below her dress and shrugged.

"Yes," Froelich said. "War is like that."

"Uncle Fabrizio says I must have faith," Sofia said. "Do you have faith, *Tenente*? Do you go to the church?"

Froelich hesitated, not wanting to reveal his Judaism yet. It wasn't shame, but the truth had broken spells before, and he thought it might alarm or frighten her away, like too quick a movement near a butterfly. He thought of all the times he'd been to his friends' catechisms and communions in Berlin, which saved him from a lie.

"I've been a few times, yes," he said.

She looked at him as if she wasn't sure, then touched her fingers to the spot above her breast.

"Well, the faith is here. Is it not, *Tenente?*"

"Yes, that's where it is."

She looked down at her pot and smiled again.

"My ice has turned to water." She reached out and straightened a wrinkle at the top hem of his blanket, and in doing so her fingertip brushed the back of his hand. Then she blushed and retreated a step, and waved at him from where she stood and said, *"Arrivederci, Tenente."*

"Arrivederci, Sofia." He waved back and watched her leave again, and looked down at his knuckle, as if she'd painted something there that marked him hers.

Fourteen

ONE DAY IN EARLY OCTOBER 1943, MAJOR
Nigel Wallace Butler entered the life of Second Lieutenant
Bernard Froelich, and would remain there for some time.

Two weeks had passed, with days and nights of intermittent
rain and sunshine, thunderclouds and brilliant moons. During a brief surgery, Captain Lefkowitz had removed Froelich's
leg bolts, stitched the flesh wounds rendered by his drill, and
had the orderlies get him on his feet. Fabrizio's contraption
had been removed, and with his leg tightly bandaged but not
cast, Froelich had begun to stalk the courtyard on a pair of
wooden crutches. Charlie Harris was encouraging and often
lent a shoulder. Pennington and Hedges grunted their ap-
provals, yet cast their eyes away.

Sofia had visited him often, albeit briefly, as if she didn't
want the others she was caring for to think that she felt more
for this one man. They chatted and exchanged pleasantries,
and here and there a laugh or two, and seeing her that way

made Froelich feel things that he knew he shouldn't. Yet still
he held the revelation of his heritage in check, and began to
hope his leg might never heal, and entertained the fantasy
that perhaps his war would end right there in Agrigento, and
he would stay.

Then Butler came and slapped him from his reveries.

The major made his entrance early one morning. He strode
in through the monastery's archway, stood ramrod still and
scanned the wounded like a hunting hawk. Froelich was sitting on his cot, crutches propped beside him, sipping tea and
munching on a hardtack cracker, and when he felt Butler's
eyes upon him, something in his guts clenched and he knew
that the officer had come for him.

The major made straight for him, his gait like a parade
ground march. He wore a smartly cocked green beret with a
silver flash resembling a winged phoenix. His woolen uniform had buttoned pockets and was girded by a white belt
that matched the puttees over polished black boots. On the
shoulder of his left sleeve Froelich saw the black-and-red patch
of Combined Operations—upthrust spearheads, a Sten gun,
and an eagle—and above that a rocker tab said No.10 Commando. A Webley pistol was holstered to his belt, butt forward for the rapid draw, and his dress shirt underneath his
tunic showed a primly knotted tie.

But it was Butler's eyes that rang Froelich's alarm bells, cold
and gray and lacking in all poetry. Above them, sharp reddish eyebrows matched the close-cropped hair that showed,
and below them, a sharp nose pointed to a pencil mustache.
His smoothly shaven ruddy face seemed as polished as his

boots. He was medium height, muscular, and looked pent up like a leopard.

The major stopped at Froelich's cot, looked down at him and said, "If I'm not mistaken, Lieutenant, my rank's superior to yours."

Froelich put his tea tin down, pushed himself erect, and saluted.

"Good morning, Major."

Butler returned the salute, held it for a moment, then released him to attention.

"Froelich, isn't it?"

"Yes, sir. Bernard, second lieutenant, formerly with the 51st out of Cairo."

"Good. I'm Butler, Nigel, major, Combined Operations."

"A pleasure, sir." Froelich tried to smile.

"Neither yours nor mine," Butler said, and Froelich noted he had yet to blink. "But we're going to make do."

"Forgive my asking, sir. Make do with what?"

Butler's glare told Froelich that his question was impertinent.

"I've read your jacket, Froelich. I hear your German lilt. One of Bertie Buck's SIGs, were you?"

"Yes, sir." Froelich glanced down at his bandaged limb. "But now, with this leg…"

"I have eyes," Butler snapped. "Your surgeon captain tells me that you're healing."

"Slowly, sir, yes."

"Well, speed it up."

Froelich held his peace, but he knew that Butler's words

portended nothing good. He stood there waiting, knowing it would come.

"You're a Hebrew, aren't you?" Butler said.

Froelich's mouth went tight. "Yes, sir. I am that."

Butler raised his gunstock chin as if scenting something foul.

"I've got a lot like you." The major sneered. "I'm Number Ten, Inter-Allied Commando, commander of Troop Three, also known as X Troop. They're all members of your tribe. Germans, Austrians, a few Alsace French. Not a troop I favor, but orders are orders. We've got ourselves a task, and you're going to be part of it."

Froelich hiked his shoulders, an apologetic shrug. "I'm not sure that I'll be ready, sir."

"You'll be bloody well ready when I say you are."

Froelich swallowed and his jaw rippled.

"One week, Lieutenant," Butler said. "And then you're under my command. Are we clear?"

"Crystal, sir."

"Good." And then Butler removed a pair of brown leather gloves from his trouser map pocket and pulled them on while he examined Froelich's bristly jaw and throat. "Shave closer, Lieutenant Froelich," he said. "And heal faster."

The major executed a perfect about-face and marched away. And Froelich watched him, and realized that all the men around him had gone silent, and many eyes were upon him, and he cursed the man's departure with a whisper.

"You can go straight to hell, Major. I intend to have this bloody limp forever."

Fifteen

ON A DEWY AUTUMN MORNING, THE FIRST one in that last week of Major Butler's promised freedoms, Froelich was summoned to Captain Lefkowitz's office.

It was no more than a wobbly kitchen table with lathed legs and a cracked ceramic top in the shade of an orange tree, upon which the captain updated piles of medical files and penned V-mails to his longed-for wife. All of it was dusted with the fine gray ash of his cigars, as if he were the last accountant working in Pompei.

Froelich, dressed in a fresh battle uniform and a pair of desert boots salvaged from a man who'd lost his mortal struggle, appeared before the captain's table with only one crutch, and remembered that he'd better not salute. The captain smacked a file with an ink stamp, filled in the date, and jerked a thumb at the monastery's entrance.

"You got a visitor, Lieutenant," he said, and Froelich stiffened, thinking it could only be Major Butler, but it was not. "Ice girl figures she's a nurse now. Thinks you need fresh air and exercise." Lefkowtiz squinted above his steel-rimmed spectacles. "I'm gonna allow it, but only 'cause a pair of gimps can't get in too much Dutch." From the side of his table, the captain picked up an M-1 carbine on a leather strap and handed it to Froelich, but he didn't release it until he said, "Back by curfew, and don't make me send the MPs after you. Got it?"

"Yes, sir." Froelich slung the rifle over his back and stalked beneath the brace of arches toward the sunlight, feeling he'd been summoned by a generous heart and knowing he could not decline, nor did he want to.

She was there, just beyond the monastery's portico, waiting on the slab stone drive. Her eyes were closed, her small face lifted toward the sun like a blossom storing up its warmth for winter. Her long curls fell unfettered and her dress was different, a pale green sleeveless frock, and again she wore one small brown shoe, but her bottom was perched upon a strange contraption.

It was a scooter of some sort, something made by caring hands, and only for Sofia. Its base was a polished board of chestnut with two large caster wheels. At its front was a waist-high wooden mast, topped by an ornately lathed handlebar with a gleaming bicycle bell, and in its middle was another shorter mast, affixed with a springed bicycle seat. A woven basket hung from the handlebars, and her wooden crutch was clipped at an angle from the scooter's base to the forward mast, like a pickax to a jeep.

She felt him there and turned to him and smiled.

"*Buongiorno, Tenente,*" she said.

"Buongiorno, Sofia."

"You may leave your crutch. I have something for you better."

He leaned his crutch against the monastery's wall. In truth he didn't need it and was only hobbling with it still in defiance of Major Butler's order that he heal, but Sofia didn't know that. He came to her and she presented him a homemade cane laid across her palms. It was a polished wooden pole with a Bakelite tip, and its handle was a shiny German 20 millimeter shell casing, driven perpendicular through a drilled hole at its top.

"Uncle Fabrizio likes you," she said.

"I like him too," said Froelich as he took the cane and admired it. Sofia gripped her handlebars and pushed off with her foot, and he tapped the cane tip on the stones and walked beside her. A gust of breeze swept her hair behind her ears and lifted the fringe of her dress, and he saw that her small stump was snuggled in a lemon-colored knitted cap, and he quickly looked away again. The morning air smelled like palms and roses, and somewhere a mother cooed her comforts to a crying infant, but there were no other sounds except the clacks of Sofia's wheels.

They wound their way along the narrow Via Spirito Santo, whose downward angle made the going easy, even though some clumps of rubble still lay in the gutters. She'd seen his glance and tucked her dress to cover up her stump, and without looking at her Froelich said, "That's all right. It's pretty."

She blushed and said, "No, it is not."

He didn't offer a retort, because you couldn't really make a blown off leg look better, and he was quiet for a while until the silence grew too heavy.

"What's your family name, Sofia?" he asked as he looked up at a line of wash hanging from a broken balcony, like the first spring sprouts popping in a scorched garden.

"It is Bellina."

"You see?" He smiled. "Pretty. Did Fabrizio's wife knit the cover for you?"

"No, one of the monastery sisters. My aunt Lucia is gone."

"I'm sorry." He hoped she hadn't fallen to an Allied shell, though he knew it made no difference.

"Fabrizio loved her very much," she said. "I loved her too. They had a carpentry shop where he fashioned tables and chairs, but it was Aunt Lucia who sold them with her smile and her charm, and all the people came for her. She had blond hair, like you." She looked at him, and then away again, and pushed off with her shoe. "Fabrizio hated to be in the army and far away from Lucia. She died there in the shop in a bombing, I do not know from who. I never thought a man could weep so much. Now he makes things in our home, in the salon. It is always thick with sawdust." She shrugged. "But I say nothing, you know, because he does not care. I think he believes that she still lives there in the dust."

She stopped the scooter and tipped her chin toward where the road rose higher, and said, "Up there." But then she turned the scooter to the left, and he knew there'd be no invitation to her home, and somehow he was glad. He wasn't ready for another sorrow.

Via Porcello was steeper, its dusty cobblestones angled sharply in descent. The houses on both sides were a mosaic

of mustard stucco and quarry stone, some collapsed from shellfire and others nearly perfect, and many walls were pocked
with ordnance strikes that left imprints like white starfishes.
With the Germans gone, and Mussolini's bandits too, the
townsfolk had begun to sweep the rubble, and all the piles
gleamed with empty cartridge shells as if the clouds had rained
a hail of brass.

Sofia's scooter had no brakes, and though she dragged her
foot it picked up speed, and Froelich hurried after to her to
save her from a spill. He yanked his cane tip off the ground
and charged to her left, his rifle bouncing at his spine, and
he shot his right hand out and gripped the springs beneath
her seat and slowed her. To both of them the gesture felt as
intimate as holding hands, and they laughed yet didn't look
at one another, and though Froelich's leg ached with the effort he ignored it.

"*Grazie*," said Sofia.

"*Prego*," he replied. "I think it needs some brakes."

"Brakes?"

"A mechanism, to stop it."

She smiled and said, "Perhaps that is why I called for you."

They carried onward carefully, and Froelich stopped and
smeared them tight against a wall as a jeep came rushing up
around a corner. Its horn was broken and its GI driver yelled
"Beep, beep!" as he grinned and waved and roared past them,
scurrying a pair of panicked cats. Then they turned down one
final steep escarpment, and broke out onto the wide thoroughfare of Via Atenea, and for the first time Froelich saw
the layout of the town, most of which was up behind them.

Agrigento was like a corpulent old woman, her buttocks

spread out on a hillside by the sea, her old toes dipping in the shimmering aquamarine waters. Her frock and skin and folds were cracked and dusty with the war, but her tired fingers bloomed with fruits and flowers, and waving palms were pinned like wedding garlands in the curls of her gray hair. She'd been a beauty once, and would be soon again, and Via Atenea lay across her ankles west to east, busy with the Lilliputians who'd bring her back to life.

There were matrons on the lane, some in modest black caftans, some in worn flowered dresses, yet all with heavy shoes to weave between the rubble hillocks. They carried baskets of fruit or precious eggs upon their kerchiefed heads, or waddled with jerrycans of water, and when they chatted with each other in Sicilian, a version of Italian mixed with the island's ancient history of Arabic and Greek, Froelich didn't understand a word. There were men as well, some working in the street with wheelbarrows and shovels to make the cobblestones alive again, and they wore cocky soft brimmed caps, baggy trousers and suspenders over soiled white undershirts from which their chest curls glistened. There were no cars yet, and bicycles were still precious, and the only one Froelich saw was serving as the steed to a corpulent policeman.

He released Sofia's seat as they were on flat ground again. She turned the scooter to the left and peddled with her foot.

"Come, *Tenente*," she said. "I shall show you my tree."

"You can call me by my name, Sofia."

"I like *Tenente*. It tastes correct."

"Tastes?" He smiled.

"On my tongue. Is this not good English?"

"Yes, it's just fine."

He saw the tree when they reached the Piazza of Victor
Emmanuel, and he stopped walking because he'd never seen
such a thing before. It rose up from a wide plot of broken
bomb rubble, with a trunk of intertwined gray roots like the
bulging veins of a wrestler. The trunk was thick as a lighthouse tower, and fifty feet above, it exploded in a hundred
arms that held a gargantuan mushroom cap of glistening ficus
leaves. And from all of that a filigree of vines cascaded down,
waving in the seaside breeze like the veils of harem dancers.
The thing was so enormous that it cast a giant shadow like a
pool of spilling ink, and it was untouched by the war, and he
wondered how that could be.

"It that your tree?" he marveled.

"*Sì*. Would you like to meet her?"

Froelich swallowed, because something in the way Sofia
said that reminded him she'd lost her mother too, and he said,
"Yes, I think I would."

She led him down a gentle grade, and now he used the cane
and was grateful that he had it. The piazza was empty, for
there were no cafés or magazine vendors or ice cream shops as
there would someday be, and Sofia's tree was like a lush island
rising from a sea of wartime wreckage, with dented ammunition cans, irreparable canteens, and useless punctured jeep
tires discarded on the run. Yet someone must have thought the
giant shadow was inviting, and had dragged a wooden bench
under the tree to face the sea, and that was what the couple
swam for, and without conference, chose that place to rest.

Sofia plucked the picnic basket from her handlebars and
Froelich helped her lay the scooter in the dust. He unslung
his rifle and they slid onto the bench, side by side yet almost

with shy hesitance, as if it were a swing on their watchful parents' veranda. Yet the wood was thick and smooth and warm, resting on its hips of iron legs and feet, and it cupped their backs and spread out generously beneath them. The giant ficus' fingers waved in breezes from the ocean and fluttered downward at their faces, as if to say "Welcome, children. What have you to tell me?"

Sofia set the basket on the bench between them. The gesture seemed to Froelich like the placement of a bundling board, a barrier between illicit lovers. She peeled away a checkered square of cloth, and he saw a heel of bread, two green apples, an oval of white cheese in cheesecloth, a corked water bottle, and an oilskin sack. She handed him an apple, opened the cheesecloth on her lap, drew a paring knife from the basket, and began cutting careful slices.

Froelich looked at her profile, her soft curls haloed by the sun, her graceful yet determined jaw, her full lips and the shallow furrow between her eyebrows as she worked. He thought she had the beauty of a classic sculpture, and only damaged because some cruel careless hands had dropped her on the way to her museum perch. And sitting on that bench beside her, he thought of Lili then, and he knew he had to tell her, to see if she would stay. He leaned over his knees and looked out at the sea. There were warships there, but far away. His apple stayed unbitten.

"Do you know what a Jew is, Sofia?" he asked.

"*Ebreo,*" she said, "as from the Bible."

"Yes. I am one."

"Would you like an olive?" she asked, and her question told him everything.

"No, not yet, thanks." He turned the apple in his fingers.

"You should eat something, *Tenente.*"

He took the offered olive from her pouch and ate it, and she seemed happier with that.

"I was born in Germany," he said, squinting once more out to sea. "The Nazis killed my father. My family owned a store in our village. It was also our house. He was home alone that evening, and they barricaded all the doors and burned it, all of it. I came home and saw it but I couldn't save him."

And he was seeing it again, there beyond the warships and far across the sea. Sofia saw it too and she'd stopped her cutting.

"They took me to prison that night." Froelich's voice was dull, but it tremored. "They took all the Jewish men in Gestern, and the teenage boys too. I was wild and fought them, but it was too late." He meant that his father was already dead, and he didn't say how badly he himself had been beaten, or thrown in the prison's dungeon hole and doused with ice water, by men who'd once been family friends and now were Brownshirt thugs. "They took the women too, my mother and my sister, but not to prison. They made them march very far to a warehouse, like cattle. It was very cold. They kept them there until they thought the men were weak enough from fearing for their families."

Sofia waited, no longer preparing their repast. Her fingers lay lifeless in her lap.

"I am sorry," Froelich said, because he thought he'd spoiled everything.

"Please say it, *Tenente,*" she whispered. "All of it, as I did for you."

"All right," he said. "My mother made me leave for Palestine. Do you know where that is?"

"East, across the sea."

"Yes. That's how I joined the British Army. That's how I came to be here. I don't know what happened after that, to my mother and sister."

It was enough. He didn't need to tell her that in Palestine, he'd received a letter from the last Jewish prefecture in Berlin, telling him that his mother and sister had finally been rounded up with all the rest. He didn't want to confess that he'd almost shot himself that night with the Enfield rifle he'd been issued. It all felt indulgent now.

Sofia didn't say that she was sorry, for what else could she be but that? The two of them were so alike, mangled lilies floating in the same roiling pool, and with his burden lifted Froelich took a slice of cheese and ate it, and then they shared the bread and olives and sliced the apples for dessert and drank the water bottled from the purer streams beyond the town. They didn't say a thing through all of it, until at last Froelich sat back and gripped the carbine lain across his lap.

"Sometimes," he said, "I wish more than anything that I was not a Jew."

"Sometimes," Sofia said, "I wish more than anything that I lived in America, where the war never visits."

"Oh, it visits there as well," he said. "It visits the homes of soldiers' mothers and fathers, when the priests come to their doors."

"How old are you please, Bernard?"

"Twenty-three." He was so pleased she'd finally used his name.

She reached across her basket and touched the back of his hand. Her fingernails were cut down to the skin, like a child's, and clean. She still looked at the sea.

"We are young, but we know too much, no?" she said. "We live between two beauties. Cruel life with all its wonders, and death with all its peace."

A church bell rang then, from somewhere higher in the town. It rang twelve times, heralding the noon, and Sofia sighed and said she had to pack their things away and go. After all, she said, she was an ice girl, and soldiers would be needing ice.

They headed back the way they'd come, but that was fine because their autumn morning had been full and lovely, and longer than a summer's day.

Sixteen

THERE WAS A GUNFIGHT IN THE MOUNTAINS near Cammarata, halfway up the winding thoroughfare that ran from Agrigento to Palermo. It took an understrength platoon of US Rangers by surprise, as by that time almost all the German and Italian troops who'd not been killed or captured had fled to Italy across the Straits of Messina, in a massive flood of matériel and men much like the Allies' debacle at Dunkirk.

Some sixty thousand Wehrmacht troops, along with even more hardcore Italian brethren, had foiled Patton and Montgomery and lived to fight another day. The entire Hermann Göring Panzer Division, the 15th and 29th Panzergrenadiers and 1st Parachute Division, had all withdrawn with perfect discipline, "encouraged," as it were, by General Hans-Valentin Hube's order that if you stained morale or showed up at the water's edge without your tank or rifle you'd be shot.

Yet twenty-seven German paratroopers hadn't crossed that

road in time, and cut off from retreat, had burrowed in the hills near Cammarata and held out there for weeks until they'd nearly starved. They tried their breakout, were slaughtered by the Rangers for their efforts, and their only four survivors were brought to Agrigento and the monastery's garden.

The Allied wounded didn't like it, but Captain Lefkowitz was first and foremost a physician, and only after that a soldier and a Jew, and he told his boys to just shut up and eat it. He treated all four Germans, planted them on cots at one far corner of the garden, and had Charlie Harris and two more MPs watch the Krauts like hawks. Then he gave each one a plaster leg cast, even if they didn't need it, and painted each one up with brilliant Stars of David, which made his other patients grin.

With all the drama and the ruckus, Froelich slipped away again unnoticed, to find Sofia waiting as he hoped he would. She hadn't summoned him or sent an invitation, yet there she was, standing on the monastery's drive, haloed by the morning sun. She wore the same green frock, this time with a lemon sweater that matched her hidden stump cap, but Fabrizio's scooter was nowhere to be seen. With his rifle strapped across his back again, Froelich used his cane and walked to her and felt his smile aching.

"Buongiorno," he said. "Where is your ice today, Sofia?"

"It is Sunday, Tenente Bernard." She tainted familiarity with rank, as if they'd been too intimate before. "A girl must have her Sabbath, no?"

He didn't know that it was Sunday, but then all the church bells in the town began to ring at once, some very close, some far away, like mockingbirds echoing each other's songs, calling everyone to feed.

"And where is your scooter?" he asked.

She cocked her head. "Scooter?"

"The thing with wheels."

"Ah. I cannot climb with that, you know."

He knew all right. The day before he'd had to carry it for her when their way back to the monastery was all uphill, and it was heavy and he'd sweated and she'd felt ashamed. Now she turned away and began to walk, and he marveled at her agility with just a single crutch. All the men with wounded legs were forced to use a pair of clumsy poles, yet she pressed hers against her stump and walked with rhythmic grace, as if she'd been born that way.

Their crutch and cane tips clicking, they strolled along the road, but Sofia didn't lead them down to picnic once again beneath her tree. More facades of shell-shocked homes were piled in the street, with here and there a dusty child's rag doll, abandoned shoe or broken dinner plate. Above on tilting balconies, some flowers had been placed in terra-cotta pots, and hand-washed underclothes and sheets waved from wires flung by one rooftop neighbor to the other. Sofia stopped where on the right, an alleyway of thick stone stairs rose steeply up.

"Via Politi," she said. "The way up there is difficult."

"I think I'll manage it," Froelich said, and smiled, and they climbed.

The way was narrow, with interlocking faces of stone and stucco houses and apartments on each side. Scrawny cats with large eyes and wary tails foraged in the piles of wartime refuse, and Froelich felt for them and knew they dreamed of milk.

Agrigento's plumbing had yet to be repaired, and rivulets from chamber pots crawled down the stony stairs, gleaming with the drops of lemon juice and olive oil meant to camouflage the scent. The morning air was tinged as well with cooking fire smoke, wild basil and oregano, and it all seemed quaint and peaceful except up at the top where a church appeared. Bombs had hollowed out its organs, with only one wall left, and carved into the brown facade was a framed oval window with a pastel painted sculpture of the Virgin Mary. The glass was shattered and she had no arms.

Sofia stumbled as they summited. Froelich caught her by her upper arm until she steadied on her foot, and then released her though he wished that he were bold enough to not. Indeed the climb had been a challenge, with her crutch armpit rubbed too much and his wounded leg still sore, and both their foreheads glistened. She turned them left onto the Via Antonio Restivo, a wide flat boulevard with no more climbing.

"This is my street," she said, a little breathless.

"Your tree, your street," he said. "I'm beginning to think you own the town, Sofia."

She looked at him and said with utter innocence, "I make everything mine, *Tenente*. Everything I like." And because she kept on walking, she didn't see his blush.

A hundred yards away the thoroughfare split left and right, and in the middle was a skinny row of flats jutting toward them like the prow of a vessel. The first one was a three-story structure of bright yellow plaster, standing out among the drab grays and browns of all the rest. Its walls were buckled, its green framed windows crooked, and it was fatter on the bottom and reminded Froelich of an English nursery rhyme about an old woman who lived in a shoe. Its ground floor double doors and windows were thrown open to the air, and as they neared, Froelich heard the whine of Fabrizio's lathe.

Sofia surprised him then as she stuck two fingers in her mouth and produced a whistling shriek. The lathing stopped and Fabrizio came out. He was wearing his Italian army boots and trousers and a soiled white singlet, his sinews gleaming, and covered head to foot in sawdust. He grinned with pleasure, walked right up to Froelich, grabbed his hand and shocked him with a bristly kiss on both his cheeks.

"I amma so pleased to see you walking, Bernardo," he said.

"It pleases me as well," Froelich said, and matched his grin, and he showed Fabrizio that he was using his walking stick, of which there was no twin in all the world.

"*Prego, entri.*" Fabrizio pulled a stained handkerchief from his pocket and wiped his calloused hands as he led Froelich into the house, with Sofia close behind.

The salon was square, with cream plaster walls and braided moldings of olive wood. The walls were spidered with cracks that Froelich knew were from recent concussions, for he sensed that Fabrizio would never have allowed his beloved Lucia to live in such disrepair. At the rear was a slim stairway leading to some lofty perch somewhere, and sunlight streamed through all the windows, its shafts swirling with glinting sawdust like tossed confetti at a wedding. There was a flowered sofa on the right, and on the left a long dining table, with Fabrizio's pedal powered lathe on top, and drills and hammers and files and mallets, and all around were pieces of his works in progress, all swathed in gritty silt.

Froelich looked at all of it and searched for words, but he

felt Sofia touch his arm as if suggesting silence would be better, and Fabrizo said, "My wife, Lucia, she loved the smell," and that was enough for all.

Fabrizio went into an alcove kitchen and came back with a bottle of pale Catarratto wine and three fat oranges. He handed those to Froelich, gathered up three wooden chairs, and they all went out to sit in the sun on the cobblestone apron before the house. They peeled the oranges and shared the wine, and no one wiped the bottle's mouth before passing it on. The war had made such cautions foolish.

"I have heard, Bernardo," Fabrizio said, "that you are not long for this world."

Froelich raised an eyebrow. "In English, my friend, that means I'm going to die."

"Oh, no, not that," Sofia said. "Uncle is speaking of the British major."

"Ah, Butler," Froelich said, though he had no idea how they knew about that, and again he felt the major's presence like a spectre.

"Yes," Sofia said, then she gently chided her uncle in Italian, and he frowned and said, "*Mi dispiace*, Bernardo."

"That's all right," Froelich laughed. "Yes, he has plans for me."

Fabrizio made a fist. "We shall defeat him!"

"Oh, I don't think so," Froelich said, and he looked at Sofia, who spoke to the orange she was peeling and whispered, "Well, we shall all be friends, for this time."

They finished their oranges and wine, and Fabrizio wiped his mouth with his handkerchief and said brightly, "I have a thing for both of you." Froelich smiled because in English the idiom meant affection, but he knew Fabrizio meant something else, and the Sicilian got up and disappeared around the northern corner of the house.

Froelich turned to find Sofia gazing up at something on the house's southern side, and he rose and walked a few feet so he could see it too. Just below the terra-cotta roof he saw a small balcony, with a simple iron railing painted emerald green, entwined with papery purple bougainvillea overflowing from a flower box.

"That is my room," Sofia said, because she knew that he would ask.

"How do you get up there?" It was very high, higher than the roofs across the way.

"I climb the stairs," she said.

"It must be very difficult. It must take some time."

"There is no hurry for me."

"What can you see from up there, Sofia?" he asked.

"I see the sea. I see the moon. It is where I pray. It is my *balcone dei desideri*, my balcony of wishes."

He didn't ask her what she wished for, and she offered nothing more.

Fabrizio returned then, wheeling a small motorcycle. It was an olive green 1934 Moto Guzzi, like an army messenger's machine, with a bulbous headlamp, a black leather bicycle seat and behind that, a small pillow hobnailed to a piece of plank strapped atop the rear fender.

Fabrizio set the Moto Guzzi on its central kickstand, which looked like a large bear claw, and stood back and folded his arms and grinned broadly.

"Can you ride it, Bernardo?" he asked.

"Yes, I think so. My father had one, though it was German."

"They are all the same," Fabrizio said.

Froelich handed Fabrizio his walking stick, mounted the motorcycle and played with the controls. With just his smiling eyes, Fabrizio summoned Sofia and helped her settle on the pillow, and showed her where he'd welded a stirrup for her foot because the machine had not been meant for passengers. He slipped the carbine from Froelich's back, fixed the strap across Sofia's chest so she could have the rifle resting on her spine, and tucked her crutch into a canvas holster on the frame that he'd made from half a weapons case. He gave them a water bottle and three more oranges.

"I shall have your cane, Bernardo," he said to Froelich.

"And I shall have your motorcycle, and care for it." Froelich smiled and kicked the starter over, and the Moto Guzzi coughed and rumbled and settled to a throaty purr.

"*Tienilo stretto.*" Hold him tight, Fabrizio said to Sofia, and she blushed but she did. She wrapped her slim arms around Froelich, and he felt the pillow of her chest against his back, and they left.

They rode along a quiet morning thoroughfare of gently bumping cobblestones, a long descending lane where Luigi Pirandello had once pursued his muse for poetry and plays, and Froelich found his balance fast and Sofia held him tight and trusted all his turns. And then they found the sea, and a small slim dusty road that led west and away to Siculiana, and Froelich opened up the throttle, and they flew. The glistening waves rushed by, the seagulls cawed and darted in their wake but couldn't catch them, and the sweet and salted air whipped Sofia's hair about his neck, and she grinned and laughed and he laughed too.

And there they raced their fates, just above the earth, and just below the clouds of gauze and blue, with nothing darkling in their past and nothing promising a future. But for the first time, in a very long time, Sofia had her legs again, and Froelich had his heart.

Seventeen

FROELICH AND SOFIA HAD NO PLANS, BUT they had a water bottle, three oranges, a motorcycle, a rifle and a day, and all of that was treasure in the middle of a war. The coastal road was empty and serene, with blurs of lichen-covered shoulders on the right and sands of gleaming sea-shells on the left, and beyond that a boundless ocean with all its promise.

Few ventured out that way, as the guns had barely fallen silent, and the train tracks were still curled from German saboteurs and the engineers had not yet clawed up all the mines. The Sicilians were still wary, finding comfort in the herd, so the western fringe of Agrigento, beyond which lay Siculiana, was like the lip of a roaring waterfall that tumbled away to rock and foam and wild imagination. But Froelich and Sofia were young, and even though they'd lost that precious sense of childhood immortality, they dared to swim beyond where it was safe.

Froelich didn't know where they were going, so he let
Sofia tell him with her finger. She hugged him tightly till
they came to any fork, then perched her hand below his chin
and wagged her digit left or right, and he grinned and did
as he was told. When at last Agrigento was lost behind them
and it seemed that nothing else of humankind could flourish,
Siculiana rose up like some creature from a Scottish fairytale
unfurling from the mist. Hundreds of feet high, it appeared
upon twin promontories like dromedary humps, both clustered with crooked houses as if some tikes had thrust their
matchbox collections willy-nilly into mounds of mud. Nestled in between them at the top was Siculiana's red capped
duomo, tipped with a gleaming cross.

"Where are we going, Sofia?" Froelich called over his
shoulder.

"It is named Siculiana," she answered in his ear. "That
small city in the sky."

"Is there something there?"

"There is something everywhere, *Tenente*."

"No, I mean something special."

"Perhaps the next step on your stairway, I do not know,"
she said, and with that she hugged him tighter, but only for
a moment, as if she knew he'd have to leave soon and she'd
have to let him go.

The dusty road dipped into a cactus valley and flattened
out, and they stopped the Moto Guzzi, its engine gurgling.
The town above was surely smirking down, as every narrow
lane between its stony huts looked too steep for even mountain mules. But Froelich gunned the engine, Sofia gripped
him round his neck, and they raced upward, spewing stones

and dust, careening left then right, banging echoes off the walls as gold toothed matrons popped their heads from windows to glare down at these careless children shattering their morning, until at last they burst onto the summit of the town.

It was a cobblestone piazza the size of a cricket field, surrounded by a crown of mismatched homes, their pimply faces painted with pastels mixed from turmeric and pomegranate. In the middle sat a massive granite duomo with a dozen wide stone stairs rising to the church's yawning door. Palm fronds flickered in the breeze, birds chirped from the rooftops, and the only other sounds were the murmurs of six old men hunched on wire chairs in the duomo's shadow, reminiscing about their youths as they smoked and shared a flask of grappa. If the war had passed this way, its rubble and its blood had all been scoured, as if it never was.

Froelich parked the Moto Guzzi, and with its engine silenced, he and Sofia turned their heads to the crackling of a distant tune. It seemed to come from somewhere west of the piazza where the houses opened onto blinding sunlight from the sea. He took his rifle, she her crutch, he set his cap, and they set off to find that source of harmony.

They came upon a long *terrazza* of crushed white limestone, its seaside fringe lined with palms and olive trees where it dropped off in a slope down to the ocean. Near that ledge, an old gramophone with an ivory crank and large brass horn sat upon a wine barrel. The record turning on its spindle was Ozzie Nelson's 1931 croon of "Dream a Little Dream of Me," and Froelich's jaw went slack because his father had owned that very platter, and had played it repeatedly.

Sofia touched his arm and drew his eyes to the left, where

an elderly woman was prancing to the tune. She had broad
hips, an ample bosom, a bulging black frock, and curiously
blue clogs, and she was hanging laundry on a makeshift rack
of broomsticks. With every turn of her imaginary partner,
she drew another clump of wash from a tin laundry tub and
draped her baggy bloomers without shame.

"Morning, suh!"

Froelich spun around and almost swung his rifle up, and
Sofia gasped and touched her chest.

A British sergeant had appeared out of the blue, stomping
to attention and saluting. He was short and husky in a khaki
battle uniform, sleeves rolled neatly to his biceps. He slung
a Thompson submachine gun, carried a sloshing jerrycan,
and wore canvas gauntlet gloves, the signature of men who'd
learned the hard way about touching red hot gun barrels.

"Morning, Sergeant." Froelich returned the salute.

"Sorry to give ya a start, sir. I'm Gutman, Fritz, but the
blokes all call me Fritzy." He had unkempt brown curls, green
eyes and a wrestler's grin, and Froelich realized the Tommy
helmet on his head was actually a straw hat.

"Froelich, Bernard, second lieutenant."

"I see that, sir." Gutman nodded at Froelich's epaulette
pips, then at Sofia. "Morning, mum." She smiled in reply.

"What's your task here, Gutman?" Froelich asked.

"Waiting for you, sir." The sergeant smiled.

"For me?" Froelich pulled his chin back.

"Righto, sir. But meantime, town morale, fetching water
for Signora Facci's wash and such." He cocked a thumb over
his shoulder.

"From the sea?" Froelich asked.

"Reckon she fancies the briny scent, sir, though we haven't a common word between us. It's all hand signals and guesses."

Froelich looked at the old woman, still prancing happily as Nelson sang on about fading stars, reluctant departures, and longed-for kisses. He turned back to Gutman.

"That's your mission, is it?"

"Oh no, sir. We've got another proper one, but it's all hush-hush and we haven't got a clue just yet."

"I see. And who's 'we,' Gutman?"

"The blokes in the castle."

"Castle? What castle?"

"*That* bleedin' castle, sir."

Froelich followed Gutman's finger and turned east to look. The *terrazzo* where they stood was like the thumb of a man's right hand, with the remaining fingers cupping the town. Between the thumb and all the rest, a deep crevasse plunged down then up the other side, where one last promontory sprouted medieval battlements and towers, straining toward the sea. Even in the yellow light and warm azure sky, the castle's stones and parapets looked black and cold as gloomy tombs, chilling Froelich's spine just as Ozzie Nelson's croon turned to scratches.

"She is Castello Chiarmonte," Sofia said as if the castle had a gender like a ship. "The Arabians constructed her in the century fourteen, and Great Frederick had the wedding of his daughter there."

"The lady knows her land." Gutman dipped his hat brim at Sofia.

"She has been a happy home," Sofia added, "and a most powerful fortress, and a most terrible prison."

"She's more a bleedin' prison now," Gutman muttered.

"What's up there, Sergeant?" Froelich asked.

"Well, Jerry had a Würzburg radar station, got all pocked up by Spitfires. Now it's lots of dingy rooms, a ghost or two, and us and all our kit. The men all flee whenever possible. Would you like to meet them, sir?"

"What men are they?"

"I believe they're *your* men, sir." Gutman cocked his head. "Isn't that why you're up here?"

Froelich looked at Sofia. She smiled lovely innocence and shrugged.

"Of course," he said.

Gutman brought the jerrycan to Signora Facci, filled her laundry tub and blushed when she pinched his cheek and kissed it. Then he led his new lieutenant and Sofia back to town, gripping his Thompson at the ready, looking left and right and all about.

"You act as if expecting ambush any moment, Sergeant," Froelich said behind his back.

"That's why I'm still alive, sir," Gutman said, and Froelich thought it might be good to have this man around.

They crossed the main piazza, passed between two buildings the color of flamingos, and descended a steep road beyond which the hills and sky seemed hung there like a tapestry. At the bottom where the road elbowed to the right, a low stone building was tucked into its crook, and outside on its apron sat a long wooden table.

Behind the table stood a young nun in a white apron and winged cap, and next to her a British soldier, with black hair, brooding eyes, and a plain white scar running from one sideburn to the corner of his lips. His Sten gun was slung across his back and he held a trench knife with a knuckle-duster handle, which looked odd beside the gentle sister, except that he was cutting strings off Red Cross food parcels and the table was surrounded by happy urchins. They had red curls, black curls, bare feet, filthy fingernails, ragged clothes and white teeth, and were hopping up and down with glee as they snatched their treats and stuffed their bulging cheeks.

"That's Private David Rosenberg." Gutman thrust his chin out as they neared. "Seems a dandy, but he's deadly with the blades. Got all scarred up by Nazi ruffians at his Berlin *gymnasium*. He likes to help the sister, she likes having him about, and there's no danger there of hanky-panky, right sir?"

Just then Rosenberg saw Froelich, put the trench knife down and saluted. Froelich returned it and said, "As you were, Private," and Gutman led them onward.

Farther on along the lane they came across a fountain. It was sitting in the middle of a crossroads, bathed in sunlight, while everything surrounding it was shadowed. The fountain's ten-foot marble dish had a rim for sitting, and in the middle was a sculpted mermaid arching from her tailfin, head and tresses thrown back, spewing fresh clear water from her mouth into the sky, where it tumbled back and bubbled in the bowl.

"How the devil does that work?" Froelich said as he stopped dead in his tracks. There were surely no electric water pumps in Siculiana.

"I've no idea, sir," Gutman said. "Can't be from a stream. There's nothing higher than us here."

"Perhaps a mule turns a wheel somewhere, *Tenente*," Sofia ventured.

But Froelich didn't really hear their answers as he stared at
a strange tableau. Another British soldier was sitting on the
fountain's ledge. He wore commando woolens, a cocked beret
with the Combined Operations flash, had rust-colored clipped
hair and the lithe form of a sculler. A Sten gun lay across his
lap with a daisy in the barrel, and he faced a middle-aged
woman in mourning black, mirroring his posture. Between
them floating in the fountain was a toy sailboat. They were
both smoking cigarettes and sipping cognac from chipped
crystal snifters.

"That's Corporal Horst Felder," Gutman said in confiden-
tial tones. "He's a brawler from some Rhine town south of
Bonn. Doesn't chatter much, but he's been cheerin' up that
poor widow, lost her only son in Libya. Speaks fluent Italian, don't ya know."

Froelich watched them for a moment and said, "Let's leave
them be."

"Right you are, sir."

Gutman turned them left into a slim dark alleyway that
descended further. A bleating goat ran past them with a jangling bell around its neck, chased by a screeching barefoot
boy with a switch. Froelich felt Sofia next to him and keeping
with his pace, but he only glanced at her and smiled thinly,
and he quietly unslung his carbine and held it by his hip. His
leg should have been aching him by now. It didn't.

The alleyway broke out into a wide cul-de-sac, and Gutman raised a finger and they stopped. The war had reached
this shady spot, where a piece of heavy ordnance had exploded
in the middle of the circle, perhaps some errant bomb from
a Mosquito angling for the Würzburg station. Not one win-

dow anywhere was left intact, and at the far end of the turning a clock shop had its face blown out.

Above the missing door a crooked sign said Rusotti Orologi, and out in front another of Gutman's charges sat on a wooden bar stool. He was muscular, shirtless, deeply tanned, and wore a Tommy helmet and his British dog tags. His perch was surrounded by mounds of empty ammunition crates, one of which he was using as a worktable, and the rest were covered by many clocks of all shapes and sizes, and all of them ticking. He had blond curls, a jeweler's loupe in one eye, burn scars from his collarbone to the top of his throat, and was repairing something with a sapper's screwdriver.

"Arieh Ben-Zvi, private," Gutman said to Froelich. "Palestinian Jew, mother took him over there from Munich long before the war, then she died from malaria at one a those kibbutzes. Basement bomber, don't ya know, caused a lot of ruckus with the Brits. They locked him up in Acre prison, then let him out to join the ranks as a sapper! Funny blokes they are. He hates the uniform. Only wears it when he must."

"And I suppose he's partnered with…"

Froelich trailed off as a tall striking woman emerged from the shattered clock shop. She was in her thirties, had a bobbed black shiny haircut and wore an Italian pilot's coverall and boots, as if she admired Amelia Earhart. But Froelich guessed the outfit had belonged to her husband, and he was dead.

She set a teacup down in front of Ben-Zvi. He nodded, kept on working as she disappeared into the shop, and then he realized his sergeant was standing there with an officer and began to rise.

"As you were, Private," Froelich said as the three of them approached.

"Thank you, sir, morning, sir." Ben-Zvi resumed his stool, looked at Sofia and touched his helmet brim. "Morning, mum. Looking smart as ever."

"*Buongiorno, soldato*," she said. Froelich looked at her and she shrugged and blushed.

"Muster and inspection at fifteen hundred hours, Private," Gutman said.

"Yes, Sergeant."

They all had to raise their voices above the cacophony of clocks.

"I want a count of all your Mills bombs, and all the fuses checked."

"Already done, Sergeant. Trimmed 'em all down to four seconds."

Gutman grinned. "That's cutting it close."

Froelich looked over Ben-Zvi's shoulder. The woman was inside the shop, watching through a broken window. She was smoking a long white cigarette in a ruby holder.

"Right, then," Gutman said. "Chop-chop, carry on."

"Sir." Ben-Zvi saluted Froelich from his perch, and Gutman turned and led them up a rising road once more, where a herd of mewling cats went rushing over the next rise as if some careless fisherman had spilled sardines.

"They're all very…unusual," Froelich said as they walked.

"Well, that's your lot, sir," Gutman said, and it wasn't lost on Froelich that *lot* meant herd as well as fate.

"I'm not sure at all they're mine."

"Oh, they will be when the major's finished fishing. There's nine of us. I think he wants a dozen."

"Would that be Major Butler?"

"The very he."

"What do you know of him, Gutman?"

"Nothing much, sir. Hard as a railway spike. Plucked us all from outfits all along the theatre. We've all got traits in common."

"What traits are those?"

"All combatants, all Jews, all speak German." Gutman stopped and cocked an eyebrow at Froelich as if they both knew that meant something dire. Sofia stumbled into Froelich's back and had to grip his shirt to keep from falling. *"Scusi,"* she whispered as Gutman said, "We're all lost boys, sir. All orphans."

"You as well, Sergeant?" Froelich asked, as the image flashed before his eyes of his weeping mother in their doorway, clutching her ladle.

"Far as I know, sir. Was sent to London on a kinder transport."

"Where are you from?"

"Ich komme aus Wien," Gutman said in German. *"Ich bin der einzige Zivilisierte hier."* I'm from Vienna. I'm the only civilized one here. He grinned and winked.

Froelich turned away and they kept on walking, and he suddenly felt ill and couldn't bear to look at Sofia, as he realized that he too was exactly like these boys, desperate and bereft and lonely, longing for the nurturing that no one but their mothers or their sisters or their gentle lovers could ever give them. He hadn't thought before that she was serving as a substitute for what he'd lost, but perhaps she knew, and offered it because her heart was just that large, and he felt awful shame that he was using this poor girl for comfort, just like all the rest.

Except for one thing. He loved her already, and that was different.

The narrow road began to angle up again toward the piazza, and Froelich wanted to take Sofia's waist and help her, but he wouldn't touch her with Gutman there. The sun was high now and long shafts of it lanced another crossroad up ahead, painting the dusty intersection in yellow fire.

A man appeared from the right, crossing to the left, another British soldier, this one smartly uniformed with a perfectly smeared beret. He was well above six feet, with flaxen hair, cobalt blue eyes, a ski slope nose, and a lion's jaw. He had an oxen's yoke hunching his neck and shoulders, from which hung two wooden buckets full of bricks, but he clipped along and smoked a pipe as if the bricks were cotton. Behind him a tiny barefoot girl appeared, with wild sunbleached hair and a soiled yellow dress, and she skipped and chattered in Italian as she beat his bulging calves with an orchestra conductor's baton. They disappeared, and Gutman carried on as if the sight were normal.

"That one's Corporal Manfred Hasenbein," he said. "Northern coast of Deutschland, fishing family. Got the strength of a Frankenstein concoction. He's a Jew but doesn't fancy it. Only way the Brits would take him on, though."

"And so it is with all of us," Froelich said.

"Right you are, sir."

They emerged again onto the main piazza. The Moto Guzzi was still there, but the six old men were gone and the square was filled with an ethereal sound of angelic Italian so-

pranos, accompanied by the keys of an untuned piano. Froelich stopped and looked at the duomo because its door was
open and it seemed to be coming from there.

"That's Private Wolfgang Steinberg in there, sir," Gutman
said as he led them toward the stairs. "Born in Salzburg, quite
the pianist. Boys call him Beethoven. He's got the girls' choir."

"The girls' choir?"

"Yes, sir. Their conductor was killed at Catania."

Froelich hesitated. He'd seen enough and needed no more
visions of orphaned young men and bereft women. "I think
the lady's climbed enough today." He nodded toward Sofia,
then fished in his pocket and handed out his oranges.

"Much obliged, sir." Gutman peeled his fruit and then
barked "Steinberg!" like a gunshot.

The choir stopped singing. Boots quick-marched from inside the church and Steinberg appeared above in the doorway,
saw Froelich and saluted. He was tallish, gangly, with deep
dark eyes and eyebrows, slabby lips, and thick brown hair. He
carried a Bren light machine gun posted smartly by his heel.
Froelich returned the salute and Gutman called up to him.

"You're behaving proper in that house of worship, right?"

"Of course, Sergeant."

"Good lad. Inspection at fifteen hundred hours."

"Yes, Sergeant."

"You seen the triplets anywhere about?"

"No, Sergeant. Sorry."

Gutman looked at Froelich. "We've also got three cousins
Butler snatched from the Pioneers, sir."

"Right, soon enough," Froelich said. He was done for
the day.

"Steinberg." Gutman looked up again. "Play something nice for our new subaltern here."

"What would you like to hear, Sergeant?"

"Do I look like I know?" Gutman laughed.

"Miss Bellina?" Steinberg looked down at Sofia, and Froelich felt even more the outcast fool.

"Puccini perhaps, Private?" Sofia said.

"Oh yes, mum!" Steinberg disappeared again.

They finished up their oranges. Sofia gathered all the peels and put them in her dress pocket.

"Well, sir," Gutman said, "if you'll release me, I've got to keep these blokes to standard."

"Thank you, Sergeant."

Salutes exchanged, Gutman headed off across the piazza toward Castello Chiarmonte, gripping his Thompson and looking left and right, until he was gone. And then a single voice rose from inside the church, shortly buoyed by ten others and Steinberg's old piano. They were singing Puccini's magnificent "Nessun Dorma," and it rent the air and filled the square and burst upon the mounts of Siciliana and splashed the distant sea, and Froelich saw there were tears in the corners of Sofia's eyes, although she smiled.

He led her back to the Moto Guzzi, helped her sit, cased her crutch, and gave her his rifle. She hugged him again, and tightly, as if she thought he might be fragile for the moment. And just before he started the machine and they rode away he said, "You know these men, Sofia. You know all of them."

"Well, yes, Bernard," she confessed. "After all, everyone needs ice."

Eighteen

ON THE DAY BEFORE THE LAST ONE OF MAJOR Butler's week, Sofia failed to come, although she'd promised, and Froelich's happy morning turned to brooding as the few hopes that he had all bled away.

He'd returned her and the Moto Guzzi to Fabrizio, and had forgotten the Castello Chiarmonte as they'd shared the carpenter's concoction of homemade fettucini drenched in an Alfredo sauce, and then he'd recovered his cane and in the evening tapped his way back to Santo Spirito, whistling "Dream a Little Dream." After that he'd lain upon his cot, fingers laced behind his neck, staring at the stars until at last he fell asleep, and didn't dream at all that night, and woke up with the birds and cats and smiled as he used a medic's signal mirror and shaved in radiator water from a hobbled jeep, and brushed his teeth with GI Pepsodent.

But after breakfast with the other wounded and recovering men, as hour turned to hour, he smoked and paced and brushed off Charlie Harris's attempts to buck him up, and Captain Lefkowitz's comments on his almost perfect gait. He found himself muttering and bitter and betrayed, until at noon he heard the Moto Guzzi's now familiar throat, and shed his childish tantrum and self-pity in a molting of shame.

From his table in the courtyard, Lefkowitz this time issued him a paper pass, and held it fast before releasing it and warned him through a cloud of stogy smoke.

"Listen, kid. Whatever's on your mind you better stow it. This war ain't over by a long shot, and if you think they're gonna leave you here in paradise jockeying a desk, forget it. You ain't the paper pusher type."

Froelich knew that it was true, said, "Thank you for the day, sir," and took his pass and rifle, but not his cane, and left.

Sofia stood there on the monastery's apron once again, this time wearing the blue flowered dress he'd seen her in at first, and he realized she had only two. The empty motorcycle was parked beside her, and knowing that she couldn't ride it herself, he knew Fabrizio had delivered her and gone.

He was so happy and relieved to see her that he couldn't speak, and so desperately wanted to envelop her he couldn't move. But then he walked to the machine, helped her on her perch, handed her his rifle, cased her crutch, and mounted up.

"Where are we going?" he asked, knowing that whatever she decided he was hers.

"Past my tree and to the sea, to see your priest," she said, and he didn't ask as he kicked the engine over and she hugged him and they left.

Neither of them noticed Captain Lefkowitz standing underneath the arch, sucking his cigar and muttering, "Kid's a goner," before he turned away and went back to his work.

Froelich's priest, or so Sofia called him because she knew no other word, was the last surviving Jew of Agrigento. His name was Elijah Moncalvo, and his grandfather had been a rabbi in Palermo, from whom he'd inherited a mantle of wisdom and traditions. Fabrizio knew Moncalvo because he'd built for him a holy ark, the ornate cabinet that held the sacred Torah scrolls. Moncalvo's scrolls were half burned because the Germans had torched a home of secret Jewish Sabbath worshippers in Trapani, including his wife and child, and that was all that had survived. He'd been at sea that day. He was a fisherman.

From Sofia's giant ficus they wound their way down switchbacks to the stony beach below the town, where Moncalvo had a fishing shack the size of a single horse stable. It had three walls, the fourth open to the sea, a palm frond roof, a shaky dining table pushed out into the sun, and many fishing rods, nets and lines, hooks and barbed harpoons, copper pots and crooked towers of books. To the right side of the shack an iron grill crackled with sparks and smoke that smelled like fir and lemon. To the left sat a thick-hulled wooden fishing boat in blue and white and orange stripes, like a Portuguese bark. It had no wheeled carriage to get it to and from the water, but when Froelich saw Moncalvo he knew he dragged it, like Samson hauling on the pillars of the Philistines' temple.

Elijah Moncalvo was like no priest or rabbi Froelich had ever seen. He was a bear, very large, with shoulders brown and sinewed from hauling heavy nets, and calves like hairy melons from wading through the sea. He had an enormous black-and-silver beard, forelock curls, eyebrows like bottle brushes, a fishing cap that made for a yarmulke, and a voice like an alpine horn.

"Why are we here, Sofia?" Froelich asked as the Moto Guzzi gurgled into silence.

"We are here, Tenente Bernard," she said, "because I think you cannot lead the men of Castello Chiarmonte, if you have shame."

He made to protest that it wasn't so, but Moncalvo had already seen them and came pounding across the stones and broken seashells in a giant pair of homemade sandals. *"La mia bellissima principessa!"* he roared as he ignored Froelich, plucked Sofia from her seat by her small waist, spun her around, and gently set her down. He cupped her head in his bear paws and kissed her forehead. She gripped his beard and pulled him down and pecked his cheek, which was hairy almost to his eye sockets.

"Questo èil mio tenente," Sofia introduced Froelich to Moncalvo, and the fisherman laughed because she'd used the possessive.

"Il tenente di Sofia!" he roared. Sofia's lieutenant! And he pumped Froelich's hand and clapped him on the shoulder and nearly knocked him over. *"Venite, venite, venite!"* Come, come, come! he bellowed as he turned away and lumbered to the shack, and they followed.

"Does he speak any English?" Froelich asked Sofia. Moncalvo heard and waved his porcine arms.

"I speaka da English. I speaka da Italiano, Francaise, that bastardi language Tedesco, and da Yiddische."

As they neared his shack, Froelich saw the dining table was shaded by a canopy of black cloth stretched from the palm roof to high poles in the sand, much like the Bedouin tents he'd seen in the Sahara. Moncalvo suddenly blocked their entrance, as if there might be wolves within, but he only wanted them to wait while he prepared a welcome late breakfast.

First he pulled three empty milk cans from the shack and set them out as stools, at the ends and middle of the table. Then he set the table with dented copper plates and chalices, and metal forks from fallen houses and meat knives made from Italian bayonets. He set down a glass carafe filled with pulpy orange juice he'd crushed with his own hands, then blue ceramic cups into which he poured black coffee from a Turkish finjan, and while whistling a Ladino tune, splashed a dash of arak into each. He led Sofia to her milk can perch, bowing like a maître d', and Froelich to his, but offered them no napkins—that's what sleeves were for—and then he served the fish.

They were *tonno rosso*, small red tuna native to Sicilian waters. He'd seasoned them with salt, pepper, and olive oil, filled their cavities with garlic and thyme, and left them on his grill until they crusted, then turned them over with his giant spatula, an American GI shovel. He slabbed them on the plates along with sliced tomatoes, olives, and raw onion, and squeezed a lime above each one with his sausage fingers, and sat down in the middle with great satisfaction.

Moncalvo closed his eyes, laced his fingers and said, *"Baruch atah Adonai, Eloheinu melech ha'olam,"* and the rest of the Hebrew grace before a meal. Then he looked at Sofia, crossed himself and laughed like a water buffalo might, and they ate and it was wonderful.

No one spoke until they were done and settling their bloated bellies with Moncalvo's arak coffee. He pulled a pack of Italian Alfa cigarettes from his vest pocket, clamped two in his hairy lips, lit them with a wooden match, and handed one to Froelich without asking. In his world all men smoked. He squinted at the glimmering sea, and then at Froelich.

"Tenente Bernardo," Moncalvo said, "you were born to be who you are. You can no escape the fate. You can no escape your biblio. The Jew is not a lion, the Jew is not a lamb. He is what he must be on the day God needs him. You will not be the first Jew to have pain, and you will not be the last. You will not be the first Jewish warrior. Gideon and David and the Maccabees were before you. But when God himself puts a mountain at your feet, and a sword in your hand, you must climb it, Bernardo, and fight, even with a bucket of tears on your back."

He held Froelich's blue eyes with his own blazing gaze until he saw the glimmer that he wanted, then he slapped the shaky table and got up, and with his hairy hands pushed his ravaged dinner plate and cups to the far side. A handkerchief appeared and he swiped the oils and juice and spittle from the wood, then went into his shack, opened the chestnut ark Fabrizio had made and came back with the Torah scrolls.

Their purple velvet covering was gone, taken by the Germans' fire, and the fringes of their holy parchment pages were singed black at the top and bottom, yet it didn't matter. He laid them down as a father would his firstborn infant, and he turned the wooden scroll handles until he saw the spot he wanted. He took Froelich's cigarette and his own and crushed them underfoot, then motioned Froelich to his side, slung one massive arm around his shoulders, and with the other hand picked up a steak knife bayonet, wiped it on his pantaloons, and jabbed it at a paragraph.

"Can you read da Hebreo, Bernardo?" he asked.

"Yes, I think I can."

"Thenna read it, all of it."

And Froelich did, while Sofia watched him, but it was as if she wasn't there.

"Adonai ro-ee, lo echsar."

The Lord is my shepherd, I shall not want.

His recitation was hesitant and stuttering at first. He'd had no use for prayer since he'd turned thirteen, but some such things are carved into the brain forever, and his voice grew stronger as he arrived at the 23rd Psalm's heart of the matter.

"Gam ki elech b'gai tzel mavet, lo irah rah, ki atah imadi."

Yea, though I walk through the valley of the shadow of death, I will fear no evil: for thou art with me.

He carried on, while Moncalvo nodded with each phrase as if Froelich were his own son and they faced a Sabbath congregation. And when Froelich intoned the final words, "And I shall dwell in the house of the Lord forever," Moncalvo didn't say *Amen* but turned and rumbled "Bravo!" and kissed Froelich on both cheeks. Then he reached beneath his vest into the waistband of his pantaloons and slammed a Pietro Beretta Model 1934 pistol on the table. He took Froelich's right hand, placed it on the pistol's body, smeared it there with his hairy paw and said, "Kill for me some Germans, Bernardo. I am old and they are gone. Amen."

Froelich took the pistol, checked the action, tucked it in his waist, and shook Moncalvo's hand. The fisherman pulled something else from his pocket, a small black velvet pouch, pressed it into Sofia's small hands, and kissed the top of her head. Then suddenly he waved his arms as if having no idea why he'd allowed these young reminders of his long-lost love and youth to stain his cave and bellowed, *"Un uomo deve lavorare, figlioli! Andate a giocare!"* A man has to work, children! Go away and play!

Sofia grinned at him, though Froelich was still pensive as they climbed aboard the Moto Guzzi and coaxed it into life. Moncalvo backed away and receded toward his shack, but they saw his eyes were glistening as they left.

They rode all afternoon, as if the Moto Guzzi were some fairy-tale horse and could take them to a world beyond their own, as if the hours they had left could be stretched into a decade. They rode south along the shoreline to the beach at Lido Cannatello, where Froelich took off his desert boots and socks and Sofia her small shoe, and they held hands and waded in the waves and laughed and washed their young pink faces in the brine, even with Moncalvo's pistol reminding them of who they were.

They rode northeast to Favara and on the way stopped before a sagging roadside farmhouse, where an old woman exchanged a wad of liras from Froelich's pocket for a wicker bottle of wild grape wine and two pears, and they munched the pears and drank the wine on the way back toward Agrigento as the early-evening sun blushed to gun-rust orange. When Sofia turned Froelich from the road, and up a slim lane lined with prickly cactus, he saw the shattered yellow plaster house, its roof split open down the middle as if a giant ice pick had been swung, and Froelich knew it was her childhood home, and they both fell silent.

He stopped the Moto Guzzi, turned the engine off, and waited to see if there was something left Sofia wanted. But she didn't leave her perch and only said, "Fabrizio has promised to rebuild it. Someday I think I would love to live here again, yet not alone," and they rode on.

They arrived, from the north, at the Valley of the Temples, the ancient graveyard of majestic relics. Beyond its columns, painted tangerine by the fading ocean sun, Froelich could see the skyline of Agrigento and his heart beat faster because he knew he didn't have much time. He drove Sofia to the Temple of Olympus and took her hand and helped her with her crutch up the hill of shattered statuary, where the letters of dead men still fluttered here and there across the ground or wrinkled in the bushes from the breeze. He helped her sit beside him on the great marble stairs, but he could find no words and they looked only at the distant sea.

She took Moncalvo's small black pouch from her dress pocket. Froelich watched her slender fingers as she opened it and withdrew a long silver chain necklace with a gleaming Star of David dangling from it. She opened the chain and held it up and looked in Froelich's eyes.

He took off his officer's cap. She gently placed the chain over his head and around his neck and tapped the star against his chest with her finger, and he tipped her chin up with his trembling hand and kissed her. It was like the touch of warm rose petals, for both of them. It was like the first long pull of clear cold water after an endless trek in the desert. It had a hundred tastes, of lime and wine, of sea salt, fruit and thyme, of awful happiness and deepest sorrow, and they held it there for as long as fate allowed.

Nineteen

MAJOR BUTLER'S WEEK DIED BEFORE THE seventh day. Froelich's glorious anticipation of seeing Sofia one more time, his heart buoyed like a feather on their kiss, was drowned just after breakfast by the roar of a jeep outside the monastery's courtyard.

Soon after, a British sergeant major stomped in beneath the arches. He was tall and broad, wearing North African theatre shorts, a heavy Enfield, a large wax-tipped red mustache, and a Highlander beret with a pompom. He marched up to Captain Lefkowitz, who was making early rounds, saluted and inquired, then spun and headed straight for Froelich's corner cot.

All the men, who by now knew Froelich well and liked him, elbowed up on their cots and craned their necks to watch, including two of the four Germans. They saw the sergeant major snap to and salute. They saw Lieutenant Froelich rise, return the courtesy, and then stoop. They all knew what it meant and they nodded at one another, sighed and smoked and watched him as he packed.

Private Charlie Harris interceded, not to try to stop the transfer process, which was something only General Sir Bernard Montgomery could do, but to somehow make Froelich understand how much he'd meant to him, how the love and loss of Tommy Robbins was something they would always share, how he almost wished that leg had never healed so Froelich could stay. But all he managed, as he stood there watching Froelich pack the few things that he had into a ruck, was to say as sure-voiced as he could, "I'm not gonna like seeing your back, sir," and Froelich stopped and looked into his gleaming eyes and shook his hand and said, "Nor I, yours, Charlie. Nor I, yours."

Pennington and Hedges, who'd never gotten over nearly taking Froelich's leg, halted in their rounds and nodded at him as he took his cane and followed the sergeant major through the cots. Men saluted from their prone positions, some shot him a thumbs-up, and there were calls of "See ya in Piccadilly, sir" from the Brits and "So long, sir" and "Take it easy" from the Yanks. Two of the monastery's sisters smiled and made small waves from beside their aproned bellies, and Father Castillo, who'd just arrived to bless the critical cases, caught Froelich's eye, crossed himself, then blew the blessing to him across the courtyard as if it were a kiss.

Froelich and the sergeant major arrived at Lefkowitz's desk. The captain stood and frowned when Froelich returned his carbine, but grunted in approval when Froelich tapped the Beretta in his belt. Lefkowitz snapped an order at the sergeant major. "Fall back ten paces, Jock," which he obeyed, but once alone there wasn't much to say.

"Don't worry about the skirt," Lefkowitz said, his knuckles on his hips and smoke curling from his lips. "I'll make sure she's okay."

"Thank you, sir," said Froelich. "For that, and all you've done. For all of us."

"Aw, crap," Lefkowitz scoffed and shook his hand very hard. "See ya after the war, kid. I'm in the phone book."

"After the war, sir."

They saluted, Froelich joined the sergeant major, and as Lefkowitz watched them walk away he muttered to himself, "Don't fuggin' break him. I just fixed him."

They drove away from Santo Spirito with Froelich knowing in his heart that he would never see that place again. The sergeant major, ramrod stiff behind the windscreen of the jeep, introduced himself as Brendan Connor, but Froelich only nodded and looked straight ahead, and didn't dare search the narrow lanes, for he was terribly afraid that he might see her. The idea that she'd soon arrive, bright and smiling and hopeful at the monastery's apron, only to discover he was gone, was too much to imagine, and he didn't dare try to move words past his thickened throat.

The road to Siculiana wasn't lovely anymore, just eleven miles of scrub and dust and cactus to endure, and the town itself was nothing without her. They drove through the piazza at the top, where no more crooners sang from Signora Facci's gramophone, nor from Steinberg's duomo choir, and they rode up Via Roma, the last bumpy cobblestoned way to Castello Chiarmonte. At the end of it, where no more Siculianans lived and it was gloomy in the shade of drooping palms and cypress, Connor parked the jeep beside an iron gate. It was high and curved across the top, its uprights looked like rusty medieval spears, and the year 1935 was welded to its face. They dismounted, and entered.

The rest was climbing, stairway after next of cracked stone slabs, because the castle's courtyard and all its structures sat atop the seaward summit. High tilting walls loomed over them of parapets and barred windows without glass, and archer's shooting posts in rows atop the towers, and one final staircase with no balustrade jutting from the side of a tall wall. At last they reached the top, where Private Steinberg, the one with the knuckle-duster knife and cheek scar, was posted as a sentry and now looked very smart.

The courtyard was a long rectangular stone terrace the size of a children's equestrian ring, surrounded by the remains of what had once been the fortress's grand entrance, armories, royal living quarters, servants' hovels, and a stable. Froelich looked up to see the machine-gunned remnants of the German Würzburg dish atop a bowman's tower. Except for Steinberg, there seemed to be not another living soul around. Compared to the monastery's warmth, the place was a glacier.

"Right this way, sir," Connor said in a voice that sounded like a Scottish bullfrog, and he marched them toward a low stone hut with a pate of clipped wet straw, rapped on the wooden door, announced the lieutenant, and left him to his lion.

But it wasn't the cave that Froelich expected. Major Nigel Butler was a meticulous man, and he'd painted all the stony walls inside with olive army vehicle enamel, and all the heavy timbers with whitewash "kalsomine." Tactical maps were posted on the walls along with one framed black-and-white of Winston Churchill, and one of Rudyard Kipling. Paper files were arranged in open ammunition crates, a metal pail was full of hand grenades, and a Sten submachine gun hung from a hook. Butler's desk was a chestnut monster that looked like it had been shipped to him from Bangalore, and as Froelich stood there at attention, he imagined the sufferings of whoever had hauled it up there.

"Morning, Major," Froelich said, completing his salute.

Butler looked up from a file he was reading with his cold gray eyes.

"Ah, Froelich, you've graced us with your presence."

"Reporting for duty, sir, as ordered."

"You mean, reporting as delivered, don't you?"

Froelich said nothing. He looked straight over Butler's head, per the formalities, and gripped his cane top in his hand along with his faint hope that he still might get out of this. Butler cocked his head. His reddish eyebrows looked like rusty splinters of steel.

"You've still got a crutch," he said.

"Well, sir, as I explained when we first met, the leg…"

"May I see it?"

Butler opened his palm as if demanding his child return stolen coins. Froelich passed Fabrizio's cane across, and Butler twirled it in his hands, admired it, then thrust the lower half below his heavy desk drawers and yanked the top half upward with such violence that it snapped in half, cracking like a gunshot. He dropped the broken halves into a wicker wastebasket and said, "You don't need this. My men saw you doing very well without it."

Froelich ground his teeth, his face flushed and furious. Butler rose, donned his peaked cap smartly, pulled his leather gloves on, and picked up a swagger stick.

"We're about to have the first formation of your men, Lieutenant," he said as he walked past Froelich, opened his door, and turned to finish off. "It's time for you to start behaving as a British officer. It you're not sure how that's done, I shall demonstrate. Follow me."

He walked out into the sunlight. Froelich stalked after him. The major posted in the middle of the courtyard, thirty feet from the castle's once grand entrance, now a blackened maw with splintered doors. Froelich fell behind and to the right, and noticed something strange tucked beside the low courtyard wall. It was a heavy wooden rowboat, maroon and white and long, and he had no idea what it was for, or like Butler's desk, how it had gotten up there. Sergeant Major Conner raised a trench whistle to his lips and blasted on it hard.

The men came on the run, and no longer in motley uniforms or singlets or straw hats, but in regulation trousers, shirts, and polished boots, smart overseas caps the Yanks called something vaginally obscene due to their shapes, and sleeves all rolled precisely to their biceps. Their cocktail of weapons were Enfield rifles, Sten guns, and one heavy automatic Bren.

There were twelve of them, and they quickly formed two ranks of six before the major, spaced themselves as Sergeant Gutman bellowed orders, stomped to attention and saluted to his "Preeeeesent arms!" then stood there waiting, stiff as rigored corpses.

"You men," Butler began without a greeting, "shall, as of dawn tomorrow, begin training for a mission. You shall not ask its nature, nor shall I tell you, nor shall any of your training cadre, shortly to arrive. This officer, Lieutenant Froelich, shall be your new subaltern. Sergeant Gutman shall be his noncommissioned in command." Butler raised his swagger stick and smacked it on his palm. "Henceforth, you are all restricted to quarters here. There shall be no more jaunts, no further fraternizing with your locals. No one in, no one out. Am I clear?"

"Yes, sir!" the dozen barked.

"Very good. Get your last rest. You shall need it. Carry on."

Butler stalked off to his office with Sergeant Major Connor at his heel. Gutman dismissed the men, walked up to Froelich and smirked.

"Looks like I was right about this being your lot, sir."

"Spot on." Froelich's face was grim.

"Come on then, sir. You're in the smaller stable." As Froelich followed him he added, "And no, sir, don't ask me how they ever got the horses up and down. Place is a bleedin' puzzle."

The stable wasn't that exactly. It was the former quarters of some nineteenth century groomsman, constructed of dark sweating stone, the floor a carpet of moldy hay, with a high ceiling and a loft for saddles, horseshoes, reins, ropes, and bridles, many of which were still up there. Below the loft was the groomsman's wooden bunk, no mattress but a folded army blanket and a leather saddlebag for a pillow. If you lay there you could look out at the sky through one tall empty window shaped like a bishop's hat, with a single iron frame bar running up the middle and no shutters.

Froelich sat hunched on that bunk for most of the day. He smoked nearly all his cigarettes, horrid filterless Astras that were rumored to be half sawdust. Gutman brought him a metal file box from the major that contained the personnel records of all twelve men, each with a small black-and-white facial photograph taken by a CID photographer. He looked at the contents for a minute, then paced and smoked and cursed Major Nigel Butler. Gutman then delivered combat rations, bully beef, hardtack, water, and peaches. He ate only the peaches, then urinated in a "chamber pot" bucket and decided he'd discard that later.

As the day grew long, he lay down, exhausted by his inner turmoil, and slept on his back for hours. When he suddenly awoke it was deeply night, and heat lightning was flashing the stable with pale blue ribbons. He hadn't had a dream in a long while, but this one was vivid as bloodred roses on polar ice. It had been Sofia, her back to him and her pretty dress torn from her shoulders, perched on an iron bench to which she was strapped, playing a white piano on a pile of smoking rubble.

He got up and staggered to the window as he splashed his face from a tin canteen. He looked out, and down, then back inside and at the loft. He climbed the wooden ladder and found two large coils of equestrian rope and bound the ends together. He climbed down, triple knotted one end to the window's bar and hurled the rest into the night, where it fell forty feet and whipped against the wall.

He made sure his pistol was tightly tucked, then slid down

the rope as Bertie Buck had taught him, with it looped around his left calf and over his boot top, where he braked it with the other sole.

When he got to the bottom, he went out the gate and stole the sergeant major's jeep.

Sofia saw him from her balcony of wishes, to which she'd retreated after failing to find him at the monastery and wandering the ruins of her town and her heart for the entire day. Fabrizio had borrowed a small slat van and gone to Palermo for the night, to a sawmill where they had acacia lumber with which he hoped to make more of a life for them. She'd thought about taking the Moto Guzzi and racing to Siculiana to find Bernard one last time, but she knew she couldn't ride it.

She hadn't eaten. She'd climbed her narrow creaking stairway at sunset. She'd stared across the rooftops and the beaches and that tiny ribbon of road, hoping, yet seeing nothing, until at last she'd fallen asleep, curled up on the plaster, wrapped shivering in a thin woolen shawl that matched her stump cap.

She felt him more than heard the jeep. She heard it more than saw it. She threw off the shawl and came to her knee and gripped the railing that flowed with her bougainvillea, and from the way it raced toward her, even at a mile in the night, she knew. Her pulse rose, her slim fingers and her knuckles went white against the iron, then starlings fluttered in a rush from down there far below as the jeep careened up Luigi Pirandello and she leaped upward.

She grabbed her crutch and nearly tumbled down her flights of stairs. When she reached the bottom, breathless with her teal flowered dress askew, she stumbled into the salon in utter darkness but for the faintest leak of moonlight, and she saw the jeep outside on the crooked little house's apron. The door flew open and Froelich was there in silhouette and breathless, as if he'd run from Siculiana instead of driven, and she saw him hesitate, unsure, and she whispered, "Fabrizio has gone away to Palermo."

In a second they were one, their hands on each other's faces with the desperate joy of blind castaways who'd nearly died yet at last had found one another, their lips taking in the only nourishment they cared for. They kissed each other from those lips to foreheads, eyes and cheeks and throats, and it wasn't enough, not nearly, and they fell onto Fabrizio's couch, slathered as it was in sawdust, and tore at each other's clothes. Soon their dress and uniform were gone, their pulses pounding, yet he hesitated to touch her missing place and she whispered in his ear, "It does not hurt me, *amore mio*, it feels as if it is still there," and then they melded with a surge and cry that was nothing like lust, but only the stunning lightning just before a downpour of relief.

They lay there for an hour, entwined in each other's arms, their fevered skins caked with lathe dust. They told each other what they felt, how much they loved, made promises they knew they could not keep, and lied about a future. At last they had to dress because Froelich knew his time was short, and Sofia hurried for a photograph to tuck inside his pocket, and she fetched them water and they drank it and kissed again and long in Fabrizio's doorway.

Froelich returned to the jeep, and started it, and couldn't look behind again and didn't. Sofia climbed her narrow stairway to her balcony, and stood there on her foot, trembling in her rumpled dress.

And she watched the muted glow of his exhaust, until it was gone, and she wept.

PART THREE

PEENEMUNDE

Courage, like death, seldom appears where it is expected.

—BEN MacINTYRE
Rogue Heroes

Twenty

Castello Chiarmonte

"I COULD HAVE YOU BROUGHT UP ON CHARGES."

Ramrod stiff, his thighbone aching from the midnight drive and climb, his armpits damp and left chest pulsing at the pocket where Sofia's photograph lay next to Tommy Robbins' unread letter, where both would lie as long as Froelich lived, he stood in Major Butler's office facing his monstrous desk. Froelich's squinting eyes were locked above the major's chair, blurring at the pins and lines of all his maps, but the major wasn't there.

Butler stood to Froelich's left, his back to his lieutenant, fingers twined below his spine as he faced his only window to the courtyard, where Sergeant Major Connor barked and Fritzy Gutman and the men stomped around in British high-knee drill, which made them look like angry toddlers who'd just been told to nap.

"I could have you field court-martialed, Froelich," Butler said. "I could mount a breakfast hearing of myself, Connor, and whichever idiot sentry saw you, as a witness, and
use my Webley as a gavel and have you hanged by high noon
for desertion."

Froelich didn't move or speak or nod, or even grunt a
"yessir." Butler's threats meant nothing in that cold officious
cavern, empty of Sofia. He only saw her eyes, only felt her
fingers on his skin, only smelled the scent of her, and sawdust.

He'd driven back to Siculiana straight from Agrigento.
Or had he? The sky had been a blurry blanket of stars and
the road a futureless ribbon. He'd returned the stolen jeep,
climbed that last railless stairway, nearly toppling to his death,
and at the top found Corporal Manfred Hasenbein, the giant
fisherman he'd first seen hauling bricks. Hasenbein had faced
him with a bayoneted Enfield, and took a while to put it up.
Froelich couldn't ask him to keep silent, nor would Hasenbein have done it. Officers were not his cup of tea.

"Do you hear me, Froelich?" Butler turned around. "Are
you mute?"

"Loudly and clearly, sir."

"It's an inauspicious start, you prancing off to have a final
dalliance with your crippled paramour. Don't you think?"

Froelich only ground his teeth and tapped the air with his
chin, a signal that he'd heard.

"That alone's enough to have you thrown in the glasshouse
for fraternizing. Besides the jeep, my orders, and the horrible
example to your men."

They are not my men, Froelich thought. *I do not want them.*

I only want her, and Moncalvo can go to hell with all his preaching and prayers.

He thought then of Moncalvo's wife and child, and was stabbed by the idea of such a loss and felt ashamed. He simply was not the man so many wanted him to be, or thought he was, or expected. German boy. Lost. Orphaned. Weak.

"You're weak, Froelich," Butler said, and walked behind his desk and slapped his swagger stick on its polished wood.

God. Does he read minds too?

"You and all your lot. Overly emotional, hearts on sleeves, first ones begging to be loved, last ones to fight. Intelligent and idiotic. Knowing nothing of the world and why you're hated so, and always *so* surprised."

Froelich knew that he was speaking of the Jews, and his fists were clenched like boa constrictors around a throat, because so much of him believed that Butler's words were true. Weak Jew. He'd only killed one Nazi thus far in the entire war. There would have to be many more to prove Butler wrong and even that score. But at the moment, the major's was the only murder on his mind.

Butler placed his knuckles on his desk and leaned toward Froelich. His eyes were cobra-like, the tips of his short mustache wet with tea. Instead of a tie, he was wearing a dickey made of green parachute silk.

"Would you like to make your brethren proud, Froelich?"

"Of course, sir."

"I don't mean your biblical coreligionists. I mean your men. Proud of themselves and their performances, before they die."

"When are they going to die, sir?"

"None of your bloody business yet." The major's voice

rose a fraction of a pitch, but that was all. He'd been through Sandhurst. Officers should never shout, the exception being battle cries above gunfire. Yelling was for sergeants major and the like. "They haven't had a minute's worth of proper training. That's about to change."

Froelich didn't want to train them. He wanted Agrigento and all that was there.

"You realize that your men all know that you're a truant."

"Yes, sir." Hasenbein had surely spread the word by now.

Butler leaned closer, eye to eye, his voice a whispered hiss.

"I issue orders, quite specific orders, orders of good discipline and proper branch behavior. And who amongst them dares to disobey? Their subaltern. Their lieutenant. That snotty fellow from the fatherland who regards his Berliner birthright as a license to enjoy the flesh, while they can only daydream on their sweaty cots."

Froelich's face flushed hot pink. His fingers twitched beside his trouser seams. Butler eased himself into his chair. It was wooden with a heavy slatted back and arms, iron wheels, and a springed seat. It creaked.

"Do you know the military theory of collective punishment, Froelich?" He wasn't really asking. He picked up an Italian bayonet and bounced the blade tip on his desk like a drumstick. "The theory is, when an insubordinate, like you, veers off course, we punish all his comrades and make it clearly known why. Eventually, with enough such torment, the collective beats the perpetrator, at times beneath a blanket with socks full of rocks, until they've set him right. He either ups his game, or finds himself discarded as a casualty. Have you ever seen this, Froelich?"

"Once, sir. At Sarafand in Palestine."

"Effective, wasn't it?"

"The boy wound up in hospital, bones fractured."

Butler smiled. "Yet the collective were forever bonded, were they not?"

"Hard to tell, sir. They mostly died in Ethiopia."

Butler's face grew dark, his glare hooded by his reddish eyebrows, and he jabbed the bayonet into the wood. Apparently his desk was not that precious.

"Well, we're going to do something different here. We shall take examples from the Phoenicians and the Persians, the ancient Roman legions and the Spartans, none of them remotely like your lot, but still." He rose from his chair, thrust his hands in his uniform pockets, and fixed Froelich with an icy stare. "You shall send these men down to the sea today, in full battle kit. Once there, they shall march waist high in water for a mile and return here the same way. Not once, Lieutenant, not twice, but all day long, till evening mess. Are we clear?"

"I understand, sir."

"Good. Your suffering over this shall not be theirs to know. But *their* suffering shall be all yours."

Butler pulled a trench whistle from his tunic pocket and blew it hard, stinging Froelich's eardrums. Seconds after that the door flew open, Sergeant Major Connor stomped to attention inside its frame, where he barely fit, and saluted with his ham shank palm.

"Yes, sir?"

"Sergeant Major Connor," Butler said. "Escort our apparently religiously privileged lieutenant to the men's formation, and ensure my orders are obeyed. He'll happily relay them to you."

"Sir!"

Connor stepped aside, Froelich saluted Butler, and walked out into the morning's blazing light. The sergeant major made to close the door when Butler said, "And Connor, after that, bring me the distributor cap from your jeep. There's a good chap."

Butler locked the door. It was a heavy wooden barn affair with crossed slats, ancient grommets, and an iron dead bolt. He returned to that space behind his desk, the one where Froelich saw only Sofia, yet Butler saw someone else. He gripped a wrist behind his back and looked at his wall maps.

There were three of them, one each of Siculiana and its environs, Agrigento, and a barren patch near Castelvetrano that had an airfield. They were British artillery maps, their keys in miles and kilometers as well, because the Germans and Italians used that measure, but they were merely obfuscations for the major's guests. He unpinned the middle one, turned it over and tacked it up again, and for the next twenty minutes studied its details of northern Germany, near the Baltic coast. Then he turned around again and sat.

From his desk drawer he pulled a stack of black-and-white aerial photographs taken by a valiant Spitfire pilot who'd barely made it back. Such photographs were made by dueling cameras in the airplane's belly, their offset lenses creating a three-dimensional effect. He slipped a stereoscopic viewer from the drawer, set it on the photos on its metal legs, and inspected every detail for half an hour, until at last he murmured, "Not bloody likely," and put everything back.

He cleaned his Sten gun thoroughly. Thousands of rounds had been fired through it, but when he was done you'd have thought it brand-new off the Royal Small Arms Factory floor. Yet he was only stalling until he could stall no more.

At last he pulled a key from a buttoned tunic pocket, unlocked his bottom drawer, uncorked a bottle of Sicilian grappa, and filled his teacup. He loaded a straight stemmed briar pipe with Prince Albert from a tin, tamped it with the bottom of an Enfield shell, and lit up with a wooden match.

He creaked back in his chair, and drank and smoked until the room was overcast with clouds of swirling charcoal blue, pierced by fiery yellow rapiers from the window and the courtyard sun. And then, armored and all ready, he pulled the silver framed photograph from the drawer's last recess, propped it on his desk, and faced it.

She was beautiful, but in his way, not the fashion magazine way. She had wavy blond hair to her slim shoulders, with a flapper curl over one eyebrow, something still in fashion though the Roaring Twenties roared no more. Her eyes were silver blue, which he knew too well from memory, though the garden portrait was in black and white. She didn't have a perfect nose. It was bent, as if the doctor of her deliverance had accidentally elbowed it, but it was perfect for him.

She was smiling broadly, just after a laugh. She wore a white lace dress. It could have been a wedding dress. It wasn't. Just below her long neck was a delicate gold chain and a gleaming cross.

He looked at her for ten minutes. Then he reached out, tipped the picture over on her face and said, "We never learn, do we."

Twenty-One

THERE WAS A BALLERINA'S GLOW, THERE WAS an athlete's perspiration, and certainly there was a farmer's heavy sweat. But for soldiers clothed in wool and leather, crushed by weights of canvas, steel and powder, there was something altogether different under the Sicilian sun.

It gushed from every pore. It slithered from their scalps. It sprang from armpits, ran down spines, crawled between their buttock cheeks and slipped into their boots. It smelled like everything they'd had for breakfast. It soaked their uniforms and bloated their weight. It stung their eyeballs, chafed beneath their helmet straps and battle harnesses, and dripped from nose tips onto panting tongues and lips, but quenched no thirst. It wasn't sweat. It was the liquid exorcism of their tortured souls.

Froelich took the lead, even though he knew that was the opposite of Butler's intent. The major'd meant for him to take a castle perch, wield only binoculars, and like a tennis umpire watch his soldiers struggle, all because of him. Not a chance. What could Butler do to him? Rip him from his one true love? Kill his parents and his sister, burn their house and pack him off with all the guilt? Dispatch him to a war that wasn't his, with nowhere left to go if he survived it?

All right. The firing squad. Have at it.

The way from Castello Chiarmonte to the shoreline was a thousand-foot slope, forty-eight degrees of boulders, thorns, and scree, with no path suited even for a mountain goat. Froelich's pistol didn't have an honorable weight, so he'd drawn a Sten from the castle's armory, a canvas battle harness with six full magazines packed into its pouches, a helmet, and a tin canteen. All the dozen men had followed suit, hefting heavy Enfields, except for Fritzy Gutman with his Thompson and the musician Wolfgang Steinberg with his long and awkward Bren.

"There's no rush," he'd said to the formation just before they left, knowing they'd be at it all day long and their game and eager smirks would soon be crushed, because he'd done this all before, in Palestine and Africa, time and time again. "Keep your proper distance, line astern, and no one passes me, no matter what."

The front rank held the men he'd met some days before, Sergeant Fritzy Gutman with his sloppy grin, the dandy David Rosenberg with his trench knife and white cheek scar, the brawler Horst Felder, who somehow spoke Italian, the basement bomber Palestinian Arieh Ben-Zvi, the giant Manfred Hasenbein and "Beethoven" Steinberg.

The second rank were men he'd only just met. Three of them were cousins, Hans, Gustave, and Moses Bloch, who looked like dark-haired triplets just emerged from a collective bar mitzvah. They were from Alsace and had escaped from Nazi occupation in a stolen boat they'd rowed across the English Channel, after all their parents were trucked off to Natzweiler-Struholf concentration camp. The fourth man was a chubby lad, Erich "Ricky" Schonberg, whose constant jolly quips belied the pain of losing everything he loved in Hamburg, and the last two were Paul Green and Felix Braun, who stuck together, rarely said a word, and who Gutman called Frick and Frack.

Froelich didn't want to know them. None of them. They were all Ottos, or Tommy Robbinses, soon to be just memories in his world, or he in theirs.

"Follow me," he'd said, and they were off.

The way downhill, and sharply, was not as easy as a novice troop might think. Froelich took it carefully, rock to rock, knowing that if someone turned an ankle, one of these poor sods would have to sling him on his shoulders, just like Elsa the gazelle, as no one would be left behind. The morning sun was bright but not yet wicked, his aching thigh warmed up, and the sounds behind him, which he'd hear until his end of days, were the comforts of a cavalry without horses. Boot stomps, weapons slings creaking and clacking, panting lungs and the occasional slip and fall and quick recovery, punctuated by a grunt, "bloody hell."

They arrived at the bottom, a slim beach of ocean polished rocks and broken seashells. Froelich held his hand up and they stopped.

"Sergeant Gutman," he said, and Fritzy sprang up to his shoulder. "Estimate a mile down the beach."

"Yes, sir." Gutman shot an arm straight out, raised a thumb and squinted like an artist plotting a bucolic painting. He'd learned to judge a mile in North Africa by the size of panzers in the distance. "See that wrecked old fishing bark down there, just before the waves?"

"I do."

"That's about a mile, sir."

"Very good."

And the men were happy for a moment. An easy walk along a flat and gleaming beach, with a nice sea breeze and all those pretty gull sounds just like Brighton. Fancy that.

But Froelich turned due west and walked into the sea. Surprised, yet unalarmed as yet, the men followed, and the cool and shallow water felt so good on soles already stinging from their tramping that they laughed and couldn't help but quip.

"We're going for a bath!" said Ricky Schonberg from the back.

"You need it, Ricky," Ben-Zvi called back. "Your farting has turned grim."

"You should talk, Ben-Zvi," Horst Felder grunted. "There's not a bar of soap in all of Palestine."

"*Arschloch.*" Asshole, Ben-Zvi hissed back and the three Bloch cousins chortled like hens.

"Sergeant Gutman," Froelich said as he waded farther out, "tell them to shut up. It's not a party."

Gutman barked, they all fell silent, and soon they couldn't speak even if they'd wanted. Froelich kept on going till they were all waist deep and the ocean's slimy bed was sucking at their boots. And only then, with weapons high and biceps trembling, he turned them left again, and they began a mile's horrid slog, their uniforms soaked below with seawater, their faces soaked above with stinging sweat, and their lungs gasping for mercy from their gods and mothers. No day at the beach.

At last they splashed ashore and Froelich let them sit, or rather crash, in the shade of the bark's twenty-foot hull, which had been punctured by machine gun bullets in some forgotten seaside spat.

"Helmets off," he said as he looked down at them, fists on hips and dripping. "Each pair of you, share one canteen. Empty it, and keep the other full. Commandos never slosh."

A few young eyes grew wide. The word commando wasn't on their menu of ambitions. Tommy helmets plunked into the sand, throats gulped steamy water. Someone raised a hand and Froelich smirked. They thought it was a classroom.

"Yes, Private Bloch?" It was one of the triplet cousins. He didn't know yet which was which, but they all were Blochs.

"Sir, is this bit over now?"

"You'll soon be fighting Germans. Think they'll take pity on you and let you rest at teatime?"

"No, sir."

"It shall be over when it's over." Froelich turned to Gutman. "Ten minutes, Sergeant."

"Yes, sir."

Froelich climbed a small escarpment off the beach and sat down on a rock. He didn't smoke, or drink his water, because he had no sharing partner and he could wait. His body had learned that. He leaned his Sten across his soggy knees and looked out at the sea, through figure eights of cawing gulls, and only saw Sofia. That sensation of their becoming one, wherein the glorious force of nature had shown her face, was something he might never feel again. His new men couldn't fathom that his icy blue-eyed stare was heartbreak. They thought it was a combat leader's machine gun killing glare, which was all they needed from their shepherd.

"He's hard," said David Rosenberg in the shade beside the bark. He touched his cheek scar. He always touched it.

"Like lizard lips," Horst Felder said as he rubbed his rust-hued hair. Brawlers rarely nodded at the strengths of other men, so that was something.

"SIG, the rumor has it," Wolfgang Steinberg said. He was splayed out against the hull, head back, still breathing hard, with his sand-coated Bren beside him. "God I hate this gun."

"What's SIG?" Ricky Schonberg asked. His chubby cheeks were still bright pink from the exertion.

"Machlakah ha'Germaneet," said Arieh Ben-Zvi in Hebrew.

"Speak bloody English," the giant Manfred Hasenbein snarled. Of all the men, the morning's stroll had barely raised his pulse rate. "Or German, but not that bloody Bible babble."

"No German," Fritzy Gutman snapped. "Not unless the major clears it."

"We never want to speak German again," said Moses Bloch, which appeared to be a collective oath by him and his two cousins.

"Never," Gustave Bloch said.

"Or even French," said Hans Bloch.

"You'll speak German when you're ordered." Gutman lit a cigarette.

"So what's it mean then, Arieh?" Ricky Schonberg asked.

"German platoon," said Ben-Zvi. "That's likely what they're making us."

"Oh, shite," Paul Green muttered.

"Oh, sod it," Felix Braun agreed.

"Frick and Frack, at last alive!" Horst Felder grinned.

"German bloody platoon," Hasenbein growled. "Lots of crazy Jews, all dead."

"You know, Manfred," Ricky said, "if you hate your bleedin' birthright all that much, we could have your *shvantz*'s foreskin sewed back on you."

"Never had it cut, Schonberg." Hasenbein shot him a frightening wolf's grin. "Bend over and I'll show you."

"All right, that's enough." Fritzy Gutman tossed his smoke away and got to his feet. "Kit up."

The way back down the beach was easy after slogging through the waves, even though the sun was higher. It was funny how the dreaded monotone of stomping boots on flatland could sound like chirping music when the trek was dry. But as their uniforms steamed off, their straps and slings chafed more, their weapons seemed to fatten and Castello Chiarmonte loomed above them and they gulped and knew they'd have to climb.

"You think the major's watching, sir?" Fritzy Gutman said to Froelich as they quick-marched that beach mile.

"Like a hawk, with binoculars," Froelich said, thinking of Papa and how he'd always done that very thing with him and Greta.

The first return climb was a trial, yet respectable. Froelich kept it slow, the formation didn't stretch too much and they all made it to the top. He gave them fifteen minutes to relieve themselves in the castle stable's makeshift latrine, a collective urinal made from a pig trough and feces buckets dug into the floor, refill their canteens and snatch a cracker and a scoop of marmalade. And then again, before they'd half recovered, they were off.

The men admired him the first time and despised him halfway through the second. Their legs had turned to jelly, their lungs to fire, the sun had taken center stage and sang an aria of filthy brightness, and the tide had pulled the ocean back, which made them have to wade much farther out to get the proper dunk. *Bloody barmy officers!* Ricky Schonberg fell and nearly drowned, but Hasenbein caught him by his helmet brim and dragged him up, while Froelich never slowed or seemed to give a damn and left it to the men to babysit each other and kept going. Two more hours for that round trip iteration.

In the early afternoon he gave them respite at the top, after having Fritzy Gutman stand them in formation and straighten up their uniforms and weapons. He dismissed them to the shade beneath the castle's entrance archway, telling them to eat, but not too much. He saw Sergeant Major Connor standing on a parapet, a pair of tanker's field glasses hanging from his muscled neck. But Connor only nodded at him, and Major Butler wasn't on the scene. He didn't need to be. He had his gargoyle watching.

Froelich went into his quarters, sat on his bunk, smoked a cigarette, ate a can of peaches, then removed Sofia's picture and Tommy Robbins' unread letter from his pocket, and hid them underneath a saddle in the loft. The tide would soon be rising. He couldn't bear to have them ruined or lost, and he trusted no one not to toss them.

He went back out to the men and ordered them on their

feet. They were shocked. They hadn't finished lunch. Gutman sidled up to him and whispered, "Sir, they've got a good
five minutes yet, by your watch."

"Weren't you at Alamein, Gutman?"

"I was, sir."

"Did the Stukas wait until you'd had your lunch?"

By the third time there was murder in their eyes. No one
spoke. No one joked. They moved like beaten pack mules,
heads down, hopeless. Paul "Frick" Green cried. Felix "Frack"
Braun squeezed Paul's neck to shut him up. No one laughed
about it. Ricky Schonberg passed out on the beach before
the final wade. Fritzy Gutman ordered that Horst Felder the
brawler and David Rosenberg the knife boy take his harness
and his Enfield, sling his arms about their necks and drag
him through the water. He was fat. Rosenberg had his trench
knife, he always had it, and imagined it plunged hilt deep in
Froelich's back.

At the formation's point on the last return trip down the
beach, Froelich knew his feet were bleeding in his boots and
his thigh throbbed like his temples from the sun. But it was
nothing after the Sahara. They had to learn to take it too. He
hadn't let them rest beside the bark this time around. They
never would have gotten up. He thought perhaps it might
have been wiser not to let them carry ammunition because
he felt their hatred burning through his back. *Good. So what?*
Hatred brewed the finest fuel.

On the cliffside going up, "Beethoven" Steinberg collapsed.
Manfred Hasenbein cursed him thoroughly in German, *"Du
blöder Hund steh auf!"* But when he didn't get up the giant
handed his Enfield to Ben-Zvi, picked up Steinberg's heavy

Bren, slung its strap around his neck, then threw the musician over his shoulder and went on up. The Bloch cousins got behind Manfred to help and pushed his muscled rump. He cursed them too. Horst Felder dragged Ricky Schonberg all the way by hauling on his garrison belt and twisting his ear until he squealed.

Froelich turned to watch them for a moment. Gutman, close behind, grinned at him. He nodded back. He had them.

The sun was all but gone when they collapsed into the castle courtyard. They couldn't stand, not even Hasenbein. Froelich let them sit or lie and simply breathe, and even empty their canteens on each other's sunburned faces or down their gullets.

"Well done," he said, standing once again with fists on hips, though his legs were trembling. "Change your uniforms. Freshen up. Mess in one hour. I shall hunt for rum."

They blinked at him, helped each other up, and limped into their quarters. Gutman stomped a boot in front of Froelich, saluted smartly, and held it until Froelich gave one back and said, "All right, Fritzy, bugger off."

"You're a card, sir." Gutman smirked as he left.

"I've heard that before."

"Lieutenant Froelich!"

He turned to find Major Butler, carrying his swagger stick and glaring at him.

"Suh." Froelich saluted.

Butler looked him up and down.

"I intended for you to punish the men, Froelich, not your damned *self*."

"Well, as they say at Sandhurst, sir. An officer must bleed from the front."

"You didn't go to Sandhurst. And it's *lead* from the front."

Froelich's smile was tight. "I know, sir." He snapped one more salute, spun on a heel, and left.

Twenty-Two

AT DAWN THEY RODE TO CASTELVETRANO, A
pleasant northward drive along the coast, even more so because they were not walking. Their transport was a rumbling
Bedford QL 4x4, the canvas covered truck dubbed Queen
Lizzie early on by some grim trooper happy to be riding.

Fritzy Gutman had the wheel with Froelich to his left,
squinting at the sunlit sea and smoking, with the rest of the
eleven bouncing on the benches in the back. They'd all slept
like the dead, having crashed onto their cots just after evening mess, except for Ricky Schonberg, who'd sat up yelling
after midnight with both his calves bunched up in painful
charley horses, the curse of infantry. Horst Felder had held
him down while all three Blochs massaged his legs until he'd
stopped his wailing.

But now they felt like chauffeured princes, bellies full of
breakfast, puffing cigarettes, groaning with the road bumps
and each other's farting, while their kit bags and weapons slid

across the swaying metal floor like wrenches in a plumber's toolbox. The trip, they'd heard, was fifty miles. They wished it would be more.

Just before first light, Sergeant Major Connor had nudged Froelich awake and handed him a map. Froelich hoped the way would take them back through Agrigento and perhaps he'd see Sofia, if only for a wave and smile of longing, but the X that marked their target was far the other way, at the south end of an airfield where Connor said they'd find three tents, and the next leg of their training.

All right. Lover's luck was something he'd had only once, and expected nevermore.

They drove through Montallegro, whose hilly streets were lined with bushy headed palms. They drove on through Sciacca, closer to the coast, where crooked salmon-colored buildings nearly spilled into the surf, the morning cove was end to end with rainbow boats, and the air smelled marvelous with fish and boiling black coffee.

But then they turned northwest and the ground grew flat and brown and empty. Airfields weren't built in pretty places. Froelich put the map away as American P-39 fighters and C-47 Dakota transports buzzed the truck, floated down a long wide strip of tar and gravel, and bounced onto the ground to take a rest and drink long draughts of petrol.

"Looks like we're here, sir." Gutman pointed at a clump of tents that looked like upside down green flower pots sitting in a cactus garden.

"Paradise it's not," Froelich said. The tents were at the airstrip's southern tip, set back from the tarmac, and so far from the hangars that those looked like cinnamon cubes way down at the other end.

He got out and crushed his cigarette underboot. It was hot, dusty, and windy, with tumbleweeds rolling all about like dirty dandelions. Fritzy climbed down, told the men to leave their kitbags, take their guns and form up. They groaned because they knew the best was over.

Froelich marched them toward the strip. First they saw a twelve-man tent, another with its walls rolled up and filled with steamer trunks and crates, and a third for staff and cadre. They passed a wide square plot of sand, with three large wooden boxes of ascending heights, and a strange contraption resembling a child's swing set made of wooden beams. It had a pair of iron eyelets screwed into the horizontal spar, yet no ropes or swings.

"They're gonna hang the lot of us," Arieh Ben-Zvi mumbled from the rear.

"You, for certain," Horst Felder said. "They missed your arse in Haifa. Now's their chance."

"*Ja*, they only hang the Jews," Hasenbein grunted. "Saves on ammunition."

"Shut your cake holes," Fritzy Gutman warned.

Then Froelich saw Major Butler, who'd arrived there first with Sergeant Major Connor in two jeeps, now parked between the tents, the odd contraptions, and the airfield's runway. There were also three more men, all sergeants, looking very fit and dangerous. One of them was Indian. He had a wickedly curved khukri knife tucked into his garrison belt.

Froelich formed his men in double ranks and saluted Butler, who returned it with a flick. The major and his cadre were lined up in front of a long plotting table, and the sergeants stepped aside, leaving Butler there alone. The table had some objects on it. One large green turtle-shaped bundle, a smaller one beside it like its baby sister, and all sorts of straps and belts and shiny clasps and buckles.

"Oh, bloody *hell*," Ricky Schonberg groaned from the rear rank.

The green turtles were parachutes.

"Gentlemen." Butler curled the word in such a way that Froelich heard it soggy with disdain. "These three sergeants are your training cadre."

He flicked his swagger stick at each in turn.

"Sergeant Deighton, Archibald. Sapper extraordinaire, Royal Engineers."

The explosives man was film star handsome, with dark eyes and eyebrows, a pert nose and upturned lips that broke away to dimples, all topped by a perfectly pulled beret. But the playboy image was deceptive—sappers had nerves of iron. Butler flicked at the next.

"Sergeant Gurung, Bahna. Indian regiments, Ghurka Rifles. He shall teach you hand-to-hand."

Froelich looked at Gurung and thought no one might survive instruction by this man. All of five foot five, he was a brown postal box of muscle wearing an Australian bush hat, with rattlesnake eyes, a slim mustache above a frowning mouth, and a neck wider than his rippling jaw. Such Nepalese commandos had awful reputations.

"And Sergeant Winston, Jeremy," Butler dubbed the last, who had the form of a rugby player and the drooping brows, flat nose, and expressionless mouth of a numb hockey goalie.

He wore a brimless parachute helmet, and his shoulders were crisscrossed with ropes and web straps, as if he'd arrived straightaway from a raid on Dieppe.

"Your parachute instructor," Butler said as he surveyed Froelich's wide-eyed lot. "He'll have the floor, with assistance from sergeants Deighton and Gurung, until you exit from your aircraft." He raised his chin as if he'd smelled a foul whiff. "I know you're not accustomed to such courage, but do your best to shed your history of subjugation, Old Testament obsessions, money lending, and the like, and step up."

"Good Christ," Horst Felder whispered from the ranks. "Nazis to the north of us and more right here in candyland."

Beethoven Steinberg elbowed him to hush, while Butler, with a nod, turned them over to Winston, who Froelich thought looked far too eager and somewhat daft.

The rest of that day's training was somersaulting madness. Sergeant Jeremy Winston had all the patience of a cowboy in a brothel, and a vernacular so fraught with slang that half the time his charges scrunched their noses, shrugged at one another, and simply aped his moves. He had them stack their weapons, strap on para helmets from a trunk, and spread out on the sand lot, along with Froelich, whose rank was instantly irrelevant.

"You blokes are gonna learn to fall," he barked as he paced before them, fists on hips, while Gurung the Ghurka and handsome Deighton the sapper stood back and watched with folded arms and grins, as Butler and Connor jeeped off down the airstrip in a cloud of dust. "And not like *this*." He lunged at David Rosenberg, shoved his bony chest, sprawled him flail-

ing on his back, and resumed his pacing while the shocked
boy gasped for air, too frightened to get up.

"You'll think me a bender by tea," Winston snarled. They
knew the word meant harsh drill instructor, yet that was already clear. "But I can tell ya, the wind is gonna take your
brolly." *What the hell was that? A parachute?* "And when it does
and slams your arses on the ground, you'll not make a box
up of it. Clear?"

"Ye...yes, Sergeant," they mumbled.

"I can't bloody hear ya!"

"Yes, Sergeant!"

"Right, then. Boots together, bend your knees, fists beside your ears, elbows touching. Not like *that*, you wankers!
Like *this*. Now on my signal, fall to your right, onto your
calf, then hip, then shoulder, and throw those legs the whole
way over. Up!"

They did it to the right. They did it to the left. They did it
twisting backwards, and then full frontal as he shoved them
from the rear. They were pathetic. They looked like drunken
toddlers falling down the kindergarten stairs. They did it for
an hour of gasps and grunts and groans.

"Ya bloody sorry sods!" Winston yelled as his eyes gleamed
like Jack the Ripper's. "It's a parachute landing fall, not a bath
at Bristol! How'd the lot of you make it past the trick cyclist?"

He meant the parachute regiment's psychiatrist, whose task
was to weed out questionable candidates. But none of Froelich's dozen had been examined by a mental health professional, who likely would have failed them all.

"Pardon, sir." Winston touched his helmet brim at Froelich. "Don't mean you."

"Quite all right, Sergeant," Froelich rasped. His thigh was throbbing like the day that Lefkowitz had hammered it. "Carry on."

"Thank you, sir," Winston said with genteel deference, then screamed again, "To the left. Up! To the right. Up! To the rear. *Up!*"

Another half an hour and they were soaked in sweat, shirts askew, caked with sand, bruised and sore and slinging saliva as they gripped their knees and tried to remain upright. Gurung and Deighton fetched two jerrycans of water. The dozen had to help each other swig with trembling arms, and finished every drop.

"All right then, the boxes," Winston called as his two grinning aides dragged the wooden cubes onto the pitch.

"*Gott im Himmel,*" Ricky Schonberg whined. "I can't lift another boot."

"Secure that bloody hatch!" Winston spat at Ricky, which all the men thought strangely nautical, but no one dared to comment.

He lined them up behind the lowest box, had each one climb up, then shoved them in the rump to give them a sensation of velocity and height. That made for better executions and a blessed bit of breeze. But the next box, three feet high, was harder, and the last, at five feet up, cranked their knees and bounced their helmets on the ground, until at last they crawled away from every fall like judo novices at the hands of a merciless sensei.

"All right." Winston nodded, somewhat satisfied. "You can all pike off for a cup and a wad. Fifteen minutes. But don't you blokes be tardy back or I'll have ya in the moosh."

His slang was clear as Greek, yet they all got the gist of it and staggered off for tea and biscuits, while Froelich eyed his watch and wondered if they'd all survive the day.

In the afternoon, following a desultory meal for lack of appetite, Winston sat them in a semicircle before the plotting table. He wore the full rig of a harness, T-5 parachute in back, reserve chute in the front, and weapons case beside one hip. He waddled back and forth like a monkey with an itchy bum and explained procedures on the aircraft.

"Now just before your suicides," he said, "you'll get up off your arses, form up in your stick, hook the snap link of this static line to the cable in the roof, and shuffle towards me where I'm standing at the tailside door. Right?"

He mimed the whole procedure, which might have been hilarious had all of them been drunk and raucous at some jolly postwar party, but they were not.

"Oh, God," Beethoven Steinberg moaned. "Why do we have to know this?"

"Why do you think?" Hasenbein growled back. "It's bloody crystal clear."

"Bugger all the why," Ben-Zvi cursed. "Question's how the hell do we get out of it?"

The Bloch cousins nodded all three heads at that. Paul Green and Felix Braun sat silent, hip to hip, looking very pale.

"Lads, look sharp." Froelich snapped them back to focus as Winston carried on.

"Now, when you reach me, hurl the snap link down the cable, and don't get it bollixed up underneath your pit 'cause the bastard'll tear your arm off."

"Oh mercy," David Rosenberg whined.

"Now turn and grip the door, like this, and when you feel me whack your bum, hurl those knees into the breeze, head down, legs together, and hug that belly brolly like you're shagging Buxom Betty from the rear. Clear?"

"Good Christ," Horst Felder whispered.

"Ach, Mutti," Ricky Schonberg moaned, begging for his mother.

"And now, gents, here's the key. If all goes well, the static line'll drag your brolly from the pack and pop it like a blossom. But it'll be the dead of night, black as a chimney sweep's bunghole, so you won't see your canopy. Count longways to three, and if you're still whistling like a Stuka and your bollocks haven't yet been shoved up in your guts, turn your face away and yank this grip right here and pray."

Winston pulled the ripcord of his reserve parachute, a small jellyfish drogue burst straight out from his body, and the entire silk canopy spilled onto the ground like some otherworldly creature vomiting its organs.

"Don't worry about steering." Winston grinned with his finale. "You won't see a bloody thing anyways, and the ground'll tell ya when she's there. But when in doubt, pull it out. You're a meager lot, and we can't have any of ya makin' holes in Hitler's garden."

At that point, Paul Green fainted dead away.

Twenty-Three

THE MEN REVIVED PAUL GREEN WITH CHEEK slaps, cold water douses, and feeble lies. After that they headed for the gallows. That swing thing loomed much larger, since now they understood that Sergeant Winston had a predilection for instruments of torture.

The five-foot-high wooden box was set up in the sand behind the swing set's cross spar. Hanging in midair below the spar was an Irving parachute harness of white webbing, with two ropes running from its shoulder straps up through the beam's iron eyelets, and down again to the fists of Gurung and Deighton, who flanked the box on either side.

"All right, bandits," Winston said to Froelich and his crew, who stood there now on shaky legs wishing that the sun would set. But at least he'd called them something other than silly sods or wankers. "This here's the swing lander. It'll teach ya proper attitude." He didn't mean a positive viewpoint. He meant position in the air. "Volunteers?"

"Take me first, Sergeant." Froelich stepped forward.

"*That's* what I like to see, sir." Winston grinned.

He buckled Froelich in the harness, with one snap link across his chest, then yanked his leg straps so high in his crotch that Froelich coughed and thought his testicles might burst.

"Jolly good, sir," Winston said. "Now climb up on the crate and take your in-the-door position."

Froelich did as he was told and faced his men below, some of whom had knuckles in their mouths.

"Now, when I say go, leap for all your worth and set yourself for landing. Sergeants Gurung and Deighton'll hold your carcass, sir, until I think you're ready for the fall."

"Göring and Donitz, he means," someone muttered in the ranks.

"*Stimmt*," someone else agreed in German.

"Pipe down," Gutman snapped.

"Go!"

It wasn't half unpleasant. Froelich jumped and swung, his boot toes arced into the sky, a dozen upturned faces flashed by, and he thought he'd have another breezy swing to get his legs together. But, exchanging winks, Gurung and Deighton freed their ropes and he shot through the air, slammed onto his back and plowed a furrow as his men fled sideward like a school of smelts.

"Not too shabby," Winston said as he yanked Froelich to his feet. "You're still alive. Next!"

Some fell on their knees. Some fell on their necks. Ricky Schonberg pulled his legs up far too high, smashed down on his rump and nearly cried. The cousins Bloch were perfect and landed with the springy grace of kangaroos. Only Manfred Hasenbein was far too large to manage, and when he leaped, Gurung and Deighton went sailing up into the air. The men all laughed at that, which Winston didn't care for, so Hasenbein was forced to have another go. This time Winston waved his sergeants off, they didn't touch the ropes, and the giant German speared into the sand like a javelin.

Winston had them all do one more round, which everyone but Froelich thought was just to satisfy his sadism. Froelich knew better. He'd been mentored by Bertie Buck, God bless his soul wherever he might be. "Bleed them when they're training, march them when it's raining, then watch them hold the line and charge, when the ammunition's waning." He wasn't sure if that was really Buck or Kipling, but he'd understood the point, and walked his ranks and whispered in their ears as they gritted their teeth and groaned.

"Steady on, lads. Don't give him what he wants. Show that bugger we Jews are tough as any blasted *shagitz*."

They nodded and kept it up. Their lefty was calling them "lads" and breaking out his Yiddish.

At last the sun was large and orange and nearing the horizon. Finished with the swing, they thought the day was over. It was not.

Winston went to fetch his jeep, drove it back and aimed it at a long flat patch of sand and scrub. Gurung and Deighton climbed into its tub and, facing rearward, braced their boots, tossed the harness on the ground, gripped its ropes, and grinned. They were wearing gunner's gloves.

"All right then, squaddies," Winston said. "Last bit. Odds are when you smack the ground the wind'll snatch your brolly and you'll be dragged along, sucking Mother Nature's tit. So reach up, grab one riser, drag it down and show the bitch who's boss."

"Of course," Horst Felder sighed.

"Bleedin' sadist," Ben-Zvi cursed.

"I'll kill him if I'm able," said Hasenbein, and meant it.

"Chins up, lads," Froelich called, though he imagined scabby bloody horrors when he and his men would be dragged and bounced across the thorny ground. "Have at it."

Each man got harnessed up. Each got dragged behind the jeep, not so fast as to break their bones, but enough to feel as though their guts were scrambling like eggs as skin was peeled from knees and elbows. Yet every one of them, including Green and Braun and Schonberg, managed to reach up and tear the ropes from Gurung's or Deighton's grip, then got up on their feet in clouds of roiling dust. Winston was surprised, and satisfied.

"All right then, you'll do," he said as they stood all wobbly in formation, mouths and eyes and noses stuffed with sand and snot. "Wash up, pull your knickers from your cracks and have a bite."

Major Butler and Sergeant Major Connor returned from the hangars, their jeep laden with combat rations and, shockingly, bottles of Heneger low percentage beer. Froelich and his men rinsed their skinned hands with jerrycan water, salved their cuts and scrapes with stinging iodine, made a circle on the ground and slumped. The evening air grew cool. They mostly ate and smoked in silence, and wondered where they'd all gone wrong. They tidied up, fell onto their bedrolls in their tent, and slept despite the terror of knowing what was next.

Froelich lay outside the tent, alone and underneath a woolen army blanket. He stared up at the stars, and then Sofia's picture, and touched his pocket to make sure Tommy Robbins' letter was still there. Exhaustion took him fast.

The plane arrived with morning. It was a C-47 Dakota, mottled green and brown, with long bladed wings, roaring twin engines, a nose like a whale, and lifeless square glass eyes. It looked enormous as it taxied toward them down the strip, then turned in a hurricane of prop wash and showed its yawning jump door.

They'd all had early breakfast, but nothing more than tea boiled on a wood fire, two biscuits, and a plop of marmalade. Winston lined them up beside the plane, while Gurung and Deighton climbed aboard and tossed out parachutes and harnesses. Then the sergeants kitted each man up, without a quip or disparagement, all serious business now, tightening harnesses and helmets, parachutes in front and back, and handed each his static line as twenty-four legs trembled, and Froelich's too.

After that, Winston, Gurung, and Deighton donned their rigs as well, while Fritzy Gutman muttered, "At least the nasty triplets'll be dying with us," but no one laughed.

They climbed the plane's short ladder, one by one, into the dark and rumbling belly of the beast, wincing at the smells of fuel oil, cigarettes, and scrubbed up vomit. Winston sat them on the metal benches, six across from six, with Froelich closest to the tail and open door. Beside him Ricky Schonberg hunched head down, bobbing over his knees as if praying only to wake up, while all the rest looked at the ribbed vibrating ceiling and the long steel cable that would be the only link between them and survival.

The three sergeants posted near the tail, standing up and gripping fuselage spars. Froelich looked around at all his men and their glassy eyes and knew that he must say something, even though his mouth was dry as flour and hellish images flashed behind his eyes of torn and tattered silk above him, his boots below barreling toward the ground, his reserve parachute twisting up and tangling in his shredded main as he screamed and screamed...

"Steady on, lads!" he called above the engines as the stench of fuel made his stomach turn. He forced a grin and shot them a thumbs-up, and half returned the gesture. The rest were staring at their boots.

The engines roared louder. The plane began to move, and they all gripped the benches and their bladders.

Then all at once it stopped.

The engines cut, the propellers fluttered down to utter silence, and Major Butler and Sergeant Major Connor appeared from the darkened cavern of the cockpit. Butler tipped his cap back, and fists on hips, nodded at the men.

"All right, that's quite enough," he said. "We can't afford to have you spear yourselves into a tree, or break a leg or skull. You are too few."

Mouths agape, they blinked at him, and Froelich did too.

"You shall only need to jump just once," Butler went on. "We only needed to know that you will. Go have a proper breakfast."

And he and Connor were gone. Froelich whipped his head around to see the sergeants grinning as they doffed their parachutes. His men cursed and moaned and slapped their foreheads and each other's knees. Ricky Schonberg vomited some bile on the floor.

Froelich unstrapped Ricky's helmet, took it off the boy's head, ruffled his sweat-soaked hair and said, "Ricky, you're one hard Jew."

Twenty-Four

AT CASTELLO CHIARMONTE, FROELICH AND his men became again the thing they hated most.

Sergeant Major Connor barked them from their breakfast in the stable and they assembled in the castle's courtyard, field caps smart, weapons tight, eyes squinting in the lemon light, expressions grim. Their plight at Castelvetrano had made it clear that there was nothing good afoot, and even bleaker fates should not surprise them.

Facing them were Ghurka Gurung, handsome Deighton and half-daft Winston, beside a hefty pile of lumps and clumps covered by a brown tarpaulin, which somehow had appeared between the time they'd staggered to their cots and woken up. Froelich snapped them to attention as Major Butler strode out from his quarters, crisp and pressed and dark, and claimed a spot between them and the baleful bundle.

"Lieutenant Froelich," Butler said, and whipped his swagger stick across the ranks, "have your sergeant relieve them of their weapons."

Froelich gave the order, and soon their Enfields, Stens, the Bren, and Gutman's Thompson were piled in a court-yard corner.

"Right," said Butler. "Now have them strip."

"All right, men," Froelich said as he wondered what cruel plot was next. "You heard the major. Down to briefs."

No one quipped or snickered as they shed their British uniforms. They knew they weren't going for a swim, and soon they stood there, shoulders back, fists by thighs, naked but for baggy underpants. Except for Arieh Ben-Zvi, who often shed his shirt in spite of regulations, their youthful skins were tanned in soldier patterns, nut brown arms and necks and faces, with pale white legs and bellies, like human zebras. Their boots and folded clothes were ordered at their feet, and Froelich's too, and he had that sting of memory that never leaves a prisoner of war.

Then, like cabaret magicians, Butler's sergeants yanked the tarp away to reveal a treasure trove of Wehrmacht booty. There were Mauser 98 rifles, P38 pistols, MP40 Schmeisser submachine guns, a heavy MG42 *Maschinengewehr* machine gun, an MP43 *Sturmgewehr* assault rifle, stick grenades and mounds of ammunition. There were stacks of German news-papers and magazines, Luftwaffe *Soldbücher*, messkits and canteens, turtle shell helmets adorned with diving eagles, heavy boots, pantaloons and green paratrooper tunics that had short legs cut just above the knee. All had been recov-ered from the corpses of the 1st Parachute Division holdouts, the ones the US Rangers had killed at Camarata, except for

Gutman's gramophone, which sat there too beside a box of German records.

Froelich's men blinked and swallowed at the booty, as Major Butler cracked his swagger stick against his boot.

"Henceforth, my filthy Jewish dozen," he said, "you shall be Germans. You shall speak it, march it, read it, write it, and dream it. You shall learn these weapons as you know your Enfields, Stens, and Brens. You shall drill it till we're all alarmed by nightmares of invasion. Am I clear?"

"Yes, sir," the men intoned together.

"Try that again, in *character*."

"Jawohl, Herr Major," they croaked.

"Feeble, but you shall improve, and quickly. We haven't got much time." He turned to Froelich. "Lieutenant, there's a bottle of peroxide in this lot. Pick your darkest five and pale their hair. But not you, Froelich. You've got that Nazi look down pat." He spun a heel and went back to his quarters.

Yet no one moved across that chasm of emotional resistance. Those things that lay before them were the very ones they'd fled, the costumes worn by demons who'd upended all their lives, the weapons used to terrorize their families, friends, and futures. Froelich looked at them, his frozen naked boys, and knew their hearts because in Cairo at Buck's training camp, he'd felt that same skin crawling chill and knew he had to slap them into action.

"All right," he snapped. "For all our mothers. The uniforms. Have at it."

They moved like startled patients escaped from an asylum, saying nothing as they picked through boots and socks and belts and leather harnesses, finding things that fit, finding rank tabs proximate to what they'd been as British soldiers. And soon they were wearing *Feldmützen* field caps and *Fallschirm-jäger* tunics, many rent with bullet holes and crusty stains of blood, looking like a squad of Wehrmacht ghosts who'd returned to haunt the Jews who dared to wear them.

Froelich faced them, now dressed in a paratrooper *Leutnant* tunic, an Iron Cross below his throat. He looked down at his uniform, probed a bullethole, looked up again, and smiled.

"We're a holy lot," he said, which eased some grins. "We'll mend them later. Now, the weapons. You three Bloch boys, Braun and Green, shall have the rifles. Hasenbein, the MG42 machine gun and a pistol, with Schonberg as your second. For all the rest, the Schmeissers." He planned to take a Schmeisser for himself, but also keep Moncalvo's Beretta, for promised vengeance. "All right, let's do it, and leave the ammunition."

As the men retrieved the guns he turned to Winston, Gurung, and Deighton, who were looking at him as if he'd morphed into a loathsome spectre, while Sergeant Major Connor stood aside and preened the corners of his mustache.

"You three sergeants," Froelich said, and pointed at the gramophone. "We'll have some atmosphere. Snap to it."

The sergeants hurried to the gramophone, perched it on the courtyard's waist high wall, fetched a record from the box, and spun it. But it wasn't lovely strains of "Dream a Little Dream." It was a German paratrooper's battle ode, "In Crete During Storm and Rain."

Auf Kreta bei Sturm und bei Regen,
Da steht ein Fallschirmjäger auf der Wacht.

Er träumt ja so gerne von der Heimat,
Wo ihm ein holdes Mädchenherze lacht.

In Crete during storm and rain,
A paratrooper stands on guard.
He likes to dream of home,
Where a tender girl's heart awaits him.

It echoed from the castle's walls. It curdled the men's guts. And they marched to it, all morning long.

Froelich's English disappeared. His *Hochdeutsch* German rang their ears. He taught them close order drill, yelling, *"Achtung! Stillgestanden! Links um! Rechts um! Kehrt um!"* until their stomping boot heels ached and their heads were dizzy from the spinning. He taught them weapons drills, shoulder and present arms, clutching rifles straight and true, slinging Schmeissers from their necks, with Hasenbein's heavy MG42 jutting skyward like a broomstick, as only he could manage it. He bellowed *"Vorwärts Marsch!"* and they stomped in close formation, and then he made them goose step as if Josef Goebbels himself was right there watching with a steely eye.

At mess there was no letup, as while they ate he made them read aloud from *Signal*, each snapping to attention to report the latest Nazi news. Then he walked amongst them while they drank and chewed, and taught them slang they'd never heard at school. A *Blumentopf* was a flowerpot, but also a grenade. Your mother's *Küchenteller* cake plate was here an antitank mine. *Rückenwind* was not a tailwind, but a fart, and *Briefkarten* turned from mailbox into whore.

Then they learned their weapons, every bit from bolts to

breaches, rates of fire, clearing stoppages, stripping and assembling. And then he made them goose step more, all throughout the afternoon, and called them *"faule Hunde,"* lazy dogs, and punished them with calisthenics until they got it right and cursed him all the more.

And finally, near sundown, after all the men had proved that they could execute each order Froelich barked, and properly salute when done, he formed them up and ordered Connor, in German, to go fetch Butler, which raised the sergeant major's eyebrow, but he did it.

Butler strode out from his lair. Froelich stomped up to his face, saluted and said, *"Herr Major, ihre Kommandos."* Then he snapped an about-face, had the men perform eleven perfect drills, and ended with them thrusting out their arms with pointed palms and shouting *"Heil Hitler!"* which thundered in the castle's sundown courtyard as Butler's training cadre shook their heads and whistled low.

Major Butler tipped his chin up, looked at Froelich and said, "We might survive this after all."

He turned and left, and Froelich smiled at his men and winked. And he realized in that moment, that he'd become the man who'd taught him all of this, a man he'd loved and lost. He'd become Bertie Buck.

Froelich didn't visit with the men after evening mess. A British subaltern might mingle briefly with his soldiers to share a joke and pump up their morale, but no German troop commander would have done so.

Outside the stable in the dark he summoned Fritzy Gutman, while inside the men sat on canvas cots and smoked, drank tea boiled on a hay and tinder fire, and by its flickering light patched their bullet punctured uniforms with sewing kits and laughed as the three Bloch cousins, David Rosenberg, and Felix Braun tried to bleach their hair but still looked awfully Semitic. He spoke to Gutman low, in English.

"Make sure they stick to German, Fritzy. It's not a costume party."

"All right, sir. But you think we'll all pass muster? I mean, what's the play?"

"I've no idea, but I suspect it's some sort of raid and this is just to get us past the guards. If we're caught, we shan't survive interrogation anyway. They'll just kill us all."

Gutman smiled. "Good thing you're not a morale officer, sir."

"Right." Froelich smiled back. "Off you go."

Fritzy went into the stable, yelled, *"Kein Englisch!"* and the men grunted and returned to their mother tongue. But Froelich didn't leave. He leaned against the outside wall, lit a smoke, and listened.

"Unser Leutnant denkt er sei Leibstandarte." Our lieutenant thinks he's SS Panzer, Horst Felder commented.

"I trust him," Ricky Schonberg said. "He'd done all this before."

"I trust you to schlep my ammunition, Schonberg," Manfred Hasenbein growled, "and not much more."

"Arschloch," Ricky said, and someone laughed and Froelich heard some tinny object bounce off Ricky's head.

"Twenty press-ups for that, Hasenbein," Fritzy Gutman snapped. The giant got down in position, and while he did the press-ups the men abused him and applauded when he'd finished.

They all sewed onward for a while, then David Rosenberg, who'd finished his patches and now preened his trench knife, looked over at Horst Felder.

"So where'd you learn Italian, Felder?"

"Father had a leather firm in Rome. Worked there in the summers."

"Bet that Eyetie widow fancies it." Rosenberg was trying to be lewd.

"She lost a son, idiot," Felder snarled. "She's about as randy as your nun."

"Rosenberg doesn't fancy that sister, Felder," Arieh Ben-Zvi said. "He only fancies *you*."

That drew peals of laughter, and though Froelich couldn't see Rosenberg's deep blush, he knew it.

"You're the only one amongst us getting shagged, Ben-Zvi," Beethoven Steinberg said.

"That's right, Ben-Zvi," said Hasenbein. "How's that sexy clock girl in the sack?"

A moment passed as everyone stopped working and looked at Arieh Ben-Zvi, hoping for some pornographic vision. But he alone kept sewing, and muttered quietly, "It's not like that. I only hold her when she cries."

And just like that they fell to somber silence. Ben-Zvi's confession had shattered all bravado and torn away the masks they needed desperately to carry on. They were, they knew too well, nothing but lost boys, orphans playing soldier. And Froelich, standing still outside the door, stopped smoking and just listened, nearly breathless.

"I miss my girls," Beethoven Steinberg said about his church choir. "They don't know why I left them."

"They know," Ricky Schonberg said.

"That little girl, Teresa," Manfred Hasenbein muttered. "She has nothing. She lives in the gutters."

"It's peacetime here now," Moses Bloch said to Hasenbein. "She'll be all right."

"I miss my sisters," Paul Green said. His voice was choked and sunken.

"My nun is not a nun," David Rosenberg said, and everyone looked at him. "She pretended it to keep from being raped by the Germans."

"All right you tossers that's enough," Fritzy Gutman said, though he was forcing remonstrations in a sea of sorrow. "Steinberg, whistle up a tune and let's all get this done. God knows what the lieutenant's got planned for us at dawn."

Steinberg nodded and began to sing Marlene Dietrich's "Du, Du, Liegst Mir im Herzen," and with the sort of brash enthusiasm that's common to the futureless, uniformed young, they sang. And outside the stable, Froelich crushed out his cigarette and vowed to be much harder on these men.

He wanted them to live...

For his part, Major Butler had retreated to his quarters and locked himself inside. He'd shed his dickey and his tunic for a comfy carob-colored cardigan, and his pipe clouds swirled between his oil lanterns, while the overture of *Rigoletto*, broadcast from Catania, crackled from his wireless. Its heavy strings and trumpets full of portent matched his mood.

The garden portrait of his girl sat propped upon his desk,

but he only let her watch and didn't look at her. Instead, he paced around a large plotting table which, with its bedsheet coverup removed, revealed a meticulous model much like the train sets he'd loved to build once as a child.

The model was an island in the shape of a five-foot-long thumb, and it matched the aerial reconnaissance photo that he usually kept hidden. He'd made it out of papier-mâché, using strips of newspaper, flour, and water, and it was hardened now and ready. Near the island's northern tip was a small oval track made of braided radio wire, with a .30-caliber shell in the middle poking skyward. Farther down, toward the knuckle, there were buildings made of matchboxes, trees of scissored chicken feathers, and toothpicks for antennas.

He walked around the table, pipe in teeth, a small can in one hand, paintbrush in the other. Sergeant Major Connor had found those things for him in Agrigento, bartering with a kindergarten teacher in exchange for bars of chocolate. The island and its structures were already glistening green and gray and brown, and now he made the surrounding wooden waters blue.

But his eyes were barely focused, the gin had made them bleary, and he didn't really hear the mournful strains of Verdi. He was hearing the girl's father in the drawing room of their estate near Sheffield, where Butler stood in uniform, having come to ask politely for her hand, and Sir Edward Strathmore stood with his back to him, looking out the window at his foggy acreage, while he smoked a cigarette in a silver holder.

"I'm afraid you're not our kind, Butler. Terribly sorry, old chap. But it's just not on, nor shall it ever be. I'm sure you understand..."

Butler knew exactly what he meant. And it wasn't something he could help. It wasn't something he could change. Sir Edward's declaration and those words were what they were, the way he heard them every single night, the way he'd hear them evermore.

His tired eyes glistened in the lamplight, and he kept on painting.

Twenty-Five

SOFIA'S LETTER ARRIVED IN FROELICH'S HANDS by the strangest of all carrier pigeons. He awoke at dawn, with shafts of early sunlight lancing through his prison window, his woolen blanket thrown off in fits of nighttime sweats, and the splinters of a dream about the Sahara spinning off into the air like a flock of moths he'd startled from a closet.

There beyond his naked feet stood Sergeant Major Connor, his ramrod form filling the doorway like some highlands messenger. His tam-o'-shanter beret was tucked into one epaulette, his great face pink and shiny with a shave, and his thick red hair and waxed mustache almost seemed ablaze.

"Morning, sir," he brogued.

"I'm up, Sergeant Major." Froelich sat up on his bunk, bare chested, looked at his watch and saw it wasn't even five. He caught Connor's gaze fall briefly to his ID disks, and Sofia's silver Star of David nestled there beside them.

"You've got some time, sir," Connor said. "It's not muster for a while."

"All right. What's on your mind?"

Connor marched into the room. He opened a tunic pocket and presented Froelich with a small pale blue envelope.

"This came by way of the bread man, sir," he said. "I intercepted it. But that's just between us two, if you don't mind."

Froelich took the envelope and nodded in conspiracy. This man was hard as iron, yet also made of other things that he kept hidden. But Froelich had no chance to thank him as Connor spun and left. Alone again, he turned the envelope and saw that it was penned with just his name in graceful female script. Afraid of what was in it, he set it on the bed, pulled on his trousers and boots, basin shaved in jerrycan water, and finger-combed his hair. Then he took a breath, sat down on his bunk again, and opened it.

My beloved Bernard,
I write to you this night, from my balcony of wishes. There is a pretty moon in Agrigento. She is shining like a jewel in the waves. I see you in her face and I hear you in her sister sea. I remember every day we had together, and all the words we said under my tree. I pray for you in the church. I beg from both our gods to keep you safe. I will wait for you forever. My heart is yours, Amore mio, wherever you must be.
Fino ad allora,
Sofia

He found it hard to breathe. The letter fluttered in his rifle-calloused fingers. He saw her lovely face and heard her gentle voice and felt her, and everything he'd never been allowed to be, and everything he wanted, filled his swollen heart and tried to overflow his eyes, and it took every bit of strength he had to stop it. He was going to survive all this, he swore, for her if not himself. He'd return one day and find her, no matter what the world did to defy them, and even if she were the only thing surviving, like a battered flower breathing in the sun after a hurricane.

He folded the letter and placed it in the pocket of his Wehrmacht tunic, beside her picture and the testament from Tommy Robbins that still he hadn't dared to read. He blessed Connor in his mind, ate a can of Spam with cold dark tea, then finished dressing like a proper German officer, took his Schmeisser and went back out to face the war.

The morning formation was a near disaster. By the time Froelich arrived, his Wehrmacht kitted Jews were bracing at attention and blinking in a storm of shouts from Fritzy Gutman. The sergeant was pacing back and forth, red-faced and furious, calling out the roll once more in German, the spittle flying from his lips.

"Hasenbein?"

"Präsent, Unterfeldwebel!"

"Rosenberg?"

"Präsent, Unterfeldwebel!"

"Schonberg?"

There was no answer, even as Gutman called out Ricky's name again. Then he strode to Froelich, saluted, and reported with a pained expression, *"Elf, Herr Leutnant. Einer fehlt."* Eleven, sir. One missing.

"Einer fehlt?" Froelich said, and then in English, "Oh, blast."

By that time Butler had appeared, along with Winston, Gurung, and Deighton, and Sergeant Major Connor was standing to one side, scanning the horizons with his field glasses.

"What the hell is going on here, Froelich?" Butler demanded.

"We've got a missing man, sir." Froelich's face was pink with shame and ire.

"What? One day in German kit and already a deserter? Where the hell is he?"

"I don't know, sir."

"Well, you bloody well better find him! And if he's outside of these walls without a pass, which I certainly did *not* authorize or issue, prepare yourself to muster up a firing squad!"

Froelich's spine stiffened. No matter what, he wasn't going to shoot Ricky. He'd shoot Butler first.

"There, sir!" Sergeant Major Connor barked. He'd dropped his glasses to his chest and was pointing off above the heads of the formation, past the stables toward the distant crumbling tower of the radar station. On its parapet stood a small figure facing toward the ocean, his shoulders draped in something like a fringed white shawl and bobbing like a nauseous tourist at the rail of a storm-tossed schooner.

"What the hell's he doing up there?" Butler raged.

And Froelich, with both relief and consternation, squinted off at Ricky in the distance and said, "I think he's praying, sir."

"He's...what?" Butler drew his Webley and fired one shot in the air, wincing all the faces, and Ricky spun around, hopped once like a rabbit, and disappeared. Fifteen seconds later, flush faced and breathless, he charged into the courtyard, his Schmeisser clutched in one hand and his rumpled tallis in the other, and he stomped to attention before Froelich and Butler, shaking like a mound of Jell-O.

"What in God's name were you doing, man?" Butler jammed the pistol back into his holster.

"Sorry, sir, so sorry," Ricky stammered. "Morning invocations, sir. I had to find a spot and face the right direction."

"The right *direction*?" Butler twisted to his left, shot an arm out to the east, and spat, "Jerusalem's *that* way, you bloody idiot!"

The men lost all composure and exploded into laughter. Even Sergeant Major Connor had to bite his lip to hold it in, and Winston, Gurung, and Deighton had to turn away, but everyone could see their shoulders shaking.

"*Achtung!*" Froelich yelled, and his men snapped out of it and braced, and Ricky ran back to his place in the formation as he stuffed his prayer shawl into a Wehrmacht pocket.

Butler glared at them as if he'd love to see them drawn and quartered. Then he turned to his Ghurka hand-to-hand instructor, said, "Sergeant Gurung, hurt them," and stomped off to his quarters.

Gurung didn't need to be encouraged. He shed his British tunic and bush hat, and now in just a singlet, his muscles bulged like a Greco Roman wrestler. A minority himself, he held no animosity for any man who wasn't snowy white or Christian, but these Jews were dressed in things he hated. He'd battled all across North Africa, seen good mates die at the hands of filthy Germans, and those uniforms were like Persian battle pennants to a Spartan.

"If you please, sir." Gurung sneered at Froelich. His voice was like a snorting boar. "Weapons down."

Froelich gave the order, and all the men except for Hasenbein and Felder, gulped as they disarmed. Fritzy Gutman pointed at the courtyard's hard-packed earth and stones and said to Gurung, "Shall I have them fetch some blankets?"

"No," Gurung growled. "The ground in Germany is frozen."

"You may demonstrate on me, Sergeant Gurung," Froelich said as he too removed his tunic.

"With pleasure, sir." Gurung grinned.

They faced each other on the pitch in front of the formation. But Gurung had no clue about Froelich's pugilistic talents, or that Bertie Buck's instructors had taught him Judo and a score of deadly tricks. Gurung only saw a sinewy subaltern, an easy meal. He drew his wicked khukri knife, gripped it overhand, and snarled, yet before he could utter a word of instruction, Froelich flipped him.

Froelich slammed into him, chest to chest, gripped his knife wrist with his left, thrust his right arm underneath his armpit, spun, and hurled him over his shoulder. The men all gasped, and so did Gurung as he smacked onto his back and raised a cloud of dust. Yet undeterred, he tossed his knife away, leaped up, and balled his fists.

Froelich kicked him in the solar plexis, gushing air from Gurung's lungs, then gripped his upper singlet, swept his leg, and slammed him on his back again. Then he crashed down on his ribs, buttocks first, one thigh across his throat, gripped his wrist two-handed, leaned way back, and arm barred him until Gurung choked and smacked the earth with a flailing palm in full surrender.

"Ignore the major's order," Froelich hissed to Gurung's wide-eyed face. "You hurt them, I hurt you. Are we clear?"

"Yessssir," Gurung wheezed.

"Good show. Now carry on."

After that, Froelich interfered no further. He'd stilled whatever bloodlust Gurung had, and the Ghurka fireplug returned to cool professional. He didn't let the men deblouse because their tunics would be good to grab for leverage, but first he spread them out across the pitch and taught them boxer basics.

"Caps in pockets, fists beside your cheeks, now punch as if you mean it... Not like that, Steinberg! Thumbs outside the fingers. We're not tickling the ivories. Left! Right! Harder!"

They battled shadows until the sweat was popping on their foreheads. Then he made them blade their hands and break imaginary collarbones, and they looked like clumsy cooks chopping nonexistent salads.

"Pair off, men. We'll have some hip throws."

Gurung used Gutman for his demonstration. He gripped Fritzy's lapels, turned and hurled him over his hip, and the men all laughed because that looked like jolly fun, though soon it wasn't.

Horst Felder threw Steinberg down so hard that Beethoven screamed, jumped up, and slapped him. Arieh Ben-Zvi bounced David Rosenberg's skull off a rock, and when he went to help him up, Rosenberg bit him in the ankle. Ricky Schonberg, no matter how he turned and twisted, couldn't budge Manfred Hasenbein, so instead he grabbed him in the crotch and squeezed, and Manfred howled and punched him

in the face and Ricky curled into a whining ball. Hans and
Gustave Bloch went at it, but far too civilized for Gurung,
who berated them as fussy dandies until Hans wound up on
Gustave's chest and tried to choke his cousin. Paul Green
and Felix Braun threw each other twenty times until they
both lay on their backs, moaning, and when Moses Bloch
found himself without a partner, Fritzy Gutman faced him
and Moses dropped right to his knees and begged his sergeant
not to break him.

"Bunch of bleedin' birds," Gurung cursed them. "Now
go and fetch your mess tin knives and let's see you murder
sentries."

They limped off to the stables, returned with dull utensils,
and came at one another, bruising ribs and kidneys amid a
choir of shouts in English, French, and German.

"Stick me with it, Felder!"

"Well, stop running backwards."

"*Es ist ein Messer, kein Penis, Steinberg!*"

"*Ma soeur pourrait faire mieux!*"

"Squat down, Hasenbein! How'm I supposed to reach your
throat?"

"Ow! That's my bleedin' liver!"

"*Du kämpfst wie eine Jungfrau!*"

"Gimme back my knife, damn you!"

"Try it from your knees, Schonberg. That's your favorite
position."

"Oh, yeah? Take this you fucker!"

By noon they were battered, bloody, black and blue, uniforms askew and soaking wet. But they'd showed some spunk
and Gurung was quite satisfied, though he kept a skeptical

expression, as sergeants always do. He put them back into formation, joined Froelich side by side, and arms folded, they looked them over.

"What's your take, Gurung?"

"Three killers, sir. Hasenbein, Ben-Zvi, and Felder. A couple of disasters, but the rest will do."

"That's fair enough."

Gurung smiled up at Froelich. "Well, as you ordered, sir, I didn't hurt them."

"No, you didn't." Froelich smiled back. "They did it *for* you."

The afternoon was all about explosives, with Deighton laying out a smorgasbord of dastardly devices on a table. The men were happy to be sitting down for class, though smoking was forbidden, and Deighton's calm demeanor and resemblance to the film star Cary Grant made them feel at ease, till someone pointed out that he only had nine fingers.

He showed them how to use their potato masher hand grenades, then moved on to the ugly phallus headed Panzerfaust, an antitank, shoulder-fired weapon for which you had to be horrifically close to target to be effective. Then he transitioned to claylike bricks of high explosive called Composition B, and the Number Ten pencil detonators that you inserted in the clay to set them off.

"Pay close attention, gents," he said. "You squeeze the copper tube, it breaks a glass vile, then cupric acid eats away the retaining wire until it breaks, and the spring-loaded striker fires the percussion cap. Depending on the type, it'll take ten minutes to an hour."

"You can do it if you've still got all your fingers," muttered Beethoven Steinberg, who cherished his piano digits.

Deighton smiled and held up his left hand, which was missing his ring finger. "I didn't lose it that way."

"How'd it happen, Sergeant?" Moses Bloch asked.

"I bailed out from a Lancaster, hooked my wedding ring on the door, and left it in the plane."

"Oh, God." Ricky Steinberg quickly slipped off his bar mitzvah ring and stuck it in a pocket.

Then Deighton moved on to larger items, satchel charges in canvas carry bags, with lengths of pyrotechnic fuse and percussion cap igniters. And he discovered that many of his students were not your average joes, but had been the prima donnas of their high school science classes.

"What's the burn time of those fuses by the meter, Sergeant?"

"What's the overpressure value of Comp B?"

"How about the deleterious effects of water?"

Deighton finally had to fend off all their intellects, and he closed the session with a laugh and said, "Lads, don't rack your brainy heads with all that stuff. Just make sure it all goes bang, and try like hell not to be there when it does."

That shut them up, and they sat there with the sober images of blinded eyes, shattered eardrums, flying arms and legs, and blackened faces.

Froelich drilled them for the rest of all that day in German. He gave each one a *Soldbuch,* recovered from the corpses of their "tailors," and had them memorize their names, concoct biographies that closely matched their former lives before the war, and recite them under mock interrogation. He told them, as he'd learned from Bertie Buck, that close to truth was always the best cover, and he let them grow their hopes and didn't mention that if they were caught, their false particulars would be irrelevant because their captors would probably just shoot them.

After mess that night, Major Butler ordered Froelich to take his "FJDs"—his filthy Jewish dozen—and test their weapons. Most of them had never fired German rifles or machine guns, and until you pulled the trigger on live ammunition, it would be like sitting on a bronco yet never opening the gate. You had to feel the kicking of the beast and hear its howl to know you could control it.

But they couldn't do that in the castle's courtyard, so Froelich had them climb down to the ocean, and Butler sent Winston, Gurung, and Deighton along to keep an eye out. After Ricky Schonberg's insubordination, he didn't trust them.

They lay down on the beach, stuffed their ears with wads of bore flannel, and banged away at ocean waves and shadows, with tracers zipping through the night and muzzle flashes sending seagulls screaming. Deighton had them hurl grenades, which slaughtered schools of fishes. Winston kicked the men when they fumbled changing magazines, and Gurung banged them on their *Fallschirmjäger* helmets with a pistol butt, to ensure that they could function under pressure.

When they were done, all weapons cleared and safe, Froelich was about to lead them back up to the castle when Fritzy Gutman suddenly dashed off into the darkness and returned with a surprise that posed a problem. An elderly Sicilian couple had been crouching in a furrow, witnessing the cacophony and horrified that Germans had returned to Siculiana.

He had them by their sleeves, like a groom escorting parents to a wedding neither wanted.

"Oh, bloody hell," Froelich groaned when he saw them.

The poor old woman was in terror, in a printed frock and kerchief, rain boots, and clutching a straw fishing basket. Her husband's spindly hair was wild, his eyes like saucers, and he held a wooden fishing pole with a squirming sardinella still dangling from its hook. As the throng of horrid Germans gathered round, the trembling elders slumped to their knees in the sand and babbled in Italian.

"They've seen us, sir," Fritzy Gutman said to Froelich. "They'll blow our covers. What shall we do?"

"I'd shoot them," Winston said as if referring to a pair of rabid raccoons.

"For heaven's sake man, no," Froelich uttered, and then he called out, "Felder!"

Horst Felder ambled up, yet so frightening in his German paratrooper outfit that the couple closed their eyes, laced their bony fingers, and began to pray. But Felder eased onto his knees, took off his helmet and said, *"Non è un problema. Non siamo tedeschi."* It's no problem. We're not Germans.

"Che Dio ci aiuti! Tedeschi!" the couple cried.

"Non," Felder insisted. *"Siamo inglesi."*

"Non! Tedeschi!" The couple wagged their heads as if in Satan's clutches.

Felder looked at Froelich. "They're not buying it, sir. Think we're Germans."

"Well, they're not blind," Deighton said.

"Men." Froelich turned to his commandos. "'God Save the King.' Sing it."

It was a full-throated chorus, twelve hard looking Wehr-macht troops, gun barrels still hot and smoking, singing "'God save our gracious King, Long live our noble King, God save the King!'"

The couple opened their eyes, slack-jawed and blinking. Froelich gave them each a bar of chocolate, but still they held each other's hands and trembled.

"You'd better tell them something," Froelich said to Felder. "Make it up, but make it good."

Felder began to spin a tale in Italian, and at last the couple nodded and their trembling mouths turned to cautious smiles. He touched his finger to his lips, sealing their secret pact, and they agreed and crossed themselves. Then he helped them up and shooed them off, and they went stumbling away into the shadows, holding hands and mumbling.

"What did you tell them?" Froelich asked as Horst got up and brushed himself off.

"Swore them to secrecy, sir. Told them that the fate of all of Italy is in their hands, because we're off to capture Mussolini."

The men all laughed and Froelich slapped his shoulder. "Well, done. That should do nicely." Then he frowned and turned to Winston. "But we're *not* actually going to do that, are we?"

"Damned if I know, sir." Winston shrugged. "Your guess is good as mine."

And they all returned to the castle, still none the wiser.

Twenty-Six

CASTELLO CHIARMONTE HAD A CRUMBLING
chapel. It was there beyond the stables, astride the northern
wall before the radar station, a gloomy medieval cavern of
tangerine stone with only half a roof, as if the Lord had pried
it open to see if anyone still cared.

The chapel had a single stony arch inside, dividing holy
priests from congregants, and high above its podium was a
blistered oil portrait of the velvet cloaked Madonna, holy
child on her lap, smiling down upon her flock. The chapel's
only window was tall and broad and barred, because for many
years the only prayerful were prisoners, and Siculiana's winds
whipped through it, swirled around the rain-stained stony
floor and out the broken door. There were no pews, though
its recent German occupants had dragged in sodden picnic
benches, perhaps defying Hitler's spurning of religion.

No one sat there now in meditation, and no one prayed

there now in supplication, but it was the perfect place for Major Butler's first and final battle briefing.

"All right you men, pay close attention. This isn't Sunday school or Hebrew catechism."

Froelich ground his teeth at that, but also wondered if the major really hated Jews or just said such things to prod them. Anti-Semites salted all the British ranks, yet if that were Butler's case, why the hell had Combined Operations given him the mission? He was no happy shepherd to the Jews, like T.E. Lawrence had been to the Arabs.

"This, gentlemen, is the isle of Usedom. It is located at the most northeastern tip of Germany on the coast of the Baltic Sea."

He tapped his papier-mâché model with a long wooden pointer, where it lay before his congregation on its table like a coffin at a wake. Behind him, tacked below the Madonna, was a large map of Europe and the target area, both sides flanked by aerial reconnaissance photos, all with bright red arrows spearing points of interest.

Froelich and his men sat tightly grouped along the benches. They'd been allowed to smoke, and cigarettes and Hasenbein's pipe fogged the morning shafts of sunlight. Sergeant Major Connor stood beside his master, searching every face for fidgets, while Winston and Deighton guarded from the chapel's rear as if ensuring no one bolted, and Gurung watched the doorway with a Thompson. Moses Bloch had been dispatched to guard the castle's gate. He'd be filled in later.

"This model represents the island's tip, a place called Peenemünde," Butler said. "It is a highly secret Nazi installation where the Germans are developing a ballistic rocket called

the A-4, or *Vergeltungswaffen Zwei*, Vengeance Weapon Two."
He tapped the model's .30-caliber upright shell, which he'd
painted black and white and finned with little cardboard tri-
angles. "It is a five-story missile, with a 925 kilogram warhead of amatol and a range of more than two hundred miles."

"*Gott im Himmel*," Ricky Schonberg whispered.

"Sounds like science fiction," Beethoven Steinberg muttered in wonder.

"The only fiction," Butler snapped, "may be your ability
to foil its murderous intent, so pay attention. Right?"

"Yes, sir," Steinberg said.

"Now, the Wehrmacht have approximately four thousand
scientists and technicians at Peenemünde, most of whom reside
here on the island's eastern middle at a place called Karlshagen."

"Four *thousand*." Arieh Ben-Zvi whistled. "I think we're
gonna need more ammunition."

"Do you mind?" Butler snarled at Ben-Zvi, and Sergeant
Major Connor scorched him with his eyes.

"Shut it," Fritzy Gutman warned him.

"Sorry, sir. Carry on, sir."

"*Thank* you. Moving on," Butler said, and tapped a lower
spot. "Another mile south of Karlshagen is a slave labor camp
at Trassenheide, with three thousand prisoners who build the
Jerries' rocket towers and engineering structures. However,
they are not of interest."

"He surely's got no interest in 'em if they're Jews," Paul
Green whispered to Felix Braun, who elbowed him to shush.

Butler looked up from the model and slapped his pointer
in his palm.

"Now, this past 18 August, in a nighttime bombing mission dubbed Operation Hydra, six hundred RAF Lancasters dropped 1.5 million kilograms of high explosives on Peenemünde. The mission's primary objective was *not*, as one might assume, the V–2 production facilities, but to kill as many Wehrmacht officers and scientists as possible. However, reports from Austrian resistance reveal that while 180 Germans died in the raid, so did more than six hundred slave laborers." Butler let that bit sink in. "Sadly, we were off the mark, and the only significant demise was deputy director Dr. Walter Thiel, while commanding general Dornberger was spared, as was chief rocket scientist, Dr. Werner von Braun. The cost to us was also high, as we lost forty bombers, although one happy note is that as a result of our surprise, General Hans Jeschonnek, Luftwaffe chief of staff, shot himself in Berlin."

"One almost sympathizes," David Rosenberg muttered.

Butler ignored the quip and said, "And now the plot grows serious."

"It's already sounding bloody serious," Horst Felder commented.

Froelich leaned to Fritzy and said through gritted teeth, "Tell them if they don't shut up, I'll shoot them," and Gutman turned and hissed, "Stand *down*."

They looked at him and pursed their lips like truant schoolboys.

"In two nights hence," Butler carried on, "Operation Hydra II commences. That second bombing mission is of no import here, except in terms of timing. Our concern is this man."

Sergeant Major Connor handed Butler a manila envelope, from which he withdrew a glossy black–and–white photograph and showed it to the men. It was a facial portrait of a middle-aged balding man in glasses, wearing a civilian suit. His face was jowly and sad.

"This is Dr. Otto Roth. He is a mischling, a partial Jew, like some of you. Hitler sometimes makes exceptions for the talented, despite the tainted bloodlines."

Manfred Hasenbein stiffened in his chair and clenched his fists. Ricky Schonberg gripped his thigh to still him.

"Otto Roth is a highly skilled physicist, a contemporary of Germany's leading nuclear scientist, Dr. Werner Heisenberg. HQ's concern is that Dr. Roth has been tasked at Peenemünde with developing an atomic warhead for the V-2. Should he succeed, London shall be in the crosshairs, and all the Allied efforts turned to dust."

"One *cannot* split the atom," Hans Bloch whispered to his cousin Gustave. They'd both been vying for magna cum laude before being banished from high school. "Not even Albert Einstein could do it!"

"Private Bloch," Butler snapped. "I know you all believe your brains are far superior to those of other mortals, but you've been deprived of news while in the trenches. Not long ago, at the University of Leipzig, Werner Heisenberg devised an aluminum sphere containing powered uranium metal and heavy water, and inadvertently blew up his entire laboratory building. But please, *do* lecture us on your amateurish theories of improbability!"

Hans blinked and swallowed and said, "Terribly sorry, sir. Nothing further."

"How kind," Butler scoffed. "Now, if I *may*. The objec-

tive of our mission, henceforth called Operation Scepter, is to
locate Dr. Otto Roth, and either get him out, or kill him."

They were all so stunned that no one had a quip or comment. They sat there staring at the major, jaws slack, eyelids
twitching. Then all at once Ricky Schonberg began to laugh
as if someone had just called out "April Fools!" He raised a
chubby finger.

"Sir, are you having us on? You are, right? Like you did
on the parachuting plane..."

"I am *not* having you on, Schonberg," Butler spat. "This
thing is running, even if you pray otherwise from now till
doomsday!"

Ricky's shoulders slumped and he went pale. This time
Hasenbein gripped his thigh to steady him.

"Now, through the same Austrian underground agents,
Otto Roth is aware that we intend to have him, and he's ame-
nable. However, he knows nothing about Hydra II, nor the
date or timing of his rescue." Butler flicked the pointer at a
row of matchbox houses that were painted white with green
roofs. "He resides here in Karlshagen, building number three,
second floor, apartment A. He has been instructed, as a signal,
to have a bottle of wine always showing on his windowsill."

"Red or white, sir?" Horst Felder blurted out, and Fritzy
Gutman turned around and snarled, "I'll kill you Felder, I
swear I will."

"Chardonnay, you idiot," Butler said to Felder. "It's good
for fish or scorched flesh, preferably *yours*." He moved his
pointer to a spot just south of Karlshagen, where he'd fashioned a small building and a roadblock made of wire and a
toothpick. "Note that after Hydra I, the Waffen SS posted a

contingent here at this entry control point, with their command HQ up here, north of the residential structures. We assume their task is to protect the scientists' enclave. I dare say they shall not be friendly."

"And that's where we come in, sir?" Arieh Ben-Zvi asked. "That's why our German guise?"

"Exactly," Butler said, and he turned and faced the map below the Madonna. "And that is also why we cannot parachute directly on the island. Too many Nazi eyes. We shall drop here, on the mainland to the west, and cross the only bridge, here at Wolgast, which leads to Peenemünde."

"We, sir?" Froelich said as his brow furrowed. Until that moment he'd thought that only he and his commandos would be going. Perhaps Butler, Connor, Winston, and Deighton might pass muster costumed up as Germans, but Ghurka Gurung surely wouldn't.

"Yes, *we*, Lieutenant Froelich." Butler turned around. "Tell us. How was it at Tobruk, that you SIGs got the SAS through German lines?"

"We pretended they were our captives, sir."

"Precisely, Froelich. We shall be your prisoners."

Froelich looked at Sergeant Major Connor, who smiled and preened his great mustache. He already knew this. He'd known it all along.

"You and your men shall be a patrol of *Fallschirmjägers* from the 2nd Parachute Division," Butler said, "ostensibly attached to the Luftwaffe's Erprobungskommando 16 at Peenemünde West. The cadre and I shall be a quintet of British saboteurs you've captured in the forest near Katzow, across the inlet." He smiled like a lemur. "Happy All Hallows' Eve."

"If I might, sir," Froelich said, though something cold was balling in his belly as he thought about the last time that he'd tried this and had wound up on his knees in Africa, moments from a firing squad. "Once we're through the gate, and once we've got our man, how do we withdraw?"

"That's the easy bit, by submarine. HMS *Sealion* will surface off the eastern coast across from Trassenheide. Commandos from Special Boat Service will take us off in LCRL inflatable dinghies." Butler looked at his watch, and then from the same manila envelope, withdrew an aircraft manual and tossed it onto Froelich's lap. "There's our transport, a captured Junkers JU-52. We shall depart from Castelvetrano. The aircraft's being fixed with an extra three hundred liters of fuel in a belly drop tank. Clear, thus far?"

"Yes, sir."

"Good. Devise your plan, Lieutenant. Brief me in two hours."

Butler handed off his pointer to Froelich, cocked his chin at Connor, and he and all his crew departed.

Froelich took a breath, rose, and faced his men and said in German, *"Wir machen diesen Hagganah-Stiel."* We'll do this Hagganah-style. He meant the fledgling Jewish defense force in Palestine, where challenges to officers were customary. *"Ich will jede Frage hören."* I want to hear every question.

The men got up and gathered around the model. Hans Bloch came in from sentry duty and Froelich handed him the Junkers manual, telling him to work the ranges, weights, and measure with his brainy cousins. Fritzy Gutman started with a question.

"Shall we have some sort of muster signal at the dropping zone, sir?"

"Not a torch," Beethoven Steinberg cautioned. "Some sort of noise."

"A whistle." Horst Felder put two fingers in his mouth and made a piercing warble. He'd been a pheasant hunter.

"Yes, that's it," said Froelich.

"What's the range from the dropping zone at Katzow to that bridge at Wolgast, sir?" David Rosenberg asked. "We'll need to time that march."

Froelich gestured at the wall map. "Steinberg, take a string and measure it."

"Shall we bloody up the prisoners, sir?" Arieh Ben-Zvi posed. "Kill a chicken from the pantry and take a bottle of it with us?"

"Right," Froelich said. "Gruesome. Good idea."

"Sir, we won't need all the troop in Karlshagen," Manfred Hasenbein said, pointing his pipe stem at the model. "We should divvy up, slice off a diversion section to cover the withdrawal."

"Right," said Ricky Schonberg. "With the MG42, in case the show gets buggered."

"That's us, Ricky. Machine gun crew." Hasenbein grinned at him. "Means we'll be the last ones out, if we're still alive." Ricky's eyes went wide.

"What if they've got sentries on that bridge at Wolgast, sir?" Paul Green asked.

"They surely will," said Felix Braun. "The SS doesn't leave such things to chance."

David Rosenberg had drawn his trench knife, examining

the blade, and said, "Once we cross that bridge, sir, some of us should blow it, in case we're tumbled and they ring for reinforcements."

"Good point," said Froelich. "The major must be of that mind. Explains the class with Deighton."

"We can't make it in one flight, sir," said Moses Bloch as he and his two cousins looked up from the Junkers manual. "We shall have to refuel somewhere on the way."

"Salzburg," Beethoven Steinberg suggested. "Luftwaffe aerodrome."

"That's daft," said Ricky. "Salzburg's just across the road from Berchtesgaden." He meant Adolf Hitler's private mountain hideaway.

"We're not popping in for tea with Hitler, Ricky," Arieh Ben-Zvi scoffed. "Besides, what's your plan then? Pissing in the tanks when they run dry?"

"Keep the ideas coming," Froelich said. "Even if they're blather, I want to hear them."

It went on like that into the afternoon, with Froelich taking detailed notes, scrapping plans and making new ones. He sent someone to brew up tea and bring back marmalade and biscuits, and they argued, counterplotted, and shared dark jokes while planning every detail to the minute. When at last Butler returned with Connor and the rest, he took a seat up front, arms folded, while Froelich took the podium and presented.

"So then, sir," he said. "Operation Scepter." He tapped the pointer on the map below Madonna. "Beginning with the aircraft. The range from Castelvetrano to Peenemünde is 1,515 miles. The Junkers' range with extra tank is only half of that, and with her cruising speed of 153 miles per hour,

that means a journey of ten hours, without weather. We shall
have to land at the Luftwaffe aerodrome at Salzburg to refuel."

"All right, Froelich," Butler said. "And how do you pro-
pose to pull that off?"

"I shall bluff, sir."

"Bold, but I shall see about a set of phony orders. Now,
what about the pilots after drop?"

"They'll only have enough fuel left to make it out to Bon-
holm Island in the Baltic."

"That's Denmark, Froelich. It's German occupied."

"I know, sir. Can't be helped," Froelich said, knowing it was
cruel and damning the Junkers' crew to certain capture. "Perhaps you'll put them in for the Victoria Cross. Moving on."

After that he went through every detail, step by step, minute by minute. He called on every section leader to recite
their tasks, and whenever Butler scoffed or challenged them,
they had a perfect train of logic and a backup. It was clear,
after an hour, that Froelich hadn't left a morsel on the table,
and when at last he said, "That's all, sir," Butler rose and took
his pointer back.

"Impressive," Butler said, though it seemed the compliment
was sticking in his throat. "Study it, review it, prepare your
kits, and be asleep by midnight. We leave at dawn."

He marched off for the door, taking Connor, Winston,
Deighton, and Gurung along with him. Yet before he left
he turned and said, "I suggest you all takes gloves and heavy
sweaters. It's going to be cold."

Froelich didn't sleep that night. No one else did either. But
he was all alone in his stable master's quarters, with no one

there to share his fears or hopes, and just a blank cold moon outside his prison window, which said nothing to commiserate.

He cleaned his Schmeisser and his pistol, tucked some chocolate bars and hardtack in his battle harness, and sharpened up his German bayonet. He didn't pray, because the only thing he believed in was Sofia, and with that he lit a candle, set it on an ammunition crate, and with his pencil wrote a letter.

My dearest Sofia, he began, then hesitated, and went on.

I cannot promise you a future. I can only promise that I love you.

He balled it up, began again, and then once more. Yet every time it was the same, as that was all he really had to offer. But then, a few more sentences.

This war is like a dream, and we are in it. But like all dreams I hope someday that we will wake in sunlight and in each other's arms. Please know that you are all I've ever wanted.

He signed it, *Yours Forever*, with his name, folded it up carefully, placed it in a small brown army envelope and sealed it. He wrote *Sofia Bellina* on its face, and shuddered with a sigh because he had no known address for her, nor any way to post it.

"Would you like to post that, sir?"

Froelich turned to find Sergeant Major Connor once more standing in his doorway.

"I would, Sergeant Major. But how?"

"Meet me at the sentry's gate, sir. Five minutes." Connor left.

Froelich waited, staring at his watch until the five ticked over, while he wondered why this man might be serving as the priest to Romeo and Juliet, and decided that it didn't matter. He tucked the letter in his pocket and walked into the castle courtyard.

All was dark. The stars were high and bright, a black breeze swept across the stones, and the only light was from a single oil torch flickering from a stick beside the men's stable. Across the courtyard Butler's window also glowed with something burning orange, but that was all, and Froelich saw that Connor stood beside the stone wall gap that posed the only portal to the town.

He walked to him. Connor held a German rifle. Whatever sentry Fritzy Gutman had posted there on watch, Connor had dismissed him.

"Take your letter to my jeep, sir," Connor whispered in his brogue. "The major's still awake, so please be hasty. I'd like to keep my rank if you don't mind." He smiled and stepped aside.

Froelich took the broken stairs that hugged the castle wall. He hadn't felt the aching in his thigh for days, but felt it now, and he wondered how he'd ever make that parachute jump and stand up afterward, but he'd have to, for his men if nothing else. He reached the bottom, stumbled in the dark, regained his footing, and walked between a grove of palms whose leaves were clicking in the wind. Then he saw Connor's jeep gleaming in the lot before the castle's open iron gate, and standing there beside it was Sofia.

His heart pounded in his chest. He nearly fainted. Her eyes glowed and she touched her fingers to her mouth and made a sound like angels would when God at last appears. She wore a threadbare coat, open to the printed flowered dress he loved and always would, and she staggered forward on her crutch and he ran to her.

They did not speak. They clasped each other, crushed each other, and they kissed and clutched each other's hair, then pressed their lips across their cheeks and eyes and foreheads, imprinting memories that never could be taken ever more. Froelich pulled the letter from his pocket and crushed it into her trembling happy hands, and they drank each other's eyes and said each other's names, but that was all.

Then Froelich heard the engine, and he looked past Sofia's flow of curls and dainty shoulder. There was Fabrizio, sitting on his motorcycle, smiling. They turned and went to him, arm in arm, and as three they hugged each other where Fabrizio sat, as if they'd all been family born together and were still somehow breathing blessed air, even with the war.

Fabrizio gave Froelich two fresh oranges. That was all he had. Froelich helped Sofia on the motorcycle, and kissed her one more time, and gently, to remember. Fabrizio turned and gripped the front of Froelich's German tunic, without comment on the Iron Cross that gleamed there. His eyes were full and he whispered, "Come back to us, Bernardo." And then he turned the motorcycle and drove it through the gate, and they were gone.

Froelich turned away, a calmness in his soul, and that was all he needed. He climbed the stairway, breathing in the night, thinking that if this was all there was to be, he'd found that place that few men ever dreamed of. He reached the top, where Connor stood there looking off to things inside his mind that Froelich couldn't know. Connor turned and smiled down at Froelich, and nodded.

"Thank you, Sergeant Major," Froelich said.

"A pleasure, sir."

"Tell me. Why did you do it?"

Connor shrugged. His smile held.

"I just reckoned that you're going to die, sir. We all are, aren't we?"

Twenty-Seven

THE GERMAN BEAST ARRIVED AT DAWN. IT was nothing like the American or British transport airplanes with their comely curved nacelles, rounded snouts, and gently sweeping ellipses of graceful wings. The Junkers JU-52 looked as though it had been sliced from arctic ice, all square angles in its fuselage and wingtips, its razor tail and iron cockpit windows, with a machine gun sprouting from its dorsal as if the Teutonic theory of aerodynamics was to murder heaven, rather than seduce it.

It taxied down the strip at Castelvetrano, its three enormous engines and propellers whipping up dust devils, the roaring creature leaning back upon its fat black wheels, nose tipped up in haughty challenge. And when Froelich and his men first saw it, from where they'd climbed down to the runway from their Bedford truck, indeed its steely skin painted like a lizard, with Maltese crosses and a tail-emblazoned swastika, frightened each and every one of them, though no one said it.

The plane was followed by two lorries full of parachutes. It stopped and cut its engines, and so did they, and the drivers and their quartermasters left their cabs and stood there speechless for a moment. They too were secret soldiers from Combined Operations, yet they'd never seen a pack of German paratroopers standing on an Allied strip as if it were Oktoberfest in Munich. Then Major Butler and his cadre arrived in their two jeeps, also dressed as horrid Germans, and the quartermasters looked as though they might turn tail and run.

"All right you men," Butler called out in the frigid morning air. "Stop staring like you've all seen Jacob Marley's ghost. Have at it."

That snapped the spell. The quartermasters broke out all the parachutes, plus a weapons canister resembling an aluminum torpedo. With the help of Deighton, Winston packed the canister with the Mauser rifles, MG42, British Stens, the MP43 *Sturmgewehr* assault rifle, ammunition, and explosives. But then Froelich interceded and said to him, "Myself, Gutman, Felder, Rosenberg, and Ben-Zvi shall all be jumping with our Schmeissers."

"That's mighty risky, sir," Winston objected. "I can rig 'em underneath your pits, but they might snap your ribs ya know."

"Better broken ribs than all of us jumping in unarmed."

Winston looked at Major Butler for support.

"Just bloody do it, Winston," Butler snapped. "It's Froelich's show."

The canister went underneath the Junkers in its bomb bay and Froelich formed the men into a line, along with Butler and his crew. Each man swung a parachute onto his back, and while Winston tightened every strap and buckle, they shivered and their breaths steamed in the air, yet no one made a quip or comment. But Winston didn't snap the reserve chutes to their bellies, and said to Froelich, "The dodgy Germans don't use reserves, sir. We'll pile them in the back and don them only after Salzburg."

"All right," Froelich said. "That's your bailiwick."

Winston had them carry the reserves, and with their static lines clenched in their teeth like bridled horses, he turned them all to face the Junkers' door. He waddled to the metal ladder, then bowed and swept one arm like a butler at a ball. "By your leave, gents, all aboard."

One by one they struggled up the ladder. Fritzy Gutman was the last, and he turned and said, "Goodbye, Sicily. I loved you for a while," and went inside the gloomy cavern. Someone slammed and latched the door, like the locking of a coffin. The men squeezed themselves onto the tube and canvas benches and passed back the reserves to make a pile near the tail, where Gurkha Gurung covered up the pile with a tarp. In Salzburg, he'd have to cover himself too. There were no Nepalese *Fallschirmjäger*, as far as anyone knew.

The engines coughed and spat blue smoke outside the airplane's rows of small square windows. The Junkers rattled like a freight train. Froelich waddled forward to the nose, passing Major Butler, who was chewing on his pipe and examining a map, with Connor there beside him. He squeezed into the cockpit, where the pair of RAF pilots were dressed in Luftwaffe leather jackets, jaunty airmen's caps, black earphones, and gloves. He tapped them on their shoulders and they turned. They were very young, but so was he, and that seemed normal.

"Good morning, gents," he called above the engine roar. "I'm terribly sorry about the arrangements."

He meant the fate they had to face, and knew it. In Denmark, chances were high that they'd be captured.

"Oh, that's quite all right, Lieutenant." The pilot grinned. "I think our odds are still better than yours."

And they were off...

The skies above the ocean were magnificent. The air was cobalt blue, the clouds were here and there yet small and soft like curled up sleeping rabbits, and below the plane the greens and tans of Sicily fell away to rows and rows of glistening gentle waves. They headed north and low, across the Mediterranean toward distant Rome, and the swelling sun of later morning warmed the vibrating steel fuselage, and the shafts of yellow streaming through the windows made the future brighter, if only for a moment. The thrumming of the engines thwarted speech, except with closest neighbors, yet there was nothing much to say and they all relaxed their bones.

Froelich signaled from his perch up forward that everyone should loosen up their chin straps, and two canteens of lukewarm tea were passed around for modest sips, along with tins of crackers. The piss pot followed that, a wide-mouthed milk flask, and finding shriveled penises between their thigh straps made them point and snicker like schoolboys on a field trip. With jangling nerves they used up half their cigarettes, and even Steinberg smoked, although he never had before. Manfred Hasenbein crossed his ankles on the deck, lit his pipe, leaned back against the bulkhead, pulled a folded copy of *Berliner Morgenpost* from his trouser pocket, and read it like a father in his Sunday morning salon, which engendered peals of laughter. They knew that soon their smiles would be gone.

An hour later, when the coast of western Italy was looming in the cockpit windscreen, Froelich felt relieved that soon at least they'd all be safe from Allied hawks hunting Nazi airplanes. Half the men were sleeping, chins on chests, dreaming of other worlds before the war and after, when suddenly an alarm bell rang inside the cabin, triggered by the pilots. The men all snapped awake and Major Butler struggled up, jammed his face into the cockpit, then turned and cupped his fingers to his mouth and yelled to Froelich, "Spitfire!"

Froelich felt a rush of panic. He jumped up from his seat and smeared his face against a port-side window, and there it was above, diving toward them in its murderous intent. He couldn't have the pilots radio the Spitfire and claim they were not Germans. That had only worked once in his life, and barely so, and then the pilots banked the Junkers hard to starboard and dove down toward the ocean, and he crashed onto the floor as a cannon shell pierced the roof and exploded out a window right next to Ricky Schonberg's head.

"The machine gun!" Froelich yelled to Manfred Hasenbein and shot a finger at the dorsal turret, as all the men tried to plug their faces deep between their knees.

"He's a Brit, sir!" Hasenbein yelled back in protest.

"He'll kill us all if you don't do it," Froelich shouted. "Drive him off!"

The Junkers pitched and rolled and screamed as Hasenbein struggled toward the ceiling turret. He pulled the saddle down, yanked the hatch, and as it had no canopy the wind roared through the fuselage and snatched his *Berliner Morgen-*

post from his pocket, which pinwheeled through the cabin and shredded into tatters, smearing gawking faces with its news. He climbed into the metal gun frame, totally exposed, cursing as the howling wind slapped his cheeks and streamed his eyes. He racked the MG15 machine gun and swung it. The Spitfire had turned back, heading toward him, but his trembling finger wouldn't pull the trigger even though he knew by God he had to.

Then all at once another shape appeared, a black shadow darting from a cloud, and the Spitfire's tail exploded in a hundred pieces. It rolled onto its back and went spinning toward the ocean, too fast for its pilot to get out and use his parachute, and as it burst a plume of water, a German Messerschmitt BF-109 came roaring over Hasenbein's head, so close he thought that he could touch it.

He gripped the turret's frame and slumped there while his heart still hammered. A moment later, the leopard-colored Messerschmitt appeared just off the port side, cruising in its pride beside the Junkers. The German pilot in his leather cap and goggles grinned at Hasenbein and saluted. Manfred, though he was crying, nodded and returned the gesture back. What else could he do but thank him? He wiped his eyes, slipped below, and closed the hatch.

It grew dark near the Alps. Whatever feeble conversations they had forced before were gone now from all their brains. Froelich walked the line inside the claustrophobic fuselage, trying to buck up the men and ensure they still were focused, but the wind whistled like a banshee through Ricky's punctured window, the heating runnels in the Junkers' floor barely warmed their boots, and somewhere deep in Austria, it snowed.

The Junkers bucked on through the storm another hour. The pilots' windscreen wipers flicked off nails of hail, bursts of lightning flashed the frosted wings and they hunched and squinted at their compass, fuel gauges, and altimeter, trying not to smack into a mountain. The airplane shuddered up and down as fists of turbulence assailed it, and soon the men were gritting teeth and trying to control their wretched stomachs.

Near the tail, Felix Braun tore off his helmet, bent over and vomited inside it. Sergeant Deighton took it from him sympathetically and poured some canteen water in the steaming mess, but having nowhere to dispense of it he had to spill it on the metal floor, where almost instantly the bile froze in chunks of half-digested crackers. No one cursed at Braun, as half of them were close to hurling too, and Hasenbein and Major Butler flamed their pipes to quell the stench, and everyone felt bad for Felix because soon he'd have to don that putrid helmet once again.

Nearing Salzburg, the pilots took the Junkers down below the pelting clouds and summoned Froelich to the cockpit. He peered beyond the spinning nose propeller, seeing nothing but a blackened bowl braced by the craggy peaks of Berchtesgaden and Bad Reichenhall. With Allied bombers pounding every Nazi airfield, the Luftwaffe wouldn't light the strip unless they had to.

He took the pilot's microphone, pretended he was him, and called the tower.

"*Salzburg, das ist JU-52, alpha 269, Kommandotruppe 13, die zum Tanken hereinkommt. Beleuchte deine Landebahn an.*" Salzburg, this is JU-52, alpha 269, Commando Troop 13, coming in to refuel. Light your runway.

"Kommandotruppe 13?" the crackling tower queried.

"Ja! Mach es jetzt!" Yes! Do it now!

Froelich held his breath, but then they did it, and a double line of landing lights lit the snow-swept strip dead ahead. He gripped the cockpit's door frame, the pilots dropped the flaps and cut the engines, and the Junkers' tires bounced once, and then again, and they skewed and skidded to stop in a cloud of propwash blizzard, almost at the very end.

Froelich quickly doffed his parachute and made sure his Iron Cross was there below his throat. Butler handed him an envelope stamped with Wehrmacht seals and swastikas. He slung his Schmeisser and headed toward the door as headlights from some rumbling vehicle flickered through the fuselage, and he saw Gurung at the back snuggling in the pile of reserve chutes, where Winston covered him up with the tarp and sat on it.

"Gustave has to shit, sir," Moses Bloch pleaded for his cousin.

"So do I," said Arieh Ben-Zvi.

"Hold it," Froelich snapped. "Everyone can shit in Germany."

He opened the door, a swirl of frothy snow burst into the cabin, and then a face appeared and looked around.

"Who are you?" the Luftwaffe sergeant demanded.

"Geh mir aus dem Weg." Get out of my way, Froelich barked, and hopped down on the runway.

Lights blazed in his face. Troops were hunching there with

rifles. Froelich shoved the envelope into the sergeant's chest and growled, "Read it."

Shivering in his great coat, the sergeant looked at Froelich's blazing eyes and opened the orders.

"Kommandotruppe 13?" he said. "I haven't heard of it. And you are... Lieutenant Heinkel?"

"Yes, and you've forgotten your salute, you idiot!"

The sergeant clicked his heels and snapped a trembling glove up to his brow. "Excuse me, sir."

"We're headed for Berlin. I need fuel *now*. Get it."

"But sir, we have no notice of..."

Froelich snatched the paper from his hands and flicked the bottom with his finger.

"Whose signature is that?" he barked.

"Adolf... Hitler...sir."

"That's correct. So call him up and wake him. I hear he *loves* that. Now move!"

The sergeant turned and skulked away, and used the radio inside his Kübelwagen, and soon a fuel truck appeared. Froelich felt a weakness of relief crawl up his legs, yet stood there glaring and impatient. It took half an hour with frozen hoses pumping life into the wing tanks, during which he backed up to the Junkers' door and slipped one hand inside and raised a thumb, so everyone would know the bluff was working.

At last the tanks were locked, the fuel truck pulled away, and the sergeant once more presented himself to Froelich, this time with the proper posture.

"Lieutenant Heinkel, my captain said that I should have a look inside before you leave, sir."

"Tell him he can come down here himself and look inside my *ass*."

With that he climbed back in the airplane, slammed the door, and saw his men were grinning at him from the benches. Fritzy Gutman said to him, *"Sie sind eine Karte, Leutnant."* You're a card, sir, and Froelich smirked and strode into the cockpit and said, "Let's get the hell out of here, before they call the Führer."

The weather worsened east of Regensburg. The roiling thunderclouds could not be skirted, as they towered from the German valleys to the lightless heavens, and adding injury to insult, a headwind slapped the Junkers' face as if Zeus himself were punishing Athena. The airplane bucked and whined and struggled, its propellers whipping snow across the wings like windmills churning salt, and the men bounced on the benches, gripping anything they could to keep from tumbling to the floor. Froelich couldn't promise them improvement, as that was up to God, and besides the roar was just too great for speech.

No one ate a cracker. No one sipped from their canteens. And for the first time since the start of the adventure, the flight was so much worse than the fear of parachuting, that all they wanted was to get out of the fucking airplane.

Somewhere north of Nuremberg the storm began to clear, and the pilots dropped the plane to just a thousand feet so its exhausted engines could bite some thicker air and save on fuel. They weaved the plane along the twisting valley between Erfut and Gera, where through the frosted windows the lights of villages and farmers' huts looked like fireflies struggling in black water, and when they broke out on the flatter plains near Leipzig, a panicked battery of antiaircraft 88s tried to shoot them down. Again the Junkers jerked from left to right, slamming all the men against each other as arcing orange tracers rose to slay them, but they bolted through the iron maelstrom. And finally the clouds were swept away and the sky was full of stars outside Berlin, where far below the fires glowed like wild barbecues from British bombers.

The copilot emerged and cupped his mouth to Major Butler's ear, who passed the message down till Fritzy Gutman yelled in Froelich's face, "Thirty minutes, sir." Froelich signaled Winston, who passed out all of the reserves and waddled through the fuselage, rigging every man and slapping each one's helmet. For Froelich and the other four with Schmeissers, he strapped the weapons over their left shoulders, then tied them to their harnesses with short lines from his rigging pocket, and yelled for each to hug them like a baby hugs his mum. Then he pulled their static lines and clipped them to the ceiling's taut steel cable, and Ricky Schonberg closed his eyes and swore he wouldn't open them again until he felt the ground.

Major Butler summoned Froelich with a wave, and Froelich came and bent his face to him.

"I shall lead the pack, Lieutenant," Butler shouted.

Froelich shook his head and shouted back, "These are *my* men, Major. If you do, you shall find yourself alone."

Butler's face turned red, yet he relented, and the copilot appeared again, thrust up all the fingers in one glove and yelled, "Five minutes!"

"On your feet, lads!" Winston shouted, and as they struggled upright, clenching anuses and bladders, he marched Froelich to the jump door and grabbed his static line and snapped it. Froelich turned and looked at all his men, raised a thumb and nodded, though his legs were shaking terribly. Then Winston opened up the door, slammed it against the outer fuselage and locked it, and the wind roared into the cabin like a hurricane.

Froelich took position. He gripped the metal door frame bars and stared into a freezing night of nothingness, while the typhoon slapped his cheeks and whipped his uniform. The plane was roaring at a thousand feet, with all the stars blurring by like comets and the land below a racing rug of blackened trees and whiteness. His pulse pounded in his throat as Winston gripped his harness, and then the thundering engines cut to drones, someone shouted something, Winston smacked his buttocks, and Froelich saw Sofia's face, and jumped.

Twenty-Eight

NOTHING IN HIS LIFE HAD EVER BEEN SO QUIET.
It felt like he'd been stuffed inside an empty oil drum from
dawn till midnight while a pack of evil elves banged on it
with hammers, and now the elves were gone and he was sitting in the middle of the sky on a gently swaying hammock.

His thighs ached from the yank and his neck was sore from
whiplash, but above him his parachute rippled like a silken
bed sheet and the Junkers was a mumbling bird slinking off
into the night as it disgorged a line of kicking legs and blos-
soms. He didn't have much time, so he reached up, clutched
the risers, pulled them to his ears, tucked his head down, and
jammed his boots together. The ground below looked soft
and white and gentle, but then the shapes of rocks and trees
were growing in his sight and rushing by, and he closed his
eyes, forgetting everything that Winston taught him, and
smacked into a hillock like a sandbag. The Schmeisser banged
his ribs and took his breath away, the parachute collapsed,

then caught the wind and tried to hang him, but he just lay there for a moment in the snow, looking at the stars, absolutely stunned to be alive.

He found his boot knife, reached up and sliced the shroud lines till the parachute surrendered, rolled onto his knees, doffed the harness, and freed his Schmeisser. He yanked the canopy into a messy ball and quickly stuffed it in the snow as best he could and got up on his feet. His breaths were steaming in the air like a puffing locomotive, and he was standing in a great white meadow surrounded by enormous pines. If no one had been hung up in a tree, it would be a miracle. He heard Felder's warbling whistle and started toward it.

On the far side of the meadow the men were gathering around the weapons canister and had already cracked it open. Hasenbein was shouldering the MG42 with nonchalance as if he'd hiked there from a picnic, Arieh Ben-Zvi was pulling out explosives, Rosenberg and Steinberg were still trembling with adrenaline and pissing in the snow, and in the moonlight Ricky Schonberg's face was paper white from the horror of his leap into the night.

To one side Major Butler and his men had shed their German costumes, revealing British uniforms and donning woolen caps. They were fixing Sergeant Major Connor's left arm with a sling to make him look less threatening, and smearing chicken blood on faces, necks, and knuckles. As Paul Green and Felix Braun rushed up breathless, Froelich counted all the heads and whispered, "Who's missing?"

"The bloody Blochs, sir," Horst Felder whispered back.

"I saw a brolly in a tree," Winston said from where Ghurka Gurung was bloodying his nose like a theatre makeup artist.

"Cock up on the landing," Hasenbein snarled. "Why'm I not surprised?"

"Never mind," Froelich said. "Check your weapons, fix grenades and ammunition, take the Stens from the prisoners."

Butler and his men had forgotten about that bit in the excitement. They surrendered their Stens, but didn't like it.

"There they are, sir!" Paul Green pointed. Hans and Gustave Bloch were trudging toward them through the drifts with Moses in the middle, his arms slung around their shoulders and his teeth bared in a grimace.

"Broke his ruddy leg," Gustave panted as they arrived.

"We had to cut him down, sir," said Hans.

"I'm so sorry, Lieutenant," Moses groaned.

"Get your weapons, Blochs," Froelich ordered. "Then the rest of you cover up the canister."

Major Butler walked to Froelich and said lowly, "You should leave him. Any German would."

"I am not a German," Froelich said, then turned to all his men. "Quickly lads, gather round."

They formed a semicircle in the snow, with Ben-Zwi and Felder facing outboard, squinting at the woods. Froelich looked at each, making sure their German gear and arms were proper. Moses stood there on one leg propped between his cousins, trying not to groan. His fractured lower right knee was cruelly crooked.

"From now on, only German," Froelich said, "at least when we're speaking to the prisoners, which only one man shall do. Right?"

"Right, sir." Gutman nodded.

"*Nur Deutsch. Verstanden?*" Froelich glared at the

"Jawohl," they all replied.

He pulled a compass from his pocket, turned until he faced the south and said, *"Gehen wir, schnell,"* and began to march off through the snow.

"What shall we do with Moses?" someone whispered.

"His name is Fritz," Froelich said over his shoulder. "Carry him."

They walked a mile south-southeast, heading for the mainland's shoreline, with Froelich in the lead, glancing at his compass. Navigationwise, the plan was simple. Cross the bridge, traverse three miles, come to a "T," and turn left for the Nazi residences. He kept his British prisoners in the middle between his point and rearguard Germans, their fingers laced behind their necks. Hans and Gustave Bloch took turns piggybacking Moses. The drifts were shin deep, they trudged through clouds of their own lung steam and soon they all were sweating, yet still it was much better than the waves at [c]uliana and no one bitched about the march.

The bridge at Wolgast first appeared beyond a copse of [bla]ckened elms, a 150-foot affair of gleaming girders topped [with] wooden planks. Concrete stanchions propped it up from [the] waves of Peenemünde's narrow channel, which looked [dark] and freezing cold, yet being full of Baltic salt there was [no ice]. On the far side of the bridge, starlight glimmered off [the he]lmets of some sentries and their rifles, and beyond that [Peene]münde hunched below the night, a flat expanse of bris[tling tr]ees like a hairy sleeping serpent.

[Froel]ich led the men into the woods, raised a fist and took [a knee, a]nd they all followed suit. He turned to Fritzy Gut[mann, wh]ispered, "Ben-Zvi and Steinberg," and Fritzy passed the message back and soon both men were crouching there beside him.

"You two know your task," Froelich said in German. "When we cross, take the rear, then slip away and climb down the embankment. Set your charges in the middle." He tapped his watch and showed it to Ben-Zvi, then aimed a glove due east across the island. "In one hour, if all's quiet, bugger off and head straight that way for the beach. But if you hear gunfire first, just blow it." He looked at Steinberg's sallow face and gripped his arm because the boy was shaking. "You'll be all right. Give yourselves sixty seconds for your fuses and get out the other side."

"Yes, sir," Steinberg croaked.

"*Leutnant*," Ben-Zvi whispered. "You know if you can't make it to the beach, this bridge is your only way out."

"And if we cock it up and they summon reinforcements," Froelich said, "this bridge is their only way in."

Just then a peal of thunder rumbled from the blood, which was strange because the skies above were cloudless. The men all squinted through the woods, where two great flaming balls of orange rolled above the trees of Test Stand VII, followed by enormous gouts of smoke and the roar of the fuel engines. From the middle of the hellish conflagration the black-and-white spear of a V-2 rocket slowly climbed the sky, then raced off toward the moon, spitting fire from its tail, and disappeared into the night with a final whine.

All the men gawked at the sight. They'd never seen anything like that before, and Froelich turned to find his two sappers there beside him.

"Well, if you believe in God, Froelich," Butler said, "that was your holy signal."

They marched across the bridge like Teutonic knights stomping from Valhalla, prodding at their bloodied prisoners and cursing them in German, who damned them back in English. The Blochs put Moses down and gripped him under his pits, skating him across the creaking timbers, while below them underneath the planks Ben-Zvi and Steinberg worked their way along the horizontal girders, gripping angled uprights that were bolted to the bridge bed like a jungle gym. As Froelich and the odd contingent neared the other side, a German corporal and two privates dressed in winter camouflage and white helmets stepped out to challenge them.

"Who goes there?" the corporal called. He had a pistol in his hand.

"Second Parachute," Froelich called back. "We've got British prisoners. Taking them to Karlshagen."

"We've heard nothing about this, sir," the corporal said.

"Your lack of intelligence isn't my concern," Froelich snapped. "Stand aside." And he stormed right past them.

They held their breaths, yet no one said another word and the sentries only watched them. They broke out from the bridge onto a plowed tarmac road that weaved between tall firs, their fir tops rustling in the wind and weeping snow, and Froelich turned as he walked faster and said to Hasenbein, "Manfred, take the cripple." Hasenbein gave the MG42 to Ricky Schonberg, fell back to the rear, pulled Moses from the Blochs' sins and slung him over both his shoulders like a fireman's mummy, just as Froelich turned the march into a run. They pounded down the roadway for nearly twenty min-

utes, spewing breath and sweating, their weapons banging ribs
and hips, with five men suffering the added weights of captured British Stens. Their boots slapped tarmac as they raced,
their helmets bounced and punished skulls, and they gasped
and prayed that it would end, but Froelich had a clock inside
his head and only took them faster. Then at last they skewed
around a long right-curving bend, the roadway stretched and
straightened through a tunnel of trees leaning inward like
a wedding arch, and lights winked up ahead and Froelich
halted. The men skidded to a stop, bent over, gripped their
knees and tried to breathe, sweat dripping off their chins and
noses.

"Put me *down*," Moses groaned to Hasenbein. "My testicles."

"Shut up," Hasenbein snarled. "You won't need your balls
just yet."

Froelich moved them to the shoulder and let them gather
their composure. His thigh ached in the cold, but he had the
thought that warfare in the winter was preferable to desert.
He raised a pair of field glasses and peered ahead.

At the piney tunnel's end, a white sentry pole was lowered
across the road, with leopard smocked SS sentries on both
sides and floodlights overhead, painting the roadblock in an
oval yellow glow. To the right he saw a gatehouse built of
timbers like a mountain hut in Linz. From a flagpole on its
slanted roof a red-and-white Wehrmacht battle flag snapped
in the wind, with a black swastika and corner SS lightning.
Communications wires ran from the eaves, draping from the
block to a twelve-foot wooden pole, then another and another, weaving left and north beside the road to Rohr.

He panned his glasses left, and through the trees he saw the distant clusters of white buildings. Somewhere there was Dr. Otto Roth.

"The Blochs to me," he said to Fritzy. "Just the ones with legs."

Hans and Gustave jogged up from the rear. Hans had his Mauser rifle and the Panzerfaust, and Gustave gripped the MP43 *Sturmgewehr* assault rifle. It was heavy and his arms were shaking. Froelich pointed through the trees.

"Cut the telephone wires quickly, then set up where we planned," he whispered. "If we return in peace, just fall in line. If we're on the run, let us pass, then let them have it."

Wide-eyed and grim, they nodded and tiptoed off into the woods. Froelich looked at Major Butler, who nodded too, and the Brits resumed their prisoner postures and they marched.

The sentry pole loomed larger. The four sentries turned and bared their rifles. Froelich heard Bertie Buck's voice inside his head, *"Here we go,"* and someone shouted something and an officer stepped out from the gatehouse. He was an SS lieutenant, wearing pressed woolen grays, a peaked cap, double lightning on his collar, and an Iron Cross below his throat. One black glove was posted on his pistol holster and spread his jackboots on the far side of the pole, chin tipped in challenge.

Froelich stopped before the roadblock, raised a glove and "Heil Hitler. Guten Abend."

"Heil Hitler." The SS man had blond eyebrows, a dueling scar and ice green eyes. "And you are?"

"Winkel, Klaus, Second Parachute, attached to Erprobungskommando 16."

"Heinkel?" The SS lieutenant smiled. "Like the airplane maker?"

"An uncle." Froelich smiled back. "And you are?"

"Plauder, Jurgen, Waffen SS." The Nazi peered over Froelich's shoulder at his cowed and bloody prisoners. "And these?"

"British," Froelich said. "We caught them in the woods outside Katsow."

"Why didn't you just shoot them? You know the Führer's order about these damned commandos." He sneered and thrust his chin at Gurung. "Especially that black one."

"Well, I once had tea with Field Marshal Rommel," Froelich said. "He asked me how the Führer expected us to glean intelligence from dead men."

"Oh you *did*, did you?" The SS officer laughed. "Well the' Heinkel, come on in."

The sentries tipped the pole up. Froelich led his troop the pool of light. Plauder pointed north along the roa

"Our command post is up there on the north sid residences. I'll call and tell them that you're coming. stapo goon will *love* this."

He went into the gatehouse. Froelich glanc who looked up at the sky as both crossed their r praying that the Blochs had cut the wires. If the post and Froelich failed to show, alarm ringing. Froelich almost lit a cigarette, b fingers. Plauder came back out again.

"My goddamn telephone's not worki disgusted. "Well, I shall escort you."

Just what we fucking need, Horst Fe and Ricky exchanged eye rolls. Ar walked right up to Felder and said, "Do I know you, Corporal?"

Felder braced to attention. "I don't think so, sir."

Lieutenant Plauder thrust his palm out. *"Soldbuch."*

Felder fumbled in his pocket and produced the soldier's booklet, while Froelich's finger tightened on his Schmeisser trigger. Plauder flipped the booklet open.

"Stiegel, Karl," he said as he perused the pages. "From?"

"Cologne, sir." The sweat was crawling down Felder's armpits.

"I know it well," Plauder said. "Such a beautiful cathedral. My aunt lives in the flats across from the main entrance."

Felder swallowed. "I don't recall the flats there, sir. Only the market."

"Ah, yes, correct." Plauder gave the *Soldbuch* back, then turned and jutted his chin at Hasenbein and his burden, Moses Bloch.

"And what's with that man there?"

"He fell over a tree stump," Froelich said.

"You should have shot him too," Plauder quipped. "Leave him here. I have a medic."

Froelich had no choice. He cocked his chin at Hasenbein, who eased Moses down into the snow to lean against the gatehouse. Moses' eyes were wide and terrified, and he gripped rifle like a life preserver. Froelich said to Felix Braun and Green, "Holtz and Manheim, you two stay with him." stepped aside.

hmidt!" Plauder barked at one of his four sentries. up the rear so no one goes astray."

ohl." The private ran to the back of the formation.

Fritzy looked at Rosenberg and touched the hilt of his belted bayonet, and Rosenberg nodded and fell back.

"Forward," the SS officer snapped, and they all began to walk.

Froelich strode beside Lieutenant Plauder, with Fritzy and Horst Felder close behind, hefting clanking captured Stens, then Butler and his cowering cadre, then Hasenbein and Ricky Schonberg, and finally Rosenberg and Schmidt the SS sentry. Plans flashed through Froelich's mind, *What if this? What if that?*, yet there was nothing they could do but improvise. Up ahead, on both sides of the road, long white buildings loomed, two stories high with rows of darkened windows and weak light bulbs glowing over entrance doorways.

Third one on the left, second floor. Look for the wine.

"I thought the Second Parachute had gone to Russ Plauder said as he walked on Froelich's left and they p the first building.

"Yes, but my unit drew the lucky card."

"Indeed you did."

A burst of hollow gunshots echoed in the distan west. Froelich's stomach tensed, yet Plauder kept

"Someone's trigger happy on the mainland," "Or they're hunting boar again."

"Fresh hog's better than our shitty ra quipped.

"*Natürlich!*" Plauder laughed.

At the rear of the formation, Ricky Sch fell back to the sentry's right, taking his berg took his cue, slipped behind the se ugly trench knife from his belt. He'd taken off his gloves. His palms were slick with sweat.

"So, where are you from, Schmidt?" Ricky smiled at the SS sentry, though his cheek was twitching.

"Düsseldorf." The sentry smiled back. "And you?"

Rosenberg slapped a hand across Schmidt's mouth, tore him backwards, then drove the trench knife overhand straight into his heart and dragged him, bug-eyed and kicking, off into the woods between the buildings. A moment later he rejoined Ricky, shaking and without his knife, his eyes glassy. Ricky squeezed his neck to steady him and whispered, "Never mind."

"So how's the service with the *Fallschirmjäger*?" Plauder asked Froelich. They were nearing building number three.

"Wonderful, if you like broken legs." Froelich's heart was pounding. He glanced up at they passed the building's entrance and saw the bottle on a windowsill, silhouetted in a greenish glow.

Plauder laughed. "Well, not everyone can be SS. After all, we're Hitler's favorites."

And Froelich grabbed him by his tunic collar, slammed him backwards up against the wall, drew Mancalvo's pistol, and jammed the barrel underneath his Adam's apple as Plauder's skull banged against the concrete.

"Yes, you are, *Arschloch*," Froelich hissed, then whispered, "elder."

Horst leaped forward and stabbed his Schmeisser barrel Plauder's stomach. Plauder grunted hard and groaned.

"he tries anything, kill him," Froelich ordered as the unshouldered all the Stens and gave them to the Brits.

"With pleasure," Felder said as he took Plauder's P38 pistol. The SS lieutenant's eyes were flashing back and forth.

"You shits," he croaked. "You're all stinking German Jew pigs, aren't you?"

Ghurka Gurung understood that much in German, and he drew his wicked khukri knife from underneath his tunic, walked up to Plauder, laid the blade along his throat, and hissed in English, "Do I look like a Jew to you?"

"Froelich," Major Butler hissed. "For God's sake, man, let's *go*."

And just then, the bridge at Wolgast detonated.

Twenty-Nine

IT WAS AN AWFUL THING, THE WAY FATE TUM-
bled and cascaded, as it often does with cold indifference, on
no more than a sneeze.

Below the bridge, on both sides of its middle stanchion,
Beethoven Steinberg and Arieh Ben-Zvi had finished roping off
their satchel charges and crimping firing caps to sixty-second
fuses. Ben-Zvi's hands were steady, as he'd done this all before, but Steinberg's hands were slick and shaking, and his
rifle slipped away and went tumbling down into the water,
end over end. Both men froze like foxes in a hunter's beam.

The sentries on the far side heard the splash. One walked
out onto the bridge, got down on his belly, and leaned over.
He spotted Steinberg, yelled "Saboteur!", and upside down,
aimed and pulled the trigger of his Schmeisser. Steinberg
could do nothing except ball up on his girder as the weapon
barked and bullets sparked off steel and blew away his left
thumb and forefinger.

The shock of staring at his ravaged hand and splintered bone was far worse than the pain. No matter what followed, he knew that never again would he play the piano. He looked across at Ben-Zvi's slack-jawed stunned expression, cried, "Arieh, get out," then gripped the percussion cap in his blood-soaked left palm, and with his trembling right finger, yanked the ring pin detonator and the fuse spat fire.

Arieh could have saved himself and jumped into the water, but he wouldn't leave his mate to die alone that way. He pulled his ring pin too, the fuse ignited, he called out to Beethoven, "I'll see you in Jerusalem," and climbed up on the bridge.

The three sentries were stomping toward him, brandishing their weapons yet bewildered by his *Fallschirmjäger* uniform. Arieh marched straight at them.

"Was zum Teufel ist los mit dir?" What the hell is wrong with you? he shouted as he cocked his Schmeisser. "We're engineers inspecting your damned bridge!"

He opened fire on the first one and sent him sprawling on his back. The second sentry yelled something as he crouched and shot Arieh in the chest. Arieh grunted, dropped his Schmeisser, collapsed onto his knees and then his face. He thought once about the pilot's widow, Gina, and how he'd only held her and wished it had been more, and he closed his eyes as the bridge erupted in a plume of orange flame and spinning timbers, and disintegrated all of them.

In Karlshagen, Froelich, Major Butler, and Fritzy Gutman charged up the building's stairwell. Lights were flicking on and spilling from apartment doorjambs, with urgent voices calling. Froelich saw the *A* beside a doorway on the left, gripped Mancalvo's Beretta, and kicked it open, splintering the lock.

Dr. Otto Roth was standing in his kitchen nook, his back against a lime-green stove, shaking. His white hair was wild, his metal spectacles smeared from worried fingers. He was wearing a white dress shirt, woolen trousers and unlaced shoes, and his hands gripped the stove beside his chubby hips, knuckles white as bone. Froelich flicked his eyes across the flat, an engineer's abode of tea-stained furniture, photographs of rockets, and bookshelves overflowing.

"What do you want?" Roth croaked in German as he stared at the Nazi officer before him. "I have done nothing!"

"We're here to take you, Dr. Roth," Froelich said in a voice that sounded anything but soothing.

Butler shoved his way past Froelich. "We're British, man," he snapped in English.

"Nein!" Roth cringed. "I don't believe you!"

Froelich jabbed his fingers in his tunic, behind his Iron Cross, pulled out Sofia's gleaming Star of David and showed it to the quaking physicist.

"Do German officers wear these?"

Roth stared at it and slumped. He looked like he might faint. Fritzy Gutman turned from where he was peering out the doorway with his Schmeisser and said, "Sirs, can we please go?"

"Get your coat, Doctor," Froelich said.

Roth shook his head. His jowls flapped. "Not without my daughter!" And then he shouted, "Lisl!"

To the left inside the flat another doorway opened. A girl stepped out into the salon, perhaps nineteen, petite and pretty, with her black hair pulled into a ponytail and her dark eyes wild. She was a wearing a buttoned fir-green woolen coat and snow galoshes.

"Oh bloody hell," Butler groaned. "No one mentioned this!"

"I will not go without her," Roth announced in English. "If you force me I will never talk. Never!"

"All right, all right," Froelich said. "Your *coat*."

"For God's sake," Butler spewed.

Roth pulled a woolen greatcoat off a kitchen chair and struggled into it as he said, "Lisl, the suitcase."

"He doesn't need a bloody suitcase," Fritzy said, nearly singing it.

"It has all my papers." Roth threw his hands up. "Don't you want my papers?"

"Good Christ." Butler rolled his eyes as the girl retreated and came out again, hauling a large brown leather suitcase as if she and father were going on a lovely train trip.

Butler grabbed the case, Froelich gripped Roth's elbow, Fritzy herded Lisl out the door, and all of them went rushing down the stairs into the street.

They burst out from the building. Froelich's men had taken up positions on both sides of the road, weapons at the ready, the Brits all crouching there with Stens and facing north, with Hasenbein, Ricky and Rosenberg aiming south back toward the gatehouse. The western sky flickered with the distant blaze of burning timbers, and from the left and north a siren had gone off, the hee-haw warble of what the Germans called "Green Henry."

Horst Felder still had Plauder smeared against the wall, and when the SS officer saw the girl, then Roth, he understood exactly what was happening. He punched Felder in the face, grabbed his Schmeisser barrel, twisted it around, and yanked it so that Felder's finger jerked the trigger. The gun exploded, spitting bullets at the rescue crew. One broke Fritzy's elbow as he threw Lisl to the road and smeared her with his body, another cracked the side of Froelich's helmet and sliced the flesh along his skull, and another punched through Butler's rib cage as he dropped the suitcase and fell onto his face.

Cursing, Felder kneed the SS Nazi hard inside his groin and wrenched the gun away, just as Froelich marched right toward them, blood streaming down his cheek, pistol fist extended, and shot Plauder in his forehead. The SS man's expression matched the death's-head emblem on his cap as he collapsed onto his back, and Froelich shot him in the heart, and then once more, the debt paid for Moncalvo's wife and children.

"I'm all right." Major Butler's tone sounded impatient. Froelich turned to see Sergeant Major Connor helping Butler up.

"Oh just peachy, sir," Connor said as he slung Butler's arm around his neck and handsome Deighton gripped him on the other side.

Fritzy's left arm dangled and the blood was dripping from his sleeve, but he had Lisl on her feet and her father was beside her, fussing over her bruised knees, while Rosenberg gripped Roth by the elbow. Sergeant Winston had the suitcase, which somehow had stayed closed. A burst of wild gunshots reached them from the south, and then another.

"Move!" Froelich shouted like a cannon, and they all began to stumble south away from him, back toward the gatehouse.

Lights were flicking on in all the buildings, with panicked neighbors calling to each other and a woman wailing. Froelich stood there staring north beyond the buildings, where engines rumbled, drawing nearer. One sounded like a motorcycle.

Hasenbein approached him with the MG42 as he slammed its breech on a belt of bullets. Ricky was beside him, wide-eyed with his knees knocking. Both had belts of ammunition draped around their necks like prayer shawls.

"Go now, sir, or you won't make it," Hasenbein said, looming over Froelich. "We've got this. Right, Ricky?"

"He's right, sir," Ricky said. "Go."

Froelich looked at them, imprinting both their faces in his mind.

"We'll wait for you," he said, though nothing in his heart told him they would come, and he turned and hurried off.

Manfred got down on the damp and freezing roadway facing north, popped the machine gun's bipod, lay down behind it, and slapped a spot beside him with his palm.

"In the middle of the road?" Ricky whined as he got down next to Hasenbein and pulled out both his hand grenades.

"Best for fields of fire." Manfred smiled.

"God help us," Ricky moaned while his shaking fingers made a spare belt ready.

The engine sounds grew louder. Past the rows of buildings up ahead, something turned a corner and headlights painted the facades. Then a motorcycle showed with a machine gun in its sidecar, followed by a roofless Kübelwagen packed with further guns and bobbing helmets. Hasenbein and Ricky held their breaths until the SS troops were nearly on them, and then they opened fire...

When Froelich and his bleeding stumbling crew arrived back at the gatehouse, everyone was dead. The three remaining SS sentries were sprawled beside the gate pole, limbs twisted in strange postures, rifles flung into the snow, one shattered by a bullet. Close across the roadway, Paul Green and Felix Braun lay on their backs, extinguished eyes staring at the sky, their blood already thickening on the ice with empty shell casings glittering everywhere. Moses Bloch still sat where he'd been left against the gatehouse wall next to the doorway, with a German medic's corpse, his red cross armband plain to see, sprawled facedown across his lap.

Dr. Roth's daughter screamed and nearly swooned when she saw it. Froelich flung an arm at Fritzy and Rosenberg. "Take the Roths back behind the gatehouse," he ordered, and they did it, and Lisl mewled and Roth stumbled and tried to shield her from the horror. Froelich looked at Green and Braun and knew he couldn't even bury them. A grenade whumped from the north, and Hasenbein's machine gun rattled in the distance like a jackhammer.

Hans and Gustave Bloch burst out from the woods beside the roadway, as the rest spun and crouched and nearly shot them. The Blochs were trembling and pale and breathless.

"We couldn't help it, sir," Hans gasped to Froelich. "The sentries got suspicious with all the ruckus, we heard them arguing with Paul and Felix, then a gunfight started and we had to come outside and shoot them."

"Never mind," Froelich said, then yelled to everyone, "Take cover."

Hans and Gustave ran to pull the medic's corpse from Moses. They yelped with joy to find him still alive, checking himself everywhere for bullets holes and crying. The medic had sliced his pant leg open, where a shard of bloody broken shin was poking through his skin. "Can we please go home now?" he begged as Hans and Gustave hauled him up.

"Get him back behind the gatehouse too," Froelich snapped.

Froelich glanced around at his position. It wasn't good. Across the roadway from the gatehouse side wall, Ghurka Gurung, Sergeant Winston, and handsome Deighton were hunkered behind tree trunks at the wood line, Stens jutting north, with extra magazines beside their boots and potato masher hand grenades they'd borrowed from their *Fallschirm-jäger* comrades. Sergeant Major Connor and Horst Felder had eased Major Butler down beside the gatehouse wall as if they dared not drag him farther. Froelich went to him as he looked at his watch. It was getting very close to 1:00 a.m.

Froelich knelt in front of Butler. The major's woolen cap was off and steam wisped from his ruddy hair. His British tunic was laid open where the Schmeisser bullet had exited his chest and Felder tried to staunch the wound with a combat bandage, yet Butler's every breath made it froth with bloody bubbles.

"I'm so sorry, sir," Horst Felder was saying to Butler. "That was all my fault."

"Nonsense," Butler wheezed. Some blood was pooling at his lips. "Fate takes its turn when we least expect it."

"Lieutenant," Fritzy called from behind the gatehouse where he and Rosenberg were quieting the Roths. "We really should be going."

"He's right, Froelich." Butler looked at the lieutenant's

troubled eyes. Hasenbein's machine gun had stopped barking. It all went very quiet.

"But Steinberg and Ben-Zvi," Froelich protested.

"They're not alive, Froelich. They'd be here if they were." Butler smiled. "But no more Huns will come across *that* bridge." He reached out with a pale hand and gripped the front of Froelich's German tunic. "Take the Roths and go. We'll keep the Jerries off you right from here."

"What about the prisoners at Trassenheide, sir?"

"Silly boy. You can't save everyone, you know." Butler coughed up blood and smiled wider. "I think we did all right, for Jews."

Froelich stared at him, then blinked. *"We?"*

"That's right. I had to do it my way, Froelich," Butler said. "Had to make you hate me, had to make you prove to all of us you weren't weak or cowardly. I'm Bernstein, not Butler. Just another Jew, like you."

Froelich sat back on his haunches in the road, his world turned inside out and upside down. He looked up at Sergeant Major Connor where the giant stood beside him, grinning broadly underneath his great mustache. "We all are, sir," he said. "I'm Cohn from Glasgow, not Connor from Dundee."

Froelich spun around and looked across the road at Deighton.

"It's Danzig," the sapper called and smiled. "Stole Deighton from a school chum."

"Weinberg, here," Sergeant Winston added with a grin. "Had you on real good, sir. Didn't we?"

Froelich looked at Ghurka Gurung.

"Not him," Connor said, "though we've been trying to convert the stubborn sod."

Gurung smirked and shrugged at Froelich.

"I'm so bleedin' lost," Felder whispered as he tried to manage Butler's wound, but everything was soaked in red and the lung was pumping hisses like a punctured tire.

Butler yanked on Froelich's tunic and snapped him back to focus. He pulled him close again, smiled with great effort now, and whispered.

"Sometimes a man can find religion in strange places." He coughed and shuddered. "Now get them to the boat, Bernard. That's your mission."

The men all snapped their heads around and raised their guns as Hasenbein and Ricky Schonberg came pounding down the roadway from the north, Hasenbein with nothing but a pistol.

"Where's the bloody MG42?" Connor barked.

"Burned out both the barrels," Hasenbein panted.

"And *all* the ammunition," Ricky yelped. He looked like he'd gone mad.

"There's a bloody whole lot more of 'em," Hasenbein warned as he and Ricky blew right by and went scrambling for cover.

"*Go*, Froelich," Butler ordered one last time. "We'll see you all in Piccadilly."

Froelich got up on his feet and called out to the Blochs behind the gatehouse. "Blochs, leave the Panzerfaust here."

"And the MP43, if you don't mind," said Connor.

"Right," Froelich said, and turned and looked at all the cadre. He nodded at them and they answered with their thumbs poked at the sky, and he took off with his tattered remnants.

They hurried southward on the lightless gloomy roadway for a quarter of a mile, Froelich in the lead, blood still crawling from his helmet, with Fritzy in the rear, his shattered arm dangling as he twisted backwards, left, and right, his Schmeisser at the ready, just like Froelich had first seen him with his Thompson. Hans and Gustave carried Moses in a sling of arms and gripping wrists, because Hasenbein was just too spent to haul him. Ricky Schonberg and Horst Felder propped Otto Roth underneath his armpits and he moaned and lost a shoe but no one cared, and Rosenberg let Lisl take the suitcase by herself because she was young and spry enough.

Froelich turned them sharply left and through a line of whipping trees and brambles, and suddenly they broke out on a wide and endless strip of rocky beach, curving north and south, with nothing but black Baltic waves curling out to the horizon. They stopped, panting plumes of steam and staring at the ocean. And then they saw a flashing in the distance, the signal from the deck of a rocking vessel, the submarine HMS *Sealion*. From behind them through the trees and north came the screech and impact of a detonating warhead, then a chorus of tight gunfire and a roar of answers.

"Take them, Fritzy," Froelich barked at Gutman, and Fritzy snapped at all of them and pushed them toward the water. Froelich watched them go, and saw at last the hulking shapes of rubber boats bobbing on the waves beneath the starlight. They hadn't made it close to shore yet, but Fritzy wasn't waiting. Froelich heard Lisl screeching as they waded out into the icy surf, and Rosenberg snatched the suitcase from her and propped it on his head, but he heard nothing from his men. They'd done all this before.

He turned and stared back at the woods. The treetops far away around the gatehouse glowed and flickered with the echoing of gunfire, and to the north, high in the skies from Denmark, he saw the tiny shapes of a great armada, winging toward their target.

He turned and ran across the beach and broke into the surf, the shock of freezing ocean crawling to his waist, and saw the rubber boats with everyone aboard and thanked Butler for everything he'd made them do, and why he'd done it, and thanked those days of torment back in Sicily, and blessed Siculiana.

And then two large men in black from head to foot were grabbing him and hauling him into the rocking rubber boat, where he fell down on his face amongst a crowd of sopping feet and knees and guns. He flipped over on his back and looked up at the twinkling heavens.

"You're all bloody daft," said one SBS commando.

And they turned away, and rowed.

Afterward

London, April 1944

FROELICH NEVER OPENED TOMMY ROBBINS' letter. In the end he felt he didn't have the right to do it, and brought its still sealed secrets to Tommy's mother in the neighborhood of Canning Town, one of the poorest of the city's eastern districts, though proud and wartime stubborn. After all, the letter was addressed to Mrs. Margaret Robbins, not to him, and Froelich held his faith that his friend would never hurt her with its contents.

Wearing British Army woolens, the patch of Combined Operations on his shoulder, Froelich walked the rubbled streets searching for her flat, which wasn't easy. The Germans hadn't yet unleashed their last-gasp V-1 buzz bombs and V-2 rockets from the coast of France, and thanks to men like Froelich, those warheads would never be atomic, but Canning Town was suffering the "Baby Blitz" of early '44. Bleary-eyed residents spent their nights sleeping on Tube platforms, and by day the Civil Defence and fire brigades cleared broken bricks and quietly removed the fallen, amid the sorrowed gazes of the priests, along with prayers. Yet the women still pushed their prams in foggy sunlight, the paper boys in jaunty caps still hawked their news in reedy cries, and London hadn't yet surrendered, nor would it.

He found her in a redbrick flat whose cheek had fallen to the street but still had all its mouth, and he took a breath and climbed the stairs. The bullet scar above his temple was well healed and mostly covered by his hair, but as he removed his officer's cap, he hoped she wouldn't see it. She wore a kerchief and had Tommy's straw-hued curls and kindly eyes, and although she'd known about his passing for some time, she seemed alarmed for just a moment, then happy to see Froelich, as if he were the last part of her son still living. She touched her chest above her simple dress and bade him come inside.

She made him tea. They sat down at her simple table. There were purple flowers on her windowsill and pictures on her sideboard, one of Tommy, but Froelich didn't look at it. He lit a cigarette for her and one for him, and then with trembling fingers made old too fast by hardships, she read the letter. Then she folded it, doing all she could to keep composure, and looked at him.

"If you please," she said in a hushed tone with Tommy's East End accent, "what's your Christian name, Lieutenant?"

"It's Bernard, mum."

Her tired eyes were brimming, but she touched his hand across the table.

"Thank you so much, Bernard. Tommy says you were his stalwart mate. He told me that he did his very best, and that I should be proud and always comforted by that."

"He was very brave, Mrs. Robbins."

"How did he die, Bernard?" she asked.

"In Sicily, at hospital. His wounds were just too much. I'm sorry."

She nodded and looked out the window past her purple flowers, yet still touched Froelich's hand. It was quiet. The German ordnance fell mostly after dark.

"He wanted me to tell you one thing, though," Froelich said.

"What was it?" she asked.

"That in truth, he always loved to dance."

The tears spilled from her eyes and ran down her trembling cheeks, but even so she smiled.

"I knew it," she said with gentle triumph, and turned back to him. "Will you come again, Bernard?"

"As often as you like, mum, while I'm still here."

"Please do," she said. "Please do." And then she rose and he did too, and she hugged him and he left.

Froelich and the men of Operation Scepter had been sequestered since arriving back in England. Combined Operations was headquartered at the War Office in central London, but they were billeted and worked at Wormwood Scrubs, a two-hundred-acre ugly plot of open land west of the city. The Scrubs was known for its prison, a medieval looking structure noted for its cherry-colored entrance arch, flanked by two brown and white mosaic towers resembling the queens of a gargantuan chess set. Early in the war, all the prisoners had been packed off elsewhere as MI5, Military Intelligence, took over.

Now the cells and guardrooms were occupied by spies, secret soldiers and combat trainers. Rear echelon troops who typed and messengered throughout the city were brought out to the Scrubs in groups to hurl their hand grenades and stab at sandbags with their bayonets, and women of the Home Guard practiced antiaircraft drills with cannons, all still preparing for a German onslaught that would never come.

Froelich and his men slept in a single prison cell of peeling lime-green paint and metal bunks, pleased that it was heated, and the door was never locked. They couldn't speak of where they'd been or what they'd done, but command staff whispered they were heroes, and called them only X Troop. By day they labored at two rows of metal desks inside a former guardroom, where dispatch messengers delivered intercepted Wehrmacht communications from GCHQ at Bletchley Park for them to translate. No one knew how the cipher wizards out at Bletchley had broken the German codes, and no one asked. The missives were voluminous and they worked six days a week, sometimes were granted passes to the city on the seventh, but always in the company of a sergeant major, the only exception being Froelich's visit to Tommy Robbins' mother. It wasn't that they were not trusted, just that they were precious.

Manfred Hasenbein had never learned to type, nor would he, but he could translate, and Ricky Schonberg did the pecking for him. A clacking Smith Corona was so much better than an MG42. Horst Felder worked in silence, still brooding over Major Butler, as he always would. Fritzy Gutman, his arm still in a sling, managed everything one-handed, and David Rosenberg was jaunty and prolific, perhaps because an SAS lieutenant had gifted him a Fairburn-Sykes commando blade in place of his beloved trench knife. Hans Bloch kept his chin up, even though Moses had been relieved of service for his injury, and Gustave had requested and been granted dismissal from the unit so he could care for him.

Froelich worked alongside all of them, as until orders came down for another mission there was no other task. They never spoke about the friends they'd left and lost at Peenemünde, though they did say *kaddish* for them once, the Hebrew prayer for the dead, and the faces of those men would always be behind their eyes. They smoked, sipped tea, chewed biscuits, and interpreted the reams of German messages. Sometimes they laughed when Wehrmacht officers shared lewd comments about their mistresses. Sometimes they cursed when SS bastards bragged of executing French Resistance. And once a week, Froelich wrote a letter to Sofia. He addressed them care of the US Army field hospital, Monestero Santo Spirito, Agrigento, Sicily, hoping that the wounded there still thirsted for some ice. He knew he never would receive an answer, as orders forbade him marking a return address, yet he kept his faith that Agrigento slept in peace, and so did she, and someday he'd return to her, in one form or another.

By April there were rumors of invasion of the Continent. A great Allied armada was forming on the southern coasts of England. The London pubs were overflowing with American GIs, all courting British beauties, and the jealous English boys wished only they would leave, and soon enough they would, though no one knew the date or target yet of that ominous departure. One day a motorcycle messenger arrived and handed Froelich an instruction. He was to travel to the War Office and present himself to the father of Combined Operations, Lord Louis Mountbatten.

He arrived there on an evening at the date and time requested, chauffeured in a jeep by a corporal driver who complained of being stuck in London rather than the front, and Froelich only smiled because he'd done the very same in Cairo. He felt some trepidation at being summoned by Mountbatten, a cousin to the Queen with an enormous wartime reputation, yet assumed it wasn't disciplinary, but if it were, no matter. The War Office, in Whitehall, just across the way from the prime minister's residence at Number 10 Downing Street, was a trapezoidal fortress of pale-yellow Portland and York stone, with seven floors, more than a thousand rooms, and corner towers resembling domed churches of the Vatican. Curiously, all the branches of the service worked there on bankers' hours, so with the exception of the wireless posts that listened round the clock, after five it was ghostly quiet.

Froelich checked his uniform. He wore only the North African campaign ribbon, yet his pride in that was solid. He passed the guards and sandbag barriers on Whitehall Place, went inside and showed his orders to a sergeant at the security desk. The sergeant rang someone, then issued him a temporary pass and said, "Third floor, Lieutenant. Q-9."

Froelich stepped out from the lift onto a long and wide arched corridor of yellow beige moldings, a speckled marble floor and bright red painted doors. The only soul in sight was a sergeant of the Horse Guards, looking very grim outside a single office of no overt significance. The sergeant looked him over.

"May I have your pistol, sir?" he asked, though it wasn't a request.

Froelich handed him Moncalvo's Beretta, which raised the sergeant's brows as it wasn't regulation.

"Don't lose it, Sergeant," he said.

"I shan't, sir." He opened the door.

No one was inside the office. The walls were blank, with one great window overlooking London and one side door on the left leading off to somewhere. There was a simple wooden desk off to the right, with a fountain pen and inkwell, a crystal ashtray on its blotter, a simple wooden office chair, and two more leather armchairs facing it. Froelich stood there at attention, waiting for Lord Mountbatten. The side door opened and a man came in, but it wasn't him. He was stocky, stoop shouldered, bald and broad. He wore a black vested suit with a gold-chained pocket watch, a blue polka dotted bowtie, and a large cigar clutched in his stubby fingers.

The man was Winston Churchill.

Froelich blinked. He thought he might be dreaming, or that he'd trespassed into some forbidden room. Churchill curled his famous slabby smile and spoke to him in his never-surrender growl.

"Excuse the ruse, Lieutenant. We knew you'd pop up here for Mountbatten, but thought that I might scare you off."

"Good evening, Prime Minister." Froelich's leg was aching. It hadn't done so in a while. He thought this rendezvous with such a man was nigh impossible, but suddenly recalled that Churchill's summons wasn't that unusual. In Cairo, when he visited, he'd often shared a drink with junior combat officers at Shepheard's and had chin-wagged there with Captain David Sterling of the SAS.

Churchill strode across the room, tipped his ashes in the tray, and plugged the fat cigar into his mouth.

"I haven't got much time, Froelich," he said. "The cabinet, you know. However, this thing at Peenemünde. Tell it, please, but summarize. You're the only one who knows just what transpired."

Froelich told it all as quickly as he could, while Churchill looked up at the ceiling in a cloud of bluish smoke and listened. The whole adventure was distilled down to a minute.

"Remarkable," the PM said. "How many of you survived it?"

"Seven, sir. The rest were lost."

Churchill fixed him with his tired eyes. He'd sent thousands of such good men to their deaths.

"You may have saved the Empire and the Allies, Froelich. Dr. Roth is now in New Mexico. They're brewing something up. However, I cannot issue medals or citations for you chaps. It's all hush-hush and we can never speak of it. Ever." He waited.

"I understand, sir."

"Good. Have you some other request, perhaps?"

Froelich's mind spun in a vortex. What could he possibly ask for? Nothing personal, he knew that much. But he also knew from rumors in the ranks and speculation in the papers that Churchill held the British Army's Jews in high regard, in particular the Palestine regiments. He was friendly with the statesman Chaim Weizmann and had lobbied with his general staff for a full brigade of Jewish soldiers, but the arguments were all against it. British generals feared the stubborn strength of combat hardened Jews who'd no doubt claim that once again, Jerusalem should be theirs, and that would whip up England's Arab allies into a lather.

"With all respect, Prime Minister," Froelich said. "I think

it's high time for your blessing of a Jewish brigade. I think we've earned it."

Churchill's blue eyes narrowed and his bulldog face looked stormy. Froelich thought that he might shout and throw him out, but he said, "Indeed. I've been saying so for years now. But if I do it, when all of this is done, you're going to make hell for us in Palestine. Won't you?"

"Most likely, sir." Froelich smiled. "But we shall try to keep it to a minimum."

Churchill laughed at that. Then his expression darkened and he looked at Froelich as if seeing someone he admired, yet also something in his past that pained him. Perhaps it was his youth in India and Africa.

"I shall do it, Froelich," he said. "You have my word."

Then he turned and walked over to the window, one hand in his vest pocket as he smoked and looked at London. Froelich thought he was dismissed. He saluted to the PM's back and made to go, but Churchill spoke again.

"Seven of you left, you said?"

"Yes, sir."

"Well, a lucky number. I fought in the Sudan with Kitchener, you know, and the Boer War as well as other places."

"So I've heard, sir."

Rings of smoke enveloped Churchill's head. He stood there for a moment, staring at his past, and spoke quietly once more.

"We all told each other that the losses would grow easier over time, yet we all knew it was a lie. The first shock of it dulls, but then, as years roll by, one's left thinking about all they've missed. That's the truth of it. One grows older, yet they stay just as they once were when they left." His shoulders slumped a bit. "In a melancholy way, war is the fountain of youth."

Churchill didn't turn around again, and Froelich took his cue and slipped away.

On the morning of the Normandy Invasion, Froelich and his men were not amongst the first wave, nor the second or the third. They didn't parachute at night beyond the beaches, or land in flimsy Horsa gliders, or wade ashore into hails of German gunfire that would surely cut them down. Their talents were too rare to be sacrificed as cannon fodder.

They'd spent the month of May in quiet preparations for Operation Overlord, all leaves canceled, though still ignorant of what their tasks would be. An officer from the Special Operations Executive, Captain Patrick Fellows, became their new master. He wasn't Bertie Buck or Major Nigel Butler, but he was jocular enough and easygoing. By day they kept up their translations and by night they shot and hurled grenades amid the rolling scruff of Wormwood Scrubs. They were all issued Stens, except for Fritzy Gutman who was allowed his favored Thompson, though they sensed that in the fields of France they'd be using German weapons.

One evening Captain Fellows called them to the guardroom and posted an MP outside the door. He presented them with German SS uniforms of the Leibstandarte Division. A secret tailor checked the fittings, an SOE clerk issued them forged papers with the same names that they'd used at Peenemünde, and a woman from the War Office documentary film section made sure their ranks and ribbons were just right.

After the support staff were dismissed, Fellows opened two

wooden weapons crates. They were packed with gleaming Schmeissers and an MG42 for Hasenbein, but there were also silenced pistols. Fellows smiled at that them wanly.

"You chaps shall be capturing or killing German generals. I know it's not exactly cricket, but there it is."

In early June they were allowed one final somber celebration at a pub in Piccadilly, with an escort and in British kit, of course, and cautioned to speak only English. Froelich sat there with the rest, imbibing ale and picking at his fish and chips, thinking how much Tommy would have loved it, and wishing Major Butler could have kept his promise. He wrote a note to Margaret Robbins and gave it to the sergeant major, promising he'd see her once again. He never would.

They crossed the English Channel on a vessel of the Royal Engineers. The skies were cobalt blue, the waves were summer gentle, and near the shores of France barrage balloons floated high above the masts of many warships like celebrations at a child's birthday. Artillery still rumbled past the shattered French villages that had suffered from both sides, and Spitfires and Thunderbolts roared overhead to gun down Wehrmacht recalcitrants, but they crossed a pontoon wharf, in British uniforms, hauling kitbags full of German tools and guises, and came ashore at Sword beach, boots dry.

They were met by sullen escorts of Combined Operations amid the detritus of days before, piles of cracked helmets, broken rifles, and fresh crosses in the stony sand. Their kit was tucked aboard a Bedford truck, and only then, Captain Fellows issued them their orders. He produced a photograph of a German officer and a single sheet of intercepted ciphers.

"Lieutenant General Vollrath Lübbe," he said. "Second

Panzer division. His tanks are wreaking havoc with the 7th Armored. He's somewhere west of Troarn. *Find* him."

That night, the twelfth of June, they changed into their German kit. Fellows wasn't going with them. He told them, with a hopeful grin, that all the British troops and some Canadians along their route had been informed to please not shoot them. He shook their hands, wished them luck, then two jeeps braced the Bedford front and back, and they drove off for the front.

By dawn they were alone, trudging up a long wide rise of trampled dewy grass crisscrossed with tank tread scars and shell craters, some filled with rain and bloody bandages. Behind them in the sea off Normandy, vessels tipped and rolled beneath a foggy placid sky, while past the ridgeline up ahead the horizon moaned and coughed with shellfire and crimson flashes in the underclouds. Froelich had the lead, his Iron Cross below his SS tabs, his Schmeisser at the ready. Horst Felder followed, then Ricky Schonberg draped in ammunition, and Manfred Hasenbein bouncing the MG42 on one shoulder. David Rosenberg and Hans Bloch had the tail, with Fritzy Gutman last, healed and slingless, turning left and right and backwards. They were a frightening vision, especially to themselves.

As they came over the top, Froelich raised a hand and they all halted. There facing them were two startled figures, only yards away and so improbable against the lurid landscape, that for a moment he just blinked and cocked his head.

One was a young German soldier, an SS corporal whose uniform was torn, unkempt, and streaked with blood above his muddy boots. He looked remarkably like Froelich had before the war, a version of his younger self, with mussed blond hair and strained blue eyes that gleamed as though they'd seen too much and never could be bright again. Yet he trembled like a thief who'd been discovered, and his fingers fluttered near a crooked pistol holster, as if he were dismayed instead of pleased to fall upon some Wehrmacht brethren on this awful plain.

The other was a girl, who could be nothing else but French, although she wore a pair of German army trousers and a cream roll-neck sweater. Her long blond hair tumbled from a field cap, her blue eyes were like diamonds, and her visage was magnificent, like some angel from a boy's imagination. She held a pair of leather reins in one small hand, and behind her, nose nuzzling in the grass, was a gleaming, glossy, raven-colored horse. The vision that the trio made was utterly incongruous.

"Was ist los hier?" Froelich said, and pointed past the young man's shoulder. "Our lines are that way, Corporal. Who is your commander?"

The young man seemed to hesitate, then stammered, "Colonel Erich Himmel."

"Kommandotruppe," Horst Felder said to Froelich, then named the SS regiment. *"Das Reich."* This Colonel Himmel had a reputation, and Froelich wondered why the boy has left his charge.

"Are you deserting?" Froelich asked the trembling corporal. "Along with this French jewel?" He kept his Schmeisser ready as he played his part, thinking they could well be spies or ambush lures of some sort.

Then suddenly the girl stepped forward, gripped the corporal's arm as if he were the last thing that she loved, and in perfect *Hochdeutsch* spoke in bold defiance.

"He was a German war hero, but now he's done," she said. "And I am racially impure, so you'll want nothing of me. This war is over soon, and you'd be wise to let us pass."

Froelich dipped his face and raised a brow. The girl had stupefying courage, and the corporal looked as though he might collapse with her outrageous outburst, yet he fumbled for his pistol in a show of desperate chivalry. Froelich stilled him quickly with his Schmeisser barrel, pointing it at her.

"A Jewess?" Froelich asked, incredulous.

"That's right," said the girl, her dimpled chin raised in prideful challenge, without a hint of fear that he might shoot her on the spot. And to prove her claim, she produced a silver Star of David from underneath her sweater, and thrust it at him as if he were a vampire.

Froelich's smile overtook his face, and a flood of admiration filled his heart. He had no idea what horrid things had made this girl so reckless, but clearly she had had enough of Germans, and all he wanted was to fold her in embrace. His men had gathered close behind, all stunned as he was, and he knew that all of them were thinking of their sisters and their mothers, the lonely girls and widows of Siculiana, the softness of their innocence, the mourning of their losses. As for the young man trembling there before him, Froelich somehow knew this Jewish girl was his Sofia, and the stallion was their Moto Guzzi, and he reached inside his tunic, produced his Star of David, and said to her in English, "It looks rather like mine."

He thought the girl and boy might faint. They clutched

each other and their horse whinnied. He told them he and all his men were British soldiers, commandos of the newly minted Jewish Brigade, but that their tailors were Berliners. Yet still the couple stared at him in disbelief, much like the old Italians on the beach at Siculiana, but then the girl made one more startling revelation as she pointed at her love.

"He's half a Jew as well!"

Froelich's eyes went wide at that. "Now *that* I don't believe," he said.

"It's true," the corporal whispered, and nodded in confession, and when Froelich glanced in reflex below the young man's waist, the French girl raised a finger and claimed, "He isn't cut."

"Neither are *you*, Froelich," Hasenbein teased as he poked him from behind, and Froelich blushed and they all laughed as beyond them the artillery still flashed and shook the ground beneath their feet. They were all standing on the precipice of hell, and he had no idea what to do with these two Jewish refugees and their handsome horse.

"They might be useful to us, sir," Manfred Hasenbein murmured near his ear.

"Right," Ricky Schonberg whispered. "Turn them loose, the Huns'll shoot him, rape the girl, and eat the horse."

"Sending them to our lines might be just as risky, sir," said Hans Bloch.

"If nothing else," Fritzy Gutman offered, "she can be our morale sister."

"Sir, the lad's a mischling," said David Rosenberg. "He's one of us, just doesn't know it yet."

Froelich heard his men's entreaties, and loved them for the

kinds of men they were. He looked at the young broken boy with pity. It was nightmare enough to have to pose as a Nazi soldier, but somehow this tormented Jewish lad had lived it, and surely had been forced to hide it for God knew how long, suffering awful terrors. Nothing in this world could cure him of his past, but for however much longer they all lived, Froelich and his men could soothe his future, and none of them would harm the girl he surely loved.

He made his decision, cocked his head at his men to fall back into battle line, and as they started forward for the front, he slipped his arm around the young man's shoulders.

"Come," he said. "Sometimes a man can find religion in strange places."

And they walked off to find whatever there was left of all their lives, and the war.

★ ★ ★ ★ ★

HISTORICAL NOTES

The Special Interrogation Group, SIG, was a commando unit of the British Army comprised of Jewish German, Austrian, French and other European volunteers. Attached to Middle East Commando, they played a significant part in the North African campaigns of World War II, in particular the battles of Tobruk, with some surviving members later designated as "X Troop" under No. 10 Commando. Captain "Bertie" Buck and Lieutenant David Russell were the SIG's commanders of record.

George Henry Lane, a Hungarian born Jew and British commando with X Troop, was captured by the Germans and expected to be executed, but was spared by Field Marshal Erwin Rommel, who'd invited him to tea. He later escaped from a German prisoner of war camp.

In October 1942, Corporal John William "Jack" Sillito was cut off from his reconnaissance unit, which came under heavy German fire during a raid on the Tobruk railway. With only a revolver, a compass, and a small water flask, he walked 180 miles from Tobruk through the Great Sand Sea and back to British lines.

The sinking of Her Majesty's Hospital Ship *Kensington* during the invasion of Sicily, is based upon the sinking of the HMHS *Newfoundland*, which took place during the invasion of Italy. Otherwise, the facts of the incidents are true and identical.

The *Kommandobehefhl*, Hitler's formal order to execute all captured Allied commandos, was issued on October 18, 1942. But prior to that, on June 13, 1942, he issued a verbal order to execute all Allied soldiers dressed as German troops, in particular German Jews. The order was relayed by word of mouth and forbidden to be documented, as even Hitler understood it constituted a war crime.

During and prior to World War II, the name Palestine referred to all the territory now encompassing both Israel and the Palestinian Authority, and therefore all Jews and Arabs of the area called themselves Palestinians. The name derives from the Roman Empire's conquest of the land of Judea, which they punitively changed to Syria-Palestina.

The Monastery of the Holy Spirit, in Agrigento, Sicily, was occupied by Allied troops after the invasion of the island and served as both a regional headquarters and Allied field hospital. As of 2019, one elder sister residing there still remembered the events.

Castello Chiarmonte in Siculiana, Sicily, still stands exactly as described and has hosted many conquerors, including both the Germans and Allies. It is a museum and its courtyard a favored spot for weddings.

The notorious Nazi V-1 and V-2 secret weapons program, based at Peenemünde, was bombed and raided multiple times under Operation Crossbow. Numerous Allied commando raids, some still classified to this day, were mounted to foil the German development and fielding of an atomic bomb. At the war's end, many Nazi scientists were smuggled into the United States under a secret program called Operation Paperclip, where they developed ballistic missiles and birthed the US space program. Dr. Ludwig Roth, head of the Peenemünde Future Projects Office, was one of those scientists.

Captain Leo Lefkowitz, the author's uncle, was awarded the Bronze Star at the Battle of the Bulge for refusing an order to abandon his wounded men to the oncoming Germans, and rescuing them all instead.

Shortly after the Normandy Invasion, Sir Winston Churchill signed the order creating the Jewish Brigade. Who inspired him to finally do so is a matter of conjecture, based on legend.

ACKNOWLEDGMENTS

The author owes a debt of gratitude to literary agent John Talbot, editor Peter Joseph, and all the staff of Hanover Square Press for their faith, skill, and patience. Subject matter and language experts John Morgan, Giorgia Winters, and Ruth Bazzano were crucial in their contributions. The friendship and support of Oren Baratz and Susan is unequaled. My wife, Lia Yang, is an angel of salvation. And finally, I am grateful for the inspiration of my late father, Sy, my uncle Erich Wellisch, and my brother David Bale, who would have loved this tale.